# Battle Song

# Battle Song

Ian Ross

HODDER &
STOUGHTON

First published in Great Britain in 2023 by Hodder & Stoughton
An Hachette UK company

1

A CIP catalogue record for this title is available from the British Library

Hardback ISBN 978 1 399 70884 5
eBook ISBN 978 1 399 70885 2

Typeset in Perpetua Std by Manipal Technologies Limited

Printed and bound in Great Britain by Clays Ltd, Elcograf S.p.A.

Hodder & Stoughton policy is to use papers that are natural, renewable and recyclable
products and made from wood grown in sustainable forests. The logging and manufactur-
ing processes are expected to conform to the environmental regulations of the country of
origin.

Hodder & Stoughton Ltd
Carmelite House
50 Victoria Embankment
London EC4Y 0DZ

www.hodder.co.uk

Nottingham

Shrewsbury

Leicester

Kenilworth

Worcester    Northampton

Gloucester

Oxford    St Albans    Ware    Pleshey

R. Thames    London

Odiham    Rochester

Winchester    Canterbury

Lewes    Dover

North Sea

0    50
miles

Ghent

Boulogne    Lille

Valenciennes

Arras

English Channel

Amiens

La Fère

Soissons

Senlis

Épernay

R. Seine    Paris

Lagny

R. Severn

1 2 5 8: Magna Carta has failed to limit the power of the king, and England is once more in turmoil. Led by Simon de Montfort, Earl of Leicester, a band of rebel noblemen compel Henry III to put his seal to a new document, the Provisions of Oxford, and to swear that he will govern only by the consent of parliament and his council of advisors.

At first it seems that their demands have been met. But in the summer of 1261, Henry persuades the Pope to absolve him from his oath, then overthrows the new rulings and seizes back absolute control of his realm. Only Simon de Montfort refuses to bow to the king's will, and departs for France in disgust.

By the following winter, Henry appears secure on his throne once more. Few are aware of the clouds gathering on the horizon. Fewer still can foresee the coming storm that will burst over England and engulf the kingdom in the violence of civil war.

# Part One

## Chapter 1
## January 1262

*The forty-sixth year of King Henry III*

Epiphany's eve, and snow lay on the slope of the castle mount. Boisterous, alight with spiced ale, the three young men scraped it up with their hands and packed it onto the steps that descended from the upper hall. With their heels they rubbed it to a smooth grey slick. Then they leaned against the railing of the bridge that spanned the moat, breath steaming, curbing their laughter as they waited for their prey.

A figure appeared at the top of the steps, lean and hunched against the cutting breeze as he emerged from the shelter of the hall. He was a squire like them, eighteen years old, with cropped hair and a short tunic. Hurrying down the steps, his arms burdened with folded linens, he did not see the trap until it was too late. Then his foot skated out from beneath him and he was tumbling backwards, the stone step cracking into his spine as he fell. Their laughter was raucous in the frigid air.

'Look at him!' the biggest of the three cried. 'Look at him, writhing like a worm! What's this worm called?'

'His name's Adam de Norton,' said one of the others.

'Adam de Nought!' the big youth said with a grin, dropping from French into the English of the common people. 'Adam de *Nothing* – he comes from nothing! Was his father a *nothing*?'

'A Welshman killed his father,' the third of them said, stamping his feet to keep warm.

Sprawled on the icy steps, Adam de Norton felt the pain bursting through him. The humiliation too. The clean linens he had been carrying were scattered in the dirt and the muddy snow; they were cloths for the feasting tables, and he knew he would be punished for spoiling them. Then he heard their words, and fierce anger flared in his blood.

'Let's see if this worm can swim,' the big youth was saying, eager in his malice. 'Perhaps the moat's a good place for him?'

'Leave him, Gerard,' one of the others said. By his tone, he was already having misgivings about this game. Adam turned his head and blinked; he had considered that one a friend.

The second youth he knew as well, a fellow squire of the household. But the leader, the one who had clearly bullied them into this sport, was a stranger to him. Gerard was stocky and thick-fleshed, with a red face and a snub nose and very small eyes. On his white tunic was sewn a red diagonal cross-lattice. A heraldic device, but Adam did not recognise it; Pleshey was full of strangers who had come for Earl Humphrey's winter court.

Gerard advanced a pace closer. Adam was still lying on the steps, his muscles bunched. He felt the pain in his back and head, but the ache was fading fast. He knew that Gerard wanted more. He wanted to assert himself, and intimidate his followers.

'Leave him – someone's coming!' said the third squire, but his friend remained sitting on the bridge railing, watching avidly. Gerard took another stamping step towards Adam, reaching down to seize his shoulder.

With a surge, Adam pushed himself upright, darting clear of the young man's clumsy grab and getting his feet beneath him. Anger drove him; without thinking, he was swinging his fist with the momentum of his movement, a wide reaping blow that smacked meatily into the centre of Gerard's face.

For a few long moments nobody made a sound. Birds cried harshly from along the moat. Woodsmoke scented the air. Gerard was still standing, bent forward and clutching his face. Spots of blood spattered at his feet, jewel-bright in the snow.

'By *dode!*' he managed to say. 'He boke by *dode!*'

The two other squires were motionless, staring in fascinated shock. Then Gerard straightened, let his hands drop from his bloodied face, and roared as he flung himself at Adam.

They went down together, locked in combat. Adam was numb to Gerard's savage blows on his chest and face. He knew he had to win. His adversary was two stone heavier than him and driven by pain and outraged pride, but Adam was agile and angry. He dragged his right arm free of Gerard's crushing grip and slammed two punches into the man's face, bursting the remains of his nose. His third blow struck his eye, and his fourth struck the stretched column of his throat. Gerard had his thumbs clamped over Adam's face, trying to gouge at his eyes. But Adam had rolled on top now, shoving himself clear. He swung his fist, and slammed another blow into Gerard's right eye socket. Blood sprayed across the dirty snow, and he felt his attacker's grip slackening. Again he struck, and again, fury powering his blows.

'Enough!' somebody was shouting. 'Enough! Stop this!' Men were hurrying from all directions, their cloaks and mantles flapping in the cold air.

Adam barely felt the arms that hauled him out of the fight.

*

'You don't know who that was, do you?' the cook's mate said, sitting under the back porch of the kitchen plucking geese. 'Or rather, *whose* that was . . . Whose squire, I mean.'

'No,' Adam replied. He set another log on the block, straightened, then swung the axe down. His whole body ached, but he would not let it show. 'I don't care,' he said. The air in the kitchen yard was so cold it hurt to breathe, but he was sweating.

'You should care!' the cook's mate said. 'That lad you mauled yesterday, young sir, is squire to Robert de Dunstanville, that's who!'

Natural John, Earl Humphrey's fool, was squatting beside the basket of goose down, trailing his fingers in the soft feathers. He raised his head at the name and whined like a dog.

'Dunstanville, hah!' said the porter, rolling a keg from the bakehouse door. 'He's here too, is he?' He paused in his work to make a holy warding sign.

'I said I don't care,' Adam told them. He swung his axe again, splitting another log into shards. Chopping wood for the kitchen fire was well beneath even the lowest of squires, but this was his punishment for brawling on the eve of a holy day. A morning of menial chores, while the rest of the household rode out to the hunt.

'Quiet down, Natural John,' the cook's mate snapped. The fool was still whining, rocking on his haunches. 'Robert de Dunstanville,' he said to Adam, gesturing with a handful of feathers, 'is not a man to cross. There are tales about him.'

'Tales?' Adam said, finally relenting. He propped his axe on the chopping block and leaned on it, breathing hard. A blizzard of splintered wood lay all around him.

'They say he murdered a priest,' the porter said from the doorway. 'Cut him down right on the steps of his own altar! He was excommunicated for that, and would have been outlawed except for the pleas of Lord Humphrey and his grace the Earl of Winchester. But his lands were seized anyhow, and now he wanders the earth like a carrion dog . . .'

'They say,' the cook's mate broke in, lowering his voice, 'that he was taken captive by the Saracens, and they forced him to renounce Christ, and now he is the Devil's Man! You see that red lattice he bears as his emblem? That's the devil's fiery flaming griddle, that he uses to roast sinners down in hell!'

Natural John let out a keening wail and buried his head in the basket of goose down. Adam was unmoved. He remembered the red-on-white lattice from Gerard's tunic – he had seen it on a shield as well. A simple heraldic design that he knew well from his lessons. *Argent fretty gules*. Something else too: a lion on a red quarter, and a blue charge. *In a quadrant gules a lion passant gardant or, with a label of three points azure . . .*

'So why does Lord Humphrey admit him to his court?' Adam asked. He stooped down, feeling the ache of his bruised ribs, and set another log on the block.

'Because Robert de Dunstanville is Lord Humphrey's bastard offspring, that's why,' the porter said. 'Or *so they say*,' he added hurriedly, with a glance towards the gateway. 'Lord Humphrey got him on old Saer de Quincy's youngest daughter, who was wed to the brother of Walter de Dunstanville, the Baron of Castlecombe.'

Adam sniffed tightly, not wanting to appear impressed. The porter prided himself on his intimate knowledge of family connections among the nobility.

'Well, he'll be leaving again soon enough,' the cook's mate said, going back to his plucking with renewed vigour. 'Soon as the feasting's done he'll be away, and his misbegotten squire and light-fingered servants with him . . . Off to wave a lance on the tourney fields overseas – that's how he gains his bread nowadays, when he isn't living off his betters . . .'

'And God be praised once we're rid of them all,' the porter muttered.

But Adam was no longer listening. He split another log, burying the axe blade in the block, then pulled the steel free with a savage tug. Heat was flowing through him, despite the chill of the morning. Gerard was equally to blame for the fighting the day before, and everyone knew it, but only Adam was being punished. The other squire was a guest at Pleshey, and had Adam not struck the first blow? Besides, a badly broken nose and two black eyes looked worse than mere bruises. Adam had spied the young man leaving the chapel after mass that morning, and his face had been shockingly battered and livid. Gerard had even had trouble mounting his horse. But he and his depraved master would ride with Earl Humphrey on the hunt, and only Adam would take the blame. The injustice was sickening.

For nearly five years Adam had served in the household of Earl Humphrey de Bohun, riding with the retinue between the earl's many estates and castles, but still he was the lowest of the squires. Lord Humphrey himself had scarcely said a word to him in all that time, except to issue orders. Often he seemed uncertain of Adam's name. Then again, why should he not be? There were over thirty squires in the household, some of them from great and powerful families. Adam himself had no great name, no fortune or ancestral estate. His father had been a common serjeant, knighted by the king for valour during the fighting in Aquitaine; he had died in Wales, serving in Lord Humphrey's retinue, and the earl had taken Adam in as a favour to his widowed mother. Now his mother too was dead, and strangers tenanted his father's lands.

Earlier that morning, watching from the sidelines as Lord Humphrey's household and guests rode out to the hunt, Adam had been all too aware of his own insignificance. He was closer to the servants than to the other squires. The noisy swirl of horses and dogs, shouting men and screeching horns had poured from the bailey yard, out across the bridge that spanned the moat and away into the dimness of a cold winter's dawn, leaving the castle to the servants and the womenfolk, and to Adam.

He took a few moments to collect up the cords of cut wood, his fingers too numbed to feel the splinters. The knuckles of both hands were still grazed, the skin split and blackened. He stacked the wood, sucked at his thick lip, then picked up the axe once more.

Counting the earl's household, the castle servants, the guests, and the resident paupers, well over two hundred people lived within the walls and moats of Pleshey. Adam knew he could make no claims for special treatment. But it angered him that he should have to toil like a common labourer, while Gerard was pardoned. While a murderous Christ-despising renegade like Robert de Dunstanville was treated as an honoured guest, merely due to some accident of birth. What sort of world was this, he seethed, when the godless and the vile were honoured and rewarded, and the honest must suffer for the crimes of others? It was not the first time he had mulled over these things. But now his grievance had a sharply personal edge.

He set about the stack of wood once more, hacking the axe down into the block with a cold destructive fury. Only when he paused, blinking the sting of sweat from his eyes, did he notice the stillness around him.

Voices came from outside the gateway to the yard, and the sound of horses and dogs. It was far too early for the hunters to have returned; barely an hour had passed since their departure. Then two men came shoving through the gateway, bearing something between them. A dog weaved around their legs, tail thwacking. Another two men followed; it was a plank they were carrying. A plank with a body tied to it.

'. . . fell from the saddle when he was struck by a branch,' one of the men was saying to the group at the kitchen door. 'His foot caught in the stirrup and the horse dragged him at the gallop . . . was dead by the time we got to him!'

'What did they expect?' another man said. 'State of him this morning . . .'

The yard was crowded now, a throng pressing through the gateway and surrounding the body as the bearers set it down. Adam pushed his way between them, his heart tight in his chest. He already knew what he would see.

The body was battered almost beyond recognition, the face a black and bloody mask. Adam's throat tightened as he imagined what had happened: the rider dragged by the panicked horse, whipped and smashed by thorns and tree-trunks, likely kicked by the hooves too. With any luck his neck had snapped immediately. The men crowding round the body hissed and sucked their teeth. Natural John was capering in the kitchen doorway, wailing in anguish.

But what drew Adam's eye was the badge stitched to the dead man's breast. A diagonal red lattice on white. *Argent fretty gules*.

'Poor lad could barely see where he was riding anyway,' somebody said. 'Eyes swollen half shut, and not in his right senses either. They should never have allowed it, after the pummelling he took yesterday . . .'

And as the guilt consumed him, Adam felt himself drawing back from the throng, letting them close in and block the sight of Gerard's mangled body. The axe hung loose from his fist, and when he glanced to his right he saw a group of riders outside the gateway to the yard, peering in. One of them, wrapped in a thick cloak, stared back at him with accusation in his eyes. A face like a blade, and a short pointed beard. Adam's blood slowed. He knew who this must be.

Robert de Dunstanville. *The Devil's Man*.

\*

The great hall of Pleshey Castle was warm and smoky, the glow of the fire in the central hearth driving back the encroaching gloom of winter. Three long trestle tables stood around the hearth, each covered with linens laundered to fresh whiteness, and the household and guests filled the benches. Adam de Norton took his place on the fourth side of the long hall, between the doors, where the meats were laid to be dressed and carved. He was one of four squires appointed to serve the high table, where Lord Humphrey himself sat. Despite the tragic events of the morning, and the premature end of the hunt, Adam seemed to have been forgiven his lapse of the day before.

'Did you see him though, when they brought him in?' whispered the squire beside him. Ralph de Tosny was one of the few in the household that Adam considered a friend.

'Briefly,' he said, wincing.

'I was away with the leading hunt,' Ralph whispered. 'But I heard what had happened. Lord Humphrey was not at all happy – they'd only just sounded the chase, and in the confusion the dogs lost the spoor—'

Then the steward hissed for them to be silent.

A blart of noise, and a group filed into the hall bearing the main course between them. Two servants carried the massive platter holding the roast boar, decked with festive holly and ribbons in the Bohun colours of blue, white and gold. Not a real wild boar, of course – such creatures were seldom to be found in England nowadays, even in the game parks of great magnates – but a huge pig dressed to look like one. Its bulging flanks dripped with honey, and its gaping snout was stuffed with a blackened apple. Musicians accompanied the platter-bearers on bagpipes, vielle and tabor as they made a round of the hall, circling the central hearth to display the boar to the diners, before taking it back to the table to be carved and dressed with piquant sauces. Adam was uncomfortably reminded of the dead man tied to the plank that morning; surely others made the connection, but none said a word about it. He tried to put the image from his mind as he carved the meat and carried the platter up to the high table.

Lord Humphrey de Bohun, Earl of Hereford and Essex, Constable of England and one of the greatest magnates in the kingdom, was in his mid-fifties, but still a powerful man and a famed warrior. He gripped his wine goblet with a corded hand, and scrutinised his assembled guests through hard and narrowed eyes. Only occasionally did his lips twitch a smile, as some words of jest or praise reached him. He spared not a glance as Adam stepped up with the platter and served the meats; Adam was glad of that, and gladder still to return to his place at the far end of the hall.

Further courses were already arriving from the kitchens. Besides the boar-pig there were rolls of stuffed venison, a rack of roasted geese and ducks, veal rolled in almonds, roast herons and partridges, glazed sheep's heads and lark's tongues in jelly, and pies stuffed with game and fowl. A torrent of meats, as if all the beasts of the wild and the birds of the air had hurried forth to fill the gullets of the diners. Between courses, the squires made their rounds with silver ewers of water and jugs of wine, fresh white loaves still warm from the ovens, and the big voider baskets to collect the uneaten food and dripping trenchers. Lord Humphrey's collection of paupers were already gathered in the kitchen yard, waiting for their allocation of alms from the master's table.

Soon the feasting would be done. The hippocras and wafers would be served, Natural John would appear in one of his amusing costumes, and then Adam himself could eat. Perhaps before the hall was cleared there would be music, or a poet to recite tales of chivalry. Lord Humphrey enjoyed hearing singing after dinner, particularly rousing songs, so everyone could join in the chorus. But Adam had always preferred to hear stories; since childhood he had loved the romances of Arthur and his knights, of Roland and Alexander, and of Godfrey de Bouillon.

As a boy, listening to the poets in the warm shadows of the hall, he would let his mind drift to scenes of distant lands and great deeds of prowess, beautiful ladies and chivalric champions. Picturing the young Roland, knighted by Charlemagne on the battlefield of Aspremont and girded with the sword Durendal that he had captured from the King of the Saracens, he would imagine becoming such a champion himself. A true heart, he had told himself, and firm convictions could win great rewards on earth besides in heaven. Childish fantasies, they seemed to him now. Roland, he guessed, had never split his knuckles brawling

in the dirt. Godfrey de Bouillon had never been ordered to chop
firewood either.

Even to be knighted, Adam thought, was a near-impossible dream.
Knighthood had to be *earned*. And where were the opportunities
for that, in the packed clamour of Earl Humphrey's court? He
knew of men who had served twenty years or more as squires
and had never been granted the accolade. That was his own likely
fate, he told himself, and found a strange grim pleasure in the
bleakness of his mood.

Ralph's nudge broke him from his thoughts. 'The lord's companions are running short,' the other squire whispered. 'I'll take
the wine, you carve.'

Adam felt the heat from the fire on his back as he took up the
knives and carved the slices of pork. His senses were flooded
with the scents of roasted meat, and his empty stomach tightened. When the platter was filled he dressed it with a ladle of
peppery sauce and carried it up to the high table. Lord Humphrey was listening to his wife, the countess, with his chancellor
leaning across to offer advice. Adam hung back, waiting for their
hushed conference to be concluded.

'But I'd heard,' a voice said across the hall, 'that the King of
France had prohibited the sport – is that not so?'

'He did, last year,' another voice said, and Adam's shoulders
tensed. He had been trying not to glance in the direction of the
right-hand table, but he knew to whom that bitter, cynical-sounding
voice must belong. 'At the time, King Louis believed that the
Pope was about to call a new expedition to the Holy Lands. But
now the Pope is dead, there is no new expedition, and doubtless the ban will be lifted before long. It only covers the French
crown domains anyway – tournaments continue in the county of
Champagne, and in Flanders and Burgundy, and the Empire too
of course.'

'Well, I consider King Louis very wise in banning them,' one
of the priests at the table primly declared, 'and our King Henry

likewise. As our holy father the Pope says, tournaments are nothing but vanity for the participants, and the cause of turbulence
and unnecessary bloodshed too . . .'

'And the Pope knows more than most about causing turbulence
and unnecessary bloodshed, I suppose,' Robert de Dunstanville
said with a smile.

Before the priest could summon a reply, Adam saw that the
countess and the chancellor had ceased their deliberations.
He stepped up quickly to the high table and began serving the
meat onto the dish that Lord Humphrey shared with his wife.
After a few slices, the earl raised his hand, then gestured to one
of the side tables. 'Sir Robert,' he called. 'Some meat from my
platter?'

Adam tensed, willing himself to appear unconcerned as he
passed down the right-hand table to stand before Robert de
Dunstanville. He looked down as he served the meat and caught
the man's narrowed eye. Then, as he made to step back, de
Dunstanville flashed out his hand and seized Adam's wrist in
a clamping grip. He twisted his arm, turning Adam's hand to
expose the battered knuckles.

'So,' he said, with a sneer in his voice. He was facing the fire,
but Adam's shadow cloaked him in darkness. His large eating
knife lay beside his trencher.

'I was sorry to hear of what happened to your squire, sir,'
Adam managed to say.

'Were you?' de Dunstanville replied quietly, still gripping
Adam by the wrist. 'Perhaps you were. But perhaps you revelled
in it a little too, hmm? Any man would, I think.'

Abruptly he released his grip, and Adam stepped back from
the table. 'Bring me wine,' the knight told him, raising his empty
cup. 'And I want to see you pour it yourself.'

Quickly Adam paced back down the hall and took the silver
jug of wine from Ralph. By the time he returned, the conversation had resumed along the table.

'Lord Edward is in France now, I believe?' one man said. 'Or he will be soon – he's been wintering in Gascony, I think. He'll surely be in Burgundy for the tournaments.'

Adam stepped up to the table once more; Robert de Dunstanville ignored him as he poured the wine.

'And you'll meet with him while you're overseas?' another man asked the knight.

'If our paths should cross, I shall not avoid him, no.'

The cup was filled, and Adam made to turn away, but de Dunstanville halted him with a raised finger, still not glancing in his direction.

'And what of our other . . . *friend*, who is in France?' Earl Humphrey said from the high table. The other voices around the hall fell abruptly silent. 'Will you see him too?'

'I cannot say, my lord,' de Dunstanville said with a shrug. 'I believe Simon de Montfort is currently a guest of the King of France, and keeps to his estates.'

'Just be careful,' Earl Humphrey said, with a vague circling motion of his hand. Adam recalled the story the servants had told, that Robert de Dunstanville was their lord's bastard son. 'Avoid becoming embroiled in any schemes,' the earl went on. 'Avoid *mischief*, Robert. I can say no more to you.'

The knight inclined his head in polite acknowledgement. Adam was already backing away along the table, the wine jug clasped before him.

'Well, you need not worry,' de Dunstanville said with a laugh. 'I shall not be tourneying at all in my present condition! As you see, my lord, as of today I have no squire. What use is a tourneying knight without a squire?'

'A sad business,' Earl Humphrey gruffly agreed. 'Unfortunate! I feel, of course, somewhat responsible. No, really . . .' he went on, as a chorus of dissenting voices came from the other tables. 'Really, I would not allow a guest to leave here inconvenienced or unprepared, after such a sad event. That one – you there!'

With a tight shock, Adam realised that the earl was gesturing towards him.

'We might hold him too at least partly responsible,' he said to Robert de Dunstanville. 'Would he serve as your squire in the place of the other?'

Adam turned in surprise and the knight's searching gaze caught him once more.

'Maybe,' de Dunstanville said. 'He looks a little scrawny for his age. But he bested my squire Gerard, who was no kitten. How clever is he at his duties?'

'Not for me to say,' Earl Humphrey replied. 'Marshal,' he called down the table, 'how proficient is the lad?'

The marshal of the household gave Adam an appraising squint. 'Oh, he knows a horse from a hound,' he said. 'And his skill at arms is no worse than the rest. Which is to say, good enough.'

'Then maybe he'll suffice,' de Dunstanville said with a shrug.

And Adam stood motionless, conscious suddenly of the gathering silence around him, the throng at the tables all staring at him, the faint crack and hiss of the burning wood in the central hearth. And he knew, as the pulse quickened in his throat and his chest grew tight, that his life was now in the hands of Robert de Dunstanville.

# Chapter 2

They left Pleshey before daybreak and rode westwards on lanes of frozen mud. The pale light of dawn exposed a flat landscape under hoarfrost, bare black trees scratching the sky, mist rising from the thawing fields. A few hooded figures in the middle distance gathered wood or hacked at the soil, but otherwise the world appeared deserted. Robert de Dunstanville rode at the head of his little retinue on a palfrey, with his iron-grey destrier thudding along beside him. Adam followed, on a plain rouncey that Lord Humphrey had provided from his own stable. Two sumpter horses came behind him laden with baggage, led by a weaselly-looking servant named Wilecok. At the rear upon a heavy cob was de Dunstanville's serjeant, a weathered man-at-arms of uncertain age called John Chyld. His chin was thick with greying bristles, he wore a grimy linen coif pulled down to his eyes, and as he rode he chewed on a roasted pig's foot taken from the kitchens.

There had been no ceremony to their departure. The castle had still been in darkness when they left, most of the occupants wrapped in their bedrolls. Only Natural John had come forth to bid Adam a stammering farewell – fitting that Lord Humphrey's fool was the only member of the household to do so. Adam was strangely moved all the same. In the four days since the Epiphany feast, he had felt himself frozen out of the community at Pleshey. Even former friends like Ralph had seemed to avoid him, as if he were already tainted by whatever curse or malediction Robert de Dunstanville bore. As if his soul were already blackened.

Now Adam could observe him more closely, he saw that his new master was around thirty years old, and as lean and hard as a rawhide strap. He was dressed in cloak and tunic of common dark blue serge, but the sword belted at his side had a silvered hilt and fittings. As he rode he tugged and teased at his short beard, or stroked at his moustaches with his thumb, as if he were lost in complex thoughts. He said nothing, to Adam or to anyone else, for the first few hours. Only when they were passing through Roding did he call a halt to rest the horses and break their fast.

'So,' he announced, as they sheltered in the lee of a blackthorn thicket and chewed on their tough bread and smoked ham. 'You'll have heard folk talking about me, back at Pleshey. What did they say?'

Adam merely shrugged. He heard John Chyld make a kissing sound against his teeth, and Wilecok was grinning to himself. But if the knight could be taciturn, so could he.

'You're right to be wary of me, boy,' Robert de Dunstanville said, in a low tone. 'I'm a man of fierce and bloody temper, and I do not like to be crossed. But if there are lies being told of me, I want to know of them. So – I asked you a question. Speak.'

*I will not fear this man*, Adam told himself. *I will not let him intimidate me.*

'They say,' he replied, the words drying his mouth, 'that you murdered a priest. And you're excommunicated.'

Sir Robert barked a laugh. 'That priest deserved what he got!' he said. 'He disrespected my late wife's memory. The excommunication I paid off with a pilgrimage to Pontigny last year. What else?'

'They say you were a captive of the Saracens. And they forced you to deny Christ.'

For a moment Sir Robert appeared to consider this. 'True enough, I was,' he said with a sniff. 'But the Saracens never tried to break my faith. The clergy of this very kingdom have tested it sorely indeed though.'

John Chyld let out a wheezing laugh and shook his head again.

'And they say . . .' Adam blurted out, feeling an angry heat rising through him, 'that your lands were seized from you, and you roam the earth like . . . like a carrion dog.'

Robert de Dunstanville gave no reply. He stood plucking and teasing at his beard, frowning. 'A carrion dog, eh?' he said at last. 'Who says this? The household knights? The other squires? Who?'

'Everyone says it,' Adam told him quietly, hoping that none would catch the lie.

'Well, damn them all to hell then!' de Dunstanville said, baring his teeth in a mirthless grin. 'God's death, let them say what they like! My lands were seized unjustly, and against all laws and liberties – they know it, and Lord Humphrey knows it too.'

Wilecok was already packing the food and adjusting the baggage. John Chyld had swung himself back into the saddle. But Sir Robert was not finished. 'A barony I had of my late wife,' he told Adam, in a strangely mild tone. 'But I lost it when she died. My own estate though, a sweet manor that was my birthright, was taken from me by the connivance of the Bishop of Hereford – a shepherd who devours his own sheep! – and William de Valence, Earl of Pembroke, the king's half-brother . . . You know of them?'

'I've heard their names spoken,' Adam replied, uncertain.

'Foreign vermin, both of them,' de Dunstanville said, 'that infest the court of our king, snatching whatever they can. Vermin, who should be hunted with dogs! And yet good men are blamed for their wiles and ruses.'

Then before Adam could respond he gave an abrupt gesture and mounted his horse. 'Many miles to Ware yet,' he declared, 'and dusk falls early.'

They rode onward, an hour and then another, their horses' hooves thudding on the road while the wind blustered around them and rattled the thin branches of the trees. They were almost at Wydford before Sir Robert spoke again.

'You must be disappointed, I suppose,' he said over his shoulder as he rode. 'You must have expected better prospects, eh? Maybe thought you'd be squire to some great lord in time, one like your own father maybe, with wide estates to inherit?'

'I have no estates,' Adam said bleakly. 'My father died, and my mother married Hugh de Brayboef. Now she's dead too, and the lands my father held of the king were granted to him and his sons.'

'Brayboef?' Robert frowned. 'I know of him. A creature of Peter de Savoy, is he not? Another foreign court favourite! Well, so we're well suited – a landless knight and a landless squire, quite alike.'

'I'm not like you at all,' Adam said, anger tightening his shoulders. 'I never murdered anyone, let alone a priest!'

'I didn't *murder* the priest – Christ's bones! I said he *deserved to die*, not that I'd killed him. His death was an accident, as the inquest found.'

Adam grunted, uncertain. He still could not tell whether de Dunstanville was genuinely angered or just taunting him.

'Anyway, what of my squire, Gerard?' the knight said, a little further down the road. 'You murdered him, didn't you?'

'I did not!' Adam said. 'His death was an accident – everyone knows it . . .'

'But if you didn't kill him directly, you'd have liked to have done, isn't that so? It felt good, didn't it, beating him like that? Think of it – all those years of anger and frustration breaking forth . . .'

'No!' Adam said, appalled by the suggestion. 'It wasn't like that at all! He mocked me . . .'

'Oh, he mocked you!' Sir Robert said with a laugh. 'And forbearance is no longer considered a virtue?'

'He mocked my *father*!' Adam said. As the chill wind carried away his words he felt a sudden remorse pouring through him. He should not have allowed himself to be provoked. De Dunstanville had turned his head, and Adam was sure the knight was laughing at him. But when he looked back again a little further down the road, his face was grave.

'Listen to me,' he told Adam. 'I don't blame you for what you did. Maybe I'd have done the same. I'm not much good at turning the other cheek. But we're more alike than you'll admit, you and I. And there are plenty more like us.'

His voice was bitter, every word sawing like a notched blade. 'Justice is dead in this kingdom,' de Dunstanville said. 'King Henry pours gifts and favours into the hands of his family and his foreign courtiers, and squanders the kingdom's wealth on foolish schemes, while honest men must live in shame . . .'

Sir Robert bit a curse between his teeth, then punched his fist into his gloved palm. 'There's a fury growing in England now,' he said. 'A fury that none shall suppress — and by God's death, when it breaks forth it will shake the throne. And the man who sits upon it.'

Adam sat upright in the saddle, surprised by the passion of de Dunstanville's words. He had heard such things said now and again by the knights of Earl Humphrey's household, but always in mutters and never with such force and clarity. The political strife that had raged through the kingdom these last four years, the struggles for supremacy and control between King Henry and his barons and great magnates, had seemed far above his head. But to speak such treason openly was surely reckless, even dangerous.

'Lord Humphrey was of a like mind once,' de Dunstanville went on, 'but he's too canny to speak of these matters now. No, these days he keeps his jaw clamped tight against anything that might sound like sedition. Only fierce loyalty to the crown will pass his lips! The times are "too delicately balanced", he likes to say. But there are others with more fire in their marrow.'

And Adam recalled the talk around the tables at the feast of
Epiphany – of Lord Edward, the king's son, and of the other
'friend in France', as Lord Humphrey had called him. Just for
a few moments, he sensed the distant loom of great events and
felt a nervous thrill pass through him. When he glanced over
his shoulder he saw John Chyld watching him with a hard and
calculating eye.

'However,' Sir Robert announced with a forced grin, 'we shall
see none of this, as we'll be far away overseas, eh! Now let's get
on, there's only an hour or so until dusk.'

Adam thought on his strange speech as they rode. The words
stirred something in him that he did not recognise, a yearning
for something he had never known and could not quite discern.
But still there was a cold savagery in Robert de Dunstanville's
attitudes, in his scorn for finer feelings, that repulsed Adam. No,
he told himself – the knight was a ranting fool, blaming others
for his mistakes and misfortunes. Never would Adam accompany
him to France, or anywhere else. Lord Humphrey had committed
him to indentured service as a squire, but at the first opportunity
he would slip away from de Dunstanville and his little retinue
and take his chances alone, far away from here. He had rela-
tives in Hampshire and Wiltshire, and during his time in Lord
Humphrey's household he had seen a lot of the Welsh Marches –
the marcher barons were always eager for trained men-at-arms
and would ask few questions about his background. Fate had
made him an outcast, but from now on he would make a new
fate of his own.

*

The daylight was almost gone by the time they reached the town
of Ware, and a cold hard wind was buffeting in from the north.
Adam had passed through the place several times with Lord
Humphrey's retinue, but never stayed the night there. The bridge

at Ware spanned the river Lea and carried the old straight road to London; Robert de Dunstanville took a few moments inspecting it, muttering to himself, and then they rode on through the marketplace towards the priory. In gathering darkness they turned off the road and through a gateway, and Adam saw the shape of a large house before him, a hall with a two-storey chamber at one end and kitchens and outbuildings at the other. As they dismounted in the yard, men came from the porch to greet them. There was firelight from within, and the smell of food; but when he made to follow the others inside, Sir Robert snapped his fingers and pointed towards the stables.

'You'll tend to the horses,' he ordered. 'You know how to do that?'

'Of course,' Adam muttered grudgingly, then gathered the reins and followed one of the servants across the gloom of the yard. Wilecok was already attending to the baggage animals, the cob and his own pony, but Adam was left with de Dunstanville's destrier and the other two saddlehorses. In the gloom of the stable, lit only by a single covered lantern, he unsaddled the animals, removed bits and bridles, combed and rubbed them down, then saw to their feed and water. He had worked with horses most of his life, and he knew enough to be careful around the destrier. The animal seemed as restive and ill-tempered as his master, and it took some time before Adam could win its trust sufficiently to complete his chores. By then it was fully dark outside, and the wind was whining around the eaves of the hall as Adam ran hunched across the yard to the warmth of the porch.

He found Robert de Dunstanville already at his supper, seated at the long table at the far end of the hall, beyond the central hearth. There were two young ladies with them – or girls, perhaps, Adam realised as he approached. Both were well dressed, in fur-trimmed clothes, and he bowed to them as he approached the table. A shield hung on the wall behind them, painted with a device he did not recognise: red with a white cinquefoil.

'This is Adam, my new squire,' Sir Robert said to the ladies, with a brief gesture. Then he motioned Adam to sit at the far end of the table and ordered the servants to bring him food and drink.

A pair of friars, the steward, and the bailiff of the estate were already seated, and shunted along the benches to give Adam room at the table. There was an older woman as well, dressed like a nun in plain clothes and a tight headscarf. The servants brought Adam a thick bread trencher, a white roll, a dish of potage with pork and venison, and a heavy flagon of fresh ale. Nobody spoke, and for a while Adam ate in glad silence, feeling the fire's warmth on his back and the food spreading comfort through his body.

'The bridge is damaged again, I see,' Robert said to the steward, pushing his empty dish aside. The fire crackled behind them, and his voice echoed slightly in the dark hall.

'Yes, sir – it was the men of Hertford,' the steward said, with an apologetic wince. 'They often come in the night and try to dig up the roadway or collapse the parapets. They argue that our bridge drains all the trade from theirs, and their tolls are suffering.'

'Your bridge is far better placed, that's why,' de Dunstanville said. 'And this manor needs those tolls. I'll ride over to Hertford in the morning with John Chyld and pull their ears, and see they give you no further trouble.'

Now that his immediate hunger was sated, Adam turned his attention to the two women that sat with Sir Robert at the far end of the table. They appeared to be sisters. One was only a child, twelve or so, with flaming red hair in a thick plait and an open, frank expression. The other was perhaps two years younger than Adam. She wore her hair bound in a simple linen fillet, with twin braids the colour of dark copper hanging to her shoulders. There was something aloof and rather distant in the curve of her lips and her hooded eyes. On one finger she wore a gold ring, enamelled with the same white cinquefoil on red as the shield on the wall behind her. Clearly neither girl was married, though both were of an age to be wed. There was no sign of a senior man around the house, no father or uncle to watch over them, and the older woman was apparently not their mother. What, Adam wondered, were they doing here, living alone in such a place? And why was the disreputable Robert de Dunstanville looking so comfortable at their table?

He felt a spike of quick jealousy, and wished it were he that sat with the women so companionably. He was watching the older girl, almost nervous, hoping and fearing that she might glance in his direction. But instead it was the younger one who spoke.

'What happened to your other squire?' she asked Robert.

'Sadly he suffered an accident,' the knight said. Adam could almost detect the sneer in his voice. 'He went on to his eternal reward, I'm afraid.'

The younger girl peered at Adam, lips pursed. 'I didn't like the old squire,' she said. 'He resembled a pig, and made a panting sound through his mouth when he breathed.'

Her sister turned, frowning, and flicked the girl on the shoulder.

'My dear and well-beloved cousins,' Robert said to Adam, in a weary drawl, nodding to them both. 'The ladies Hawise and Joane de Quincy. Hopefully we will not have to abuse the hospitality of their house for too long.'

Adam stood up, the bench shunting noisily from beneath him, and bowed again. The younger girl, Hawise, stifled a laugh. Adam's jealousy at de Dunstanville's ease and confidence redoubled.

Shortly afterwards the servants came to clear the dishes from the table, snuff the candles and lower the cover over the hearth fire for the night. The two ladies climbed the stairs at the back of the hall to the solar; Adam almost expected Sir Robert to follow them, but instead the knight kicked out his bedroll on the floor

beside the hearth and wrapped himself in his blankets with his
sword at his side. Soon enough he was snoring, with the snores
of Wilecok, John Chyld and the servants echoing from the far
end of the hall.

Adam lay a while in wakefulness, feeling the ebbing heat from
the hearth and the black cold seeping in from the winter night.
When he closed his eyes, he saw in his mind the young woman's
pale oval face, the hooded eyes, the simple elegance of her gestures. She had not spoken a word, and it grieved him that he had
not heard her voice. Snapping back from the brink of fantasy, he
told himself not to be foolish. Weariness fogged his mind, and he
slipped down into sleep.

A screen of leaves opened before him like a curtain, and he
walked from dense darkness into sunlight. He was in a meadow
beside a brook; a moment later he recognised the place. Here
was the mill, and the lower paddock, the strip fields and the
wooded flank of the hill dark above them. Years had passed since
he was last here, but Adam knew it all so well: his father's old
manor, where he was born and grew up. Joy flooded through
him as he saw the path through the meadow leading him up
towards the moated enclosure. There was the manor house, the
little chapel and the dovecot, the stables and barn. And inside
the house, Adam knew as he hurried closer, his mother would
be waiting for him. His father would be in the upper paddock,
perhaps, exercising the horses, or out hunting along the valley,
but soon he would return.

Adam's mind stilled, and he noticed the silence all around him.
No figure moved in the sun-drenched countryside. No bird flew
overhead. No smoke curled from the thatch of the kitchen or the
main house. All was empty – all was dead. Gripped by sudden
horror, Adam tried to turn back. But the dream was carrying
him onward, towards the dead house and the darkness within,
the scene of all he had lost . . .

He awoke with a cry choking his throat. *Ware*, he told himself – he was at Ware, sleeping on the floor beside the dying fire in the hearth. The strange surroundings had conjured the dream from his disturbed mind, that was all. But his heart was beating fast, and he lay a long time in the cold gloom before sleep engulfed him once more.

# Chapter 3

The tip of his nose felt frozen when he woke. He had rolled further from the hearth in the night. Sitting up and stretching his limbs, he saw Wilecok sitting beside the newly lit fire, warming the soles of his shoes. 'Sir Robert's already gone for Hertford,' the servant croaked, then yawned heavily. 'Suffice it to say, we'll not see him back before noon.'

Adam nodded, getting up and rolling his mattress and blankets. Of the ladies, and the other servants, there was no sign.

Living in the Earl of Hereford's household, Adam had become accustomed to noise and activity when he woke, and to the preparations for morning mass. The stillness of the manor house was uncanny. Throwing his mantle around his shoulders, he went out into the yard. A bright day met him, and he squinted as he made his way to the water butt, cracked the skin of ice and splashed his face and hands. Gasping, he raised his head and drew a deep breath. The sky was blue and the yard and surrounding land glittered with frost.

He could not have wished for a better day to make his escape.

The door of the stable was open, but the grooms that usually slept within had already gone. Robert de Dunstanville's palfrey was gone too, and the serjeant's cob, but the destrier and the other horses remained. There were other animals in the stalls,

which Adam had not noticed in the darkness the previous evening. An elegant-looking dappled jennet among them, which he
guessed must belong to one of the ladies of the house. The warm
and familiar scents of the stable were a comfort to his nerves,
but he had no time to waste. Robert would return in only a few
hours, and he must be long gone by then. Hertford lay to the
west, and he could not go that way without risking meeting the
knight making his return journey. To the east lay Pleshey, and to
the south was the road to London that de Dunstanville would
take later that day. Northward, then, was the only option; Adam
had no idea what lay in that direction.

Putting the thought from his mind, he found the sack of bread
and smoked sausage he had managed to secrete the night before,
and the leather flask of watered wine. He had a short-bladed
falchion slung on a baldric, a change of clothes and a purse with
three silver pennies. Hurrying, praying beneath his breath that
the grooms, or still worse Wilecok, would not make an appearance, he lifted the saddle onto the back of his rouncey and began
fastening the girth straps. In the opposite stall the destrier stirred
and stamped, already sensing departure.

'You are in haste to leave us, I see,' a voice said.

Adam jerked upright, leaving the second girth strap hanging.
The figure in the stable doorway was a bar of shadow at first,
then as he blinked he saw the marten-trimmed mantle, the hood
thrown back, and the sheen of copperish hair in the cold light.
One of her maids was with her, but hung back from the doorway.

'Robert told me that you'll be away to Waltham as soon as he
returns,' Joane said, walking further into the stable. 'It's a shame
you have to go so soon, we see so little company here.'

'I think he said he wants to reach the coast before the weather
changes,' Adam said, stumbling over the words. His tongue felt
thick in his mouth. Surely she had seen that he was preparing to
flee? He turned away quickly and finished fastening the rouncey's
girth strap. Joane had crossed to the stall where the jennet was

tethered. The horse whickered, stretching its neck towards her, and she rubbed the nose and chin.

'A bitter season to be journeying,' she said. 'But I suppose you'll want to be in Flanders for the beginning of the tournament season?'

Adam could only nod dumbly. He had very little experience of talking to women, certainly of the higher classes; Earl Humphrey had forbidden any of his young men to consort with them. He felt his lack of confidence now, tangling his nerves. A hot breath over his shoulder and he tensed; the destrier had leaned in to nuzzle at his back.

Joane's face was silhouetted in profile against the light from the stable door. 'Have you attended many tournaments, yourself?' she asked, rubbing her horse's neck. 'I suppose they must be very spectacular occasions.'

'No . . . very few,' Adam managed to say. In truth he had attended none; there had not been a full-scale tournament in England for years, as King Henry fervently opposed them. But he had heard all about what they involved: the initial jousts of the young knights wanting to make a name for themselves, the great mass charge of the opposing teams and the shattering clash of lances, then the swirling horseback melee spreading over miles of country. Spectacular indeed, he thought, and had to remind himself that he had no intention of attending any tournaments in the near future.

But he sensed that Joane was merely probing forward in the conversation. Adam refocussed his attention; he listened carefully, dreading the sound of hoofbeats from the yard, the voices of the returning men.

'I don't know how much Robert has told you of our relationship,' Joane said, and again Adam's pulse jumped, as the jealousy he had felt the night before spiked inside him. She must have caught his expression, and she smiled slightly. 'No, it's not like that,' she said quickly. 'But we think of him as far more than a mere cousin,

Hawise and I. In fact he's more like an older brother, or a second father. He's been our protector these recent years.'

Adam found it hard to imagine the bristling Robert de Dunstanville as anyone's protector, and tried to hide his expression.

'Oh, I know how he appears,' Joane said. 'He can be coarse, and he lacks gentleness ʼ . . . But he has a noble soul, even if he chooses not to show it. Life has not been easy for him. Believe me when I say that.'

'I do, my lady,' Adam said thickly. Confused, he turned away and began preparing the bit and bridle.

'My father was killed at a tournament, did you know?' Joane said, in an altered tone. Adam turned and straightened, shaking his head.

'Sir Robert was with him at the time,' Joane went on. 'They say, don't they, that anyone killed on the tournament field dies excommunicate, and must be forbidden Christian burial. So the Pope once decreed, I think, although it seems quite unchristian . . . But father remained alive long enough for a priest to hear his confession and give him absolution, and his soul is at peace now, with the Lord. Robert assured us of that.'

'He's told me nothing of it,' Adam said, shrugging. 'I'm sorry – he's not the most talkative of men.'

She laughed, dropping her head, then took several steps towards him. 'It would grieve me deeply,' she said, 'if Robert were injured or killed. Every time he goes away overseas I fear the same thing happening to him, but with nobody to attend him, and to make sure . . .' Her voice caught suddenly. 'To make sure that he dies well, if it comes to it.'

Adam was very aware of her closeness in the dim light of the stable. The horses stirred and blew around them, and he felt his heart grow still in his chest.

'I don't know why,' Joane said quietly, 'but I feel I can put my trust in you. As soon as I saw you yesterday, I felt it. Will you promise me something?'

'Of course,' Adam said without thinking. He swallowed heavily as she took his hand. 'Take care of Robert, in the jousts and the melee,' she said. 'I know he's reckless and cares little for himself sometimes. Will you be cautious for him? And if he falls . . . if he is injured, please care for him. For his body . . . and his soul if it comes to it. Can you swear you will do this?'

'Upon my oath, my lady. Upon the love of Christ.'

As soon as the words had passed his lips he burned with remorse. How could he swear such a thing? Her voice, her presence, compelled him. For a moment he could not breathe and felt his blood burning in his body.

'Would you . . . pray with me?' she asked quietly.

'What – here?' He imagined them both dropping to kneel on the stable floor.

'Of course not!' She laughed, sounding nervous. 'I have a Psalter and breviary in the house, that my father left me. You can read?'

'Latin and a little French, if the script is good.'

Adam cursed himself as he followed her from the stable into the chilly blaze of daylight. A promise made under duress, to a woman he did not know and would surely never see again . . . But an oath nevertheless. Could he break it, and live with himself? His teeth were set against the cold, biting back remorse.

'It's strange,' the woman said as she led him to a heavy door of studded oak at the far end of the house, 'I've been several times to Pleshey while the earl has been in residence, and I've never seen you, I think.'

'I was seldom there myself,' Adam told her, trying to unclamp his jaw. 'Mostly I served at his other estates. In the Welsh Marches, and at Caldicot.'

'Then you'll know his son, Humphrey the Younger?' she asked, pausing in the doorway. 'He's often in the Marches, isn't he?'

'Only by sight, my lady, and not for several years.' Adam frowned, remembering the earl's son. A vain and haughty man, crude and arrogant in his behaviour, and far too superior to pay any attention to junior squires.

Joane nodded, distracted, her features clouding for a moment, then she visibly blinked away the thought. Pushing the studded door wide, she led Adam into a dim stone-flagged room with heavy ceiling beams. She spread a rug on the flagstones, then knelt and opened a leather-covered chest decorated with brass nail-heads. From inside she took an object wrapped in silk. When she drew aside the wrappings Adam saw it was a book, with tooled leather covers and gold clasps. Joane kissed it, then laid it on a low wooden lectern and gestured for Adam to kneel beside her.

'I would never ask Robert to do this,' she said with a brief smile, as Adam knelt and crossed himself. For a moment he pictured the knight's mocking sneer, and tensed.

The book was old, the binding loose in places, but each leaf was beautifully lettered and illustrated, with rich inks and gilding that caught the light from the small barred window. Together they recited the Paternoster and the Benedictus, Adam barely conscious of his own voice but hearing only her words, the sounds of her breath. She turned the leaves, her fingers smoothing the vellum, and together they recited the psalms, and the *itinerarium* prayer from the breviary. *Nihil proficiat inimicus in nobis . . . Et filius iniquitatis non apponat nocere nobis.*

As they sat in silent prayer Adam was all too aware of the warmth of her body, so close beside him. His breath caught as she took his hand, and he felt the subtle pressure of her grip. 'Thank you,' she said.

He turned to her, all words driven from his mind, but at that point there came the sound of voices from the hall, the stamp of feet and whinnying of horses from the yard outside. The two of them got up quickly, and by the time Joane had wrapped the book and locked it safely back in the chest, Adam had already left the room.

*

The whole household assembled in the yard to watch them
depart. The steward and bailiff, the priests and the elderly nun
and all the servants stood at a respectful distance as the ladies of
the house, Joane and Hawise, said their farewells. The day was
still clear and bright, the air cold, and Adam sat bundled in his
cloak on the back of his restive horse. Robert de Dunstanville
embraced both women, then swung himself up onto the saddle.
Wilecok and John Chyld were already mounted, the baggage
packed. Adam noticed that the younger sister, Hawise, was sniff-
ing back tears.

'I'll send word from France, when I know the date of my
return,' Sir Robert said. He had an evasive air.

'You won't be back for years, will you?' Joane replied. She
shivered and drew her cloak tighter around her shoulders.

Robert just shrugged and tossed at his reins. John Chyld nodded and urged his cob forward, leading the way.

'Wait,' Joane said, and reached inside her cloak. A long glance
at Robert, but it was Adam's horse she approached. Standing
at his knee, she took his hand and pressed the keepsake into his
palm. A circular silver medal on a leather cord. St Christopher:
protector of travellers.

'Remember,' she said.

Adam did not dare look back as they rode away. John Chyld
was warbling a song, half beneath his breath, but Robert de
Dunstanville rode silently with his head down. Back through the
town they went, then they crossed the bridge and started down
the long straight highway that followed the Lea valley to London.

'So it appears you've turned my cousin's head,' Sir Robert said
after a while, not looking back. Adam made no reply.

The knight laughed. 'Not surprising, I suppose. The last young
man of any decent breeding that she saw was my old squire
Gerard. As you can imagine, he failed to impress.'

Adam remained unmoved. He could almost detect in Robert
now the same jealousy he had felt the evening before, and tried

hard not to appear too pleased with himself. He had already deposited the keepsake medallion in his saddle bag. Even so, as he rode further an uncomfortable feeling began settling over him that Joane de Quincy had entrapped him somehow. He had believed what she had told him utterly; only now did he begin to suspect that he had been subtly manipulated.

'Her mother was a princess of the Welsh, you know,' Robert de Dunstanville said, glancing back at Adam and raising a sardonic eyebrow. 'A daughter of Llywelyn the Great, and granddaughter of old King John too – royal blood flows in my cousin's veins. And she and her sister are wards of our uncle Roger, Earl of Winchester and Constable of Scotland. So best put any hot and wanton thoughts you might be entertaining far from your mind!'

'I never . . .' Adam began, but outrage closed his mouth. He felt himself blushing fiercely and heard the laughter of the two servants. Could it be, he thought, that Joane had simply been *mistaken* about de Dunstanville?

'No, she's got a good soul, Joane de Quincy,' the knight went on, after they had ridden a way further. 'Not like me. Mind you, they say her mother poisoned her first husband . . . Luckily she takes after her father.'

'She told me you were with her father when he died,' Adam said, wanting to shift the conversation away from Joane, and from himself.

'I was. He was killed at a tournament at Blythe, a good few years ago. In the first charge, it was – a lance struck his shield and slid up over the rim. The point went under his helmet edge and broke his mail coif just beneath the jaw – which goes to demonstrate that you should always keep your head down behind your shield in the charge. Don't flinch away from your opponent's lance . . . Anyway, it killed him instantly.'

'You told her he had time to hear absolution!' Adam said.

'Sometimes,' Robert said firmly, 'you tell people what they need to hear. Understand?' He raised his hand and stabbed his finger at Adam. 'If that girl ever hears otherwise, you'll suffer for it!'

Another mile passed before Sir Robert spoke again. The day had grown darker, and a damp wind was hissing through the wiry bushes on the riverbanks.

'I was squire to her father,' he said, 'when I was around the age you are now. I went with him to the Holy Land. He was the man who knighted me, in fact.'

'He did you a great honour,' Adam said, wary of Sir Robert's friendlier tone.

'Ha! Not really,' de Dunstanville said. 'We were prisoners of the Saracens by then, and they were killing all the squires, so it seemed merely humane. Mind you, once you've seen the flower of French nobility puking and shitting themselves to death on the banks of the Nile, knighthood doesn't seem quite as glamorous . . .'

Adam made a noise of disgust. 'Why must you drag everything down into the filth?' he exclaimed, before he could stop himself. 'Since yesterday I've heard you malign the Pope, the Church, the king and his courtiers, Earl Humphrey . . . even knighthood itself! You abandon ladies who regard you as their protector, and ride off to tournament . . . Do you hold nothing sacred at all?'

De Dunstanville tugged at his reins, and with a swift sidestep his horse closed on Adam's, the knight reaching out and seizing the bunched cloak at his shoulder. 'Listen to me!' he growled, all humour scoured from his voice. 'I care for little in this world, true enough. But those two girls back at Ware are more precious to me than my soul! Their father died quickly, as I said, but he made me swear that if he fell I would protect them, and so I will. If either were harmed, I would hunt the man who did it to the very deepest of the seven hells and rend the flesh from his bones!'

Adam had flinched in the saddle. Now he took Robert's hand and eased it from his cloak. 'Peace, sir,' he said. 'I give you my word, I do not doubt you.'

'Good!' the knight declared, and grinned. He tugged at his reins and started off along the road, then halted once more. 'At least,' he said, 'whatever promises my cousin wrung out of you seem to have persuaded you not to run away. Or are you just planning to do that later?'

Adam stared, wide-eyed, cursing his carelessness. Of course, Sir Robert would have noticed the horse already saddled in the stable, the sack of provisions laid ready. Adam had been so distracted, he had forgotten to cover his tracks.

'Listen, boy,' de Dunstanville said, his tone hardening again as he turned to gaze back at Adam. 'I'll have no unwilling followers with me, understand? If you want to go, go now – no need for skulking and hiding. I'm no easy master, I know that, and this is no easy road. Our way lies overseas, to the tournaments. To the school of warfare. I can't promise you much – fame and glory, if you're lucky. Pain and death, if not. And burial in unhallowed ground. But you might at least win more than those three silver pennies in your purse.'

The clouds shifted, and hard winter sunlight flooded the road. Adam turned in the saddle and squinted back the way they had come. He looked at Sir Robert again, and felt the promise he had made to Joane de Quincy weighing heavy on his soul.

'Choose, then,' Robert said. 'Go in peace, and I'll not pursue you. Or follow me, with a true heart and your eyes open.'

# Chapter 4

They entered London at noon the next day, to the clamour of bells. Passing through the great arch of Bishop's Gate, they heard the sonorous chimes of the distant cathedral bell sounding the hour of sext, and a heartbeat later the bells of St Botolph's Without rang from behind them. Then, as they rode on into the packed thoroughfare of Bishopsgate Street, came the bells of St Ethelburga's, St Helen's and St Martin's Otteswich, and each of the hundred other churches in the city following the last at a slight delay, until all the chiming notes rang together and the air reverberated with metallic tumult.

'Praise God!' John Chyld cried as he rode, raising his arms to the noisy sky. 'His mercy upon London!' And he let out a loud belch.

Earl Humphrey had come often to this city, and to nearby Westminster Palace when the king was in residence there, but Adam had never accompanied him through the gates. He had seen other cities and large towns: Bristol and Gloucester, Salisbury and Hereford. But never had he seen such a dense and teeming accumulation of people as he saw now. Fifty thousand of them lived within the circuit of London's ancient walls, so Wilecok had muttered that morning as they were leaving the abbey lodgings at Waltham. And Adam could almost believe that entire number were packed into Bishopsgate Street, or in the narrow alleys that opened like cracks between the gable-ended houses to either side. A blue haze of smoke hung overhead, shot through with beams of winter sunlight.

'Keep your wits about you, young sir,' Wilecok said, riding alongside Adam. 'These Londoners are crafty folk. I should know, suffice it to say – being as I was one of them!'

Adam nodded, reaching beneath his cloak to check the purse and knife hanging from his belt. His eyes open, his heart true, he tried to digest all that he saw around him, as Wilecok announced each new street and district through which they passed. The smell alone was almost overpowering; a fug of warm bodies and charcoal fumes and cooking food, and a stink of rotting filth, with various unidentifiable sweeter scents rising through it all. Robert de Dunstanville and his retinue were the only ones on horseback among the crowd, and at the sight of his champing destrier and the mounted men following him, the mass of people parted to let them through. Only the dogs disputed their passage, barking and weaving around the hooves of the horses.

They rode into the open area by the Stocks Market, where the ground was runnelled with blood and piss and marshy with the trampling of beasts. On into Poultry, and Adam saw wicker cages of chickens and geese stacked high, the squawking and honking of the fowl adding to the cacophony. A group of women were lugging wet clothes from a slopping basin, and as he rode past, the prettiest of them smiled and winked at him, pulling up her skirts to show her legs. She called out to him, but he did not catch her words.

'You've made another conquest, I see!' said Robert.

Adam blushed, glancing away quickly.

'Oh, not so fond of women, perhaps? Has my cousin wasted her favour on barren soil?' Robert laughed. 'Or did Lord Humphrey have you all living like monks, is that it? The sight of a woman makes you bashful?'

Wilecok was cackling to himself, leering and doffing his greasy hat at any woman he saw, but Adam held his tongue and kept his head down as they rode on through the crowded market.

They passed Mercers Hall and the tanners' market, and came into Westcheap, by far the widest city street Adam had ever seen and almost filled with market stalls and booths. A short way further and Robert led them aside into a much narrower thoroughfare, lined with buildings that leaned close above them and almost shut out the daylight. After the tumult of Westcheap it was like entering a cave. Near the end of the narrow street Robert turned again, guiding his horse through an arched gate that led to a covered passageway. Adam followed behind him, and they emerged into a cobbled yard surrounded by brick and timber buildings. A wooden stairway rose to the portal of a hall on the upper storey.

'Master Elias of Nottingham, my man of business,' Robert told Adam as he dismounted, indicating the neatly dressed man waiting at the head of the stairs. 'We'll stay here tonight, as there are matters I need to discuss with him. You'll go with Wilecok to buy provisions – be sure to return here with them before vespers.'

He took a heavy pouch of coin from his saddlebag and tossed it to the servant, who snatched it as it flew. Then, without another glance at Adam, Robert turned and climbed the stairs towards Elias, who stood with arms spread to greet him.

*

They bought dried peas and smoked sausage, a wheel of hard cheese and a tub of mutton grease, and a keg of English ale that Wilecok claimed should last them till Dover. 'After that,' he said, 'we'll be drinking that piss-and-water brew the Frenchies make.'

Adam quickly realised that his principal task was to make sure that Wilecok did not slip too many coins into his own purse, and to manage the laden packhorse that carried their purchases. Anything more would have been beyond him, amid the confusion of thronging people and animals, and the strange sights that surrounded them. Wilecok took him along Westcheap and Poultry, and as far east as Leadenhall, then back again to the great cathedral of St Paul's, all the time haggling and chaffing in a bewildering mixture of bad French, several English dialects, and half a dozen other languages that Adam had never heard before.

'Raisins,' the servant declared, slinging a jar of them into Adam's arms. 'The master does love them so – his only luxury! If he's ever at cross purposes, just feed him raisins.'

They bought a sheaf of tallow candles, spare straps and buckles, fire irons and a new cooking pot, a big canvas tent and a smaller one, with rolls of rush matting to go inside them, bowstrings and arrow heads, needles and thread, and several bolts of red and white cloth to make surcoats. They ate hot meat pies from a huckster's tray and washed them down with mugs of fresh ale from a booth beneath the bell tower of St Paul's.

'I'd be careful what you eat tonight, young sir, if you catch my hook,' Wilecok said, as he led Adam up Paternoster Street towards the city wall. 'I wouldn't even stay beneath that roof myself!'

'How do you mean?' Adam asked, frowning.

Wilecok gave him a quizzical stare, then grinned. 'Ah, you don't even know it! Well, I shouldn't be the one to tell . . . Just take a look in the screens passage, and use your head. I wouldn't let anything pass my lips in that place, suffice it to say!'

Adam blinked at the man, baffled. If Wilecok was playing games with him, he would indulge the servant no further. They passed through the city wall at Ludgate, and went down the slope and across the Fleet Bridge to Farringdon Without. At an armourer's workshop beside St Bride's chapel they collected a full mail hauberk, leg armour and a great helm that Sir Robert had left there several months before to be repaired. Wilecok also bought a selection of heavy iron lance heads. 'Pointless to buy the staves,' he explained. 'They break so many of them in the hastiludes, we're better off cutting our own ash rods once we're across the seas.'

Back over the Fleet with their laden packhorse, they were in the shadow of Ludgate when Wilecok paused. He took out the purse and weighed the few remaining coins within it, then stuffed it into his tunic and grinned. 'I'll let you find your own way home, eh?' he told Adam. 'I'm off to acquaint myself with the good women of Smithfield. Just go on through the gate and keep the cathedral to your right hand – follow the road around to Westcheap and you'll see the way easy from there. And remember . . .' He tapped the side of his nose with a gnarled finger, then traced a cross over his sealed lips.

*

It was getting dark by the time Adam found his way back to the house of Master Elias, after several wrong turnings. Several times he had wondered what Wilecok's strange warning could mean, but the thought had been driven from his mind as he tried to navigate the packed London streets with a heavily burdened packhorse. Only when he had stabled the animal and safely stowed all the day's purchases in the locked storage chamber did he think on those words again.

A servant opened the thick oak door at the head of the stairs. Once inside the gloomy panelled passageway Adam took his time unfastening his cloak and taking off his mud-spattered shoes, glancing around him all the while. Nothing caught his eye. Voices came from the hall beyond the inner door: Sir Robert and another. There were capes and outdoor mantles hanging from pegs beside the door, and when the servant stepped outside for a moment Adam shifted them aside, thinking they might conceal something. He saw only the wood panelling, but as the capes dropped back he noticed that each had a pair of rectangular linen patches stitched to the breast. The servant returned and showed Adam into the hall.

Robert de Dunstanville was sitting beside the central hearth, drinking wine and playing chess with his host. Master Elias of Nottingham was a small man, with a quick confident smile and a beard teased into two forks. Robert made the introductions, and both Adam and Elias made their bows.

'An improvement, I think, on your last young man,' Elias said. 'And the one before that — the Hainauter. Whatever happened to him?'

'He fell sick and died in Flanders, when last I was there,' Robert said. 'But yes, I certainly hope that young Adam de Norton here makes a better squire than either of my last ones.'

Adam tried to smile, but felt very uncomfortable. He had already worked out that Gerard had only been with Robert de Dunstanville a matter of months before his untimely end. The news that the previous squire had also departed his life early deepened his uncase.

A bell sounded in the passage, and servants began carrying the dishes into the hall for the evening supper. They set them on a large table at the far end of the chamber, with candles burning on tall iron stands to either side. Once Adam had joined Robert and Elias at the table a woman joined them, appearing from an inner room. She was in her mid-twenties, tall and elegantly dressed, with very dark eyes and a married woman's headcloth covering her hair; Elias's wife, Adam guessed. Sir Robert introduced her as Belia.

The meal was roast goose in a rich-smelling saffron sauce, and they said no grace before eating. Adam was sharing his mess platter with Robert, but every time he glanced at the meat he thought of the honking fowl in the Poultry market and his stomach contracted. Wilecok's sly warning revolved in his mind, and he sat sullenly picking at the bread roll beside him, which was surely inoffensive enough.

'I've had messages back from Jacob, and from Hagin,' Elias said as he ate, 'and they've agreed to your request. They'll come in with me on the loan, and we can draw up the chirograph and the other documents and have them witnessed tomorrow before you leave.'

'From my heart, I thank you,' Robert replied, inclining his head. 'You'll be more than pleased with the repayment, I hope.'

'I hope so too! And for that, we must pray to God for a keen lance and a swift sword, eh?' Elias mimed a couched lance, galloped a little in his seat, then laughed and drank more wine. 'And maybe,' he went on, 'if you are lucky, you'll meet with Lord Edward on your travels too? He could certainly aid matters, I think.'

'That remains to be seen,' Robert said. 'But I'll drink to my chances.'

'Certainly I would prefer him to the other one we mentioned,' Elias said with a frown. 'We have heard no good reports about him.'

'Earl Simon has learned from his mistakes, I'm sure,' Robert said. 'You should have no concerns about him now.'

Elias's frown remained, and the silence lengthened.

'Your squire must be eager to prove himself on the tourney field as well,' the woman, Belia, said from the far end of the table. She was sitting with one of the candle-sconces behind her, so Adam could not make out her expression, but he could detect the odour of her perfume. Sweet like roses, he thought, or musk. Her voice was deeper than he had expected, and there was a strange warmth to her tone.

Sir Robert turned to Adam and raised an eyebrow. 'Yes,' Adam said, almost coughing the word. 'I'm . . . very eager.'

'Hopefully his appetite will improve by the time he reaches Flanders,' Elias said, 'or he'll waste away before the first trumpet sounds!'

'You must excuse my new squire,' said Robert, with a touch of gravel in his voice. 'Until lately he has dwelt in the household of the Earl of Hereford. Not a place known for its social finesse.'

Adam saw the flash of Belia's teeth in the shadows as she laughed, then she raised her wine cup again. 'I'm sure you are the man to teach him, Sir Robert,' she said.

When the meal was done, Adam went to his bedroll hungry and disturbed. Robert had described Elias as his *man of business*, but he was clearly a moneylender. Hardly a respectable profession, but the knight had spoken and joked with Elias as an equal, and with his wife as well. The meaning of Wilecok's warning was growing clearer to Adam now, although he could not bring himself to put a name to his fears just yet. He lay down beside the embers of the hearth, with Robert stretched on the far side and the servants sleeping at the other end of the hall near the door. Elias and Belia had retired to the inner chamber.

For a long time Adam lay in the darkness as the dying heat from the hearth ebbed and the dark chamber filled with cold. He was listening for Robert's snore, but heard nothing; when he opened his eyes and craned his head he caught the gleam of firelight reflected from the knight's open eye. Quickly he dropped his head, closed his eyes, and willed himself to sleep.

He must have dozed for a short while, but he snapped awake again suddenly, disorientated in the dark. Lying motionless, he stilled his heart and shortened his breath, listening into the midnight silence. The creak of a door, then the sound of a tread on the floorboards. Opening one eye, Adam peered into the gloom, and a moment later made out a shadowed form crossing the floor. His breath stopped completely. The figure was wrapped in a dark cape or blanket, and advanced as far as the hearth where Sir Robert lay. Then Adam caught the smell of roses and musk, keen and distinct, and he understood.

Eyes closed, he heard the rustle of cloth and the whispered words. The straw of Robert's bedroll rasped slightly. When he dared himself to look again, Adam saw the woman kneeling beside Robert, then straddling him. Her unbound hair tumbled in black curls over her naked shoulders, and the last glow from the hearth lit the curve of her breast and the dark whorl of her nipple. Then she lowered herself over him, and her hair covered them both like a cloak.

Adam had heard the sounds that people made during sex often enough before. Several times, sleeping in communal halls, he had heard the servants rutting in the shadows, and sometimes one of the less scrupulous of his fellow squires rutting too. But this was different. He closed his eyes, tried to dull his ears, as if the sense of burning shame that flooded him could be stoppered up. But still he heard the breathy sighs, the whispered words and the gasps of urgent pleasure that sounded almost like pain.

When he opened his eyes at last the woman was gone, but the trace of her scent lingered in the air, mingling with the smell of the cold ashes in the hearth.

\*

It was mid-morning before Robert de Dunstanville and his retinue departed the house of Master Elias. A wet grey morning, with thin rain slicking the cobbles and dripping from the low eaves. Sir Robert was clearly in a foul mood, and neither Adam nor the servants said anything to him as they saddled the horses and piled the baggage onto the sumpter beasts. Elias bade his farewell from the head of the stairs, but Robert only raised his hand and grunted. Of Belia there was no sign.

They rode along the bedraggled length of Westcheap and Poultry, then moved onward through districts that Adam had not seen before, forging a path through the crowds at the junctions and spattering mud from the puddles with the hooves of their horses. Some time later they passed through a gateway, and Adam spied brown water between the houses packed on either side of the street. They were crossing London Bridge, he realised. Only when they were on the far bank, riding on through Southwark with open ground before them, did he jog his horse forward to join Robert de Dunstanville.

'You might have told me,' he said.

Sir Robert flicked a glance from beneath his hood, but said nothing.

'They were Jews, weren't they?' Adam went on.

'Oh, you noticed? I thought you were picking at your food strangely. What did you think – they'd poison you? Feed you unchristian goose?'

'But . . . they were *Jews*,' Adam said, baffled. For as long as he could remember he had heard tales of the curse upon the Jewish people, of their vicious customs and crimes, the hatred that all good Christians should feel towards them. When he was a child his mother had told him of the wicked things the Jews would do to him, if he did not say his prayers. 'It's a crime even to associate with them,' he said. 'And they . . . they have the blood of Christ on—'

'On *what*?' Robert demanded suddenly, reining his horse so hard it almost reared. 'Do you hear what you're saying, boy? You dare to speak like this to me, one who's been signed with the cross? One who's shed his own blood in the Holy Land?'

Adam halted beside him, his face burning. He realised now that he had never before witnessed Robert de Dunstanville's true wrath. Only now was he seeing a flicker of the man's anger fully unleashed. Fear flowed up his spine, and he tried not to quail.

'Oh yes, you'll have heard a few things,' Sir Robert went on, grinding the words and spitting them forth. 'Up there at Pleshey, and in Earl Humphrey's hall. Things the priests have told you, eh? You have a few *notions*, I'm sure . . . But I've seen the world, boy. I've seen things done by good Christian men that would cause Christ himself to hide his face and weep. And more noble things by far done by Jews, and by Saracens too, than by any Christian!'

Adam tried to reply but could only stammer. From the corner of his eye he saw Wilecok shrugging and shaking his head.

'As for Master Elias,' Robert went on, shaking himself like a dog shucking off water, 'I have known him many years. He's written me bills of exchange, to present to his colleagues overseas, that will grant me the funds I need to support us. We trust each other, and he's as good and true a friend as any man I know.'

'And yet . . .' Adam went on, unable to hold back. 'And yet you *lie with his wife?*'

'Ha!' Robert cried, and drew a long, pained breath. 'Belia's not his wife, you fool. She's his sister. His *widowed* sister. And I have known her for many years too, from when my wife and her husband both still lived. And while they lived, I promise you, we laid not a finger upon each other!'

'But now,' Adam said, his words halting as he frowned. 'Now, you're free to do as you please?'

'If only it were so simple! By the laws of her people and mine we cannot. If we were discovered, the harm would be greater for her than for me. Elias is aware of it, of course, but he is a good man and says nothing . . . And this, God knows, is why I have to go overseas. Go, and not return for as long as I can, and hope that when I do she is safely married again and far away, and this dangerous madness will die.'

'Then you and she . . .?' Adam began.

Sir Robert nodded, slumped in the saddle of his motionless horse. The rain dripped from his hood and caught in droplets in his beard. He gave a quick sour laugh, filled with anguish. 'Did you think,' he said, 'that love is like they tell it in the romances, and the songs of Arthur? That the good knight rescues the Christian maiden from her tower, and all ends in marriage? Life, you'll find, is seldom so convenient.'

Then he jogged his horse forward once more, and they rode on towards the sea.

*Chapter 5*

'God damn you, you great briny bastard!' John Chyld yelled, raising his fist to the waves. The stiff breeze blew his words back at him, and the sea answered with a blast of freezing spray. Clambering up from the open hold, Adam stood beside the serjeant, clutching the rail as the ship slid across the crest of the wave and plunged downwards once more. A fresh swell of nausea rose from his gut, and he fought it back. They had left Dover at daybreak on the land breeze, with the promise of a swift passage across to Wissant. But now, nearly eight hours later and with the light fading, they were still battling against heavy currents and shifting winds as they tried to beat south-eastwards towards Boulogne instead.

Adam had seen the estuary of the Severn, where the waters stretched to the horizon, but his first sight of the open sea at Dover had been daunting all the same. It was particularly daunting in this winter season, when the gales blew up and down the straits with seldom a calm, whipping the cold grey waves into spumy whitecaps. It had taken Robert de Dunstanville four days to locate a ship which was preparing to make the dangerous winter crossing. The *St Bride the Virgin* was an aging half-decked *nef*; when Adam had first seen her in the harbour at Dover he had thought her a sturdy and substantial craft, with her broad clinker-built hull, towering

single mast and timber castles at bow and stern. Now, wallow-
ing in the open sea, she seemed as fragile as a bean pod. Down
in the open hold the horses rolled their eyes and hauled against
their tethers as the bilgewater slopped around their hooves, and
with every rise and fall of the deck the other passengers cried and
groaned, wailing prayers for their salvation.

Adam felt the icy sting of the breeze on his face, and his fingers went instinctively to the St Christopher's medallion he
wore around his neck, hanging just inside his tunic. Both he and
John Chyld had tin pilgrim badges pinned to their cloaks as well,
bought at the shrine of St Thomas Becket in Canterbury. Robert
had paused there for a day to hear Sunday mass in the cathedral,
and they had all visited the martyr's tomb and prayed for a safe
crossing of the sea. Adam had no idea whether St Thomas had
any power over the elements or the billowing of the open water;
putting his trust in St Christopher seemed the better option.

Keeping a grip on the slippery windward railing, he made
his way aft towards the sheltered area beneath the stern castle.
Robert de Dunstanville was sitting in the gap between two kegs,
with his cloak pulled tightly around him and his sword across
his knees. His mood had been so foul ever since arriving at
Dover that only John Chyld had dared speak to him. He made no
response now as Adam greeted him and lowered himself to squat
against the keg beside him.

'The shipman says we may yet reach Boulogne before nightfall,' Adam said, his jaw aching from the cold. 'But we may have
to put back to Winchelsea if we cannot get any further east.'

Robert flicked a glance at him from beneath lowered eyebrows. 'Is that so?' he said in an ironic tone. Obviously he had
heard exactly the same news.

'I believe I should apologise to you properly,' Adam said, clearing his throat. 'For the things I said as we were leaving Southwark
last week. I know you implied the matter was settled, but—'

'You've been thinking on your mortality, I suppose,' Robert broke in, 'and want to make amends, eh? If it's absolution you want, talk to them,' he said, gesturing to the little knot of Franciscan friars who knelt in fervent prayer on the aft deck, their wet grey cassocks billowing in the wind.

'There's much I do not know about the world, I realise that,' Adam went on, undeterred. The ship gave a lurch, the deck plunging, and his stomach plunged with it. Another chorus of anguished cries came from the passengers. 'I'm eager to learn,' he said queasily, mastering himself, 'if I get the chance.'

Sir Robert joined his hands in a gesture of prayer and raised his eyes to the angry sky. Adam took a few moments to settle himself more securely against the kegs. Although he was now committed to following the knight, he still could not fully trust him, or warm to his grim attitudes and sardonic humour. Even so, despite himself, he was becoming strangely fascinated by Robert de Dunstanville. There was far more, he suspected, that he still did not know about the man and his shadowy past.

'Back in London,' he said, raising his voice against the whine of the wind and the deep groaning of the timbers, 'Master Elias suggested that you hoped to meet Lord Edward in France. Somebody at Pleshey mentioned his name as well, I remember. But I do not understand why.'

'Edward is a great lover of tournaments,' Robert said with a dismissive shrug. 'He often spends half the year overseas. It's not unlikely we shall meet him, and perhaps he might permit me to join his retinue.'

'But Master Elias seemed to give it a special significance,' Adam said. 'As if it would be important for you in particular.'

'By the head of St John!' the knight exclaimed. 'Can you not work it out for yourself? Lord Edward is the king's eldest son, his heir. And he has been, at certain times, far more inclined towards reform and justice than his father will ever be. But he is a dangerous man, mercurial and proud. He is known to reward those close to him, and punish any who fail to give him respect.'

'So by joining his tournament retinue you might gain him as a patron?'

'Something like that, if luck is with us.' Robert shrugged again. 'We might better help our prospects in France than by staying in England.'

'*We*, you say?' Adam asked, startled. He had not considered that he too might have a part in Sir Robert's plans.

'Of course,' the knight replied. 'You want to claim your lands back too, don't you? By placing ourselves in Lord Edward's good graces, we both might prosper. But if Edward cannot help us, there could perhaps be another who can.'

Robert's expression clouded, as if he were unwilling to say more, but then he raised his head, suddenly alert, and peered along the deck. The prow of the ship rose and crested the next wave, and along the grey horizon appeared the smudged shape of the coastline, and the distant breakwater of Boulogne harbour.

'Land, sweet God be praised!' one of the friars declared, raising his hands to the heavens, before a spray of cold spume blew across the deck and almost knocked him off his feet.

\*

From Boulogne they rode east and then south for the town of Arras. The early tournament season, Robert said, would begin at any moment; it was the last week of January, and already the heralds would be carrying word of the dates and venues from one town to the next. At Arras they would wait and prepare themselves, training for what lay ahead, until the announcement of the first tourneys reached them.

Since boyhood Adam had been schooled in the exercises of arms: riding and fighting from horseback, charging with couched lance against the quintain, jousting against another rider, and taking falls from the saddle. But never had he trained as hard as Robert directed, during that journey to Arras and in the week that followed. Every evening he staggered to his bed with aching muscles and bruised limbs, only to rise before matins and begin it all again. Robert de Dunstanville himself had changed since arriving on the continent; his mood had lifted, just as his temper had shortened. Like a battle-trained horse, he seemed to sense the proximity of violence.

'What are the principal virtues of knighthood?' he asked Adam after supper on their first evening at Arras, swigging the sour gritty wine in the gloomy hall of the inn. There was a chessboard between them, and he had already won two games.

'Courage and prowess,' Adam said promptly, 'loyalty and honour . . .' He had spent his youth listening to tales of chivalry, and knew the virtues well.

'Exactly!' Robert declared, raising a finger.

'Generosity of spirit, courtesy, a frank and honest bearing . . .' Adam went on, scratching at the flea bites on his arms.

'Yes, yes, that's enough,' Robert said, before he could continue further. 'And where would one best find these virtues displayed?'

'On . . . a tournament field?' Adam suggested. He picked up one of his pawns, frowned, and set it down on the board again.

'Yes!' Robert said with a grin. He took another swig of wine. 'The tourney,' he went on in a didactic tone, propping his elbows on the table, 'is the ideal venue for the perfection of knightly virtue. The initial jousts display the courage and skill at arms of the younger men. Then the cry of the trumpets, the shattering of lances when the lines converge, the glorious frenzy of the melee . . . all display fortitude and loyalty to one's team and leader. And, of course,' he said, raising a finger, 'honour in acknowledging defeat and paying ransom, should it come to that.' He casually moved his bishop across the board, trapping Adam's king in *échec*.

'So if tournaments are such displays of virtue and nobility,'
Adam asked, 'why do the kings of England and France so often
try to ban them? Why does the Church anathemise them?'

'Kings fear any gathering of armed men that do not follow their own banner, and owe allegiance solely to their rule,'
Robert said with a shrug. 'They believe that the tournaments
breed pride and independent spirits in their subjects. Which is
true enough. As for the Church – they fear that on the tournament
field men might see something more glorious even than God!'

And Adam, his ears burning from the blasphemy, poured
more wine from the jug. Despite his misgivings, he felt the lust
for glory stirring within him.

But he did not feel at all glorious the following morning, his
head thick as he tramped out to the frosty paddock behind the
inn dressed in an ill-fitting quilted gambeson. The body armour
had belonged to Sir Robert's former squire, Gerard; it was far
too big for Adam and hung down past his knees. Wilecok could
only do so much with shears, needle and twine, and the gambeson stank of mildew and old sweat. Gerard's sweat, Adam did
not doubt, and probably the sweat of many other former squires
as well.

An hour later, plenty of his own sweat was soaking into the
grimy linen of the garment. He was sparring against John Chyld,
both of them armed with quarterstaffs. The serjeant fought with
a slow grunting ferocity, effortlessly driving Adam back across
the stiff turf before knocking him down again and again. Adam's
knuckles were skinned and bruised, blood-red and white as he
gripped the staff and hauled himself back to his feet to begin
once more.

'I see the Earl of Hereford's master at arms is an old woman,
as I'd suspected,' Robert said, strolling across the paddock to join
them. He was already dressed in his full mail hauberk, with the
groom from the inn stables leading his horse. 'He's taught you to
stand your ground, defend yourself to a point, but nothing about

attack. I'll need more than that from you if you're going to be useful to me.'

'What more could I give you?' Adam asked bitterly. His nose was bleeding, and he wiped it with the back of his hand. As far as he was aware, squires were not expected actually to fight in the tournament. But he had been hiding his ignorance of what was required of him for so long, he did want to appear foolish by asking questions now.

'I need aggression,' Robert said. 'I know you've got the fighting spirit – you beat my old squire Gerard with your bare hands, and he was a bully of a lad. That was why I chose you to replace him! Now all we have to do is draw that spirit out of you again.'

'You didn't choose me,' Adam said. 'Lord Humphrey offered me to you, at the Epiphany feast . . .' His words died away as he saw the look of amusement passing between the knight and his serjeant.

'Oh, I chose you, don't worry,' Robert said over his shoulder, as he walked towards his horse. 'It was all agreed, before the feast even began.'

'But . . .' Adam began to say, his brow furrowing. He turned to follow Robert, but before he could speak another word John Chyld's quarterstaff struck the back of his knee and knocked his legs out from under him. Sprawling once more on the turf, Adam blinked away the tears of humiliation as he heard the laughter of the two men.

'Lesson for you,' John Chyld said. 'Never turn your back on an opponent with a weapon in his hand.'

That night, plunged into exhausted sleep on his bed of straw, Adam dreamed that a shadow stood over him, and he quailed beneath it. The shadow was his own, he knew, formed of his shame and his sense of weakness, his fear of failure. He awoke suddenly, well before dawn, and lay in the darkness scratching at his flea bites as thoughts spun in his mind. Why had Robert de Dunstanville taken him on as a squire? John Chyld could do all that was needed as an armed servant on the tournament field – did Robert want merely the appearance of knightly dignity that a squire would provide for him? Adam had no way of telling, but he knew that he could not continue to live in ignorance. He knew what he had to do.

*

As the first daylight streaked the sky, Adam was waiting at the inn door. Robert descended the wooden stairway from the upper chamber, blinked at him and then frowned, yawning heavily. 'John Chyld is not with you?' he asked.

'He's still snoring,' Adam told him. 'I want you to teach me instead.'

'I have my own business today,' Robert replied curtly, and motioned for Adam to move aside.

'All I learn from being knocked over again and again is humility,' Adam said, standing his ground. 'If that's all you want, then I'd understand. But you say you want more – so show me. That's your task, isn't it? The duty of knight to squire?'

Robert inhaled sharply, affronted. For a moment he stared at Adam in the dawn light, his wrath kindling. Adam made an effort not to flinch. Then abruptly Robert shrugged and laughed. 'So be it then,' he said. 'After matins, we begin.'

An hour later, Wilecok led Adam to the muddy stable yard at the back of the inn. In the open doorway of the wagon shed there was half an animal carcass hanging from the beam. Adam stared at the mass of old meat, clotted blood and bone. Already flies were circling around it in the chilly morning air. 'What was it?' he asked.

'Sheep,' Robert replied, striding across the yard. 'An old one. It would have been chopped up for dogmeat, so I got it for a couple of silver bits. Hopefully worthwhile.' He shoved the carcass, and it swung heavily on its hook.

'Hit it,' he said.

Adam glanced at him. He clenched his fist, and Robert nodded. Drawing back his arm, Adam punched at the carcass. His bruised knuckles slammed into the cold hard flesh and he felt the shock of the blow up his arm. The carcass swung, creaking.

'Again,' Robert said. 'This time show some force. Imagine the carcass is Gerard, eh? Imagine he's mocking you – or mocking your father . . .'

Adam set his jaw, knowing that he was being goaded but feeling the anger building inside him anyway. He struck again, then a third time, catching the carcass as it swung back towards him. His fists ached in the cold.

'Stop.' Robert exhaled, hooking his thumbs over his sword belt. 'You're flailing,' he said. 'Your attacks come from your shoulders, and from your arms.'

He stepped closer, then raised his hand and planted his palm in the centre of Adam's chest, below his breastbone. 'From *here*,' he said, pressing slightly. 'You attack from the core of your body, using every muscle.'

Stepping away again, he drew his sword, then reversed the blade and presented the hilt to Adam. 'Now do the same with this,' he said.

Adam took the sword and weighed it in his hand. He had used such weapons since he was a boy, but this one was different, a true fighting blade. The grip felt worn and somehow alive, despite the cold. Drawing a deep breath, trying to feel the energy gathered beneath his sternum, he raised the sword and struck. The tip gouged the meat and rebounded. Circling, Adam struck again.

'Think of how you use the blade,' Robert was saying as Adam continued his attacks. 'The tip, the upper span near the tip, the lower span nearer the hilt. You've seen the unmaking of a stag or hind, after the hunt?'

'Yes,' Adam said, pausing.

Robert took the sword from his hand.

'You go about the human body in the same way,' the knight said, gesturing with the blade, tapping Adam's collarbone, his upper arm, his hip. 'Directed cuts, knowing the weak points, the bones and the cleavages of muscle—'

'But you don't seek to kill your opponents in the melee?' Adam asked, slightly unnerved at the cold touch of steel against his body.

'Of course not – one cannot get a ransom from a corpse! The object is to unhorse them, take them alive. But in order to do that you must beat them, and quickly, before they can evade you. The method of attack,' he went on, swinging the sword wide, 'is to direct all of your force and fury against your opponent, *immediately*. Do not spar with him or defend yourself – attack, as if you mean to kill.'

He pivoted on his heel, sweeping the sword round in a rapid cut. The honed steel seemed almost to sing in the air. 'Even if your weapons are bated – blunted, that is, as they should be in tournament,' Robert went on, 'you must assure your enemy in his heart that they are facing imminent death and dismemberment. You must appear to him,' he said, bringing the blade up level to Adam's throat, 'as a spectacle of utter violence and destruction. Then his bowels will turn to water and his muscles to lead, his limbs will be unstrung, and you will have beaten him before he can raise his arm against you.'

Robert turned once more on his heel, and with a sudden roar of fury he slashed at the hanging carcass, the tip of his sword opening the meat from top to bottom. Wheeling his arm, he delivered a second scything blow with the centre of the blade, hacking through flesh and bone and splitting the carcass entirely in two.

Adam had flinched instinctively, his heart skipping, and taken two steps back. The severed chunk of meat dropped to the ground. The top half, sliced open, was still swinging wildly.

'Usually I prefer to use the axe in the melee,' Robert said, wiping his blade. His eruption of killing fury seemed to have entirely burned away. 'It creates still greater fear in an opponent. But now,' he said, reversing the sword hilt towards Adam once more, 'you have a smaller target!'

Taking the sword once more, Adam tightened his hand around the grip and swung it, feeling the energy coursing through him, from the core of his body to the extremities of his limbs. *But what*, he thought, *if your enemy is not overcome at the first blow? What if he returns your attack, and all your force is spent?* He aimed a cut, then paused and stepped back.

'There's something I feel I should tell you,' he said.

Sir Robert raised his eyebrow, quizzical.

'You were right that your cousin, Joane de Quincy, made me swear an oath before we left Ware,' Adam went on, letting the blade fall. 'She made me promise . . . that I would protect you in the tournaments. And that if you were mortally injured, I would ensure that you heard the sacraments before you died, for the preservation of your soul.'

For a few moments Robert just stared, his expression shifting. Then he threw back his head and laughed. 'Truly,' he said, 'neither of you has the first notion of what happens at the tournament! You, boy, are going to have more than enough to do, without looking out for me!'

Abruptly he took a stride towards Adam, his mirth dying instantly. 'If Joane de Quincy – or you – have any care for my immortal soul, you can keep it to yourselves,' he growled. 'Once we get out there onto the tournament field, you must look to your own duties and let me look to mine, understand?'

Adam nodded as Robert de Dunstanville paced away from him, heat still flowing through his blood but mingling now with the chill of remorse.

'And if the Lord God should decree that I meet my end on the melee field,' Sir Robert said, turning once more and stabbing his finger at Adam, 'then you'll go back to Ware and you'll tell that girl whatever she needs to hear. And you will think it no sin to lie.'

# Chapter 6

'*Preudhommes!*' the herald cried, advancing before them through the crowd. 'The one who will take your measure has arrived. A mighty challenger, all the way from *Angleterre*. A champion admired by all, loved by all. Roger de Dunstanville, lords and masters!'

'Robert,' Adam hissed, following at his heels. 'His name is Robert de Dunstanville!'

'Worthy contenders, gird up your courage and look to your arms! The champion Robert de Drostanville has arrived in Lagny!'

'Be quiet,' Sir Robert ordered, tossing a shiny coin. The herald snatched it from the air, then bowed and melted into the throng.

The little town of Lagny on the Marne was, Robert had explained, an old and famous site for tournaments. Only a few miles east of Paris, it belonged nevertheless to the Count of Champagne and was therefore exempt from King Louis's ban on the sport. News of the event had reached Arras only a week before, and Robert had readied himself at once and departed without delay. Now it was Sunday evening, an hour after their arrival. The tournament was set for the following morning and the town was thronged with combatants and their retinues.

The vespers bell had already been rung, the liturgical day was over, and none of the people in the streets and squares had any religious scruples about enjoying themselves. As they crossed the bridge and approached the town gate, Adam had seen men sparring in the meadow outside the walls, or riding jousts with untipped lances in the gloom of dusk. Inside the town, the streets were packed with revellers, musicians, stamping horses and women in sumptuous gowns, all lit by the wavering glow of torches and braziers. Already it was clear that Sir Robert and his retinue were too late to find accommodation in Lagny itself; he had left Wilecok and John Chyld to pitch the tents and tether the horses in the camping ground spreading along the riverbank, and only Adam had accompanied him into the town.

Smells of spiced wine, roasting meats and perfume lingered in the air with the smoke from the torches. Robert de Dunstanville walked with a nonchalant swagger, one hand resting lightly on the hilt of his sword. Adam, following behind him, could not resist glancing to left and right, taking in everything. There were shields mounted above the doors of inns and private houses, where knights had established their retinues. Despite the February chill, tables stood in the streets, laden with cups and jugs of wine and platters of food. These were the *receptions*, Robert had told him, where the great lords and magnates competed to attract followers for the next day's combat, and to outdo each other in lavish expense. But Robert paid no attention to any of them, until he reached the main square of the town and found a table larger than most, surrounded by glowing braziers and a great pack of armed men, musicians and laughing ladies.

'Edward?' Adam whispered, noticing the banners that hung overhead: the three golden lions on a field of red, surmounted by a blue bar with three points. He caught Robert's curt nod.

Lord Edward, the eldest son of King Henry of England, lounged in a padded chair, his long legs crossed, a golden goblet dangling from his fingers. He was in his early twenties, barely five years older than Adam, but when he got to his feet he stood a head taller than most of those around him. His surcoat was of quilted velvet, lined with black fur. His thick curling hair was the colour of dark honey, and his downy beard and moustache were golden. His face was broad and fine-featured, and would have appeared handsome but for a drooping eyelid, which gave his expression a contemptuous look.

'De Dunstanville is here, I see,' he said, pointing. His voice was powerful, but a lisp dragged at the words. 'The demon of the melee has arrived! We are assured a good day's sport tomorrow, my friends!'

'My lord,' Sir Robert said, bowing. 'I bid you greetings, in God's name.'

'The demon of something,' said a knight in a red surcoat. 'Is he even here for the melee, or is he searching for another priest to murder, or another dying heiress he can marry?'

'Maybe he hopes to rob the sons of Lagny of their patrimony as well, eh?' another said with a sneer.

'And my greetings to you too, L'Estrange,' Robert replied tersely, bowing his head to the knight in red and then to his companion. 'And to you, de Leyburne.'

Many of those around Edward were knights of his own household, while others were his friends and companions, some great lords in their own right, or the sons of lords. About the women Adam was less certain; they appeared far freer and merrier than any ladies he had seen at the court of the Earl of Hereford, and dressed with much more verve as well.

Robert remained standing at the margin of the group around the raised table, glaring with fixed eye at Edward. But the king's son appeared to have lost interest in him, or was making a show of ignoring him entirely. Instead he laughed and exchanged witty remarks with the two knights who had spoken earlier, and with the other younger men who thronged around his chair. Adam saw the muscle flexing in Robert's jaw. Then the knight turned abruptly and stalked away through the crowd. As Adam followed he could almost feel the simmering heat of rage flowing in his wake.

'How I detest this empty chaffing talk,' Sir Robert said through his teeth, once he reached the far side of the square. 'I'll find another opportunity to speak with Edward. When he is less *amused.*'

'Was it true, what they said?' Adam asked, lowering his voice.

'Was *what* true?' Robert replied, halting and turning so suddenly that Adam almost walked into him.

'About your wife,' Adam said, stammering slightly. 'I didn't quite understand, but—'

'No, you did not,' Robert said, baring his teeth. 'But you should understand enough by now not to pay heed to the words of lying dogs, eh?'

For a few heartbeats they stood facing each other, the crowd eddying around them. Adam was about to ask more, sensing the shape of some greater mystery, but he feared the knight's wrath, and the urge died. It was dark by now, and the air was filled with the smoke of the braziers and torches. From somewhere along the street came the voice of the herald once more: '*Preudhommes!* A redoubtable challenger indeed – Philippe de Bourbourg is here, lords and masters! A knight to rank with the heroes of old . . .'

Adam flinched as a hand fell on his shoulder and he pulled away, startled. A figure appeared beside him. 'Robert de Dunstanville!' a familiar voice said. 'Unless I'm mistaken, you've stolen one of my father's squires!'

'Only after he killed my last one,' Robert replied, twitching a smile. 'He may look like a mild and gangling youth, but he is a bloody-handed savage, this Adam de Norton.' He clasped Adam's other shoulder, his grasp tightening.

'Is that so? . . . Then perhaps I'll get to see him in combat one of these days.'

It had taken Adam a few moments to recognise the new-comer. Several years had passed since he had last seen the Earl of Hereford's son, Humphrey de Bohun the Younger, Lord of Brecon and Baron of Kington. The man had appeared fleshy and rather indolent then; now he was harder and fitter-looking, red-faced and smiling, with a glint in his eye.

'You've only just arrived?' Sir Humphrey asked.

'And already been insulted,' Robert said.

De Bohun laughed. 'What more should one expect from Edward's friends?'

'They don't insult you, I dare say.'

'They don't insult the son and heir of the Earl of Hereford and Essex, no.'

But the earl's bastard son, Adam thought, remembering what the servants at Pleshey had told him, was surer game. Hard to believe that the lean, dark Robert de Dunstanville could be the half-brother of this man. Joane de Quincy had asked about Sir Humphrey too, Adam remembered, but he had never discovered why.

'Is the White Lion here?' Robert asked, lowering his voice.

Humphrey de Bohun shook his head. 'No, de Montfort abides with the French king. But his sons, Henry and Simon the Younger, are with Lord Edward. They'll ride in his company tomorrow, in the Duke of Burgundy's team. You too?'

Robert coughed a laugh. 'I think not. Edward scorns me, though I don't know why. He pays too much heed to the yapping of his dogs, perhaps. And his company seems large enough.'

'He has over thirty knights with him,' Sir Humphrey said. 'I myself have only nine – I'd be happy if you joined them.'

Adam thought back to what Robert had told him at Arras, and during the journey: riding in the retinue of a great lord or magnate on the melee field provided greater security, but one's first duty was always to protect the leader, who took a third part of any ransoms gained. Robert de Dunstanville preferred a more perilous, and lucrative, independence.

'I thank you for the offer, but I'll keep to my own company,' he told de Bohun, clapping him on the shoulder.

'Well, may God give you strength, and guide your lance well!'

They returned to the camping ground in darkness, and after a brief supper Adam crawled into the tent he shared with Robert. He lay for a while on his mattress, all that he had seen and thought that day still whirling in his mind. He was surprised when Robert spoke.

'You asked about my wife,' he said quietly. 'I despise a lie, so I would have you know the truth. Sure enough, she was already sick when we married. And yes, she was heir to considerable estates, but I did not wed her for her fortune. After her death the estates were claimed by the sons of her first marriage. I do not deny that I fought their claim, albeit without success.'

Adam made a sound in the back of his throat. He had feared exactly this.

'You might think me the same as de Brayboef, the man who wed your mother and took your inheritance. Others would say that, certainly.'

'I might,' Adam said in a whisper.

Robert did not speak again for some time. 'These things happen in the world,' he said finally. 'I wish it were otherwise. Now sleep – tomorrow will be long and hard for us both.'

*

Adam woke in the cold darkness before dawn, convinced that he had not slept a moment. He heard men and horses moving, hushed voices, the chime of bells. Throwing aside his blanket, he scrambled up from his mattress and crawled towards the tent door. Sir Robert had not stirred. Adam thought he was still sleeping, but then heard the whisper of breath and realised he was praying to himself, lying flat on his back with his hands clasped over his chest.

Outside, the dimness swirled with woodsmoke and the scents of damp turf and horses. Wilecok was already getting the fire started. Adam dressed hurriedly, flapping his arms around his chest to try and work some heat into his body. By the time he had laid out Robert's armour and equipment, men were already assembling and thronging towards the chapel for Morrow Mass. When Adam joined them the little building was packed, hundreds of knights and their squires and attendants gathered within and crowding around the doors, even kneeling in the muddy square outside, craning and peering for the glimpse of the Elevation of the Host, that would preserve their bodies from death and their souls from imminent damnation.

Adam knelt with them, crossing himself fervently, and his right hand reached beneath his tunic and touched the pendant of St Christopher that Joane de Quincy had given him. *Protect him, if you can. Protect him in the melee. Save his soul if not his body . . .*

Robert de Dunstanville was already preparing himself by the time Adam returned to their camp. Wilecok thrust a wooden bowl of hot potage into his hands and gruffly told him to eat. 'You won't want it, but you'll need it later.'

Adam ate as best he could, though his stomach was drum-tight and his nerves jumping. Sir Robert seemed unnaturally calm and composed as Adam helped him into his mail leg chausses and the iron greaves that covered his shins, then the long padded linen aketon and the mail hauberk over the top. A surcoat went over the mail, red on one side and white on the other. Robert laced a padded arming cap onto his head and then drew the mail coif over it, but left the ventail that would cover his lower face dangling. All of it performed in terse silence, with only muffled grunts of effort. Then Wilecok led up the horses, Adam's rouncey and the iron-grey destrier already primed for battle with ears twitching and veins standing proud. The two men swung up into the saddle. John Chyld, already mounted, followed behind them.

The sun was just coming up, the wintery glow lighting the gulfs of mist that lingered in the hollows and along the river. On the rise ahead of them the old stone walls of Lagny were ochre brown in the sunlight, and the parapets were lined with people gathered to watch the day's spectacle.

'Pay close attention to the ground,' Sir Robert said as they rode. 'If the melee spreads out, there may be fighting here — check for the wooded areas, the ditches and hollows, the places where ambushes might be laid . . .'

Adam nodded, staring all around him, but he was so distracted by the mass of riders that he could pay attention to little else. Horsemen were converging from all directions, spilling from the gates of the town and riding from the village of Torcy where the opposing team was quartered. All were armoured and dressed in bright surcoats, and many rode horses covered in mail and leather, or flowing caparisons bearing their heraldic devices. Never had Adam seen so many men armed for combat. In the cold morning sun they were a river of silk and steel, streaming pennons and flashing lance-points through the mist.

They converged on the meadow before the town walls, where the tournament field was prepared and the lists stood ready for them. Two fenced enclosures, one at either end of the broad field, would hold the opposing teams. Between them, below the wall of the town where the spectators gathered, stood wooden viewing stands for the ladies and older noblemen to sit in comfortable shelter. And all around the perimeter there were carts drawn up, also covered in people sitting and standing and calling out the names of the famous champions. Booths and stalls held farriers' smithies and armourers' workshops, leatherworkers to mend saddles and tack, horse dealers standing ready to buy and sell.

'It looks to me that the Count of Anjou's team has fewer men,' Robert said, standing in the stirrups and peering across the meadow into the pale gleam of the sun. 'It would be chivalrous, I suppose, were I to join their number.'

'But . . .' Adam said, perplexed. He glanced at the nearer lists, where the Duke of Burgundy's team was already gathering beneath his red gonfalon. Lord Edward's banners were proudly displayed there, and those of his companions, and Adam saw the blue and white of Humphrey de Bohun, son of the Earl of Hereford. Robert had already set off across the field.

'You intend to ride *against* Lord Edward?' Adam called after him. 'To ride against all the other English?'

Robert turned in the saddle and gave him a wolfish smile. *Unbelievable*, Adam thought: did the knight intend to avenge his insult of the evening before by trying to take Edward's men in the melee? Or just demonstrate his worth to the prince who had scorned him? He hunched his shoulders to trap a shudder, then took a deep breath and spurred his horse onward.

Trumpets blared and drums beat a steady pulse as the rid-.ers packed into the enclosures, their horses stamping the turf and steaming in the cold air. At the centre of the lists, beneath the blue gonfalon studded with the golden *fleur-de-lis*, was the Count of Anjou surrounded by his household knights. Robert made his way forward between them, with Adam trotting along behind him. As they neared the count, Robert stood in the saddle and called out something in a strange and guttural language that Adam did not recognise. The count heard it and scanned the crowd around him until he picked out Robert de Dunstanville. Adam, watching carefully, saw the French nobleman's expression cloud for a moment, almost as if he had taken offence. Then he spurred his horse forward to greet Sir Robert, seizing him by the hand. Adam stared, amazed. The Count of Anjou was the brother of the King of France, and one of the most prominent aristocrats in all of Europe.

'What language was that?' Adam asked, when Robert returned from his brief conversation.

'Arabic,' Robert told him. 'The count and I were prisoners of the Saracens together for a time.'

'And what did you say to him? It caught his attention . . .'

'I merely said *bring me a cup of water please.*'

Adam frowned for a few heartbeats more, then laughed in wonder. But Robert had already ridden forward to the fence that closed the front of the lists. Flags were waving from the stands and the walls of the town, and to the brassy notes of the trumpets and horns and the rolling of drums the contestants of the opposing team were beginning their grand review. Parading forth, some as individuals and others in massed companies, they turned a circuit between the stands and the opposing lists. Squires rode behind every knight, carrying their lances, shield and helmet, yelling out names and war cries, while the marshals and adjudicators strutted with their long batons. Heralds, some gorgeously dressed and others barefoot and in rags, checked their lists of names and cried out their praises of the combatants.

Adam had assumed that all the contenders would be either French or English, but among the companies there were men of Flanders and Hainaut, Brabazons and Germans from the Empire, Spaniards and Scots, a vaunting company of Italians from Lombardy and even a group of knights from distant Denmark.

'Watch carefully,' Robert said in a hushed tone, leaning from the saddle. 'See if you can pick out some fitting prey. They look proud enough now, but remember – we are the wolves who will shear them of their pretty fleeces, once the lances shatter and the ironwork begins!'

Adam, squinting into the low sun, tried not to be distracted by the glittering cavalcade of riders and all their finery. He tried instead to judge them with the hard appraising eye of a predator.

'What about that one?' he asked. He indicated a young knight, only a year or two older than himself, in silvered mail with his long blonde hair streaming loose, riding a prancing horse caparisoned with bold stripes of blue and white.

'The son of the Count of Luxembourg,' Robert said. 'Only knighted this last year. He's rich enough to make a splendid prize, sure enough. But also rich enough to surround himself with other knights to protect him. Men like that ride onto the tourney field like they're entering a pageant.'

'So he couldn't be taken?'

Robert pursed his lips. 'It would be a great deed of arms to do so. Then again, in the melee, anything can happen!'

But Adam was distracted by the next band of riders, led by a pair of proud young men whose shields bore a fork-tailed white lion, rampant on a bloody field. '*Montfort! Montfort!*' the heralds cried. 'What about them?' he asked.

Robert snorted a laugh. 'Capturing the sons of Simon de Montfort on the tourney field might be a fine deed too, depending on how it was done, but perhaps not a wise one,' he said. 'I would not want to make an enemy of the Earl of Leicester. Not at this moment in time. Their household knights, though – their pawns, we might say. Well, they could be fitting game.'

Soon enough the Duke of Burgundy's team had completed their parade, and now the Count of Anjou led his own men out. Adam glanced around at the bright colours of the painted shields and caparisons, the polished armour and glinting horse trappings. He was very conscious that he was wearing only a shabby sweat-stained gambeson, barely concealed beneath his red and white surcoat. Hefting Sir Robert's shield and lance, propping the blued-iron barrel of his helm on the pommel of his saddle, he nudged his horse forward and rode ahead of the knight out through the gap in the lists and onto the tourney field.

'*Dunstanville! Dunstanville!*' he heard the heralds shout, and joined his voice to theirs. 'Dunstanville!' he cried over the cheering of the crowd, the brassy thundering of the horns and the churning beat of the drums, and he raised the lance so the pennon streamed in the breeze. For the first time, he felt a surge of pride that lifted him in the saddle, and found that he was grinning.

As they passed the opposing lists, he noticed the knight called L'Estrange and his friend de Leyburne gesturing and hooting abuse. He heard Robert's cruel laugh, and then they were gone. The two teams had begun mustering in front of the lists, and Robert took his place in the line. All around were stamping horses tossing their manes; everything seemed primed for imminent action, but first came the initial jousts.

Riders emerged from the lines, galloping before the stands until a challenger came forth to oppose them. Most were younger men, Robert had earlier explained, recently knighted and eager to display their prowess. Breathlessly Adam watched the charges and clashes, rising in his saddle as the moment of impact approached, his chest tight with anticipation. At every moment of collision, every blow of lance against shield, every shattered shaft and staggering horse, a great cry went up from the stands and the assembled onlookers. The two rows of opposing knights sat before the lists, calling out their comments – 'faultless!' or 'good lance!' if a jouster performed with valour, hissing and tutting if he flinched and veered at the last moment, or failed to strike hard and true.

Wild cheers from the stands as the final challenger rode forth: the young son of the Count of Luxembourg, with a woman's sleeve pinned to his gilded helm. Silence as he turned his blue and white caparisoned horse at the opposite end of the field to his opponent. Then the trumpet sounded, the contenders dug in with their spurs, their horses springing forward at once and rapidly stretching out into a careering gallop. As the lances dropped to the couched position and the riders closed to impact, Adam imagined himself as the charging knight, plumes on his helmet, nothing but courage in his heart. Clear in the cold air he heard the thunderous bang of lance against shield, the splintering of wood. Then a gasping cry rose from the spectators as the young knight of Luxembourg was smashed backwards out of his saddle and hurled, loose-limbed, almost falling beneath the hooves of his opponent's galloping horse. The watching knights let out a vast exhalation of breath, filled with the sound of tongues against teeth.

'God's bones, he won't survive that,' somebody said. 'Do you see the blood spew from his helmet vents?'

As the other rider came cantering back, the fallen man's attendants ran to help him. A few moments of confusion, then one of them raised a flag. A moment more, and the stands erupted in applause as the young knight clambered to his feet to be guided, staggering, back to the lists. Such a courageous display, the spectators agreed, was almost as worthy as a victory.

The sun was high by the time the jousting was concluded and the lines had reformed, ready for the main event. 'Lace up!' the marshal cried, and the knights pulled on their constricting great helms and tied the chinstraps. Adam dismounted and took his place before the fence of the lists, two spare lances gripped tightly. Still he felt the nerves twitching and flickering around the pit of his stomach, where his morning's breakfast lay like a stone. The day was cold, but beneath the horrid gambeson the sweat was pouring down his body. At least, he thought, he was not alone in his discomfort; ahead of him, one of the younger knights leaned from the saddle, made a choking sound, and vomited. The others around him laughed as he wiped his mouth and put his helmet back on.

'You know what's expected of you, right?' John Chyld said, standing beside Adam with another couple of lances. The grizzled serjeant was chewing something as he spoke, and Adam's gut contracted. The rich scent of fresh horse dung came from the lists behind them.

'I know, don't worry,' he said with a brusque shrug. 'We hand Sir Robert new lances for as long as he needs them, and then when the melee breaks up and spreads I go out onto the field and . . . *secure the captives*.'

John Chyld nodded. 'Some places nowadays,' he said, still chewing, 'let the squires ride onto the field. Not here – you'll have to leg it. Make sure you don't get ridden down or get your head knocked off by somebody else's squire . . . And you know how to secure the captives, right?'

'Tell them the name of their captor and demand that they yield,' Adam said, trying to sound more confident than he felt, 'then conduct them back here to the lists and hand them over to you.'

'That's the way,' John Chyld said, and spat out a fragment of bone. 'Just make sure they give you their oath of surrender, then bring them in nice and douce-like.'

Out on the open field the heralds and marshals were still dashing back and forth, brandishing their rods and lists of names, but now the opposing lines appeared to be properly arranged. They did indeed resemble the pieces on a chess board, Adam thought, set out for the game to commence. The heralds retreated to the safety of the stands, and five hundred paces of open ground separated the two lines. Horses shifted and blew, pawing the rutted turf, primed for the sound of the horns.

The flash of a flag, a blaze of brassy noise, and two thousand mounted men in armour surged into motion. Adam felt himself stretching upward, staring wide-eyed as Robert de Dunstanville vanished into the mass; he tried to pick out the red and white colours, but in the dazzle of horses and men and banners and caparisons he could not. The advancing line receded from him towards the centre of the field, the pace gathering from a trot to a charge. Five rapid heartbeats, then six. *Pater noster, qui es in caelis, santificetur nomen tuum, adveniat regnum tuum* . . .

Then, out in the middle distance of the field, the charging lines met. An explosion of thunderous noise; lances on shields, shattering wood, screaming men and horses, the roar from the stands and the surrounding spectators. Craning upward, Adam saw a score or more riders pitched immediately from the saddles, others clinging on as their mounts stumbled and staggered. Many horses down too, kicking as they rolled, their riders trapped beneath them. Desperately he tried to pick out Robert de Dunstanville's colours, but the centre of the field was lost to a milling chaos. Then, just as suddenly the mass of men split apart as the charging line broke through and began to turn and wheel for the second attack.

Chaos in front of the lists too, the squires and serjeants pressing forward, raising their spare lances and yelling the names of
their masters. Adam felt himself jostled, and shoved back with
his elbows. 'Dunstanville!' he shouted. '*Dunstanville!*'

Mounted men rushed from the fray, their horses kicking up
the turf, riders snatching lances from the waiting squires. Then
Robert was right there in front of Adam, leaning from the saddle
and bellowing from inside his helm. Adam lurched forward, and
the knight snatched one of the lances from his grasp. Already
Robert was turning once more, the destrier's front legs off the
ground, hooves swinging dangerously close to Adam's face.
Another knight cantered past, hanging semi-conscious from the
saddle as the blood streamed from beneath his helmet and spattered his horse's haunch, and his squires ran to assist him.

'Go, boy, go!' John Chyld was shouting in Adam's ear. Out
across the field Robert was charging again, lance lowered; as
Adam stared, he clashed with another rider, his lance bending at
the point of impact. His opponent was reeling, almost unhorsed,
his shield destroyed, only the high cantle keeping him in the saddle. John Chyld was still yelling. Gripping his second lance in
both hands like a pike, the padded skirts of his gambeson flapping
around his knees, Adam ran.

The whole field was in motion now, the melee swirling outwards half a mile or more from the stands, breaking up into fierce
jostling knots of combatants. Keeping clear of the kicking hooves
and swinging blades, Adam stumbled forward, searching for a
glimpse of Robert. Already a few dozen men were being led back
to the lists as captives, their horses trailing behind them. A few
dozen more were being carried from the field; injured or dead,
Adam could not tell. Over the constant bleat of horns and roll of
drums, the roaring and cheering from the distant stands, there
was a sound like nothing Adam had heard before. *The ironworks*,
Robert had called the melee – now Adam understood why. The
air reverberated with the clash and grate of metal, like a hundred

smiths wildly pounding at their anvils, a hundred armourers beating steel. Louder even than the yells of combat, the crack of shattering shields and the panicked din of the horses, the metal thunder pulsed with its own savage intensity.

A horse crashed to the ground in front of him, and Adam veered to escape its thrashing hooves as it rolled. Beyond it he saw a knight, his lance gone, reach from the saddle and grab another rider by the helmet rim, hauling him back over the cantle until his feet slipped from the stirrups and he toppled over his horse's tail. Two squires in red surcoats came running in fast, barging Adam aside, yelling '*Montfort! Montfort!*' The tip of the lance Adam was carrying buried itself in the turf, and he lost his grip on the shaft. He turned to grab it but leaped back quickly, neatly avoiding a charging rider – he felt the hot breath of the horse on his back as it passed, and when he looked again the fallen lance was gone.

As the two Montfort squires secured the fallen man, Adam saw the press of combatants shift and break, and caught sight of a white caparison with a red lattice. Robert was circling another knight, standing high in his stirrups to deal smashing downward blows with his long-handled cavalry axe. His opponent crouched in the saddle, a battered shield raised over his head, unable to turn his horse and get a cut at Robert. As Adam ran closer, empty-handed, Robert's destrier lunged and bit at the neck of the opposing knight's horse; at the same moment Robert swung his axe upward, catching the man under the arm and toppling him from the saddle.

The blued-steel helm turned, silvered sights scanning the field, and Adam waved. Robert gestured at the fallen man with his axe, then turned at once and spurred his destrier forward again, in quest of further victims.

The fallen knight was lying on his back, one leg twisted beneath him, struggling to rise. Adam grabbed the dangling reins of the horse, dragging it after him as he approached the downed rider. Keeping the horse on a long rein he dropped to the ground beside the knight, then threw his weight onto the man's armoured chest, pinning him down. The man's helmet rotated to face him. Adam saw the gleam of widened eyes through the sights, and heard the thudding of breath through the vents.

'*Yield!*' he cried, his voice cracking. 'You are a captive of Robert de Dunstanville – yield and give your oath!'

Something like a groan came from within the helmet, and for a moment the fallen knight's body fell slack, his mail crunching. Then he reared up, his right arm swinging, and drove a blow with his armoured fist into the side of Adam's head.

Adam felt the explosion of pain, the flash of hot lightning that blinded his senses, then he toppled backwards into plunging dark.

# Chapter 7

Her name was Eloise. She had told him that, before he first saw her face.

But he was aware of her voice before anything, the music of her words coming and going as he lay in pain and darkness. She talked to herself as she tended his wounds, when she believed he was insensible, and sang as she sat beside the open window; he heard the sounds from the street outside, and imagined she was sewing, perhaps. How long he had lain in the upper room, flat on his back on a straw mattress with his eyes and the top of his head bound in coarse linen, he could not tell. His skull felt as fragile as an eggshell, whenever he tried to move or speak jagged shards of agony cut through him. The woman changed his dressings, wiped the wound with a warm damp cloth, and fed him broth that tasted of nothing at first, then tasted of rusting metal. As sensation returned to him, he could recognise her by her scent, the warmth of her body when she sat beside him, the feel of her breath and the touch of her hands on his bruised flesh.

But when the dressings and bandages were peeled from his face and he opened his gummed eyes, it was a man's face that he saw before him. An old man with a bristled chin, who moved his finger from side to side and then chuckled. The light from the

window pained his eyes, and Adam was happy when the man left
and he could close his lids and lie still once more.

John Chyld appeared at his bedside next, sitting in the glow of
a stinking tallow candle. 'Seems you're not dead then,' he said,
and wheezed a laugh. 'And not blinded either, though we thought
you might be. Crack like that, and blood all down you. Could
almost see the pattern of mail links stamped into your face! Your
skull's thicker than it looks. Your first tourney, and you're carried off the field insensible – who'd have thought?'

'What happened . . .' Adam managed to say, dredging the
words up from the pit of his throat. 'What happened . . . to the
knight?'

'The one who hit you? Oh, he scuttled off, but another took
him shortly after. Sir Robert argued over the capture, but since
you'd let him go there was no case. Sir Robert wasn't best
pleased by that, but he says we should remain here till you're
well enough to ride – he's already lost one squire after a bang on
the head . . .'

They were still in Lagny then, Adam realised, and only a day
or two could have passed since the tournament. Yes, an inn in
Lagny town – he had a vague pained memory of them carrying
him up the narrow stairs.

'He's unhurt then?' he asked. 'Robert?'

'Certainly. He took another capture, with his own hand, and
lost nothing. But he could have done more.'

'But he should have yielded – the knight . . . he was rightly
downed, everyone saw it. He should have given me his oath and
yielded!'

John Chyld laughed again and leaned in closer until Adam
could smell his garlicky breath. 'That is why,' he said, 'you must
be careful with knights. They talk mightily of honour and oaths,
and respect and courtesy and such, and display them to each
other when they've a mind, like rare treasures they possess. But
to anyone else, they're like beasts in the wild. Get too close to

them, and they'll rend your flesh. You may think you're one of them, and maybe one day if God preserves you, you might be – but get between them and their desires and they'll ride you down without a thought. Even our Sir Robert, if he's crossed. You'll know that, next time.'

Adam could not recall hearing John Chyld speak at such length before.

He was unaware of sleeping again, but when he next opened his eyes the room was full of morning daylight. He lay still and stared up at the worm-eaten beams and the mess of dirty thatch angled above him, until he heard Eloise enter the chamber.

'Lord, he lives again!' she said, setting down a tray with a basin and a cup. 'Half the night I was listening to you mumbling and groaning, like the devil had a grip upon you . . .' Now he could look at her clearly, Adam saw that Eloise was around his own age, with a tanned face, straw-coloured hair escaping from her headcloth, and a gap between her front teeth that showed when she smiled.

'I was talking in my sleep?' he asked, frowning and blearily ashamed.

'Not that I could understand half of it,' she said. 'What a funny style of speech you have! Do all the men of your country talk in such a way?'

'You've heard Englishmen before,' Adam said, closing his eyes again. 'We don't talk so very strangely. Your accent sounds strange to me too – it's natural.'

'I heard the Lord Edward,' said Eloise, and smiled. 'He and his chevaliers came to this very inn! A real *preudhomme* he is – like a paladin! And he speaks perfect French, as good as King Louis himself.'

'They're still here in Lagny then, Lord Edward and his retinue?'

'Oh no, they left the day before yesterday, for Paris and then to England, so they say. Your master de Dunstanville went with them.'

'He's gone?' Adam cried, starting up from the bed. 'When —'

'Gently, my sweet!' Eloise said, laying a hand on his chest and pushing him back onto the mattress with surprising force. 'He's not gone far – only to Paris to meet with some *Jews*.' She made a face, and mimed spitting over her left shoulder. 'He said he'll return in two days, or maybe three,' she said, smiling again, 'to find if you're fully recovered or not.'

Adam groaned: the exertion had made his wound flare with pain. Lying still, he drank from the cup that Eloise held for him. Wine, spiced and flavoured with herbs. It spread heat through his body, and he took the cup from her and drained it to the dregs. Next she soaked a cloth in the basin and wiped at his wounded head, then cleaned his face and shoulders. At some point during this process Adam realised that he was naked beneath the blankets. Had John Chyld or Wilecok stripped him of his clothes? The thought that Eloise herself may have undressed him brought the warmth back to his face.

'Who is Joane?' she asked, as she dabbed with her cloth. Adam tensed, and her eyes met his. 'You were saying her name as you slept,' she said. 'Is she your lady love back in England?'

'No,' Adam told her hurriedly. His hand went instinctively to the St Christopher's pendant that lay against his breastbone. He had not been stripped of that at least. 'No, she's . . . someone I once met. I doubt I'll meet with her again.'

'A mystery,' Eloise whispered, smiling.

She squeezed the cloth over the basin, and the water turned pale brown with the last traces of blood. Another few dabs: the wound was clean, it seemed. 'He's a strange one as well, your master, de Dunstanville,' Eloise said. 'Such tales they tell of him! Are they true?'

'Some, I think,' Adam told her, feeling guarded once more, and still obscurely jealous of her praise for Lord Edward.

'He has a sorrowing look in his eyes sometimes,' the woman said, then paused with her cloth and appeared wistful. 'Maybe he regrets all the sinful things he's done? Or there's a wound inside him that he tries to conceal? Now – lie still and rest if you can.'

She took her tray and basin and got up, pulling the rough shutter over the window before leaving the room, and Adam lay in the dimness and tried to sleep once more. He thought back to what John Chyld had said, and wondered what else he might have muttered unawares. Laying his palm over the holy pendant, he tried to picture Joane's face, but found himself thinking of Eloise instead as he dropped into a troubled sleep.

It was late afternoon when she returned, and the shadows were gathering beneath the low ceiling of the chamber. She brought food: bread and hot leek potage, with salted ham and soft cheese, and a flask of wine. 'Your master, Robert de Dunstanville, has sent tidings from Paris,' she told him, sitting on the edge of the bed as he ate. 'He'll be away for another few days, or so that filthy servant-man of his says. But says he'll return here by the eve of St Valentine's feast. So – you have plenty more time to rest and recover yet!'

Adam just nodded, his mouth full. He had not realised how hungry he had become, and his wounded head no longer ached as he chewed or swallowed either. Eloise smiled, helping herself to a slice of ham and a mouthful of wine from his cup. 'Though it looks to me,' she said, dropping her voice slightly, 'as if you've recovered very well already.'

Swallowing heavily, Adam brushed the crumbs from his hands and then took the cup from her and drank. He felt the effects of the wine moving through him, his whole body beginning to glow. Or was it more than just the wine? He thought of the many sermons he had heard, the lectures he had received in the Earl of Hereford's hall, concerning the wiles of women, and the snares and traps they set for the virtuous.

Eloise raised her hand and lightly brushed the scar on his scalp, then stroked her fingers down his cheek and neck. 'So how are we going to fill all this time until he returns?' she said, cocking her head and smiling. She pressed the tip of her tongue into the gap between her front teeth, then made a soft kissing sound. 'Perhaps we could play a little, hmm?'

Adam frowned, wondering for a moment if she was about to produce a chess board and pieces from somewhere. His breath was very tight, his pulse very fast. Eloise took the platter of food and drink and placed it on the floor, then stood up quickly and drew her tunic off over her head. In a moment she had shed her headcloth, shaken out her long yellow hair, and then untied the laces at the neck of her linen chemise and let it fall to the floor. Naked, beaming, she stood beside the bed. Adam stared at her, terrified but enraptured, all self-control rushing from him.

'I don't . . .' he began to say. 'I mean to say, I never . . .'

'Shush,' she told him, and stripped the blanket from him. 'You don't need to say anything now.' Climbing onto the mattress, she straddled his hips, and for a moment he had a memory of Belia doing the same to Robert at the house in London. Then she pressed herself down onto him, her unbound hair falling over them both, and he was engulfed in the sensations of her body, all thought banished from his mind.

*

'It's a good thing,' Robert said, several days later, 'that you spent so much time languishing in bed. If we'd left Lagny when I'd originally intended, we would never have heard tidings of this tournament at Épernay.'

'I was not languishing,' Adam replied.

Robert laughed. They were riding eastwards, down the valley of the Marne, and the day was bright and clear. 'No,' he said. 'I heard you were engaged otherwise.'

'Yes indeed,' said John Chyld, who rode behind them. 'Man-fully engaged!'

Adam felt the heat rise to his face and tried to hide his smile. He had been enduring taunts like this since leaving the inn that morning, half in guilt and half in glory. He did not care. The memory of the hours he had spent with Eloise was still fresh inside him, printed on his mind and his body. He could still smell the scent of her on his skin. The tournament at Épernay, to be hosted by the Count of Champagne on the eve of Shrove Tuesday, had only been proclaimed a few days beforehand; afterwards, Robert had declared, they would spend the season of Lent in training at Soissons. But after Easter, Adam had told Eloise as he left, he would surely return to Lagny once more and they would be together. His heart was filled with her.

'At least now you're not encumbered with that great weight of virtue, eh?' Robert said to him. 'Think what Earl Humphrey would say about that! *Attende, Domine . . . quia peccavimus tibi*. But I couldn't really have a maiden boy as my squire, could I – so I must presume the silver was well spent?'

'What?' Adam said, jerked abruptly from his warm reveries.

'Oh come now,' Robert told him, and laughed with cruel rel-ish. 'Surely you don't think that the girl merely jumped into bed with you of her heart's desire? An inn servant from a market town, a tournament town? Was her head turned by your nobility, do you think? By your virtuous and manly bearing? Or by the coins I paid her to strip you of your chastity?'

Adam felt ice water pouring through him. He struggled to breathe, anger rioting with a sickening anguish inside him. 'That's . . . not true,' he stammered.

'A hard bargain she made too,' Robert said with a shrug. 'But worth it, then? What do you say, John?'

'Oh yes,' the grizzled serjeant said, and made a lewd kissing sound. 'That gap between her front teeth, eh? You could just van-ish into it!'

'No!' Adam exclaimed, his despair shifting to horror and disgust.

'Naturally,' Robert said, 'I had to ensure she was a good teacher, so I ordered John Chyld to determine her worth beforehand.'

'She learned him right enough, I'd say!' John Chyld added, with a gnarled grin. 'There's not much she didn't know, that one.'

'Enough!' Adam said, restraining himself from reaching for the sword at his belt. For a few moments anguished fury consumed him. He wanted only to beat and kill John Chyld, to murder Robert de Dunstanville, to exterminate them utterly . . . Both of them stared back at him, and there was a cold, hard wariness behind their mirth. Adam knew that any move he made against them now would only add to his humiliation. He pulled his mantle closer around him, swallowing down his angry despair.

'Anyway,' Robert said, nudging his horse on down the road. 'I'm sure that handful of silver will be of great use to the girl, when the child comes.'

Adam jolted upright in the saddle. 'But . . . how?' he managed to say.

'Oh,' said Robert, and made a rueful face to John Chyld. 'He didn't notice?'

'He did not notice!' John Chyld replied.

'I see you were taught as much of nature as you were of sword-play in Earl Humphrey's household,' Robert said, seeing Adam's baffled stare. 'I don't mean *your* child, you fool. She had one of them already, and another on the way.'

'About three or four months gone, I'd say,' John Chyld confirmed.

'I . . . could not tell,' Adam said. He was blushing hotly. They were quite right – he knew nothing of nature. Nothing of Eloise either, for all his fantasies of love. In all the hours they had spent together he had asked her almost nothing of herself, and thought only of his own pleasure. He had not even noticed her pregnancy.

He felt foolish, boorish, and cruelly used, and could not meet anyone's gaze.

Robert and John Chyld were still chuckling to themselves. Robert tugged on his reins and rode up alongside Adam, reaching over to cuff him on the shoulder. 'There's no shame in it, boy,' he said, with a gruff tenderness. 'No shame in love, however it is taken. Think of it as a gift, and soon we'll laugh about it together, eh?'

\*

They rode on for the rest of that day, following the winding river valley through a gentle landscape of vineyards, the ranks of bare vines scaling the slopes above the road. There was a softness in the air that was almost springlike, and after a few hours Adam felt his spirits rising from the depths of hurt despair. Robert's mood too seemed lighter; the days he had spent with Lord Edward in Paris had not yielded any result, but he had shrugged off the disappointment; now, he explained, they would hunt other game.

That night they camped beside the road amidst the vine bushes, and as he lay shivering in the gloom of the tent Adam touched the St Christopher's pendant on his chest, summoned a memory of Joane de Quincy, and swore a silent oath that he would never disgrace himself with intimacy again as long as he was in Sir Robert's service. He was unsure how sincere his oath would turn out to be, but it calmed his soul in the darkness, and calm brought sleep.

In the morning they broke camp in the dawn mist and rode on east towards Épernay. Their little travelling company had increased in number since the stay at Lagny. There were six riders now, with two extra packhorses, Robert's destrier, and a second warhorse that he had taken, with the rider's armour, during the tournament. Wilecok had been joined by a dark and entirely silent woman from Gascony; he did not bother telling anyone her name, if he knew it himself, but he claimed she was now his wife. The Gascon woman helped with the cooking and dealt with the laundry, and had been accepted without question. Adam had gone beyond being surprised at such things.

The second new arrival was a plump young Welshman named Hugh of Oystermouth, who Robert had taken on as a herald and treasurer. Whether he had any skill or aptitude in either heraldry or keeping accounts remained to be seen, but he was a very merry young man, sitting high in the saddle of his ambling pony, dressed in a dark mantle with a big leather satchel slung behind him. Upon his wide-brimmed hat he wore a pewter pilgrim badge from Santiago de Compostella, shaped like a shell.

'You should beware of Adam here,' John Chyld had told the newcomer, on their first day together. 'A Welshman killed his father!'

Hugh of Oystermouth had regarded Adam carefully from beneath the brim of his hat, pursing his lips. 'A particular Welshman, I am sure,' he said. 'Certainly not all Welshman can have killed his father. Therefore, by logic, I should not fear him!'

Adam frowned at that, uncertain whether to be insulted or amused. There was something sly and evasive about Hugh of Oystermouth, but the man behaved with such good spirits that it was hard to take him seriously. He spoke and sang Latin beautifully, while his French was barbaric. Only when he removed his hat for a moment did Adam guess the truth: his hair showed the signs of a partially outgrown tonsure. Robert confirmed the suspicion later; the newcomer had been in holy orders, a student at the University of Paris, and had abandoned his studies to try and make a living on the tournament road.

By the afternoon of the second day they were passing through a wilder district, where the road twisted and turned around wooded slopes. At the summit of one rise Robert abruptly reined his horse to a halt and leaned forward, shading his eyes from the low sun.

'What do you see?' Adam asked as he rode up alongside. Robert grabbed his bridle, holding him back.

Below them the road descended through the trees to a clearing where a ford crossed a shallow river. On the far bank was a strip of level open ground, where a lance stood with a pennon and a shield hanging from it. Beyond them, Adam could make out the blue haze of smoke from a camp fire, tents set up among the trees, the shapes of tethered horses.

'It's a challenge,' Robert said.

'He'll be one of the knights from the tournament at Lagny,' said Hugh of Oystermouth, joining them and peering down towards the ford. 'Thinks himself a hero from the romances of Arthur, I suppose! He must know this is the only road to Épernay, and anyone travelling on to the meeting there must pass here. He intends to contest the passage.'

'Could we not just find another way over the river?' Adam asked.

Robert winced at him.

'It would be a great dishonour to evade combat,' Hugh explained. 'Soon enough, everyone would discover it, and then, you know . . .'

Robert nodded briskly, then asked Hugh if he could identify the shield device.

'*Or, billety sable*,' said Hugh. '*A lion rampant sable*. I would guess . . . a vassal of the Count of Flanders?'

Robert winced again. 'Pull back down the road a hundred paces,' he said. 'We'll prepare ourselves there, out of sight. Adam – saddle the second destrier.'

'You intend to fight him, then?' Adam asked.

'No,' said Robert. 'I intend *you* to fight him.'

'But I'll lose!'

'Of course you'll lose. We don't know his name, but he's surely a trained knight and you're a green and gadling youth.' Robert had already turned his horse and was riding back down the slope. Adam followed him to the stand of trees where Wilecok,

John Chyld and the Gascon woman were waiting with the pack animals. 'You'll lose,' Robert went on as he dismounted. 'But you'll take your time losing. You'll put up a good fight, and leave him wearied. And *then* I'll fight him.'

'But that's . . .' Adam swung down from the saddle. 'Is that not against the rules?'

John Chyld snorted a laugh. Robert wore his thin sardonic smile. 'Rules?' he said, and laughed. 'There are no rules here. Only victory and defeat.'

Still troubled, Adam got on with saddling the second horse while John Chyld removed the equipment and armour from its ox-hide wrappings. Then he stood stiffly as Wilecok and Hugh of Oystermouth dressed and armed him in the spoils of Robert's capture at the Lagny tournament: a full-length mail hauberk and leggings, and an iron skullcap beneath the mail coif that covered his head. The horse was younger than Robert's charger and not as powerfully muscled, but strong and trained for battle. Adam was still resentful about Robert's comment on his youth and inexperience. But he was more troubled by the deceitful stratagem.

'He will discover soon enough that I'm not a knight,' he said. 'What then?'

Robert, who had been standing nearby eating a handful of raisins with deliberate nonchalance, turned abruptly. 'What, you don't want to fight?' he asked.

'No! No, I mean . . . It seems *unchivalrous* . . . Even unchristian.'

'Listen to me!' Robert broke in, cutting off any further objections. 'I am a tournament knight. Victory is my meat and drink. I have no lands to which I can return, no wealth that would support me in hardship. My sole fortune is my horse, my armour, and my honour. If I fight that man down at the ford and he beats me, I lose the tools of my profession. And then, you see, I can no longer be a tournament knight. And then, you see – I would have no need of a squire, would I?'

Adam shrugged, feeling the mail bunch heavily at his shoulders.

'So, do you care to walk back to Boulogne? Back to Pleshey? Care to beg Earl Humphrey to take you into his household once more?'

'No,' Adam said.

'Then we *fight*. And we use every stratagem we possess. And we *win*, understand?'

*

Barely an hour had passed, by the position of the sun, before Adam walked his horse back to the summit of the rise and began his descent towards the ford. Hugh of Oystermouth was riding ahead of him on a palfrey, in the guise of his squire, carrying a lance with a red pennon. Steadily they rode, watching the activity among the trees beyond the river.

'You'll need to cross the ford there, look, and strike the shield they've mounted with your lance,' Hugh said over his shoulder. 'That means you accept the challenge.'

'I know what it means,' Adam said. His voice was muffled by the ventail laced across his nose and mouth. Sweat dripped into his eyes, and he blinked it away. He had ridden in jousts before many times, although only with squires of his own age. He had ridden in full armour too, and on a real warhorse. But never had he done all three at the same time. And never had he faced a fully armed and properly mounted knight. He rode out from the shadow of the trees into the bright sunlight of the riverbank, feeling the horse beneath him already stirring for combat, neck arching and ears twitching. Nervous tension flowed through his own body too.

A rider cantered out from the camp on the far riverbank. A squire, obviously, older and better dressed than Adam in a yellow and black surcoat and feathered hat. He rode across the open ground and descended the riverbank into the ford, his horse splashing up water, then reined in and called in a strong Flemish accent, 'Philippe de Bourbourg holds this crossing! Who challenges him?'

'Adam de Norton!' Hugh cried in response. He glanced back at Adam and winked, then gestured him forward.

'The first to unhorse his opponent is victor, you agree?' the squire called, as he turned to ride back. Hugh of Oystermouth signalled his agreement.

Nudging his stallion forward, Adam passed Hugh and entered the ford. Water churned beneath him. Adam could sense the cold freshness of it, and suddenly yearned to stop and drink; his mouth was parched, his body flushed beneath the heavy mail. He rode on across the ford and climbed the far bank to the shield mounted on the road's verge. Raising his lance, he struck one blow with the socketed tip. A hollow thud and a clatter. When he looked up the road once more, Adam saw that his adversary had appeared.

The Flemish knight was in full mail, an iron great helm covering his head and a lance in his hand. On his shield, and on the caparison that clad his powerful black horse, a black lion stood rampant on a field of golden yellow freckled with black rectangles. *Philippe de Bourbourg*. Adam remembered the name. The first knight he would ever face in combat. His opponent was walking his horse slowly back and forth in the shadows beneath the trees. Then his squire reached him, calling something from the saddle, and he cantered forward into the pale sunlight of the riverbank and took up his position at the far end of the strip of open ground.

Adam was struggling to draw breath. He felt the weight of his armour pressing down on him, crushing him into the saddle. The weight of dread like a stone in his chest. He stuck his mailed legs out straight, heels down, pressing his feet into the stirrups and his rump firmly against the high cantle of his saddle. He felt the horse pawing the ground with its wet hooves, flexing its neck.

His arm was leaden as he raised his lance, signalling that he was ready.

A shout from his left, a flag flourished in the air. Immediately his opponent sprang forward, spurring his powerful black horse into a charge. 'Ride, man, ride!' Hugh of Oystermouth yelled. 'Ride, or he'll take you standing!'

Adam shook at the reins, digging in with his heels, and his horse erupted beneath him like a bolt shot from a crossbow. Four long strides and his gait was heavy, jolting Adam hard against the saddle, then the horse stretched out, his body flowing forward into a careering charge. Jaw set, Adam tried to remember all that he had learned about the joust: *keep your head down behind your shield rim, do not flinch or veer, aim for a point a horse's length behind your opponent's shield . . .*

He had been carrying his lance upright, holding it clear of his body. Now he swung the socket tip down, feeling the shaft pivot upwards into the couch of his armpit. He gripped it tight, angling the weapon across his horse's streaming mane and aiming it at the approaching rider.

Suddenly all thought was gone from his mind. He was flying, faster than he had ever ridden before, armour-clad and unstoppable, half a ton of muscle and steel behind one speeding lance-tip. He was invincible. Elation flooded him. He could ride straight through anything that came at him.

Then, a galloping heartbeat later, he saw his opponent – previously a distant speck of motion – double in size, and then treble. Philippe de Bourbourg was coming at him like a thunderbolt, a charging monolith, the hooves of his steed vibrating the earth, the caparison billowing around the horse's legs so the black lions appeared to prance and rear, flickering tongues of red flame . . . And Adam felt all his joy turn to stark clenching terror.

Everything in him wanted to drag at the reins, to veer aside from the death bearing down on him. Nerves screaming, jaw

tight – *keep going! Just keep going!* – he lowered his head behind
his shield rim and bunched his shoulder behind the lance.

De Bourbourg hit him like a toppling wall. Adam felt the
impact through his entire body, the wrench of pain lifting him
from the saddle. Eyes open, he saw his opponent's lance slam
against his shield and bend, the shaft flexing like a bowstave until
it shattered into flying splinters. Then the other rider was gone
in a blast of black wind, and in his panic Adam felt himself falling,
spinning from the saddle. His feet were still in the stirrups . . . he
was trapped, he would be dragged and trampled . . .

Realisation burst through him. He was still on the horse, the
saddle's high cantle barely holding him in place. Dropping back
down into his seat, he also realised that he was still holding his
lance. He had missed his aim completely – but now he had a
weapon, and de Bourbourg did not. Dragging in lungfuls of air
through the soaked padding of the ventail, Adam hauled back
on the reins and tried to turn his horse. The animal backed
so fast that it almost reared, then staggered sideways into a
crabbed turn.

But de Bourbourg was on him immediately. *His horse must have
spun like a dancer* . . . Before Adam could couch his lance the
other rider had crashed against him, swinging a sword blow that
glanced off his mail coif and rang in his head like a bell. Adam felt
the blade grate down his mailed shoulder as colours burst before
his eyes. He had no room to use the lance; de Bourbourg was
pressing against him, the black destrier ramming his own horse
and trying to force it down.

Again the sword fell, and Adam managed to parry the blow
with the shaft of his lance. Screwing at the reins, throwing aside
the useless weapon, he turned his horse and tried to draw the falchion from his belt scabbard. The knight's black destrier lashed
out again, snapping powerful teeth, and Adam's horse screamed
and tried to rear. He was slipping in the saddle and could not feel
his feet in the stirrups. Then, from the depths of his panic, rose a

sudden murderous rage. Just as he felt when he fought the squire Gerard at Pleshey, he was consumed with a fury that eclipsed all pain, all conscious thought. Ripping the falchion free, he aimed a flailing blow and managed to clip the bottom of de Bourbourg's shield.

The riders separated, horses circling and pawing. Adam heard his opponent shout something, but the words were muffled inside his helm. De Bourbourg lifted his sword high, and for one desperately relieved moment Adam thought he was declaring a truce. But then, with a savage shout, the Flemish knight spurred his horse forward into the attack once more. Adam managed to turn so his left side was towards his enemy. He raised his shield at the last moment, and de Bourbourg's blade slammed into it and hacked a notch from the upper rim. Twisting in his saddle, Adam turned the shield, the sword still stuck in it, and dragged it to one side, then slashed low and hard across his saddle pommel. He felt his falchion strike his opponent's armoured torso, the steel sliding and grating over the mail links. Bellowing from inside his helm, the Flemish knight released his grip on his sword, then leaned from the saddle, grabbing Adam around the neck with the crook of his arm and dragging him. His horse backstepped, head tossing high, and Adam felt himself slipping helplessly forward. His sword arm was flailing, but his opponent was too close to strike.

Then it was over. His feet slipped from the stirrups, his horse fighting its way backwards, and he was tumbling down into the gap between the two animals. De Bourbourg released him as he fell, and Adam slammed down onto his back with the hooves stamping and kicking around him. His head was still ringing, his shield and falchion were gone, and his mouth was full of blood. But he was grinning. He was alive. He had done his part.

*

'It was quite easy, really,' Robert de Dunstanville said later that
same day. 'I'd already made my way down to the riverbank while
you were preparing your charge, so I got to watch everything
from a place of concealment. I saw how he fought, his style, his
strengths and where he was weak. So when I came to challenge
him myself, I could overcome him without difficulty.'

Adam gave a rueful smile. His felt bruised and battered
in every limb, and wounded in places where he did not even
remember being hit.

'Of course, your own efforts tired him a little too,' Robert
conceded. 'You managed to get a few good blows in. Impressive,
really, for a mere gadling youth.'

What was truly impressive, Adam and everyone else knew,
was the speed and surety with which Robert had overcome
Philippe de Bourbourg, when he fought him less than an hour
after Adam's own defeat. After almost unhorsing him on the
first pass, he had hacked the Flemish knight out of the saddle
with three swift blows of his axe; no doubt, Adam thought,
he could have beaten him unaided. But he knew that Robert
had been testing him, throwing him into the fight to see how
he fared, before finishing the job himself. And they had won.
Together they had won: behind them now trotted the powerful but nimble black destrier that de Bourbourg had named
*Papillon* – 'Butterfly'. Philippe de Bourbourg's armour and
weapons too had fallen to the victors. De Bourbourg himself
had not taken the stratagem amiss, once he realised how he had
been played. They had left him on the roadside with his squires
and spare horses, and a promise to fight a return bout at their
next encounter.

'And now, friends, we ride to Épernay!' Hugh of Oystermouth
declared, for all the world as if he had won the battle himself. It
was hard, Adam thought, not to share his high spirits. The road
lay before them, with months of hard travelling and hard fighting
to come, but God had favoured them thus far.

Throwing back his head, the Welshman began to sing as he rode. A song from his student days in Paris, he told them. A song of youth and rejoicing, before death took them all. He had a fine voice, and after a few verses the rest of them began to join in with the chorus, Robert in a deep rolling bass tone, even Wilecok in a cracked warble and his Gascon woman in a sweet high treble.

*Gaudeamus igitur*, they sang, as they rode on down the valley. *Gaudeamus igitur, Juvenes dum sumus* . . .

## Chapter 8

The brazen roar of trumpets sounded across the field of Éper-nay, and all along the line knights lifted their helms onto their heads, took lances from their squires and nudged their chargers forward into formation. A damp noon, beneath a grey sky, but a mist of steam rose from the closely packed bodies of the horses.

Adam had almost retreated to the fences of the assembly area when he heard hoofbeats behind him and turned to see Robert de Dunstanville walking his horse slowly back towards the lists. His big grey destrier was moving strangely, stepping short on the rear right leg. Already the drums were rolling to announce the grand charge, the *estor*, that would begin the tournament.

'What's wrong?' Adam cried, running to help Robert dis-mount. The knight pulled off his helmet and propped it on the saddle bow. 'Lame,' he said, nodding down at his horse's rear leg. 'Or about to be. I could feel it as I rode.'

'But I don't understand – how can that be?' Adam asked. 'I checked everything just moments ago . . .' He cast a glance over the horse, which walked with head bobbing, ears down, blowing at the turf through flared nostrils. They were back at the lists now, where John Chyld and Hugh of Oystermouth were waiting beside the fence. From behind him Adam heard the single trumpet blast, the cry of massed voices, and felt the first thunder of the charge as a tremor through the earth.

'Wait,' Adam said, stooping to look at the rear hoof of Robert's horse. 'Perhaps there's a st—' A palm clipped the back of his head, and he straightened up quickly, heat rushing to his face. John Chyld hissed through his teeth.

The pulse of noise from the stands gained in intensity, drums and pipes competing with voices shouting the names of the contenders, but Robert led his limping horse along the line of the fence until they were out of the direct view of the spectators.

'Watch carefully,' he said to Adam, pointing away across the field. Adam could see the knights turn and charge once more against each other, some of them already galloping back to the lists to fetch fresh lances from their squires, others injured and crouching in the saddle. Those remaining on the field were meshing into the swirl of the melee, casting aside their broken lances and sweeping out their swords.

Up on the embankment behind the palisade fence, a herald in bright motley was crying out to those gathered in the stands. 'See him there, *preudhommes*! The champion Jean de Grailly! He rides like a tower, like a titan . . . Now he strikes – see him launch himself! And *yes*, already he makes a capture! . . . Now, *mesdames*, see to the right my lord Enguerrand de Coucy! . . . Witness his skill, his prowess!'

Across the field the melee was spilling away into the mist of light rain that had moved up from the river, and Adam struggled to make out the details of the combat.

'Look over there on the far side of the field, opposite us,' Robert said quietly, chewing a sprig of grass between his teeth.

'The opposing team's lists?' Adam asked, following his gesture. 'The refuge?'

Robert nodded. Only a moment passed before Adam saw a rider make for the opening in the opposite fence. A wounded knight, perhaps, or an exhausted one. Just after him came a second, dragging a captured horse on a long rein.

'Once they're inside the refuge they're safe, of course,' Robert said, and Adam glanced at him as he caught the note of cold suggestion in his voice. 'But only once they're inside . . . Sometimes there are infantry stationed to guard the refuges, but not today it seems. So where might be a good place to make a capture, would you say?'

'Isn't that against the rules?' Adam asked, before he could stop himself. He was rewarded by a scoffing laugh from John Chyld. 'But it's dishonourable surely?' he went on, undeterred. 'They're already leaving the field . . .'

'In battle, no man is safe,' Robert said. 'And so it is here too.'

Up on the fence the herald continued to cry out his commentary, gesticulating wildly. 'See him there, *messires* – the brave Sir Hugh D'Oisy! Like a hawk he attacks, striking to left and right . . . Oh, but he falls! A capture, *mesdames* . . . To the bold Sir Baldwin de Bazentin!'

Robert shrugged himself away from the fence and spat out the stem of grass he had been nibbling. For a moment or two longer he stared at the field and the swirl of the melee, then he sniffed in apparent satisfaction. 'Check my horse over again,' he told Adam. 'Give particular attention to the rear right leg.'

Adam found the stone quickly enough, a smooth round pebble wedged into the hoof beneath the rim of the shoe, and prised it free with his clasp knife. The destrier stirred at once, head tossing, and pawed the turf. 'Now get across the field and wait for me, close to the break of the opposite fences,' Robert said. He was smiling as he swung himself up into the saddle and took his helmet from John Chyld. 'Let's see what pretty birds might fly into our net.'

As Adam began to run he heard Hugh of Oystermouth scrambling up onto the fence of the lists, then his voice crying out across the field. 'Robert de Dunstanville, *messires* and *mesdames*! A new challenger has entered the fray, come to perform great feats of arms! Robert de Dunstanville is here – prepare to witness his skill!'

\*

Two days later, at an inn outside Soissons, Adam watched as Hugh calculated the takings, recording them in tight little columns of inked numbers. A certain sum for a horse, another for saddle and tack, another sum again for each weapon and piece of armour. Robert de Dunstanville had left the field at Épernay unvanquished and with two more captures, swiftly exchanged for cash ransoms. The second man had a capture of his own that he had taken moments earlier on the field, and Robert took a half share of that prize too.

For all Adam's misgivings about the stratagem they had used, watching Robert in action had been thrilling. The knight had made both his captures almost at the mouth of the opposing refuge, swooping down upon the riders as they retreated from the field. The first had tried to flee, but his wearied horse was no match for Robert's freshly rested charger. At the last moment the man had panicked and tried to turn, to fight, only to fall at once to Robert's battering onslaught. So swiftly, so violently did it happen that Adam laughed in amazement, even as he began to run to seize the fallen man. Already Robert had turned again, his horse rearing, to take his second victim. Neither had put up any resistance to Adam; both had yielded at once. It was almost as if they too had been stunned by the speed and naked aggression of the attack.

But how sordid it seemed now, Adam thought, to see all that daring and skill at arms reduced to columns of figures on a parchment scroll, every capture transformed into exact sums in *livres tournois*, and to little heaps of silver *deniers* on the scarred wood of the tabletop. Hugh of Oystermouth sat hunched over his work, scribing intently with the tip of his tongue between his teeth. Wilecok and John Chyld leaned over him, eyeing hungrily the little heaps of coin.

'Could have been we got more, of course,' John Chyld said, 'if we'd asked the full ransoms.'

'What do you mean?' Adam asked. He peered from John Chyld to Hugh, then at Robert, who sat at the head of the table. 'Tell him then,' John Chyld said.

'As you'd had some trouble, back at Lagny, in securing the captive,' Robert said in a mild tone, 'I had John and Hugh circulate a rumour before the fighting began at Épernay that I would only ask two thirds of the ransom of any capture I made. It seemed a worthwhile compromise.'

Adam looked from Robert to John Chyld and back as sour realisation soaked through him. 'There was no need,' he said, hot with embarrassment. 'You should not have made things easier for me.'

'Oh, don't worry,' Robert told him with a wry smile. 'Next time we won't. And if anyone still thinks I'm asking reduced ransoms, they'll be bitterly surprised.'

*

They remained at Soissons over the penitential season of Lent, training hard in the meadows outside the old walls of the town. Once more they fought with quarterstaffs, and by the end of the first week Adam no longer had to endure the taunts of John Chyld, or the stifled mirth of Wilecok and his Gascon woman. By the second week he had learned not only to hold his ground but to press the attack, and even to win. He learned to draw from inside himself a tightly focussed anger that felt almost like joy, an aggressive charge that he could direct outwards into action.

When the quarterstaffs were splintered and broken they changed to sword and falchion, first John Chyld and then Robert himself schooling Adam in close fighting. This was not the combat he had been taught at Pleshey, always at sword's length, shield up, feet braced. Adam learned to rush his opponent, using the pommel of the sword to punch at the exposed face and throat, using the crossguard to gouge and hook, the whole length of the blade to turn and to trip, to overwhelm. The shield too was a weapon, a blunt instrument; he learned to use the leading edge and corner to ram and strike, to batter his opponent down. It was fast and bruising, but he emerged from each bout stronger, breathless and elated, and often victorious.

Between fights, Adam rode. Robert had given him Papillon, the black destrier he had won from the Flemish knight at the ford, and Adam took him out over the surrounding countryside, riding with an open rein. He found the horse surprisingly docile for a trained battle-steed, but with only a light saddle, rather than the heavy padded war seat, he could sense the animal's flowing strength, the quickness of muscular reflexes. Already the horse was coming to know and trust him.

He rode at the quintain, slamming his lance repeatedly into the shield mounted on the swinging crossbar until he could aim straight and true almost without conscious effort. Then he rode practice jousts with John Chyld, hurtling up and down the long strip of meadow until the grass was worn to a hoof-scarred rut of earth, littered with the shattered wood of broken lances.

'Young men love the joust, it's true,' Robert de Dunstanville said one evening, after he had watched them ride. 'Easier to make a bold show to the ladies, I suppose. Only the melee teaches the true skills of warfare,' he said, and sighed, 'but I expect soon enough it'll die out completely, and real chivalry with it.'

Adam was rubbing his horse's neck and flanks with a cloth, wiping away the lather of sweat. He was becoming accustomed to Robert's grumbles about the changing culture of the tournament circuit. 'Harder to cheat at the joust as well, of course,' he said with a grin.

'Oh?' Robert said. He had a dangerous look in his eye suddenly, and Adam regretted his words. 'You believe it is cheating, then, to use cleverness in war?'

'No, I . . .' Adam began, but Robert was already striding towards his horse.

'Saddle up,' Robert said, snatching one of the unbroken lances that lay in the grass. 'And ready yourself.'

Adam caught John Chyld's wincing expression, then looked away. He took a lance, then swung himself into the saddle. Robert had already ridden to the far end of the meadow. Neither he nor Adam were wearing mail, only padded linen aketons, and their lances were mere untipped shafts, but Robert had a tensed vigour to his movements that Adam recognised from the tournament field.

As soon as he reached his position and turned, Adam saw Robert raise his lance and then spur his horse forward, his hair whipping out behind him. Papillon responded with only a touch of the spur, and a moment later they were galloping, Adam holding his breath tight, trying to pretend this was John Chyld he was jousting against, or the quintain, or . . .

With only a horse's length between them, Robert gave a wild cry and threw his lance, hurling it underarm like a clumsy javelin. Adam reeled back, swinging his own weapon upwards to deflect the missile. The horse beneath him buckled, almost stumbling, and Adam realised as he dropped his lance that he was no longer holding the reins. The black destrier reared, spinning so fast that Adam was almost thrown from the saddle, and before he could regain his balance he found himself galloping in the other direction, dragged behind a triumphant Robert de Dunstanville.

'Seize the reins and they're yours,' Robert shouted over his shoulder. 'Just don't try it yourself,' he went on, as they slowed to a canter and then to a walk once more. 'A squire with a broken neck is no use to me!'

\*

They arrived at Senlis one Sunday in early June, when the wheat was ripening in the fields. King Louis of France had dropped his ban on tournaments shortly after Easter, and had now gone so far as to sponsor one himself. He had sent out heralds to summon all the greatest and most chivalrous knights in Christendom to his town of Senlis, north of Paris, to contend for martial fame and glory, on the second Monday after Pentecost, the feast of St Boniface.

Already, as the vespers bell rang, the narrow square before the cathedral was awash with colours and heraldic blazons. Everywhere was the blue of the French king and his brother, the Count of Anjou, covered with golden *fleur-de-lis*. There was the black and the yellow of Brabant and of Flanders, and the blue and yellow of Burgundy. There were eagles and there were fishes, there were bears and boars and stag's heads. But most of all there were lions. Lions *rampant*, *passant* and *gardant*, in all the glorious colours of heraldry, flourishing through the narrow stone streets as if the whole town had been transformed into some exotic menagerie from the pages of an illustrated book.

From the open window of an upper chamber that overlooked the square, Adam stared into a sea of red. The deep royal red of England, where three golden lions prowled with paws upraised and tongues flickering. And the brighter sanguine of Simon de Montfort, Earl of Leicester, where a single white lion with a forked tail danced rampant on a bloody field.

'Here he comes now,' said Hugh of Oystermouth, perched on the wooden bench below the windowsill. 'The great man himself, like a king in his glory.'

Flanked by his household knights, with his sons riding before him, Simon de Montfort entered the square on horseback beneath his own huge streaming banner. From all sides men ran to assist him as he halted and began to dismount, crowding to hold his stirrup. Then, at his glance, they fell back and formed a lane before him, across the square towards the cathedral, where Lord Edward waited to greet him.

'Strange, isn't it?' Hugh said under his breath, as the crowd below them fell into an expectant hush. 'They could almost be father and son.'

Quite true, Adam thought. De Montfort was old enough to be the young prince's father. As old, perhaps, as King Henry himself, although he did not look it. And his sons were Edward's age, or a little younger. But as he strode across the cobbled square, Simon de Montfort did not appear in any way an old man. He stood straight, broad-shouldered, and walked with a prowling muscular assurance. His face was square and rather rawboned, with a jutting clean-shaven jaw and deep-set eyes. His hair was iron grey, and hung thick and straight to his shoulders. Beneath his red surcoat with its rampant white lion was the glint of mail, and he wore a broadsword belted at his side.

Compared to him, even the formidable Lord Edward resembled a boy.

'Is it true what they say, do you think?' Hugh muttered, leaning on the low sill of the window.

Adam's brow creased.

'You know . . .' Hugh went on, dropping his voice even further. 'That de Montfort planned to overthrow King Henry a twelvemonth past, and put Lord Edward on the throne in his father's place, and Edward was set fair to go along with it . . .?'

Adam raised a hand, hushing him. He had heard rumours of such things but they were best not spoken about, and certainly not here. If Lord Edward had been turned against his father at one point, his loyalties had swung firmly back again now. He had only just returned from a dutiful visit to the royal court in England, drawn back to France once more by the promise of tournament glories. 'He flits about the narrow sea like a gull, that one,' John Chyld had said.

Simon de Montfort, meanwhile, remained the king's principal adversary, the leader of the baronial faction that opposed Henry's will and wished to curb the power of the throne. As far as Adam knew, this was the first time that de Montfort and Edward had met face to face, since the sundering of their alliance.

Now the two men approached one another, ringed on all sides by their massed supporters. For a long moment they stood face to face, a sword's length apart. Then de Montfort raised his arms, and Lord Edward stepped forward into his embrace. The roar of voices from the men in the square rattled the shutters and startled the birds from the rooftops. Reconciled, the two leaders clasped each other by the shoulders and turned to face their supporters, both of them grinning widely. But how real, Adam wondered, was their friendship? He remembered what John Chyld had said to him, back in the inn at Lagny. *Get too close to them, and they'll rend your flesh.*

Yes, he thought, Edward and de Montfort were the real lions. Prouder and more ferocious by far than any heraldic beast, and never to be trusted.

'I can't say I favour either of them myself,' Hugh of Oystermouth was saying, as the gathering in the square broke up into knots of rowdy comradeship. 'Although they do say that Earl Simon is a close ally of Llywelyn, and I am inclined to support him, obviously, for the prestige of my nation—'

'Who is Llywelyn?' Adam broke in, frowning. A memory came to him that he could not place. Something Robert had told him . . .

Hugh stared at him, wide-eyed. 'Llywelyn, of course, Prince of Wales! You've never heard of him? Llywelyn son of Gruffudd son of Llywelyn the Great, who was Prince of Gwynedd in our grandfathers' day? Sir Robert claimed that some of his cousins are his descendants too, in fact.'

'Joane de Quincy and her sister,' Adam said, remembering the connection.

'I believe that was the name, yes. You've met them then? Do they have hair the colour of dark copper and eyes like the sea?'

'They do.'

Hugh nodded. 'Ah yes, that would be a true sign of the lineage,' he said. He had gone back to the table in the corner, where he was drawing up his list of all the contenders he had so far been able to identify, with notes of the arms and colours they bore and the numbers in their company.

Adam remained by the window, looking down into the square again. Nearly five months had passed, he reckoned, since he had left Joane de Quincy at Ware, but for a few long moments as he stared into the swirl of the crowd below him, thinning now that the principal men had departed, he saw only her face and form in his mind, and heard her voice as clearly as if she stood beside him.

'If you're looking for our master down there, he's already gone,' Hugh said from his desk. 'No doubt he followed Simon de Montfort's men, and Lord Edward. And no doubt he's already laying his plans to approach one or the other on the matter of his seized lands and estates. Which of them do you think holds most power now? To which of them might he give his support, to overturn the king's judgements?'

'What are you saying?' Adam asked, turning abruptly from the window as his vision of Joane faded. But he had not forgotten Robert's bitter outburst on the road from Pleshey to Ware, the great fury that he claimed would soon shake the throne.

'Only what you already know,' Hugh said, looking back at him with a sly smile. 'Which would prove stronger, do you think: the three golden lions or the single white lion? Which would prove fiercer, if it came to open war?'

Adam frowned, curling his lip. Surely things had not gone so far? Decades had passed since Englishman had last fought Englishman in civil conflict. No worse fate could befall the realm . . . And yet, he could not deny – his blood had quickened at the idea of it. He thought again of that menagerie of roaring beasts he had seen in the square a moment before, and pictured them brought to bold and violent life, and himself thrown among them.

'You too,' Hugh said, 'have suffered an injustice, so I hear.'

'You hear too much,' Adam told him.

'And you should open your ears a little more and hear what's happening around you!'

Adam gave a rueful smile. It was true enough. But now he had work to do – he needed to check that the horses had been properly stabled, with adequate fodder for the night. John Chyld and Wilecok had already melted into the crowded lanes of the town, and would not reappear before nightfall, no doubt. Outside the light was fading to dusk, and flights of starlings were whirling about the rooftops of the town.

On his way out of the room he paused a moment beside Hugh's desk, glancing over the rows of inked names and the few crabbed little drawings of shields. 'My father bore a lion on his arms as well,' he said. 'Granted to him by the king's herald.'

'A noble beast,' Hugh replied, bent over his work. His hair, Adam noticed, had grown out into a dense brown clump, entirely concealing the last traces of his clerical tonsure. 'In what style did he bear it?'

'*Vert, a lion rampant or*,' Adam told him. A golden lion on a field of green. 'I hope to bear those arms myself one day,' he said.

'Choose wisely,' Hugh said with a wink, 'and with God's grace you will.'

# Chapter 9

The grooms had almost finished with the horses by the time Adam entered the familiar warmth of the stables, although he noticed that they were giving Papillon a wide berth. Taking the currying comb from one of them, he rubbed the black destrier down himself.

'That one belongs to Robert de Dunstanville, doesn't it?' one of the grooms said, peering around the end of the stall. 'Fitting mount for the devil's knight, so they say.'

Adam glared back at him. 'The horse is mine,' he said, and enjoyed the man's quick dismay and stammering apology. Once the groom had retreated, Adam rubbed Papillon's nose and blew into the horse's flaring nostrils. The destrier had served him well over the recent months. At La Fère, in the week after Easter, Adam had ridden in a round-table jousting contest beneath the walls and towers of the Lord of Coucy's fortress. He broke three lances and remained unhorsed, and on the third pass drove his opponent out of both saddle and stirrups and toppled him back over his horse's rump. He had ridden cleanly, tried no tricks or ruses, and Robert merely nodded his approval. By the time they travelled north once more, Hugh's ledger was inked with fresh rows and columns, and the strongbox held another purse of silver *deniers*. Adam had felt the warmth of victory rising through him like the fumes of strong wine.

The following month, as the first apple blossom appeared on the trees, he and Robert had attended a three-day tournament at Valenciennes in the County of Hainaut. Adam had acquitted himself well, supporting Robert on the melee field and securing another captive, and he had twice ridden in the joust. Now it had been announced that the whole of the following morning at Senlis would be devoted to a round-table contest, with one event set aside for squires and young noblemen who had not yet attained knighthood; Adam knew that he would need his horse to be in the finest possible condition. Ignoring the muttering of the grooms, he went back over Papillon's hooves and mane with a coarse brush and worked down the animal's coat once more until the blackness shone in the glow of the lanterns.

As he was leaving the stable a messenger came for him: there would be a reception in the town later that evening, given by Lord Edward for Simon de Montfort and his sons, and Robert wanted Adam to attend him as his squire. He made the boy repeat the directions to the hall where the feast would be laid – a large inn on the other side of town, just outside the old walls – then sent him on his way. As he paced back up the lane to the town square, Adam recalled Earl Humphrey's warning to Sir Robert, back at Pleshey. Surely attending a reception feast given by the king's own son could not be considered *mischief*? And what could de Montfort do to help Robert anyway, living as a virtual exile in France?

A shout broke Adam's thoughts, then a sudden crashing noise and a woman's scream. Breaking into a run, he doubled the corner into the square and turned swiftly into the passageway leading to the upper room where he and Robert were lodging. Hugh of Oystermouth was sprawled at the bottom of the stairs, clasping his face as he scrambled to stand.

'What's happening?' Adam demanded.

'Vile sneaking bastard threw me down the steps!' Hugh cried. He took his hand from his face and stared at it. His palm was smeared with blood. 'Called me the son of a Welsh bitch!'

He dragged himself back into the corner as Adam pushed past him and climbed the stairs to the upper floor. Footsteps shuffled on the boards above him, then something was flung from the door of the chamber onto the narrow landing: his own mattress roll, and half of Robert's travelling luggage was already dumped beside it.

'What is this?' Adam cried, running up the last flight of stairs to the open door of the room. 'This chamber's already taken!'

'By whom?' said the man just inside the doorway. He spread his hands and mimed a searching glance around the room. 'I saw nobody here, except that swiving Welshman and his slut – and I had to drag him out by his heels!'

Adam took in the room: the baggage strewn across the floor, the bed disordered, the tousle-haired woman crouching in the corner with frightened eyes.

'I'm sorry,' said Hugh from the stairs. 'I thought you'd be away longer . . .'

'This chamber is already taken by Sir Robert de Dunstanville,' Adam said, setting his jaw and hooking his thumbs in his belt. 'You've no doubt seen his shield hanging in the window there. Who in the name of Christ are you?'

The young man standing before him was about a year older than Adam himself, with curling black hair, a sallow complexion and strangely protuberant eyes. He wore a tunic and hose of fine scarlet, with a knife in a tooled leather sheath hanging from his belt.

'I am Richard de Malmaines,' the man said with an eloquent gesture, 'squire to Sir Henry de Montfort, son of Simon, the Earl of Leicester, and a far greater and more worthy occupant of this chamber than your master, whoever he might be. But doubtless Sir Henry will be grateful to him for surrendering it without complaint.'

Just for a moment, Adam wondered whether Robert really had given up the room – was he intending to ingratiate himself with the de Montforts? No, he would surely have told Adam if he had. But Richard de Malmaines had noticed the brief flicker of doubt. He took one long stride and blocked the door, reaching out to grip the frame and lintel and bar Adam's way. He gave a sneering smile. 'Perhaps you might assist me by removing the last of your things,' he said.

Adam had taken an involuntary step back, and now felt the rough plaster of the wall behind him. In his mind he heard Robert's words: *direct all of your force and fury against your opponent, immediately*. He knew he could not risk another moment's hesitation. Throwing himself forward, he drove the heels of his palms against the man's shoulders and shoved him from the doorway. Richard de Malmaines let out a cry, caught off guard, and staggered several steps back into the room.

'You lay hands on me?' de Malmaines said. He looked down at himself in a pretence of disbelief. When he looked up again, Adam saw the glint of madness in his strange eyes. With a swift movement he drew the knife from his belt. The short stiff blade was sharpened to a wicked point. 'I'll slice your nose for that,' he said.

The woman in the corner of the room let out a keening wail, and just for a heartbeat de Malmaines glanced at her. Immediately Adam took another stride into the room, reaching down to grab the three-legged stool that Hugh had been using earlier. Whipping the stool up from the floor, he smashed it into the other man's wrist.

De Malmaines shouted in pain, the knife falling from his grip, and before he could defend himself Adam spun the stool and rammed the heavy wooden seat against his chest. Reeling, the man took three staggering steps backwards and tripped over the bench just inside the window. With a gasp of surprise he stumbled against the low sill, flailing his arms to grab at the frame. His fingers caught only air, and he toppled backwards out of the window. The woman screamed again, and took the opportunity to dart from the room.

'Christ's teeth!' Hugh said from the doorway. 'Did you murder the bastard? Have you killed him?'

His heart banging in his chest, Adam walked as slowly as he
could manage to the window and peered downwards. For a
moment he saw only the crowd of men that had already gathered
around the body sprawling on the muddy cobbles ten feet below.
Some of them were laughing, others calling out angrily. Then the
crowd parted and Adam saw Richard de Malmaines roll onto
his side and sit upright. Men hastened to assist him, taking his
arms and lifting him to his feet. Amazingly, he appeared to have
survived unhurt – Adam felt the pent breath rush from his chest
– but he gasped as he managed to stand and limped as he tried to
walk. Some of the bystanders were shouting encouragements
to him, others were hooting abuse. Several large men appeared
to be restraining him.

Adam picked up the knife from the floor, reversed it, and
tossed it from the window. 'You dropped that,' he called after it.

*

'You have a habit of attacking your fellow squires, it seems,'
Robert de Dunstanville said an hour later, as they entered the
packed and rowdy hall.

'Only when they look like they're about to attack me,' Adam
replied.

Robert twitched a smile. 'Yes, a pre-emptive attack is often
the best defence – even with a three-legged stool. Still, it was a
matter of honour and no murdering was done, so I approve. The
matter will not lie, though – best be ready.'

'I will,' Adam said. He had been ready all evening, expecting
to be assaulted in some narrow alleyway of the town as he made
his way to join Robert. A knife in the dark would have come as
no surprise. But Richard de Malmaines had not yet struck back
at him – and here he was in this very chamber, lurking darkly

behind his master Henry de Montfort, who in turn sat at the left hand of his father, Earl Simon. His eyes met Adam's across the crowded room and narrowed with a palpable lust for reprisal.

But there would be no violence here at least. The hall was a long vaulted chamber, more like a crypt or a storage cellar than a feasting place. Some of the men at the two central tables were Burgundian or Flemish, but the vast majority of them were English, crowding along the benches drinking and shouting, boasting loudly of the great deeds they would perform the following day. If any were nervous, they did not show it. Serving boys weaved between them, bearing pitchers of wine and baskets of bread, fruit and cheese, and beneath the tables dogs slunk and prowled. Above the roar of voices a trio of minstrels tried to make themselves heard on vielles and tabor. There was even a troupe of tumblers, crowded into one corner performing their leaps and turns while the onlookers yelled encouragement.

Lord Edward sat at the high table, with Simon de Montfort and his sons, and appeared far more restrained and dignified than the knights thronging the central tables. The air was thick with the smeech of candles and lamps.

'Watch carefully what happens here,' Robert told Adam. 'There is more going on than might be obvious.'

He leaned and whispered something to one of the serving boys, slipping him a silver coin, and the boy nodded and darted away towards the high table. Picking his way across the room, Robert lowered himself into a free place at the end of one of the benches. Adam noticed the others at the table shifting away from him, some with expressions of disdain or suspicion. Robert grinned at them, then took a cup of wine and drank it to the dregs.

A stir ran through the room as another figure approached the table. Adam guessed his identity at once: Sir Henry de Montfort, the son of Earl Simon, the master of Richard de Malmaines. A younger and slighter version of his father, with less of the dominance but all the assurance.

'De Dunstanville,' Sir Henry said, halting before Robert and leaning closer, one foot propped on the bench beside him. 'My squire tells me that he was grievously misused earlier this evening. He claims your own squire was responsible.' He flicked a quick glance at Adam, who was standing at Robert's shoulder.

Robert merely shrugged. 'So I heard,' he said. 'What of it?'

Sir Henry smiled coldly. 'I've forbidden my man from taking vengeance directly, to respect the peace of our hosts. But he will challenge yours at the individual jousts on the morrow.'

Robert shrugged again, as if Adam were none of his concern. 'So be it,' he said.

'Your squire is a keen lance?' Sir Henry asked.

'I've never seen him bested.'

'Tomorrow you may. My man is good.' Henry looked directly at Adam for the first time. 'Prepare yourselves,' he told them both. Then he straightened up again, and gestured curtly. 'Come, then,' he said to Robert, 'if you wish for an audience with my father.'

Adam felt the flare of blood in his face as Robert gestured for him to follow, and together they made their way after Sir Henry towards the high table. He was relieved that the matter was out in the open now, and that his conflict with de Malmaines would be concluded in the open as well, rather than by a sudden strike in a back alley. But his nerves were taut; tomorrow's match would be no simple demonstration of prowess. Honour was at stake, and perhaps his life as well.

The men at the high table were seated in high-backed chairs, with their squires and other servants waiting attendance. Dishes of food and cups of wine littered the board between them, along with an arsenal of silver eating knives and spoons. Lord Edward sat at the far end, in the tallest chair, but seemed subdued and watchful tonight. Simon de Montfort had taken the central place, and seemed effortlessly to command the scene. His second son, Simon the Younger, sat at his left hand. The others at the table were young noblemen, only a year or two older than Adam and not yet knighted.

'Robert de Dunstanville,' de Montfort said. 'A long time since last we met! I was sorry when I learned of your recent misfortunes.'

'I try to bear the slights without complaint, my lord,' Robert said. 'Many, after all, have suffered worse.'

'Indeed so,' de Montfort said, and his smile turned grave. 'You know that I will always uphold the rights of honest men. If there is ever anything I can do to assist you, just come to me.'

Robert bowed his head, but Adam had caught the quick stir of interest around the table. The two young noblemen at the far end exchanged a glance, then turned together to de Montfort, as alert as scent hounds picking up a spoor. 'If you truly wish to assist the realm, Lord Simon,' one of them said, 'you should return to England – the people cry out for leadership!' He was a hulking dark-haired youth, heavy and brutal-looking.

'My father would be only too pleased to have you at his side,' the second said. He was lean, almost delicate, with flaming red hair and a tufting beard of orange down. 'Surely the king would listen to reason, with two such advisors?' Adam recalled seeing this young man earlier in the day; his name was Gilbert, and he was the son of the Earl of Gloucester.

All eyes turned to Lord Edward, the king's son, who remained sitting silently at the head of the table, running stiff fingers through his beard. 'It's true,' he said at last, his strange lisping voice filling the silence around the table, 'that the *communitas regni* has been solely disturbed by these recent disputes, and many have suffered. My father knows it well. But he will always be the first recourse for justice. And the noble Earl Simon can return home whenever he likes – the king would embrace him as a brother.'

'He would honour me by doing so,' de Montfort said, raising an open palm. 'But as for returning, there are so many false and fickle men in England, I prefer to be here, with my friends.' He turned his smile to left and right including them all, and once more Adam had the impression of a lion sizing up its prey, waiting for the moment to pounce, to rend. De Montfort raised his goblet for the serving boy behind him to refill. 'By the arm of St James,' he said, 'let us drink from one cup, as brothers, and pray God sends justice to us all one day!'

The others growled their agreement, and de Montfort passed the brimming goblet to Robert. All of those at the table, Adam thought, were the sons of great and noble houses. Most were the descendants of those men who had followed William the Bastard across the narrow sea nearly two centuries before. Robert de Dunstanville too was one of them, for all his scorn for the aristocracy of his own country. He took the goblet, drank deeply, and then placed it before Lord Edward. Without glancing in his direction, Edward drank too. Adam, the son of a commoner raised to knighthood, descendant of nobody, was not included.

'But how can there be justice in England now?' the dark-haired young man was muttering, through the noise of revelry behind them. 'Half the nobility are in debt to the Jews! And the Jews are the property of the king—'

'These are not matters for this time or place, FitzJohn,' de Montfort's son broke in.

Adam had been standing behind Robert all this time, trying to ignore the murderous stares that de Malmaines was directing at him over the heads of their masters. Now he became suddenly aware that Simon de Montfort's roving gaze had fastened upon him. For a heartbeat he thought that de Montfort had asked him a question and was awaiting an answer. Then he realised that it was the question, not the answer, that was required of him.

'Will you ride in the tournament tomorrow, my lord?' he asked abruptly, and felt the attention of the men at the table shift towards him.

'Not I,' de Montfort replied, with the slightest hint of a wink. 'No, I am too old for such pursuits – I leave them to the young bucks!' He gestured once more to Lord Edward, and to his sons. All of them appeared relieved that the conversation had once more shifted. 'And you are . . .?' Simon asked Adam.

'My squire, lord,' Robert told him. 'Adam de Norton.'

'De Norton – your family come from Herefordshire, I think?'

'My father held land in Hampshire, my lord,' Adam said, his mouth dry. 'East of Winchester, by the forest of Blakemore.'

'I know that country well,' de Montfort said. 'You must be close to Odiham, and to the fine abbey of Waverley.'

'It's been many years since I was last there,' Adam told him. 'Since my father died, that is.'

'Adam de Norton too has been unjustly dispossessed of his inheritance, lord,' Robert added.

Simon de Montfort nodded, his jaw tightening as he tapped at the table. He fixed his eyes on Adam once more. 'Then I hope you too gain justice soon enough,' he told him. 'And I will do anything in my power to aid you. I have a good memory for faces, Adam de Norton, and I will not forget yours.'

Adam bowed, feeling the heat rise through him. Robert was already backing away from the table, but Lord Edward raised a hand.

'You'll ride in my company tomorrow, de Dunstanville?' he asked, with a casual gesture. 'I would not like to think any honest Englishman felt . . . *unjustly* excluded.'

'With your permission I would be honoured, my lord.'

They moved away from the high table together, back into the noise and revelry of the hall. Adam only had time to catch Robert's quick smile of satisfaction before he sensed a presence behind him. Turning, he saw Richard de Malmaines stalking after him, still limping heavily.

'Adam de Norton, is that your name?' de Malmaines said, when only an arm's length separated them. Adam could almost smell the anger burning in him, the desire for violence.

'Let there be no misunderstanding between us,' de Malmaines said, his eyes gleaming. 'You have shamed and injured me, so I give you proper challenge. I intend to destroy you tomorrow.'

'You intend to try,' Adam told him. At the margins of his vision he could make out the men around them turning to listen, giving them room.

'Oh, make no mistake of my purpose,' de Malmaines said. 'I swear upon the holy blood of Christ, I will tear the bones from your flesh and the soul from your body.'

Adam just smiled back, nodded once, then with an effort of will turned his back on the man and began to walk away from him.

'Hear me well, Adam de Norton!' de Malmaines called after him. 'I will *unmake* you!'

# Chapter 10

To the west of the town of Senlis lay a broad four-mile expanse of open pasture, bracketed on three sides by forest and marsh. On that land the afternoon's grand melee would take place. But the venue for the morning jousts lay closer to the town itself, in the fenced enclosure of the lists. Many days had passed since the last rain, and the ground was hard and dry, the hooves of the horses kicking up a scrim of dust that hung in the air and hazed the distant landscapes.

Adam waited in the saddle, raising his leg while John Chyld tightened the girth strap. It was still early, but already the heat was gathering. The jousts for the squires and others who had not yet attained knighthood were almost concluded; next would come the jousting of the young knights, before the field was cleared for the day's main event. In the stands and around the lists the crowds were forming, although most of those assembled were knights themselves, studying and assessing the skills and courage of their juniors and trying to pick out the future tournament champions among them.

Already they had seen Gilbert de Clare, the red-haired son of the Earl of Gloucester, blast a squire of the Count of Soissons from the saddle with his first lance. His friend John FitzJohn, de Montfort's other companion from the evening before, had ridden too, although he had only managed a draw against his opponent. Adam had watched them both, and a score of other riders as well, through glazed eyes. Now, finally, the moment had come to confront his challenger, Richard de Malmaines.

He had slept badly the night before, the taunts of his opponent revolving in his mind, surges of anger and terror startling him back from the brink of exhaustion. So many times had he pictured the confrontation, the galloping charge and the clash, that he felt now that he was once again dreaming. Blinking rapidly, tightening his grip on the reins, he tried to focus his mind and slow the rapid beating of his heart.

He could see his opponent at the far end of the dusty course. De Malmaines was mounted on a bay stallion that appeared half maddened already, sidestepping and tossing its head as it champed at the bit, spattering foam from its mouth. De Malmaines himself wore a mail hauberk and carried a red shield with the white lion blazon of his master. Adam was dressed in a padded linen gambeson faced with leather, a coif over his head, and on his white shield was the red lattice of de Dunstanville. He was mounted on Papillon; the black charger was placid enough as John Chyld checked the bridle and tack for one last time, but Adam could feel the solid muscle of the horse's back beneath him, the power in the haunches and the massive heart, ready to be unleashed.

Glancing to his right, Adam saw Robert leaning on the fence of the lists. The knight appeared relaxed, unconcerned. Surely, Adam thought, he must be feigning such nonchalance?

John Chyld passed Adam his first lance. Each rider was allowed three, one for each pass. At each end of the course the marshals had raised their flags. Adam only had to touch Papillon's flank with the spurs and the horse instantly moved up to the starting line, primed and ready for the charge.

A pause, a long breath. Dust settled. Then the flag went down, the trumpet roared, and at once the big destrier began to move.

Adam leaned forward in the saddle, the muscles of his right arm bunched as he held the reins short and tight. The horse wanted to stretch out into a run but he needed to hold back the full power and momentum of the charge until the last moment. He could see de Malmaines approaching down the worn dirt strip of the course, the dust billowing up behind him.

Adam swung his lance down, couching the shaft beneath his arm. The blunt socketed tip wavered, and he gripped the shaft and aimed. Nerves tight, he felt the power of the animal beneath him compressed into its haunches, into the muscles of its rear legs, ready to surge forward as soon as he let out the reins. De Malmaines was coming on at a full gallop, the socket of his lance aimed straight at Adam's shield.

Heartbeats before contact, Adam released the reins and felt Papillon spring forward, one leaping stride bringing his lance against the opponent's shield hard and true. He felt the blow through his hunched right shoulder and down his side, then a moment later the other man's lance glanced off his shield and skated away. A blast of dust, and de Malmaines was gone.

He had struck cleanly, and his lance was cracked in the shaft, but de Malmaines had remained in the saddle. Adam saw him cantering by as they returned up the course for their second pass. De Malmaines had discarded his own lance as well, although Adam was sure he could only have clipped him. For a moment he wanted to laugh; after all his bluster the evening before, Richard de Malmaines had not proven to be all that adept a jouster.

Back at the end of the course, Adam turned Papillon, keeping the horse moving and fiery. Hugh of Oystermouth was running from the fence of the lists as John Chyld brought the second lance.

'He's using a warhead!' Hugh cried as he arrived, breathless, at Adam's side. 'I saw his groom holding it. Sharpened steel tip. I believe he means to murder you!'

Of course, Adam thought. The first pass had been only a bluff. Now Richard de Malmaines was aiming to maim or kill, with a real weapon. Easy enough to claim afterwards that he had taken the wrong lance by mistake. Such things happen often enough, in the heat and turmoil of the tournament.

'If it's true,' John Chyld said, squinting down the course into the haze of sunshot dust, 'we must get the marshal to halt the challenge.'

'No,' Adam said. He hefted his lance, with its blunt socket tip. 'This matter must be decided, here and now.' *And let God be my witness.*

Again the marshals raised their flags, and again the merest touch of spur brought Papillon up to the starting line. Adam tried to slow his breathing, but sweat was tiding down his body and soaking into his waistband, and when he shifted in the saddle he felt the leather beneath him dampened and slippery. He shoved his feet more firmly into the stirrups, circled his gloved fingers with the reins, then saw the flags drop.

The second charge was faster and less controlled than the first. De Malmaines was approaching with uncanny speed, and Adam could make out the glinting steel tip of his lance with a strange clarity of vision. For one terrified moment he could almost feel that speeding point, with all the weight of man and horse behind him, glancing upwards off his shield rim and spearing his unprotected face, driving in through his eye or his cheek, smashing teeth and splitting flesh and bone, shattering his skull . . .

Then his enemy was upon him. Adam saw the lance head coming straight for him, and at the very last moment tugged the reins and twisted in the saddle. Papillon jinked to the right, nimble as a dancer, then veered left again. Leaning, Adam swung his lance, cracking the shaft against the head of the oncoming weapon and shoving it aside. The steel point of de Malmaines's lance passed a hand's breadth from his face, and then the two charging horses rammed together, Adam slamming the forward edge of his shield into his opponent's body.

The impact of the collision almost lifted him from the saddle, but Adam trod down hard on the stirrups and forced his rump against the cantle. Both horses reared together, each turning with the momentum of their charge, and Adam released his grip on his lance and grabbed for his opponent's head. His fingers hooked the edge of de Malmaines's mail coif and he clung on, keeping his shield pressed against the other man's body as their horses pulled apart once more. For a speeding heartbeat the two riders were locked together, de Malmaines trying to push back with his own shield as Adam hauled at him. Then, with a scream of rage, he slipped sideways out of the saddle and plunged into the dust threshed up by the horses' hooves.

Adam rode on halfway down the course, still uncertain whether his desperate stratagem had worked. Slowing, he shortened the reins and turned his horse, and only then did he see Richard de Malmaines lying sprawled in the dust, his legs flexing as he tried to roll onto his back. Marshals were running from the sides of the course, and Hugh of Oystermouth stood pointing at the fallen man's lance, crying outrage for all to hear.

*

'. . . and you'll get the hound's share, as usual,' Hugh was saying, as Adam raised his head from the bucket and drew breath. Water streamed down his face and shoulders, and he grabbed a linen towel and rubbed at his hair. Hugh had already arranged the sale of Richard de Malmaines's horse and armour with one of the many dealers who thronged the margins of the tournament ground. 'No great sum, all the same,' he said with a shrug. 'That horse was in very poor condition, sad to say.'

Richard de Malmaines himself had been carried from the field long before, with a broken collarbone that would put him out of any further participation. With luck, Adam thought, the matter was now settled and he would never encounter the man again. His victory had been uncontested – several men, in fact, had congratulated him on his daring in grappling his opponent and wrestling him from the saddle. His left arm still felt wrenched and tender, but he was struggling to hide his jubilation. Robert de Dunstanville, though, had said little about it. Perhaps, Adam told himself, his master had never doubted that he would win? He felt a shadow over his accomplishment nevertheless. All his life he had been overlooked and treated as a servant. Now, in this moment of his triumph, it would have been satisfying to be recognised as something greater than that.

But already the second round of jousting had been concluded, and the two great teams of knights were assembling for the grand melee. Quickly drying himself, Adam pulled on his tunic and gambeson and tightened his belt. As the field at Senlis was so large, it would be permitted for squires to accompany their knights on horseback, and John Chyld had already saddled and exercised one of the rounceys. As he swung himself onto the animal's back, Adam was keenly aware of the change from the big destrier he had ridden in the joust. But a smaller, lighter horse could keep up with the movement of the melee just as well and would not be too valuable to lose. Besides, Adam would not be mistaken for one of the contending knights.

Riding up behind the line of assembled riders, Adam picked out Robert de Dunstanville's colours and went to join him. The English were all riding together, grouped around the red and gold banners of Lord Edward's company. To their left was the blue and gold of the Count of Anjou's household knights. Away across the rutted turf, the opposing team were arrayed beneath flags of yellow, black and red; the Flemish and the Brabazons, the Germans and the men of Hainaut were united under the lead of Duke Frederick of Lorraine. This time, Adam knew, there would be no ruses or wily stratagems; Robert was riding for the king's son and needed to make a show of valour. Trumpet calls wailed in the distance, and drums rolled and rattled as the horses shifted in the lines.

Then the signal went up, all the horns blared as one, and the two huge bodies of knights spurred their mounts forward, first into a walk and then into a canter, building steadily to the charge that would bring them crashing together at the centre of the field. Dust plumed upwards, obscuring the riders, and Adam craned forward in the saddle, squinting. He heard, rather than saw, the moment of collision: the rending clatter of lances against shields, the thunder of metal, the screams of men and animals.

Already the line of mounted squires was jostling forward, horses champing and pawing the turf. Already the first riders were galloping from the dust cloud, turning swiftly for the return pass, some of them dragging captures. Adam felt his rouncey's twitching impatience and let out the rein. The horse started forward and he raised the spare lance, shouting out '*Dunstanville! Dunstanville!*' But everyone around him was shouting too, their voices sucked into the surrounding clamour.

Robert appeared from the haze ahead of him, empty-handed as he slowed his big grey destrier. He snatched the lance from Adam's grip. '*With me!*' he bellowed from inside his helmet as he sawed at the reins. '*With me – now!*'

Back into the dusty chaos of the melee they rode, Adam spurring his rouncey hard to keep up with the bigger horse. The fighting had spilled away quickly to the westward, out of the reeling dust and confusion and into the wide open pastureland. Knots of mounted men in combat turned and clashed on all sides, and Robert rode a wavering course between them with lance raised, his helmeted head turning as he hunted for a victim. Another rider careered in from the left, his mount slamming against the forequarter of Adam's rouncey, leaving the smaller horse staggering and whinnying. A moment later another knight knocked the rider from the saddle with a single blow of his mace.

Once his horse had recovered, Adam slung the shield from his back and drew his falchion: where was Robert? Mounted men crashed and reeled on all sides, figures on foot darting between them, and for several long heartbeats Adam was lost in the press of the melee.

Then the pack ahead of him parted and he saw Robert de Dunstanville with another rider, a knight wearing the black surcoat of the Duke of Brabant's household, galloping up behind him. As Adam watched, Robert reversed his lance over his left shoulder and tugged at the reins, his destrier rounding on the Brabazon knight with trained agility. His pursuer tried to evade him, but was too slow: Robert's lance speared in below his shield rim, shoving him up from the saddle.

Already Adam had closed with them. He turned his horse around the tail of the Brabazon's mount and came up on his right, ready to leap down and seize the man as soon as he fell. But the knight was still clinging on, halfway across his horse's mane with his feet kicking to find the stirrups. Before he could reach out to grab at him, Adam was struck from behind, a blow with a blunted sword across the small of his back that sent a jolt of pain into the pit of his stomach. The Brabazon knight's squire had ridden up in support of his master; Adam twisted, slashing backwards with his falchion, and his blade clashed against the other squire's shield. His horse shied as the squire slashed at its head, and Adam felt rage erupt inside him. He yelled, turning in the saddle and stabbing directly for the other man's unprotected face. The Brabazon squire flung himself back in the saddle, dragging on his reins, and Adam struck him across the chest with the flat of his blade. Then he was gone again, his master too riding clear as the billowing dust hid them from view.

Robert was gesturing, shouting words too muffled to distinguish. Adam glanced around, struggling to breathe as the dust soaked into the ventail covering his mouth. A burst of motion from his left, and a horse staggered and fell, throwing its rider from the saddle. One of Lord Edward's men, Adam thought as he saw the flapping red and gold caparison . . . *No*, he realised as he saw the gold harness trappings – it was Edward himself. The big charger rolled on its back, legs kicking, the broken stub of a lance jutting from its neck. The fallen rider struggled to get clear before the animal crushed him in its dying frenzy.

Where were Edward's household knights, the men who were supposed to protect him? Lost in the surge of the melee, Adam realised. Only Robert de Dunstanville was with Edward now, circling his horse around the fallen man and striking out at the opposing knight who had felled him. He bellowed at Adam again, and this time Adam understood.

Cantering as close as he dared to the stricken horse, which was still rolling and kicking, struggling to get up, Adam slipped from the saddle and ran to where Edward lay. Robert circled, holding off the other mounted men who tried to approach and claim their prize, but the foot squires of the opposing team were swarming forward out of the dust. Quickly, Adam dropped to one knee beside the fallen man. One glance told him that Edward had injured his leg, and possibly broken his arm too. His helmet had been twisted, either from a blow or from the fall from his horse, and the eye slits were wrenched round to the side. From the vents came a spume of bloody froth as the fallen man gasped for breath.

'Lie still!' Adam shouted. 'Don't try to get up!' Pointless even to try and make him understand. Adam could barely hear his own voice for the thundering of blood in his head.

But Edward was struggling, trying to get his legs beneath him, his uninjured arm thrashing and stretching. The sound of his breath inside the twisted helmet was like a wheezing bellows, cut through with high-pitched sobs. As Adam stood over him, Edward seized his belt at the back and tried to pull himself upright. Two footmen rushed from the dust cloud, both of them in padded gambesons and gripping staves with a determined look. Adam planted his feet on either side of the fallen man, twisting to shake off his grip, then took the first blow of the stave on his shield. The second cracked onto his shoulder, and he felt the bloom of pain red and raw in his chest. His throat felt scorched; he was shouting, but could hear nothing. Beneath him the fallen man – the son and heir of the King of England, but he could not remind himself of that – *the fallen man* writhed and kicked, his outstretched hand grasping now at Adam's surcoat.

Holding his position, Adam slammed his shield at one of the attackers and drove him back. A hammering blow with his falchion dropped the second to his knees. A squire screamed, 'Yield! The man is ours!' Then a galloping horse knocked him off his feet and trampled him.

Adam was hurt himself, cut somewhere – blood was in his eyes. *No, it was sweat.* He blinked it clear. The heat was a furnace, consuming him. Another strike from behind, pounding through the wadded linen of his gambeson, and he half turned and thrust backwards, feeling his blade thud against a raised shield.

Then Edward's men were all around him, their horses blocking the light, hooves kicking dust. One leaped from the saddle and shoved Adam roughly aside. A second was already kneeling beside their fallen leader. Between them, as he staggered free of the press, Adam saw Robert de Dunstanville beset by three other riders, hacking with his axe to right and left. He began to run, the strength draining suddenly from him. Like running in a dream, his legs were too weak suddenly to support him. Through the glassy haze of despair he saw Robert beaten down, two men closing on him, both standing in their stirrups to strike at him. Before the dust rose, he saw Robert buckle and plunge from the saddle, the opposing squires running in to seize him. He was too far away; he could do nothing. The choked cry of anguish died in his throat.

*

Lord Edward's grand pavilion had been raised upon a grassy sward to the north of the town of Senlis, far enough from the melee ground that the dust and havoc would not disturb the occupants, but close enough that it could serve as a convenient place to rest and take refreshment at intervals in the fighting. Beneath the patterned linen canopy the ground was laid with rush matting sprinkled with freshly cut flowers and fragrant herbs, and set with couches that would not have disgraced a lord's hall.

Now it was a scene of confusion. A crowd of men – knight, serjeants and servants – pressed around the entranceway, shoving to get a glimpse within. Lord Edward had been carried from the field, near insensible from the pain of his wounds. He would not die, so everyone claimed, although with tournament injuries one could never tell. Fear and anxiety, mixed with a strange excited anticipation, charged the air. Would the King of England's son and heir lose his life, right here before them?

By the time Adam arrived at the pavilion, the initial shock had passed. He was stumbling, breathless, still caked in dust and runnelled with sweat, his blistered hands bloody from the fighting. By sheer momentum he pushed his way through the throng around the entranceway, dragging aside the painted linen drapes and forcing his way inside. A mailed arm blocked him, shoving his back, and then men were all around him gripping his shoulders.

'I must speak with Lord Edward!' Adam cried. He raised his voice, calling over the heads of the men that blocked his way. 'My name is Adam de Norton, squire to Sir Robert de Dunstanville, and I must speak with Lord Edward!'

A word of command from within, and the wall of bodies parted.

Edward lay reclining on one of the couches, propped on cushions with a silk gown draped around his shoulders. His arm and upper body were wrapped in linen bandages, and one side of his face was raw and swollen with contusions. He had lost a tooth at least, and there was a row of ugly black stitches over his left eye. But he was alive, conscious, and drinking wine while two physicians attended his wounds and a third dabbed at his face with a sponge. A chaplain and a pair of friars waited upon him.

'My lord,' Adam said, stumbling to kneel before the couch. He recognised some of the men around him from the evening before. Gilbert de Clare was there, and FitzJohn too. 'My lord,' he said again, breathing hard, 'my master, Robert de Dunstan-ville, was captured in the melee . . .'

'By a couple of Savoyards, so I heard,' one of the bystanders said.

'A great many men have been captured in the melee,' Edward replied, the injury to his mouth making his lisp more pro-nounced. His mail hauberk and coif, leg armour and helmet still lay on the ground where they had been stripped from him, flung down with his bloodstained aketon.

'My lord,' Adam went on, staring up at the young man on the couch, 'Robert de Dunstanville was riding in your company. He was defending you when he was taken . . .' He felt the heat of many eyes upon him, the weight of their judgement.

'It's true,' somebody behind him said.

'The squire here was defending him, I heard,' said somebody else. It was Gilbert de Clare, the red-haired son of the Earl of Gloucester.

'And how was it that I needed defending?' Edward asked lightly, then winced as the attendant mopped at his stitches. 'Where were my own knights, hmm, that were pledged to watch over me on the field?'

He glanced around the circle of men filling the tent, but for a moment none dared to answer. Adam heard once more the ghastly sobbing sounds the young prince had made when he was lying injured. He felt once more the scrabbling hands gripping his surcoat and belt, the panicking grasp.

'Too many of them taken, lord,' said an older man, a clerk in a patterned robe, leaning over the couch. 'Taken, and needing ransoms paid.'

'And my own horse lost too,' Edward said, and a spasm of grief twisted his features. 'Anyway, I suppose de Dunstanville sent you here?'

'He did not, lord,' Adam said. Robert was still in the Duke of Lorraine's camp, held hostage, his best horse and best armour forfeit to his captors. No, Adam thought, Robert would never have told him to come here and beg for favours. That was his own decision.

'He wants me to pay his ransom?' Edward said in a musing tone, as if Adam had not spoken. He peered back at the clerk, who pursed his lips and shook his head. 'No, no, quite right,' Edward said. 'With my own losses and those of my household I've had to give out too much already. Tell de Dunstanville he will have to pay his own way or accept the loss. All of us here know what's at stake in this business, heh?'

*But some have more to lose*, Adam thought. Edward had already turned his attentions to the next man, and Adam felt hands gripping his shoulders and urging him to stand. He got to his feet, neglected to make his bow, then turned and stalked from the tent.

The light outside glared in his eyes. Hot resentment burned inside him, and for a terrible moment he found himself blinking back tears. *Anger*, he told himself, not disappointment. Not despair.

'Adam de Norton,' a voice said. He turned, and in the brightness he saw only the rough dark russet of a tunic, and assumed that one of the lower servants had followed him from the pavilion. Then he raised his eyes, shading them with his palm. Simon de Montfort's broad face creased into a smile, but his eyes had a searching intensity.

'Lord Edward has yet to learn the value of loyalty,' de Montfort said, gripping Adam by the shoulder and steering him away from the pavilion. 'Perhaps in time he will. You are de Dunstanville's squire, yes?'

Adam could only nod.

'I heard you did well, defending your leader like that. Quite a deed of arms, in itself. He's churlish to dismiss it. I saw you unhorse my son's squire earlier today as well.'

'I was sorry to injure him, lord,' Adam said, knowing that his tone did nothing to hide the lie.

De Montfort's smile twitched, and he squeezed Adam's shoulder tighter. 'No matter,' he said. 'It was neatly done. And you may tell your master, Robert de Dunstanville, to send the demand of his captors to me.'

'You'll pay on his behalf?'

Simon de Montfort nodded, and in his eyes Adam caught a quick predatory gleam. He tried not to shudder.

'Some of us,' de Montfort said, 'know what a debt is worth.'

# Part Two
*Eighteen Months Later*

# Chapter 11

They came boiling out of the alleyway at a run, feet skating on the cobbles as the fog swirled around them. Adam was leading; he had no idea how many were at his back. They were Flemish and French mostly, all of them with their blood up. Charging onto the town square, they cried out in cracked voices, *Flanders! Flanders!* Their enemies turned, howling in dismay as they saw themselves assailed from the rear. Adam grinned as he charged; the flanking attack through the alleyways had been his idea.

Smashing his shield into the first opponent, Adam knocked him off his feet and swung his way deeper into their formation. He was dressed in a well-fitted gambeson, his skull protected by an iron helmet with a broad flaring brim, and he was wielding an iron-headed mace. Even with the flanges blunted, it was a brutal weapon. He fought by instinct, letting the attack flow out from the core of his body, fury guiding his arm. One cracking blow brought a man to his knees; the backswing sent another dancing backwards, terrified. Adam brought up his shield just in time to deflect a swinging sword; he shoved forward, keeping the shield raised and ramming it against his attacker until the man fell back, then lashing out with his mace. At the margins of his vision he could see that the enemy were breaking, turning to flee into the narrower alleys. Already the battle looked to be won.

This was only a *buhort*, a skirmishing foot melee for squires and serjeants. It was supposedly a side event to the tournament held at Ghent between the Dukes of Flanders and Brabant, on this wintry afternoon of St John the Apostle, two days after Christmas. A mock battle, but real enough to the young men fighting in the heavily boarded streets of the town. The traditional rivalry between the Flemings and the Brabazons only stoked their aggression even further. Many of the local people liked to join in as well; the teams were more than half made up of town burghers who would never get to wear the gilt spurs. It was less glorious than the knightly tournaments of France and the Empire, but no less vicious, and with a purse of silver for the winners no less lucrative either.

His breath steaming, Adam paused and peered around him at the reeling shapes in the fog. Most wore the yellow armbands or headscarves of the Flemish team. The few that wore the black of Brabant had already flung down their arms, although some of them were still warding off the blows and kicks of the victors. Sounds of fighting came from the narrower streets nearby. Adam was beginning to feel the cold again now, the damp cold that soaked into his bones even during the rush of combat.

'*On, on,*' he called, gesturing to the men who had followed him from the alleyway. His foot slipped as he ran; righting himself, he caught a blur of movement ahead of him. A scrawny figure rushed at him from the fog, barely a boy, dressed in an oversized linen gambeson and coif and swinging a falchion. Lifting his shield just in time, Adam blocked the blow. The blade skated off the shield to collide with the shaft of Adam's mace and slide down to strike his right wrist. Adam snatched his arm back, then brought the mace up in a cracking blow to the boy's chest that almost lifted him off his feet. The boy reeled back to trip and fall sprawling on the muddy cobbles. *Good Christ*, Adam thought, *that could have been me two years ago.*

The eighteen months of hard fighting and travelling since the events at Senlis had changed him. He was twenty years old now, agile and strong, and his spare frame had filled out with taut muscle. The tournament road had taken Robert de Dunstanville and his little company from southern Burgundy and Gascony to the lands of the King of Aragon and the Count of Savoy, then across into Bavaria and Saxony and as far north as the Baltic shores. They had been mostly successful, and had covered their losses well.

Adam had fractured his ankle falling from a horse at Châlons, and suffered broken ribs in Mainz. He had lost two teeth from his upper jaw at Barcelona, and at Würzburg he had taken a cut across his brow that had flooded his eyes with so much blood he had feared he was blinded. He had unhorsed men in Mâcon and in Lübeck and in a dozen other places. He had fought on the melee field and in mock battles like this one in a dozen places more. And in all that time he had neither seen nor heard anything of Lord Edward, or of de Montfort and his sons. Certainly nothing of Richard de Malmaines. He and Robert had met very few other travelling knights from England at all. Adam preferred it that way – Robert had said nothing of the outcome at Senlis, though he had accepted de Montfort's largesse without complaint. If he missed the company of his fellow countrymen, he did not show it. As for Adam, he had learned not to think too much about the future.

In the main square of Ghent the last skirmishes were ebbing away, the few remaining Brabazon fighters either captured and subdued or fled to the sanctuary of their barricaded inn. Already the victors were cheering, banging their weapons on the wooden boards that closed off the houses, as if to summon the quailing occupants to come out and witness their triumph. A few places had opened up already; a knot of men had formed around one open doorway, passing around hot spiced cider. Adam went to join them, taking a mug to warm his hands.

*'Flanders! Flanders!'* the men in the square were shouting, brandishing their blunted weapons. Already Adam was feeling the strange emptiness that so often came to him after combat. As if, he thought, there was a crack in him, and all the strength and surety he had felt during the fight – the joy of battle, he could not deny – leaked from it and left him hollow. His bones ached, his grazed and battered hands stung in the cold air, and the blow he had taken to the wrist had already raised a darkening welt. Ignoring the flare of pain, he lifted his wooden mug and drank back the hot sourness of the cider.

*

'Philippe de Bourbourg is here, did you know?' Hugh of Oyster-mouth said, over the supper table of their inn that evening. 'He arrived at noon, while you were still breaking skulls in the main square. Robert is with him now.'

Adam just nodded. He was sitting on a bench with his back to the hearth, the warmth easing the aches in his bones. They had met Philippe de Bourbourg several times since the day he beat Adam at the riverbank. The Flemish knight held no grudge against Robert, and for a while the two of them had ridden as a team in a series of tournaments in the Rhineland. De Bourbourg still longed for the return of his black destrier, but Papillon was devoted to Adam now.

'What news does he bring?' Adam asked, massaging his wrist. He meant news of forthcoming tournaments; that was the only news that had any meaning for him.

'He says that the King of England will be coming to Amiens, on the morrow of St Vincent,' Hugh replied, looking up from the sheets of creased parchment he was studying by the light of a guttering candle.

'Why would the King of England be coming to Amiens?' Adam asked.

'Because,' Hugh replied, with an air of patience, 'he wants to meet with the King of France, and seek his arbitration! Apparently King Henry, Simon de Montfort and the barons of England have agreed to let King Louis settle their dispute, and they have sworn upon the Holy Gospels that they will abide by his decision.'

'How does Philippe de Bourbourg know about that?'

'Adam de Norton, *everyone* knows about it!' Hugh gave an exasperated grimace. 'I sometimes think, you know, that your stubborn ignorance of the doings of the great world is quite wilful. I think you are *intending* to vex me.'

Adam smiled ruefully. Hugh was easy to provoke. But in truth he had made an almost conscious effort to remain deaf to all tidings from his native land.

'Do you even know that England has been in flames these last six or eight months?' Hugh asked, leaning forward over the table and jabbing his stubby finger on the boards. 'Lands ravaged, castles seized and plundered, even churches despoiled . . . I wonder that this can have escaped your notice!'

Adam did know that Simon de Montfort had returned to England back in the spring, to rally the barons against the power of King Henry, but the affairs of England had seemed far away, like distant thunder over the western horizon.

'Aye, it's true, what he says,' John Chyld broke in. He was sitting at the far end of the table, munching his way through a boiled knuckle of beef. 'There's anarchy in England now, even the Flemings and Brabazons say it, and they are usually too busy fighting each other to notice anything else.'

'They say Lord Edward has raised an army of Gascons and Burgundians,' commented another man, further along the bench, 'and taken them to England to force the barons to yield to the king's authority. And Lord Simon de Montfort has made a pact with the Welsh to resist him.'

'Good man, by God!' Hugh said, thumping his fist on the tabletop. 'I like this Earl of Leicester more every day, I swear.

And I hear he's been sweeping through the land like a hurricane, talking of justice and reform, and when he speaks towns and castles throw open their gates, and even the heavens applaud!'

Adam took a sip of heated wine. His memories of Simon de Montfort were still conflicted. He recalled only too well that predatory gaze, that air of command, and the assurance with which he had stepped in to pay Robert's ransom. *Some of us know what a debt is worth.* The logs in the hearth behind him crackled and softly collapsed into embers.

'Well,' Hugh said, 'you can be sure that Philippe de Bourbourg's news hasn't escaped Sir Robert's notice. And he was very interested to hear what he had to say about King Henry and Lord Simon going to Amiens. No doubt he hopes their amicable meeting may lead to a change in his own fortunes.'

Adam frowned more deeply, shrugging, and Hugh's round face twitched into a smile, as he realised that this time Adam genuinely did not understand.

'Because,' the Welshman said, bending close over the table and dropping his voice to a whisper, 'part of the dispute between the barons and the king involves dispossession without trial, on the arbitrary judgement of the king and his court, do you see? So if the king is made finally to abide by the rulings of the Magna Carta and the provisions made at Oxford, that he's sworn so many times to uphold, then he would have to restore any lands improperly seized . . .'

'Which would mean that Robert's estates were restored?'

'Some of them, perhaps. That would be for the men of law to decide. No doubt they are eagerly sharpening their quills and consulting their rolls as we speak.'

And perhaps, Adam thought, his own lost inheritance too. He had never truly believed that it was possible, that Robert's plan somehow to gain the influence of some great man in restoring his fortunes would ever bear fruit. Had it come to that, at last?

Would the prospect of open war in England finally bring some hope of justice?

For a moment he remembered the manor in Hampshire that his father had held. He would be twenty-one this coming summer, and would have been of age to inherit if the lands had not been given as a gift to another man. Once more he pictured the steep wooded hills to the west, the rolling meadows cut by the stream where three mills stood – although one belonged to the priory – and the open fields that spread eastward all the way to the scrub woodland of Blakemore. He saw them now as if in a perpetual glow of harvest sunlight, a time of freedom, without want or hardship. Memories so sweet to him that he barely ever dared indulge them.

'Do you ever miss home?' he asked Hugh abruptly.

'Home? Ah well. I would be ashamed to return there, to be honest,' Hugh told him. 'My family believe I am still a student in holy orders, you see, at the University of Paris. If only they knew what a mighty sinner I have become, they would tumble into their graves in dismay. But that is Wales though, not England. And things may be changing – see here!'

He turned the sheets of parchment he had been studying in the candlelight to face Adam, tapping them intently. Adam leaned closer, seeing circles and lines, and rows of tiny inked numbers and letters.

'What is it?' he asked. 'Some strange new heraldry?'

'Hah, in a way. But this is not the heraldry of the earth, but of the heavens! It's a description of the sphere of the cosmos, which surrounds and contains the sphere of the earth, do you see? And the cosmic sphere moves, it revolves – the *machina mundi*, you know – and as it does it exerts influences upon the earth and the affairs of men, which if we are skilled we can read, and even predict.'

'It helps you read the stars then?' Adam asked, baffled. He had known an old woman who did that.

'Yes, but in a philosophical way, a mathematical way . . .' Hugh replied. 'And here, from what I can tell, the cosmic sphere is suggesting great changes in the world of men. A revolution in the fortunes of all, like nothing we have seen in an age! Kings will be turned upon their heads, crowns and thrones will fall. Perhaps it refers to the east, where as you doubtless know the great horde of the Tartar Khan is causing such upheaval?'

Adam had seen the Tartar Khan at a tournament at Ingelheim, or a man dressed as the Tartar Khan at least; he had been jousting against another knight, who was dressed as the devil. But he merely nodded, peering at the drawings upon the parchment.

'The planets of the cosmos bear upon us all,' Hugh said earnestly, tapping the sheets once more. 'Turmoil is coming, I think. Great strife and great change. We must try our best to see that we come out on top!'

That night as he lay on his mattress, trying to ignore the mumbles and grunts and farts of the other men in the darkness all around him, Adam thought back over what Hugh had said. For so long now he had submerged himself in the world of the tournaments, the long road of fighting and contending, winning and losing. Or rather, he thought, he had allowed Robert de Dunstanville to submerge him in it. But when he remembered England, he remembered the youth he had been before that strange accident at Pleshey had thrown him into Robert's company. A far more noble spirit he had been then, with all his dreams of glory still idle fantasies ahead of him.

Rolling to one side, he reached blindly into his haversack, moving his fingers around until he felt the cold touch of silver and the leather thong. The medallion of St Christopher that Joane de Quincy had given him was still there, tucked away with Adam's few possessions. He drew it from the haversack, and lightly rubbed the silver disc between his fingertips. Nearly two years had passed since he saw her last. The vow of chastity he had once sworn to himself had not stood up long on the tournament road; Adam had lain with a string of women since Eloise. But Joane de Quincy remained apart from them all. She was surely married by now, Adam knew, perhaps even the mother of children. But in his memory she remained just the way she had been that morning. Perhaps, he thought . . . perhaps if they went to Amiens, and the king and Lord Simon settled their differences and justice was restored, then one day soon he might return to England, and see Joane again? He touched the pendant lightly to his lips.

\*

'No, there's nothing to be gained for us in Amiens,' Robert de Dunstanville said a week later, as they walked their horses along the road to Aalst, across the flattest greyest country Adam had ever seen, beneath a cloud-tumbled January sky.

'The Earl of Leicester . . .' Adam began.

'Yes, well, there's the problem,' Robert broke in, turning in the saddle. 'Since your little negotiation at Senlis last year I've been feeling beholden to Lord Simon de Montfort. I wouldn't like anyone to think I was going to Amiens to support him merely because I owed him an obligation.'

'But you do owe him an obligation,' Adam said, his face bunching. Robert's perverse attitudes had never failed to baffle him. 'And what better way to repay it than by loyalty? Isn't that the point?'

'Ah, still the chivalrous one after all this time!' Robert said with a sly grin. 'Well, true enough such things are not repaid in coin. But if I show myself in support of Lord Simon, and the decision goes against him and his party, then I lose all hope of regaining what I'm owed. And if Lord Simon takes the judgement amiss, and matters should come to war in England – real red and bloody war, I mean – then we would have to be careful whose faction we supported then too.'

'The faction who fights for justice, surely?' Adam said. He could feel the annoyance rising inside him, and tried to restrain his ire. 'The barons who want to uphold liberty and the rights of all men – didn't you yourself talk of that once? *There is a fury growing in England now*, you told me, I remember it well . . .'

Robert looked back at him again, with a glance of withering condescension. '*Words!*' he said. 'These are mere words, Adam, and many men prate them that have nothing in the balance. All these great barons and earls, these magnates who follow the Earl of Leicester – they are too wealthy and powerful for even the king to bring low. If they are defeated, they'll still have their estates, their manors and their castles, their household men. But the likes of me – the likes of *us* . . . If we are defeated, we lose everything! We would be exiled forever, with no hope of gaining justice or forgiveness.'

'Then we do nothing?' Adam replied, his voice rising. He dared not turn and seek the gaze of Hugh of Oystermouth, or of John Chyld and Wilecok. He had no idea if any of them would back him now. 'This is not the way you have taught me,' he went on, trying to level his words. 'Always attack, with immediate force. Defeat your enemy before he can raise his hand against you . . . How are things different now?'

Robert exhaled, shrugging. He rode on in silence for a short while. Adam was still glowing with the fervour of his outburst, but he felt the cold seeping through him once more.

'I want to be in Lille by the end of February,' Robert declared, changing the subject very deliberately. 'There's a big jousting festival there, you know – the Fête de *l'Epinette*. It begins on Quinquagesima Sunday and stretches on into Lent. You'll like it, I think – the good burghers of Lille like to play at being men-at-arms, and consider it a great honour to be knocked off a horse and ransomed by a real knight, or even a real squire.'

'So we go to Lille and make ourselves rich,' Adam said glumly, 'and simply ignore what's happening in England?'

'We seem to have been following that philosophy very successfully thus far,' Robert said, smiling once more. 'So yes, we shall!'

*

Nearly eight more weeks passed before they heard what had happened at Amiens. How Simon de Montfort had suffered a riding accident back in England and had failed to attend the meeting with King Henry. How the churchmen and lawyers he had sent to argue his cause had failed to convince the French king who sat in judgement. How Louis had ruled that the power and authority of the King of England was to be restored in full, all agreements and provisions were to be abolished, and that any man who dared oppose the full might and majesty of the throne would be declared a rebel. And how de Montfort's supporters had replied that the whole meeting was a farce and a lie, and the oaths they had sworn upon the gospels were void, and all had returned across the sea to take up arms. England's fury was about to erupt, and everywhere men were preparing for war.

By then it was the end of February, and Robert de Dunstanville and his band of followers were already at Lille, preparing only for the lavish round of tournament festivities. There was plenty there to occupy Adam's mind: the parades of beautiful horses and brilliantly armoured riders, the flash of colourful heraldry and painted lances, the finely dressed ladies, and the rich feasting. A torrent of worldly pleasures, ahead of the sparse Lenten season to come. But all the while Adam felt his mind and his heart drifting westwards, towards that thunderstorm over the horizon. Its distant roar was almost drowned out by the hawkers' cries, the laughter of the women, the trumpets and the stamping of the horses, but he knew it was there.

At dawn on the Saturday, before the official beginning of the festival, Adam awoke to find Robert de Dunstanville sitting fully dressed on a folding stool beside the open flap of their tent. 'Get up, as quick as you can,' Robert said. 'We need to be on the road.'

'We're leaving?' Adam said, groggy from sleep but his mind already sharpening. It was cold, the meadow outside still misty in the early light.

Robert made an impatient gesture. 'We need to be away,' he said. 'I was talking to Philippe de Bourbourg and some of the Frenchmen here – they could not imagine why an English knight was in Lille when England itself is in such turmoil. I think they're right. There's a chance to make a difference, to take a grip on fortune . . . Maybe throw our swords into the scale, hey, like in that old Roman story?'

Adam stared at him, blinking and bleary. Robert de Dunstan-ville was gazing out of the tent door, unwilling to meet his eye. Never would he admit that he had been wrong. But that did not matter now. Outside, the horses were whinnying and stamping as John Chyld brought them from the paddock.

'We can be in Boulogne in three days, and England in four,' Robert said, the last trace of misgivings tugging at his words. 'After that, may God help us.'

# Chapter 12

It was the first Friday of Lent when they crossed the narrow sea, the feast of the martyrs Perpetua and Felicitas, and in England the war had already begun.

Their ship was once again the *St Bride the Virgin*, the same craft that had carried them two years before, and the shipman remembered Sir Robert well. 'I had some of the king's own royal court aboard my boat not three weeks gone,' he said in a proud shout, as the prow of his ship rose and fell across the bright waters. 'Bore them from Wissant to Dover. Bad weather in the straits that day, not like now, and all of them puking and spewing from the moment the wind picked up! But the blessed martyrs have sent us clear skies and a prosperous breeze, goodsirs, and we shall be in England before noon!'

They learned more when they reached Dover. There was fighting in the Welsh Marches, where Lord Edward and his followers were plundering manors and taking castles. But de Montfort's son Henry and the Earl of Derby had attacked and captured Worcester and put the city to the sack, and now both were marching on Gloucester. The king had been in Canterbury, they heard, but had departed for Windsor, or perhaps Oxford. Everywhere men were armed and angry, ready at any moment for battle, even if they knew little of who was fighting against whom.

By the following day they were in Canterbury themselves, and Robert sent Hugh of Oystermouth and John Chyld out into the town to gather tidings and gain what intelligence they could about the contending factions and the movements of the leaders.

'I suppose you should know,' he told Adam as they shared a Lenten meal of pickled herrings and coarse bread, 'that the Earl of Hereford has declared his full support for the king and is summoning knights and footmen to his service. His son, Sir Humphrey, however, remains devoted to Simon de Montfort. Apparently he's been scorching a trail across the Marches and the western shires, burning villages, even attacking and robbing priories and churches. My own crimes appear mild indeed by comparison . . . But let us pray they never meet on the battle-field – it would be a great impiety for a son to slay his father, or a father his son.'

Adam crossed himself quickly, hoping that matters did not come to battles at all. Now that he was here in England the prospect of war seemed suddenly very real, and quite daunting. It took him only another moment to remember that Robert too was the son of Earl Humphrey. Had he been speaking about himself?

'Even in war, men are seldom slain, isn't that true?' he asked.

Robert gave him a wry glance. 'Men of high standing are sel-dom slain – they are ransomed, as on the tournament field. The commoners are cut down like grass, of course. But once the ironwork begins . . .' He shrugged, and wiped his mouth on a cloth. 'Most of these fine men of the land know little of real combat, and nothing of war. Few have spent as long in the tour-naments as I have, either. If God is good, perhaps this whole thing will be settled at first blood, heh?'

It occurred to Adam that Robert had not yet declared upon whose side he would fight. If the king had still been in Canter-bury when he arrived, would he simply have offered his sword to the royal faction?

'What about your cousin, Joane de Quincy, and her sister?' he asked, trying to phrase his question casually. 'Will they be safe, living alone at Ware?'

Robert smirked and rubbed his beard. 'Don't worry, my cousins are safe where they are for now,' he said. 'Our uncle, the Earl of Winchester, still appears undecided in the struggle – nobody would want to provoke him by threatening his wards or family. We shall visit Ware soon enough, once we have more secure intelligence.'

But there was no more news to be had at Canterbury, and after hearing mass the next morning they were on the road again, passing through Rochester that afternoon and crossing the old timber bridge over the Medway in a thin grey rain that blurred the looming bulk of the castle keep. A day later they rode on through Southwark, and heard the bells of St Paul's pealing a strange and clamorous alarm.

As they passed St Olave's church and approached the southern gateway of London Bridge, they saw a mob gathering in the street ahead. Most were men, with a few women mingled among them, and many were armed with cudgels, axes and even short swords. The crowd drew back as Robert and his party rode closer, noticing his gilded spurs and the belted sword at his side, the four warhorses that walked behind him, the sumpter horses carrying weapons and armour and the red and white colours of the shield slung across one of them.

'Lord Simon!' a woman cried from the narrow doorway of a house. 'It's Lord Simon, the Earl of Leicester! *Montfort! Montfort!*'

'That ain't Lord Simon, you daft kettle,' replied a stocky man in a butcher's apron. 'That's just some tourneying knight returned from overseas . . .'

But the cry had now been taken up by the mob, more aggressively, like a challenge. '*Montfort! Montfort!*' they yelled, brandishing their crude weapons.

'*A Montfort!*' Robert called back, raising his hand in salute. 'And the Community of the Realm!'

Some of them cheered, pushing a lane for the horsemen to pass, while others still appeared dubious and hostile. Adam kept his gaze locked on Robert's back as he rode through the crowd towards the bridge, not wanting to meet anyone's eye. He was still unaccustomed, after two years abroad, to hearing so many English voices around him. But the passion in those voices was stranger still. He had assumed, when he heard about the trouble in England, that it was all a matter for the barons and great magnates, concerning their dispute with the king. Not something the common people would care about at all. But here they were, the common people of London, armed in the street and shouting Simon de Montfort's name like a battle-cry, while the distant bell of the great church kept clanging its unfamiliar discord. It was unnerving.

As they rode through the press of people around the gate arch, Adam saw the trails of dark smoke rising from the city on the far riverbank. They paid the toll, then crossed a drawbridge and continued through a second gateway, and the tall narrow buildings that crowded the bridge on either side shut out the view of the river. The horses were anxious and alert, twitching their ears and tossing their heads, as their hooves clashed on the roadway.

Halfway across the bridge, a chapel dedicated to St Thomas Becket stood perched above the flowing waters. More people were gathered outside the open doors, a woman among them in a dirt-spattered apron shouting wildly above the voices of the throng. 'To hell with King Henry!' she cried, in a cracked screech. 'To hell with Richard of Cornwall, and all the king's evil counsellors! To hell with the foreigners, and to hell with the Jews! Let the flames take them all!'

'We'll be staying with Master Elias again tonight?' Adam asked Robert, riding up beside him as soon as they were over the bridge and the street widened.

'Yes,' Robert replied, tight-lipped. 'He'll need our protec-tion, I believe. Besides, he has the best network of intelligencers I know – if anyone can tell us what's happening in the kingdom, he can. However,' he said with a bitter smile, turning in the sad-dle, 'if your prejudices rebel against the idea, you are free to find accommodation elsewhere.'

'My prejudices are long gone, you know that,' Adam told him.

'We shall see,' Robert replied lightly, and spurred his horse on up the street.

There was another mob gathered in Westcheap. The people here were wealthier, and carried better weapons: spears and crossbows. Some wore gambesons, or even mail, and flourished banners as if they were an army preparing for battle. The smell of burning was strong in the air, and Adam felt the nervous tension rising inside him as they rode, the heat in his blood; he almost expected to see the entrance to the lane leading to Elias's house beset by a riotous throng. But they passed through the crowds and into the lane, and found the gateway to the moneylender's premises well guarded by a gang of determined-looking young men with staves and cudgels. By the time Adam dismounted in the cobbled yard, Wilecok and his Gascon wife had already absented themselves, as if by prior arrangement.

At the top of the wooden steps, Master Elias stood waiting with his accustomed look of confident ease. Clearly he had been forewarned of their arrival. He greeted Robert with an embrace and ushered him into the house. Adam followed them; with John Chyld's help, he was lugging the pair of heavy saddlebags and the brass-bound chest containing Robert's portable wealth, most of it exchanged into silver and gold bullion. It was the fortune of two successful years on the tournament circuit, and more than enough to pay back Elias's loan with interest.

But there was no sign of Belia, Elias's sister. Robert had said nothing about her since last they departed England, and Adam had not wanted to ask. In all their time overseas

Robert de Dunstanville had not as much as glanced at another woman. His chastity had been quite remarkable, but nobody had mocked him for it. Perhaps, Adam thought, the Jewish woman had already remarried and left London? Perhaps Robert had learned of it beforehand, from one of Elias's contacts in France?

In the passageway they shed their travel-stained cloaks and shoes; Hugh of Oystermouth and John Chyld remained there, while Adam followed Robert and Elias into the main hall. A fire burned in the hearth, and once they were seated at the table servants brought cups of wine.

'So,' Robert said. 'Interesting times.'

Now that he was indoors, Elias appeared far less confident. His face was pouched with the signs of anxiety and fatigue, and he tugged nervously at his forked beard. 'You have heard the news from Worcester?' he asked.

'We heard that Lord Simon's son Henry and the Earl of Derby took the town, yes.'

'Took the town and sacked it. And they attacked the Jews, Robert. They attacked the synagogue and the records house, murdering anyone who opposed them. Scores of our people cut down in the street, while their Christian neighbours celebrated! *What* is happening, Robert? What is this madness in England now – can you tell me?'

'That bell ringing,' Robert said, craning his neck as the distant clang sounded once more. 'What does it signify?'

'All day they've been doing it. An alarm, I suppose, by order of the mayor. I hear that Hugh Despenser, the constable of the Tower, has put himself at the head of the mob and attacked properties belonging to the king and the royal clerks. The houses of Earl Richard of Cornwall too, the king's brother. Despenser is Lord Simon's man, I think?'

Robert nodded. 'De Montfort is not in London then?' he asked.

Elias spread his hands. 'Nobody can say where he is! Kenilworth, perhaps? He was injured back in January, while he was travelling to France – his horse fell and rolled on him, and he fractured his thigh. But everyone believes he will recover imminently, and appear here any time, like a comet of righteousness from the heavens. And meanwhile King Henry has gone to Oxford, to gather his loyal barons. Lord Edward, we hear, is currently besieged in Gloucester Castle . . .'

Robert snorted a laugh. 'Besieged? – *him?*'

'Yes! By the same Henry de Montfort who slaughtered our people in Worcester. What is next, Robert? Is what happened in Worcester going to happen here too? Will they call us *the King's Jews*, and burn us out? I fear this man Simon de Montfort, I can tell you. He is fierce in his faith, so they say. And no friend of ours.'

'Earl Simon is . . . a subtle man,' Robert said, fluttering his hand. 'He's made mistakes in the past, certainly, but he knows truth from lies.'

Elias cut him off with a mirthless guffaw. 'Does he?' he asked. 'Was it not Simon de Montfort who expelled the Jews from Leicester, back in our fathers' day? The first thing he did, upon coming to this country! Easy enough for you to say that he's changed. Harder for those whose families must suffer if he has not.'

'Have faith, I beg you,' Robert said, raising his palms. He looked pained by Elias's words. 'Once Lord Simon gets here, I think, all these disturbances should be quelled soon enough. Meanwhile, I put my sword at your service, my friend.'

But Elias just shrugged and grimaced, and did not appear at all convinced of his safety.

Belia joined them for their meal, and if Robert was surprised to see her, he was careful not to show it. Nor did he show any sign that there had been a connection between them. Adam watched them both carefully, alert to the silent language of their gestures, the tones of their words, but could detect nothing. Almost, he thought, as if he had imagined it all. The main dish was a plump bream, roasted in a crust of herbs; Adam was pleased that Elias observed the Lenten fast, despite not being Christian. He had not been sure what to expect, and had not wanted to embarrass himself again, or Robert either. But the food was excellent, the wine excellent too, and with the benefit of years he could appreciate what he had failed to enjoy before.

'Sir Robert,' Belia said from the far end of the table, 'I was about to ask who this handsome young man you've brought to our house might be. I did not recognise him!'

Adam choked slightly, and tried not to blush. Her face, framed by the white linen of her headscarf, had a playful expression, and her voice had the same rich depth he remembered from his last visit. He swallowed thickly.

'He's improved slightly,' said Robert. 'At least now he knows how to eat his dinner.'

When he looked up again, Adam met Belia's gaze. Her eyes held him trapped, and he felt a warm nervous discomfort rising through him. He swallowed again and looked away. But now Elias was talking once more, telling Robert of all that had happened in the last tumultuous year. England, it seemed, had been turned upside down, and all natural order overthrown.

'Last summer was the worst of it,' Elias said, dabbing at his mouth with a cloth. 'The king was at the Tower, and the queen tried to take a boat upriver to Windsor, where Lord Edward was staying. Whether her boatmen misjudged the tides I don't know, but her boat was unable to breast the rush through the bridge piers and became trapped there. When the mob on the bridge saw the queen below them they became maddened – they started throwing down bricks and rotting filth on her, turds and brimming pisspots even!'

'The things they shouted to her, as well,' Belia added, and shivered with disgust. 'Calling her a putrid slut, a witch and a sorceress. It was vile. These men must hate any woman who holds power over them.'

'It was the mayor, FitzThomas, who rescued her in the end,' Elias went on. 'He's de Montfort's man, as everyone knows, but he'll have laid in some stock with the king's side that day too. They won't forget it.'

'And the king won't forget the insult either, I expect,' said Robert. 'Or Lord Edward.'

'Him in particular. The queen, I believe, is a most phlegmatic lady. But her son Edward, we hear, thirsts for the blood of the Londoners like a sweating beast pants for water. He has sworn to break the bones and rip out the eyes and organs of everyone that abused his mother that day. A threat he has yet to act upon.'

'Well, first he must escape from Gloucester Castle!' Robert said, raising his cup.

'In part, I wish he would,' Elias replied. 'Men say that Henry is a tyrant and must be taught to behave. Maybe so, but to me those that oppose him seem as bad, or worse. At least the kings of England are pledged to protect our people, though they so often hold us in contempt. We are caught between ravening animals.'

'When the Earl of Leicester returns to London he'll restrain his followers, I'm sure,' Robert said. 'This sort of disorder does nothing for his cause.'

'But it helps those of his followers who are indebted to us,' Elias told him, with a level gaze. 'Some of them, I think, believe they might *erase* their debts simply by *erasing* the Jews. And Simon de Montfort has many young and reckless friends.'

That night Elias lodged Robert and his followers in the wing of another building adjoining his own. There was a connecting door and an enclosed wooden gallery between the two properties, and each had a separate entrance that led to the street, but they would be easy to defend if required. Adam unrolled his mattress on the floor beside the cold hearth in the main chamber, where he could see the doorway. John Chyld and Hugh of Oystermouth were sleeping in the next room, and he could already hear their snores.

'Elias is a good man,' Adam said quietly, as he lay on his mattress. 'I'm sorry I thought ill of him before.'

Robert made a gruff sound in the darkness.

'And his sister, Belia. She is . . . I mean, you . . .'

'Best say nothing,' Robert told him sharply. 'Think nothing, and if you can, see nothing. May God judge me for it, but this is something I cannot control.'

Adam made no response. He lay for a long time, his mind still. Only when he was on the edge of sleep did he open his eyes slightly, hearing a noise from across the room. Robert's form rose in the darkness, and the boards creaked as he crossed to the door, opened it, and slipped through into the next house. Adam closed his eyes again, but for a long time sleep did not come.

# Chapter 13

Sunday, and the people of London were pouring from the doors of St Paul's cathedral. Adam had gone there to hear mass with John Chyld and Hugh of Oystermouth, the three of them packed together at the back of the crowded nave, barely able to see anything of the service. Now they moved through the worshippers seething out into the cathedral yard. This was the second Sunday they had attended St Paul's since their return to the city, and Adam was still amazed by the size and raucous energy of the crowd.

'I notice that Sir Robert de Dunstanville does not hear mass these days,' Hugh said, glancing around him. 'Perhaps, do you think, he is *turning Jewish*?'

Adam hushed him with a sharp hiss and a nudge. Such things were better not discussed. 'If he had any mind to do such a thing,' he said, in a stern whisper, 'he would have done it when he was in the Holy Land, fighting for Christ, don't you think?'

Hugh merely widened his eyes and shrugged. Besides, Adam thought, there were a dozen other churches much closer to Master Elias's house where Robert could hear mass in greater peace and serenity. Perhaps he went to one of them? Adam himself mainly came to St Paul's to mingle with the throng and see if he could pick up any firm news on what might be happening beyond the circuit of the city walls. There were plenty of tidings, passed among the congregation in excited cries or panicked whispers: had the king really summoned an army of savage Scots to join him at Oxford and crush the rebellion? Was Lord Edward dead, or had he somehow escaped from Gloucester Castle and ridden to join his father? Had the king really been struck blind after penetrating the holy sanctuary of the virgin St Frideswide? And where was Simon de Montfort, the Earl of Leicester?

The crowds knew the answers to all these questions, or thought they did. They sang songs about their hero Simon de Montfort too. About how he loved truth and hated lies, and would return and drive out the king's evil counsellors, and restore justice to England. '*What's his name?*' they chanted. '*He's called MONT-FORT!*' they chanted back, as they danced in circles in the streets. In the midst of Lent, the dread of war was turning to a frenzy pulsing through them all, and de Montfort's name alone was a talisman of victory.

'Not that I hold anything against the Jews, you understand,' Hugh of Oystermouth was saying, as they emerged from the great cold shadow of the cathedral into the weak spring sunlight. 'A most fascinating people! Brave too, I would say. And we should recall what St Augustine said of them, that their scriptures herald the coming of the Redeemer, and they were the first to witness Christ . . .'

Yes, Adam thought as they circled the cathedral and walked towards the gateway that led to Paternoster Street, Elias and his household were certainly brave. He had seen them often enough leaving the house, Elias in his pointed yellow cap and both he and Belia wearing the mantles with twin patches of pale cloth sewn upon the breast that identified them as Jews. How simple it would have been for them to assume the same clothing as their neighbours, to hide their faith and feign Christianity, for a quieter and safer life. But they did not.

'I've often wondered, in fact,' Hugh was saying, 'if there might be an ancient connection between the Hebrew people and the Welsh . . .'

Adam paused in his steps, and Hugh fell abruptly silent. There was something happening ahead of them, a thickening of the crowd in Paternoster Street, before the church of St Michael le Querne, and a roar of voices raised in anger and abuse. Adam glanced back and checked that John Chyld was still behind him. The grizzled serjeant had already seen what was happening, and his thumb was hooked in his belt, close to his dagger.

There was a man standing on the brick plinth before the church doors, Adam saw as he shoved his way through the crowd. A friar, in the white habit and black cloak of the Dominicans. In a thin high voice he was calling out to the mob that surrounded him.

'Who are the fools who say, *There is No God*?' he cried. 'They are the same fools who say that the word of His Holiness the Pope means nothing! Who mock at the penalty of excommunication, and do not fear the fires of purgatory!'

'*No!*' the crowd shouted back. '*No! You are no true friar!*' '*MONT-FORT!*' others chanted, clapping and stamping their feet.

'And yet you exalt the sinners who oppose the king, when His Holiness has ruled that royal authority shall not be challenged!' the friar went on. 'What will you do when the cross stands over you? Will the sinner Simon de Montfort save you from damnation?'

A figure broke from the crowd, a heavily built man in a fine tunic and hose of deep blue, with his cloak thrown back to reveal a knight's sword belted at his side. With three strides he closed with the friar. Then with one long reaping blow of his fist he knocked the holy man from his perch. The crowd bayed and cheered.

The friar had fallen to the ground, but the man in blue grabbed him by the arm and hauled him to his knees, then punched him twice more on the head. Adam clearly heard the friar's nose break, and he saw the blood spatter down his face. Letting his victim drop, the attacker turned to the crowd and dusted his palms, and as he did so Adam recognised the man.

'To the stocks with him!' the crowd were yelling, surging forward. 'To the pillory with the false friar!'

Adam had not seen Sir Humphrey de Bohun the Younger, the son and heir of the Earl of Hereford, since the tournament at Lagny two years before. But he remembered him well enough. And Sir Humphrey remembered him too.

'Adam de Norton!' he cried, as the crowd thinned around him. He had three of his own squires and a pair of serjeants at his back, Adam noticed; his gesture of outrage had been well supported. Sir Humphrey threw his arm across Adam's shoulders, as if they were old friends.

'You're still de Dunstanville's squire?' the nobleman asked. Adam could smell the wine on his breath. 'Is he here in London then?'

'He is,' Adam replied, careful to say no more. Robert had insisted that nobody reveal where in the city they were staying.

'Then tell him he must visit me soon,' Humphrey replied, glancing at his bloodied knuckles and then idly wiping them on Adam's tunic. 'I'm lodged at the Abbot of Waltham's Inn, by St Mary's de la Hulle. Tell him, if he's sick of herrings and salt pork, that the kitchens there have the broadest possible interpretation of Lenten restrictions. There is a species of goose they classify as seafood, you know . . .'

'I'll tell him that,' Adam replied quickly, disengaging himself from the man's embrace. He had yet to break his fast, and the thought of food brought a swell of hunger. 'You've come to London recently?' he asked, before Humphrey could enquire any further about Robert.

'Arrived two days ago, from Kenilworth. I've been with Lord Simon this last week, laying our plans against the king and Lord Edward – you know he's escaped from Gloucester?'

'That's true then?' John Chyld asked.

'All too true,' Humphrey told them, his face reddening. 'Henry, Lord Simon's son, foolishly agreed to a truce! Edward took the chance to escape the castle, seize the town and hang de Montfort's chief supporters. Now he's ridden for Oxford with all his knights . . .' Sir Humphrey hissed through his teeth. 'He's a cunning one, Edward. Men have started calling him the *Leopard*.'

'That's the proper name, you know,' Hugh of Oystermouth broke in, raising a finger, 'for the lion *passant gardant,* which Lord Edward bears on his arms, of course.'

Sir Humphrey shot him a withering glance. 'Well, of course,' he said. 'But he's a subtle and sinuous beast, to be sure, and fierce as any great cat . . . Oh yes,' he said, turning to Adam again as a thought occurred to him, 'when you see Robert de Dunstanville, you might ask him about his cousin, Joane de Quincy.'

'What about her?' Adam replied, ice flowing suddenly through his veins.

'Robert agreed to support my bid to marry her,' Humphrey said, lowering his voice. 'I visited her at Ware only yesterday, in fact, to seek her betrothal. But her uncle, the Earl of Winchester, refuses to wed her to me.' Humphrey smiled again, tightly. 'Please do remind Robert to speak to the earl on my behalf.'

*

Robert de Dunstanville was in the stable when Adam found him, checking on the condition of the horses. They went together into an inner workroom, where saddle leathers and bridle tack were spread on a workbench, and Adam told him all that he had just heard.

'What of it?' Robert said, twitching a shrug.

For a moment Adam could not speak. On his journey back to the house his mood had shifted from cold desolate despair to hot anger and back again. 'Humphrey de Bohun is a vicious drunkard, that's what,' he managed to say, grinding the words. 'Only moments ago I saw him punch a holy friar in the street and then beat him senseless! But I knew him well enough, once. He is dissolute, arrogant, cruel . . . How could you support his intention to marry Joane de Quincy?'

'I too know him well,' Robert replied. 'We're of the same blood, after all . . . though we were not exactly raised together. Your description fits half the noble young men of England – who would you have my cousin marry instead, hmm?'

'Then it's true?' Adam said, feeling the grip of despair tighten inside him. 'You really want this to happen? Didn't you say to me – I remember it well – that your cousin was *more precious than your soul*? That if anyone harmed her, you would *hunt them to the deepest of the seven hells*, you would *rend their flesh*? And now you would simply hand her over to a man like Humphrey de Bohun? . . .'

'What a keen memory you have for things I've said,' Robert replied, toying with a leatherworker's awl on the workbench. 'If I'd known what an impression I was making, I'd have minded my words better—'

'She considered you her protector!' Adam snarled. He was aware that his fists were clenched, his nails digging into his palms.

'Oh, and you're her protector too now, is that it?' Robert said, rounding on him with sudden scorn. 'Listen to me – Joane de Quincy is the niece of the Earl of Winchester, who has *no male heirs*. When he dies – and he is not a young man, my uncle – any legitimate female relations could claim a share in his vast estates. She is also the granddaughter of Llywelyn the Great, who is still revered among the Welsh. A woman like that would make no mean prize, wouldn't you say? Anyone might be grateful, if such a sweet cherry fell into their lap.'

'So that's it?' Adam cried, revulsion tightening his throat. 'You've made an agreement with Humphrey de Bohun? You'll back his plan to marry Joane de Quincy if he helps you regain your lands?'

'And what would you arrange for her instead? Should she take holy orders and retreat to a nunnery, like her older sister? Or – aha, yes, I see it now!' Robert said, snarling. 'You think she would make a fitting wife for you instead, is that it? A mere squire, a serjeant's son, with no land and no fortune?'

'Who are you to speak to me like that?' Adam shouted, raising his fist as he took a step forward. The last time Robert had insulted him, he had been a raw youth, but now things had changed. 'Where are your lands, and your fortune? Where is your honour?'

Robert moved first, lunging from the bench. Adam swung at him, but with startling speed the older man had trapped his forearm in a punishing grip and slammed his body against the heavy wooden post behind him. The leatherworking awl was in Robert's right hand, the steel spike only a finger's breadth from Adam's eye.

'Speak to me like that again,' Robert breathed, holding Adam pinned against the wooden post, 'and I'll blind you.'

For a moment he maintained his grip, then with a swift intake of breath he released him and stepped back. As Robert tossed the awl back onto the bench Adam slumped into a squat, his back to the post.

'You're right,' Robert said, with quiet bitterness. 'Humphrey de Bohun would not be a good match for my cousin.' He stared towards the pale light from the barred window. 'But he's known her for a long time. After their father died, she and Hawise were sent to live in our uncle's household. Humphrey holds the castle at Kimbolton, close to Earl Roger's estate at Eynesbury – it was there he first met Joane, I think, one winter soon afterwards. He became besotted with her, though she was barely more than a child and he was twice her age and married already.'

Adam glanced up quickly, his expression tightening, but Robert shook his head.

'No, no, he did not touch her,' the knight said. 'He has some self-control at least. And his love, as he explained it, seemed genuine. But the matter came to the ears of Earl Roger, and his own father, and Humphrey was sent away to the Marches and forbidden to see Joane again. I knew nothing of it at the time – he told me when last we met, after the tournament at Lagny. I recall you were attending to other matters.'

Adam just shrugged. He had not forgotten Eloise, but he refused to feel guilty about his dalliance with her.

'Anyway, after the recent breach with his father, Humphrey must feel he can renew his attentions. But Earl Roger loathes him, and refuses to sanction the match.'

'And he wants you to persuade him? Would you do that?'

'It may be out of my hands,' Robert said bleakly. 'One day soon Humphrey will be Earl of Hereford and Essex, and could become powerful even before that, if he stands with de Montfort. I want the best for my cousin, but she needs a husband, and perhaps Humphrey de Bohun is as good as she will get.'

Adam drew a breath between his teeth. 'And she would feel the same way, do you think?' he asked scornfully. He expected a vicious reply, but the knight merely scrubbed at his beard.

'Perhaps . . . he is a better man than he appears,' Robert said. 'Sometimes we must swallow compromises that stick in our throats.'

He stepped away from the bench and paced towards the door, leaving Adam slumped miserably at the base of the wooden post. At the door he paused and glanced back at him. 'You're still my squire, by the way,' he said. 'Don't think to question me again. And clean that tack and harness properly before you eat – it's filthy.'

Seething with humiliation and anger, Adam sat at the bench for the next hour scrubbing at the harness buckles and the saddle leathers, scouring them of rust and dirt and then oiling them until they shone and his fingers ached. He was painfully aware that nothing he could ever accomplish would raise him to the level of a man like Sir Humphrey de Bohun, who had been born into wealth and prestige. Adam might move among the powerful men of the land, but he could never be one of their company. Such had it ever been, of course, and he would have been foolish to imagine otherwise. But it was Robert's betrayal that really sickened him. He had traded Joane de Quincy's future for his own personal gain. What, he wondered, must she herself think of what was happening? Would her opinions, her feelings, even be considered at all?

A shadow fell across him, and he turned sharply. A woman stood in the doorway, holding a tray with an earthenware dish and spoon. Only when she placed the tray down and drew the scarf from her face did Adam recognise her.

'Something to break your fast,' Belia said, with the shadow of a smile. 'I thought I would bring it myself, so the servants do not tell Robert.'

'Thank you . . . mistress,' Adam said. He was unsure of the correct way to address her. His stomach pinched and rolled at the smell of the food.

'Please forgive him if you can,' Belia said, lowering her voice as she stepped towards him. 'He is . . . intemperate at the moment. But he cares for you a great deal, you know that.'

'He does?' Adam said. It seemed highly unlikely.

'Yes.' Belia stood with her hands clasped before her, smiling once again. 'He told me what happened,' she went on, moving closer. 'About this cousin of his, the de Quincy girl. You have feelings for her?'

'I barely know her,' Adam said quickly, conscious of how uncouth he must sound. Remembering himself, he stood up and made a belated bow. A memory crept into his mind, a vision lit by fireglow, and he quelled it.

'Well then,' Belia said. 'We must hope for the best. And pray, I think, that the Lord God bestows wisdom on us all.' She reached out and touched his cheek, her fingers tracing his skin lightly. Then she turned and left the room.

Adam lifted the lid from the earthenware dish: stewed leek potage with salt cod. Eating slowly, his hunger dissipating, he tried not to think about Sir Humphrey de Bohun at the Abbot of Waltham's Inn, enjoying the plump roast goose set before him.

\*

Simon de Montfort, Earl of Leicester, arrived in London two days later, on the feast of the Annunciation of the Blessed Virgin. The streets were packed as he rode in through New Gate, and the bright sunlight held the first real promise of spring. Trumpets blared, the crowds cheered, and de Montfort rode in full armour upon a champing white horse with his blood-red banners raised, the rampant white lions dancing in the air above him.

Two days before, de Montfort had left Northampton, where his son Simon the Younger had seized the castle and the town and was holding it with more than fifty knights and bannerets and all their troops. King Henry was still at Oxford, boasting of his desire for peace while gathering his forces for war. Now Lord Simon had come to London, to meet with the barons and powerful men of the city. With firm jaw and stern expression he rode on through the meat market, cheered all the way, a cavalcade of knights and armed retainers behind him.

Waiting with Robert in the broad expanse of Westcheap, which was specially cleared to receive the newcomers, Adam picked out the banners of the magnates and barons assembled to greet de Montfort. He saw the red chevrons on gold, and beneath them the red-haired Gilbert de Clare – Earl of Gloucester now, following the death of his father, so Hugh had learned – sitting on horseback surrounded by his household knights. The golden fish swimming on a blue field were the arms of the Kentish baron Ralph de Heringaud, while the black cross on yellow marked out John de Vesci, only nineteen years old and already Baron of Alnwick. Adam had learned to identify most of their heraldic insignia in the preceding days, with Hugh's assistance. But he needed no help in recognising the familiar blue banner slashed with white and ornamented with little golden lions; except for the three *fleur-de-lis* on the white diagonal, Humphrey de Bohun used almost the same arms as his father, the Earl of Hereford, who was at Oxford preparing to raise them for the king.

Among them all, Robert de Dunstanville had no banner, wore no armour and carried no shield. He sat patiently in the saddle, plainly dressed, stroking his moustache with his thumb and watching everything.

Simon de Montfort rode to a halt before the assembled barons. In a ringing voice that all the crowd could hear, he greeted them in perfect French.

'Together, my friends,' he declared, 'we will uphold the cause of justice, as I have sworn to do, for the honour of the Church and the good of the realm. I would have you all remember,' he went on, addressing the magnates but including everyone around him, 'that we do not aim to deny King Henry his sovereign rights, but only to compel him to respect and observe the rights and customs of England, under the ancient law, the Oxford Provisions and the Magna Carta! If God grants us peace, then we shall rejoice — but if it must be war, then we are ready, and the Lord of Hosts stands with us!'

'And may He bring us victory in our just cause!' Humphrey de Bohun cried, and the crowd roared their assent. Adam heard the earl's statement being swiftly translated into London English, for the benefit of those who did not understand courtly French.

The assembly broke up as de Montfort moved on along the street in the direction of the Tower. As he passed, the earl glanced in Robert's direction, then paused and looked again. 'De Dunstanville,' he called through the throng. 'Have you decided to join us at last?'

Robert merely inclined his head. 'My sword is yours, lord,' he said.

But de Montfort raised himself in the saddle, peering past Robert. 'Adam de Norton,' he said, and just for a moment Adam felt the man's powerful gaze locked on him alone. 'I remember you from Senlis! And I hope you will find justice yet.'

Speechless, the heat rising to his face, Adam bowed from the saddle as the great man moved on. Moments later, Simon de Montfort had been swallowed by the crowd.

'He never forgets a name,' Robert muttered. 'It's a way of winning men's trust, certainly.'

But Adam's gaze had been drawn to the column of men following along behind the earl. More banners, more flashing shields emblazoned with heraldic arms. One stood out in particular: on a red field, three white hands displayed, palm outwards. Adam had not seen it before. Then he raised his eyes, and drew a quick breath. The young man that carried the shield had curling black hair, a handsome hawk-like profile, and an expression of utter contempt on his face.

He was a knight now, with a sword belted at his side and gilded spurs at his heels, and riding in de Montfort's retinue. But Adam could not fail to recognise Richard de Malmaines.

# Chapter 14

'Look at them,' John Chyld said with a sneer. 'Like they're off to the Hocktide revels! If Lord Edward and his gang of ironclad bastards catch this lot in the open, they'll be splayed, split and gralloched before they can draw breath!'

The collected host of the baronial army and the militia of London were marching north-west along the broad straight road from the city in high spirits and a distinctly festive mood. The militiamen in particular seemed to be enjoying themselves, hefting their spears and axes and crossbows as they ambled along in a rough column behind their appointed marshal and constable. The Londoners sang as they marched, some playing on bagpipes and hand-drums, others chanting verses in praise of Simon de Montfort and in mockery of the king and Lord Edward. It was the eve of Passion Sunday, but many had decided that the rules of the Lenten fast no longer applied in times of war, and munched on dried sausage and strong cheese as they went, while others swigged from leather flasks of fresh-brewed ale. The colourful standards of their wards and guilds stirred the air above them, together with the banners of the bishops of London, Chichester and Worcester, who rode with de Montfort in the vanguard.

Even with John Chyld's scornful mutterings, Adam found it hard not to be gripped by the mood of the troops. Only the day before they had heard that King Henry had finally raised his royal banner at Oxford. In another few days they would be at Northampton, to join the earl's second son, Simon de Montfort the Younger, and defend the town against the royal forces. The April breeze was fresh and revitalising, and after so long trapped within the circuit of London's walls and the warren of the city streets it felt wonderful to be out under the sky once more, back in the saddle and riding to war.

And war it would be, Adam thought as he rode in the spring sunlight, listening to the roaring songs of the Londoners. A nervous prospect, for all his training and experience. In all his months on the tournament circuit he had never yet killed a man, to his knowledge at least. It seemed a terrible and sinful thing to take a life. But Lord Edward, they had heard, had gathered a powerful force of knights from the Welsh Marches, cold-blooded men who knew how to fight, and how to kill. All of them with sword in hand, and no doubt sworn to as mighty an oath as de Montfort's troops.

At least the barons and their retinues looked prepared for what lay ahead. Two hundred knights, more or less, had followed Simon de Montfort from London, all of them in armour, and many on armoured horses. Robert had joined his own small company to the larger force led by Sir Humphrey de Bohun. Adam tried to quell his dislike of the nobleman and forget his tormented thoughts about Joane de Quincy. Sir Humphrey, meanwhile, was in a fine mood, laughing and calling out to men he knew from the tournament fields. He too acted as if he were attending a festival of some kind. Could he really, Adam wondered, feel this sanguine about riding to do battle against his own father?

Adam had managed to avoid Richard de Malmaines since their departure from London; as far as he knew, the young knight was not even aware of his presence. De Malmaines was riding in the company of the mastiff-like Sir John FitzJohn. Both of them,

Hugh of Oystermouth had reported, had been knighted after
the fighting on the Welsh borders. Both had played a prominent
part in the attack on the Jews at Worcester as well.

They were approaching Edgware, and the end of their first
day's march, when the news passed down the column that Henry
de Montfort, Earl Simon's eldest son, had redeemed himself of
his disgrace at Gloucester by capturing Warwick Castle, and the
Earl of Warwick too. The militiamen cheered and hooted, and
soon they were singing songs about the bold Sir Henry, and how
he pulled the nose of the coward Warwick . . .

'Ach, they're like children, they are,' said John Chyld, and
spat from the saddle of his lumbering cob. 'They won't be singing when they're looking at their own guts hanging round their
knees!'

*

Passion Sunday dawned cold and grey, and the army stumbled
from their tents at Edgware under a lowering sky to hear mass.
By the time they were on the road the hour of terce had come
and gone, and the rain was falling. The feet of the men and the
hooves of the horses churned the road to mud, and the wheels
of the baggage carts and the wagons that carried the tents soon
began to drag and stick. There was no sense of festive enjoyment
now, as the army trudged heavily onward, bent-backed, towards
St Albans.

'I hear, you know,' said Hugh of Oystermouth, breaking his
fast on a chunk of bread as he rode, 'that among the defenders
of Northampton are many of the students from the University
of Oxford. The king threw them out of the town, you see, afraid
that they would fight and riot with the fierce Scotchmen he
was bringing down to join his army. And now there they are at
Northampton, manning the walls with their slings and catapults.
Strange days these are, when even scholars must learn to fight!'

'About time they did something useful, I'd say,' John Chyld added. 'I'm sure they will terrify Lord Edward though, with their fearsome drinking and puking.'

By mid-afternoon they were at St Albans, and the column straggled to a halt in a meadow outside the town. Already men were throwing themselves down, some of them gathering wood for fires and others beginning to erect tents as a shelter from the rain, though there were many more miles left of their day's march.

'No good water, and too damp for fires,' Wilecok complained as he struggled to tether the sumpter horses. His Gascon wife added something in her own incomprehensible dialect.

'Why have we halted though?' Adam wondered out loud, but the only reply he got was a shrug. Robert had already ridden on ahead, and had sent no message back. Remaining in the saddle, Adam stood in the stirrups and peered across the meadow towards the main body of the army, which had shifted closer to the abbey walls. Blinking the rain from his eyes, he tried to make out where Simon de Montfort and his commanders might be. Then he kicked with his spurs and urged his palfrey on between the knots of muddy footsore militiamen.

He did not have much longer to wonder. News was spreading through the halted army like a racing tide. King Henry and Lord Edward had already reached Northampton; they had already attacked it, seized the town and harried the defenders back into the castle.

'But the castle could hold out,' Adam said, once Robert had told him the news. 'It's well provisioned, isn't it? Why doesn't Lord Simon push ahead and try to reach it anyway?'

'This news is a day old at least, and we're two days' march away,' Robert explained, his face drawn and anxious. 'Even if we rode ahead of the infantry, we'd not arrive there with enough strength to make a difference. It sounds like they were driven back to the castle in a rout, and routs seldom lead to valiant defences. All we'd do is share in their defeat.' He hissed with frustration, baring his teeth and cursing at the chaotic confusion of the stalled advance. Already the promise of an easy or conclusive victory had been snatched from de Montfort's forces.

'Wait here,' Robert ordered, swinging down from his horse and passing the reins to Adam. 'I'll gather what tidings I can, and decide what action we should take.'

Before Adam could ask him what he meant, Robert was stalking away towards the abbey gatehouse, where a knot of knights and barons had gathered around Earl Simon and the three bishops who accompanied him for a council of war. Adam stared after him for a moment, then dismounted too.

'Senlis!' a voice cried, and he turned sharply.

'It is you, isn't it?' Richard de Malmaines said, smiling coldly as he advanced. 'I'd wondered what had become of you. You've crawled back to England at last! I did not see you when we left London – were you hiding with the baggage train all this time?'

There were people all around them, and any confrontation could easily summon a crowd. But de Malmaines was still smiling, and to anyone who did not know them, they might appear to be old friends united after a long separation.

'I have no reason to hide from you, or from any man,' Adam said quietly.

'Nor should you,' de Malmaines said, coming to a halt a sword's length away. He opened his cloak and spread his arms, displaying the knightly belt and sword that he wore over his mail and red surcoat. 'As you see,' he said, still smiling, 'I occupy a different station to you now. It would be undignified for a dubbed knight to raise his hand to a mere squire. But if you should ever win the gilded spurs, watch for me. I will find you, and I will be the death of you, I promise you that.'

'Why continue with this mad rivalry?' Adam said, holding his ground. He had a sword scabbarded at his hip, but wore no armour and carried no shield. 'We're both on the same side now. There are greater matters at hand, surely.'

'Oh, but this is a matter of *honour*,' de Malmaines said, frowning.

'And honour was satisfied, at Senlis. You challenged me, I defeated you.'

'But *I* am not satisfied!' de Malmaines roared, taking a step forward and grasping the hilt of his sword. 'You defeated me by a stratagem, and I will not tamely accept it!' Heads turned, the angry words instantly attracting attention, and at once a circle of onlookers began to form.

Adam made no movement to oppose him. If he did so, he knew, de Malmaines could claim provocation and strike first. Breathing slowly, keeping his hands on the reins of the two horses behind him, he looked de Malmaines in the eye and held his gaze steady.

For several long moments Richard de Malmaines stood with his hand on his sword, a glinting anger in his narrowed eyes. Then he shrugged his cloak back around him and paced away towards the abbey gateway. The little circle of onlookers broke apart, shrugging and muttering with disappointment. Adam felt the cold flush across his brow, and released a breath he had not realised he was holding.

It was some time before Robert returned. He approached with Humphrey de Bohun, the two of them locked in debate; they halted before getting close enough for Adam to make out their words, but he saw de Bohun gesturing emphatically. Then he clapped Robert on the shoulders and walked away.

'Nobody knows anything.' Robert said as he joined Adam once more. 'Whether we advance or retreat, it's not going to happen quickly, and probably not tonight. We need to get the horses fed and watered and find some lodgings in the town before everyone else starts crowding in there.'

Adam nodded his agreement, relieved to be doing something at least. They led the horses back to where Wilecok had managed to get a fire going, and Adam left them with John Chyld while he crossed the meadow towards the nearest houses. By now the stalled army had spread itself around the side of the abbey grounds and into the streets of St Albans. Woodsmoke hung in the damp air, and women had flocked from the town to hawk provisions to the soldiers. Dogs barked and ran in circles, horses whinnied as their owners fed and dressed them. The sense of being at war was dissipating utterly, and as the rain stopped and a low evening sun washed the meadows, the scene began to look like a bedraggled sort of fair.

He had almost reached the main street when Adam saw the lone rider galloping across the bridge in the distance. Something about the man's haste caught his attention at once. He wore a black cloak and surcoat, but the light flashed on his horse harness and buckles, the links of his armour. Before the rider had cleared the bridge and crossed the meadows, Adam had turned to run.

By the time he arrived at the abbey gatehouse, the rider had dismounted and was surrounded by men. Adam could hear the cries of despair and lamentation as he approached. It was not difficult to determine the news that the rider had brought: Northampton had already fallen to the king's forces.

'And how did you alone escape, de Segrave?' a voice demanded. It was Gilbert de Clare, Adam noticed as he pushed his way through the throng. 'Did you run away before the attack?'

'Or did your old friend Edward let you go, Nicholas, is that it?' Humphrey de Bohun called angrily.

'Peace, let him speak!' Hugh Despenser broke in, raising his palms.

Nicholas de Segrave was a tall lanky young man. One of the midland barons, Adam remembered; his black surcoat was emblazoned with three white sheaves of wheat. His long face and thinning hair gave him a look of desperate anguish as he stood wiping his brow. 'I rode clear after the castle fell,' he said. 'My horse leaped the ditch, and I cut my way through the enemy . . . If any man doubts me, he may look upon the proof!' With a flourish he drew his sword, holding it displayed above his head so all could see the notched and pitted blade, and the smear of drying blood near the hilt.

'No one doubts your valour, de Segrave,' said Simon de Montfort, appearing from the shadow of the abbey gateway. His face was grave, but he appeared resolute. 'And though we grieve this defeat,' he said, raising his voice so all could hear, 'and I can only pray that my son and all our friends still live unharmed – this is not the end of our struggle. This is merely the fortune of war, as God directs. But I promise you this – we will not see Pentecost before all the joys of our enemies are turned to pain!'

A hand fell on his shoulder, and Adam found Robert beside him. 'Come, quickly and quietly,' the knight said in a low whisper. 'We need to be away from here, before anyone notices us leaving. We wouldn't want anyone to think we were deserting too openly.'

*

They rode through the dusk in a straggling line, Robert in the lead and Wilecok bringing up the rear with the laden baggage horses. As the sun set the clouds had cleared to show a waxing half-moon, and while there was still enough light to pick out the roads and trackways ahead of them they rode as fast as they dared. Then, once darkness had fallen, they kept the horses to a steady walk, and the noise of the hooves was loud in the hollowness of the night.

After skirting the Bishop of Ely's game parks at Hatfield they came to the valley of a river, which Robert said was the Lea. Adam could smell the water and could hear the rills as it flowed, but by then it was too dark to see it. They rode in silence, and Adam had the strong sensation that he had slipped into a dream.

A brook crossed the path, and they paused to rest and let the horses drink. Adam found Robert in the gloom beneath an overhanging tree. 'What was it that Humphrey de Bohun told you, back at the camp?' he asked quietly. 'I'm guessing it was the reason for our swift departure.'

'Sir Humphrey was talking very fervently of my cousin,' Robert replied, in a musing tone. 'He seemed to believe she was in some danger at Ware.'

'So . . . he's sending us to fetch her?' Adam asked, and noticed the quick gleam of Robert's eye in the darkness. There was something more here, but he knew that Robert would not reveal it too easily.

'Sir Humphrey spoke of sending men to Ware, yes, to find Joane de Quincy and take her to some safer place – he suggested his own castle at Kimbolton.'

Adam waited, frowning. He could hear Robert sucking his cheeks.

'But I suspect,' Robert went on, 'that his intention is to hide her away and marry her privately, while all are distracted by the confusion of war.'

'And so you're doing his bidding?' Adam said. His horse tugged at the rein, unnerved by the darkness.

He caught the curt shake of Robert's head. 'I told him to give me a few days, and I'd go to Ware myself and see what might be done. That should give us time to take Joane and her sister somewhere they can be protected, for now at least. I told Hugh of Oystermouth to stay with the army until he could determine where they were going next, then to ride and find us, at either Ware or Pleshey.'

'Pleshey?' Adam asked, startled. He had not expected to see that place again, especially now that the Earl of Hereford was with the king's army.

'The castellan is no friend of mine,' Robert said, 'but he might take the girls. And then we shall see what fortune brings.'

Adam was speechless for a moment. 'You changed your mind then, about supporting Sir Humphrey?'

'Consider,' Robert told him, 'that your impassioned outburst a few days back might have given me some thoughts. Consider that perhaps it caused me to recognise I was on the wrong path.'

'It did?'

'Of course not,' Robert said, tutting. 'I am not swayed by such things. But consider it *possible*, is all I will say on the matter.'

They climbed back into the saddle, and without another word they resumed their nocturnal journey along the river valley. The moon was low over the north-eastern horizon when they slipped past Hertford in the dead of night. Robert sent John Chyld galloping on ahead to announce their arrival, and an hour later they crossed the bridge at Ware, five riders each with a spare horse and three baggage animals behind them. Through the silent streets of the town they passed, the noise of the hooves waking the dogs in the yards. By the time they entered the yard of the manor house there was a light glowing in the porch and another showing through the hall window.

Robert dismounted and waited. Servants came loping from indoors, startled from sleep and still bleary. Adam climbed down from the saddle too, his thighs and back aching after a long day and half a night on horseback. Rubbing the nose of his weary palfrey, he watched the silhouetted shapes moving around the door and the porch. So many times he had imagined his return to Ware, and his meeting with Joane. Never had he imagined anything like this strange dreamlike scene.

She came from the house in a fur-trimmed robe, a deep hood thrown over her head. Adam knew her at once even so.

'I must apologise for the late hour, cousin,' Robert said, hushed but smiling.

Joane de Quincy drew the hood back and looked him in the eye. She stepped towards him, as if to greet him with a kiss.

Then she raised her hand and slapped him hard across the face.

# Chapter 15

With a flurry of beating wings, the falcon scaled the bright morning sky. Leaning back in the saddle, Adam tracked it as it flew. Below and ahead of him, the dogs were coursing along the riverbanks, forging through the stands of reeds and bracken.

'There,' Joane said, pointing. A moment later Adam saw the brace of waterfowl burst upwards, startled into motion by the dogs. But Joane was watching her falcon. Adam glanced up again, and saw the bird of prey wheel and fold its wings, stooping instantly into a plummeting dive. Almost faster than his eye could track, the bird fell on the second of the waterfowl, fanning its wings at the last moment and stretching out its talons. Joane drew a quick hissing breath as the falcon struck, its prey snatched from the air and propelled earthwards by the killing blow.

'Come on!' she called, leaning forward in the saddle and kicking with the spurs. She rode like a man, astride the horse with her feet in the stirrups, and wore a hunting cap with a brim to shade her eyes. Ahead stretched a grassy downhill sward, and Joane rode fast with Adam only a horse's length behind her. The falconer and the dog handlers were already closing in on the kill, striding through the reeds.

By the time they reached the falcon it was standing on the dead fowl, letting out shrieks of triumph as it bent to hack and pluck at the downy breast-feathers and the flesh beneath. It was a young peregrine, still in training, but when Joane reined in her horse twenty paces away and extended her gloved hand, the bird rose from its prey and swooped across to her, wings spread as it came to a perch. One of the dog handlers came running with a bit of meat torn from the dead fowl, and Joane pinched it in the fingers of her glove and let the falcon feed, its curved beak ripping at the hank of bloodied flesh.

'Fortunate creatures,' she said with a smile, 'that do not know the Lenten fast!'

'There is no sin in them, only nature,' Adam replied.

She looked at him, still smiling, not flinching as the hunting bird fed and then preened and stretched its wings. 'Unfortunate humans then,' she said, 'with our sinful natures.'

They rode back towards the house, the hooded falcon secured to her glove. 'Imagine,' she told him. 'For two years I hear nothing, and then only a few days ago Humphrey de Bohun, the son of the Earl of Hereford, appears at my home intent on betrothal, and telling me that Robert de Dunstanville, no less, is going to help press his claim to my uncle. And then, after hearing nothing more, Sir Robert himself appears suddenly from the depths of night with some message that I must be ready to leave imminently, for an unknown destination. Would anyone not be angry?'

Adam said nothing as he rode.

'And now he has gone to Pleshey,' Joane said with a sigh, gazing into the low morning sun, 'to persuade them to give me refuge. It seems my virtue is to be once more protected by castle walls.'

Robert had left that morning soon after dawn, after only a few hours' sleep. He hoped to ride to Pleshey and return that same day, he had told Adam before his departure. Remaining in the house until he got back seemed sensible, but Joane had insisted

on taking her falcon out for exercise, and Adam had felt compelled to accompany her.

'What did Sir Humphrey say to you, when he was here?' Adam
asked.

Joane sniffed back a laugh, and the bird on her glove twitched,
the bells on its jesses chiming. 'He tried to recite love poetry. It
was quite baffling.'

Adam smiled wryly as he tried to picture the blustering de
Bohun attempting such a thing.

'My sister could barely conceal her mirth,' Joane went on. 'Sir
Humphrey has children already, you know, by his late wife – one
of them is older than Hawise! But he hopes I might become *a
good mother to them* . . . He left soon enough for London, talking
mightily of Simon de Montfort, the Earl of Leicester. I rather
wondered whether he might recite love poetry to him too.
You've met him yourself?'

Adam nodded. 'He's a forceful man,' he replied. 'I've heard it
said that he is too fond of wealth and fame. But he always seems
to know what must be done, and how it should be done. Almost
as if he has already seen the shape of the future.'

'We hear a lot about him,' Joane said. 'There's no real company here, but the travelling friars bring us all the news of the
wide world. This Simon de Montfort seems like a great wind
sweeping through the land, shaking all the trees. Bringing down
the rotten fruit and the ripe all together.'

Adam looked at her from the corner of his eye. Hugh of Oystermouth had said something similar once, he remembered,
although he had not expressed it so well. Joane was handing the
falcon and glove across to the falconer, who had ridden up beside
her.

'A race,' she called to Adam. 'Back to the stables!'

At once she let out her reins and set the spurs to her horse,
and the animal surged forward into a canter. Adam dug in his
heels and set off after her, his bigger palfrey gaining fast. Joane

had taken off her jaunty hunting cap, and her hair whipped out behind her in dark auburn braids. Over the years since last they had met, Adam realised, his idea of her had remained static, like a painted picture in a church or on the pages of an illustrated manuscript. But the quiet, nervous girl who had asked him to read with her from the Psalter and pray for Sir Robert's protection was gone. He had feared he would be disappointed to find her changed; instead he was awestruck. Never had he expected this wry dancing intelligence, this confident vitality. As they rode neck and neck towards the house, he saw her grinning back at him and knew that she could reads his thoughts exactly.

'I didn't recognise you either at first, you know,' she told him, as they walked the horses back into the stable yard. 'I believed that Sir Robert must have lost another squire, and that rather awkward gangling youth I knew once had met his end on some tournament field in France.'

'I think he did,' Adam told her.

She slid a glance at him. A half-smile. 'Perhaps so,' she said, and swung her leg to dismount. 'But I'm sure it was all very chivalrous, and you had a great many stirring adventures.'

He thought of Eloise and tried not to smile. Was that what she meant? 'There were many . . . great deeds of arms,' he told her. She almost laughed, but stifled it quickly.

They walked together across the yard towards the house, as the grooms led the horses to the stable. 'And now you're a follower of Simon de Montfort as well, I suppose?' Joane asked, changing the subject abruptly. 'You believe what he says of the king, that he's the enemy of his people?'

Adam took a moment to compose his reply, sure that in some way he was being tested. 'If you mean that the king should be bound by the law, then yes I believe it,' he said. 'If you mean that the king should rule with the consent of his parliament, as he swore to do, then certainly. And if he does not, then yes . . . the king is the enemy of the people.'

'And so you would make yourself the king's enemy?' she asked lightly. 'The enemy of the sovereign anointed by God?'

'If that's what justice demands, then yes,' Adam said, trying to sound more confident than he felt. 'Besides,' he went on, 'it is the king's advisors who lead him astray . . . And if it comes to a trial by battle, God will judge the outcome.' He realised as he spoke that he had never made such a certain declaration before, and neither had Robert. He realised too how much he was risking. Was this what he truly believed? *Yes*, he thought. *Yes, it is.*

Joane had turned to look at the stable, perhaps to hide her expression. For a moment Adam wondered if she doubted him, and felt offended. Was she impressed by his resolve, his bold attitude, or simply amused?

'I envy you,' she confessed as they walked on towards the house. She did not seem eager, suddenly, to go back inside. 'To feel so active in the world, to hold chivalry as something real, not just an ideal . . . It must be glorious.'

Adam could not answer. Her words made him feel more humble than enviable.

'Sadly,' she went on, 'women are condemned to passivity in these matters. Still, I can imagine . . . I too dream of going on pilgrimages and adventuring in foreign lands.' She gazed towards the horizon, narrowing her eyes, as if she might see rising there the spires of Lyonesse, or the towers of far Antioch.

'Perhaps, if you were married to Humphrey de Bohun . . .' Adam forced himself to say. The words were clumsy and bitter in his mouth, but he needed to see her reaction.

'Oh, so you're his advocate too now?' Joane said sharply.

'Not at all. And neither is Robert, as you must surely know.'

'Then I'm glad I have some support,' she said, pausing in the porch before the doors to the hall. 'Too often nowadays I feel like hunted game.'

'You have other men hunting you as well then?' Adam asked, feeling a prickle of renewed jealousy.

Joane glanced at him, her smile returning. 'My uncle,' she said, 'has threatened to cut the arms and legs off any man who touches me. He would have sent both Hawise and me to a nunnery years ago, like my older sister Anne, had he not sworn to my father he would see us wed. But he resents us, you see, and he's gone out of his way to surround us with thorns.'

\*

Later that day they dined with Hawise, the chaplain and steward, and the elderly nun whom Adam had seen during his last visit. Wilecok and his Gascon wife had joined the bailiff and the manor servants at the trestle table at the far end of the hall. The chaplain pronounced grace before the meal, and read from the *Liber de Contemptu Mundi* of Pope Innocent III as they ate.

'The sky grows very dark to the east, and there's a wind rising,' the steward said to them, once the dishes were cleared. 'I am afraid Sir Robert will have a wet ride back from Pleshey.'

'That's if he returns today at all,' Joane said, under her breath. She waited until the steward and chaplain had left them and the nun had gone to pray, then exhaled loudly. 'They only joined us because you're here,' she told Adam. 'And if Robert doesn't return, they'll surely be back for supper. They need to watch over you, you see.'

'He'll return,' Adam said. The shutters were banging at the windows, and he could hear the trees whipping in the gale outside. As he listened further, he heard the tap of hail against the roof overhead.

'I don't think he means to come back today at all,' said Hawise, with a sly smile. She was fourteen years old now, and sleek as an otter. She kept the falcon beside her as she ate, fixed to its perch with a slim gold chain, and stroked its breast feathers. The bird rotated its head, large eyes open and alert, as if the upper corners of the hall might at any moment fill with starlings.

'Whatever do you mean?' Joane asked her.

'Well, is it not obvious?' her sister asked. 'Robert has intended to throw you two together! Why else would he leave you both here and ride off to Pleshey? Surely he means that you should fall in love, and be . . . married in the sight of the Lord.'

'Hawise!' Joane cried, blushing suddenly. 'Be *quiet* . . .'

'Married how?' Adam asked, keeping his composure.

'In the flesh, you know,' said Hawise with a diffident shrug. 'If there is consent and love, then there is union. And no man could sunder you then. Not even Uncle Roger, or Humphrey de Bohun!'

'Hawise – *that's enough*!' Joane hissed. 'You have no idea what you're talking about . . .' She was staring down at the tablecloth. Adam cleared his throat lightly.

'Well, you don't *want* to marry Humphrey de Bohun, do you?' Hawise said, getting up from the table. 'And who else is there? Anyway, I've seen the way you keep looking at each other.'

And with that she left the hall and went up to the solar.

Adam and Joane sat in silence for a few moments after the girl had gone. Joane snorted a laugh suddenly, and Adam grinned. 'Married in the flesh,' said Joane, then gave a long sigh and stared down the room. She could not meet Adam's eye.

'Do you think she really knows what it means?' Adam asked.

'Oh, I think so. As do we all. But she cannot be wed before I am, so it matters to her, I suppose.'

'And not to you?'

Joane looked at him directly. Her pale grey eyes caught and held the light. 'I would rather be free to live as I please, if I had the choice,' she told him.

\*

With the wind and hail gathering force, Adam went out to the stables with Wilecok to secure and feed the horses, in case the night proved tempestuous. With his cloak pulled up over his head Adam stood in the gateway of the stable yard and stared off down the rutted road to the town, in the direction of Pleshey. Nobody was in sight, and he knew that few travellers would risk the roads in such weather. If Robert had left Pleshey already, he would need a pressing reason to continue his journey.

'He'll get here if he can, I'm sure,' he told Joane. 'But we might have to wait until tomorrow.' They were sitting together at the high table once more, drinking wine as the hall was slowly engulfed by darkness. Only the glow from the hearth and the single candle on the table illuminated their end of the chamber, where Joane's father's shield hung on the wall, the white cinque-foil radiant in the darkness. A notched old sword was mounted below it, and a hunting crossbow. At the other end of the hall, Wilecok and his wife and a couple of servants were eating a late supper at the trestle. Hawise had already gone to bed for the night. The storm thumped and wailed around the eaves of the hall, rattling the shutters.

'It's strange how much you've come to resemble Sir Robert,' Joane said. 'You've taken on some of his mannerisms. You've even come to look like him at times.'

'I have?' Adam said, unsure whether this was praise or criticism.

'You must have changed your mind about him,' Joane said. 'You didn't care much for him when you came here before, but I think you admire him now.'

'I suppose I do,' Adam replied, careful with his words. 'He's a hard man to like. A man of twists and turns. If you could only see him on the tournament field — I know you hate such things, but even so, he is . . . *magnificent*. But I think he is struggling to be just and true, and to get what he desires from life.'

'And you?' Joane asked, dropping her voice a little and swirling the wine in her cup. 'What is it you most desire in life?'

'To be knighted,' Adam said without hesitation. 'And to regain the lands my father once held . . .' He hesitated, unsure how to express himself. 'But more than that,' he went on, 'I want to be found worthy. Not to fail or be weak, when the test comes. Whatever the test may be.'

'I believe we all desire that,' Joane said, gazing at the flickering flame of the candle. 'Many people don't have the awareness to recognise it though.'

At the far end of the hall, Wilecok and the others at the trestle had finished their meal and were playing dice by rushlight. Intent on their game, they appeared oblivious of Adam and Joane. Adam was fighting to still his mind and concentrate on the moment. Those women he had known before were like Eloise, simple and direct in their affections, and he had taken a simple and direct approach to them. Joane de Quincy, he knew, was different. But he found their conversation so easy that he felt no need to try and summon the eloquence of poetry, or to remember lines from the romances he had read or heard. It seemed enough to be direct and simple with her too.

'You've really never had another suitor?' he asked her, guarding his nerve.

Joane laughed to herself, then took another sip of wine. 'With my uncle's threat of murder and dismemberment, and Humphrey de Bohun's threat of additional murder, and then the surety of murder by Robert de Dunstanville for any who survive, is it any surprise that none have been foolish enough to try?'

'It would surprise me,' Adam said.

She gazed at him for a long moment, twisting the ring adorned with her family emblem, then drank again. 'It may shock you,' she said, 'but there was one. Not a suitor, exactly . . . One of my uncle's squires – this was on his estates in Scotland, three years ago. We were both little more than children, and it started in play, but we became lovers in time. My uncle discovered it, and sent the squire away. He died soon afterwards, the squire, and it was said that I had poisoned him out of spite. Then my uncle said I was a putrid little slut and the spawn of a Welsh witch, and if I ever looked at another man, he would seize me by the ears and fling me off the sea cliffs. That was when he sent me and Hawise to live here, in solitude.'

Adam waited a moment, digesting what she had told him. He tried not to be shocked, and found that he was impressed instead. 'What was he like,' he asked quietly, 'this squire you loved?'

'Perhaps a little like a gangling youth I once met, who read from the Psalter with me,' she told him.

Hardly daring to breathe, he reached across the table and laid his hand over hers. She turned her wrist, and their fingers met.

A crash on the outer door resounded through the hall, followed by the banging of a fist. Adam got to his feet at once. His sword lay scabbarded on the floor beside his chair, and he reached down and grabbed it.

'Robert?' he asked.

'No,' Joane said. 'He would not beat at the door like that . . .'

One of the servants was already running into the passage to look through the sliding opening in the front door and see who was outside in the porch. Before he reached it there was another crash, a splintering of wood, and the servant staggered back into the hall with a cry of alarm.

Three figures followed close behind him, heavy-set men bundled against the storm in thick cloaks, sodden wool coifs on their heads. Two carried drawn swords, while the third had a crossbow, spanned and loaded. As he entered the hall he raised it and aimed directly at Adam's head.

Joane screamed, and the falcon woke and burst upwards from its perch, wings flapping. Adam drew his sword and flung the scabbard aside, but the crossbowman was tracking him as he moved, his fingers curling around the trigger.

It was Wilecok's Gascon wife who moved first. With a shriek of fury she flung a wooden mug at the man with the crossbow. He turned, his weapon swinging, then released the trigger and shot the bolt wildly towards the ceiling beams. Adam was already closing on him, sword raised to cut him down before he could reload, but the two other men surged forward with their blades. From the corner of his eye Adam saw Joane bend sharply and then straighten; he thought for a moment that the bolt had hit her, but then he realised that she had taken the hunting crossbow from the wall and spanned it, and now held it loaded in her hands.

The first swordsman lunged at him, a clumsy stab, and he knocked the blade aside and slashed back. The man danced away from him, weapon swinging. Behind him the crossbowman was bent over his weapon as he spanned it, a fresh quarrel clamped between his teeth. The second swordsman was craftier. He slid along the wall to Adam's left, then aimed a chopping blow at his shoulder. Adam turned on his heel, dodging the man's sword and then bringing his own blade slicing along his forearm. The man fell back against the wall with a howl, bleeding from a long cut. The noise filled the hall in echoes.

Wilecok and one of the servants were holding the first swordsman at bay with a fire iron and a cleaver. But now the crossbowman had spanned and reloaded his weapon, and was raising it to take aim.

'Stand clear!' Joane cried. Adam chanced a quick look over his shoulder, then dropped to a crouch as she shot her own bow from the far end of the hall. He heard the meaty *thwack* of impact, and saw the crossbowman stagger and reel, his loaded weapon falling. The trigger released, the bolt shot forth and deflected from the floor beside the hearth, striking sparks off the flagstones before burying its head in the wall.

The injured swordsman let out a roar as he surged to his feet; Adam stepped quickly back and dodged the blow, knocking aside the man's swinging weapon. Then he drew back his hand and punched the iron pommel of his sword into the man's forehead, dropping him like a stunned beast.

He turned just in time to see the last of the attackers give up the fight and fling himself into the passageway leading to the door. A moment later the sound of his running footsteps came from the yard outside. Breathing heavily, Adam surveyed the room. Joane stood white-faced and staring. The falcon was still shrieking from its perch. The crossbowman was lying flat on his back, Joane's bolt projecting from his eye.

'Christ's nails!' Wilecok said, staring at the dead man. 'That was some shot!'

# Chapter 16

Robert de Dunstanville returned to Ware the following morning. He had left Pleshey at first light and ridden hard; John Chyld was still on the road behind him. In the porch he gave the corpse of the dead crossbowman a long look: the grimy sheet that covered the body was tented grotesquely over the jutting bolt, which nobody had cared to remove. Drawing a hissing breath between his teeth, Robert paced through into the hall.

'You've been keeping yourselves amused while I was away, I see,' he said, rubbing at a spatter of blood on the wall that Adam had not noticed.

'It was Earl Roger that sent them,' Joane said from the high table. She had been sitting there most of the night, a crossbow laid ready before her. They had all spent the hours of darkness in nervous vigil, convinced that the man who had run away would return imminently with reinforcements. 'Earl Roger, our own uncle,' Joane went on. She gestured to the wounded captive who sat in the corner, securely tied and with his arm bound in blood-soaked linen. 'Ask him if you don't believe me.'

But Robert had no need of corroboration. The wounded man, in any case, was unlikely to tell them much more. Once he had recovered from the blow on the head that Adam dealt him he had been quick enough to confess everything, much to Wilecok's disappointment. The weaselly servant had been heating a variety of implements in the fire for some time, just in case persuasion was required.

'Of course,' Robert said, pressing his fingertips to his brow. 'Earl Roger will have heard that Humphrey de Bohun was planning to seize Joane, and sent his own men to stop him. They'll have seen the stable full of strange horses and guessed that de Bohun's men were already here . . . They used the oaken bench from the porch as a ram to break the door, by the way – the latch must have rusted. It'll need repairing.'

'The steward's already sent for a carpenter from the town,' Adam told him. The steward and the chaplain had both appeared before first light, ready to read the matins of the day, and both had been genuinely appalled at what had happened in their absence. They would testify that the attackers were mere brigands, taking advantage of the confused state of the kingdom to prey upon defenceless ladyfolk in their homes. There would be no trouble about the dead man, at least.

Adam nodded towards the captive, who was already looking pale and feverish. 'What do we do about him?'

'Best give a drink of water and turn him loose,' Robert said. 'That wound's likely to kill him if it gets infected, and he'll just be one more to bury. If he lives long enough, he can run back to Earl Roger and tell him what happened.'

Once the captive had been sent staggering off into the noon daylight and the carpenters had repaired the door, the kitchen servants appeared with hot vegetable broth and bread fresh from the oven. Adam ate hungrily, noticing with a guilty pang that the cooks had used marrowbone to thicken the stock. But surely, he thought, God would forgive the lapse after such a night? Hawise joined them to dine, very disappointed that she had slept through the attack on the house, and particularly that she had missed the spectacle of a man being shot in the eye right there in her own hall.

Joane, though, was silent and distracted, and ate little. All knew that she bore no guilt for the death of the intruder, but it was a killing all the same, and the shock of it weighed upon her. She had not slept at all, and her face was waxen pale with dark patches below her eyes.

'What happened at Pleshey?' Adam asked Robert as they ate. Perhaps, he thought, that might draw Joane from her grim reflections.

'The countess was in residence, worse luck,' Robert said, dunking bread into his broth. 'She was first inclined not to allow me through the gates, and was then inclined to hang me from a gibbet as a traitor and rebel.'

'She's been after the opportunity to do that for many a year,' John Chyld added.

'Fortunately,' Robert went on, chewing bread, 'the castellan persuaded her that they had no evidence I had joined Simon de Montfort's cause. So I was able to convince her that for the sake of Christian charity alone she should give shelter to Joane and Hawise de Quincy, until the current warlike state of the land is changed and order restored.'

'I won't go,' Joane said. She had not spoken for so long that the sound of her voice made all pause.

'You will go, certainly,' Robert replied sharply, poised with his spoon raised. 'I have not just ridden all the way to Pleshey and back on flooded roads for you simply to refuse.'

'I will not go,' she said again. 'I will not seek charity from the Countess of Hereford, or from you, or from anyone.'

'God's *brains*!' Robert swore, throwing down his spoon. 'Can you not see the danger here? Did last night's escapades not reveal it? Tomorrow or the day after, Humphrey de Bohun's men will be here, if Earl Roger's men do not return and take you first. They'll drag you and your sister out by your hair if they need to!'

'No!' Joane cried, standing up suddenly, her knuckles white. 'This is my home. You cannot simply order me out of here against

my will — you are not my father, or my guardian! I never asked
for your help in any of this!'

'No, but I gave it for your father's sake!' Robert yelled, standing up so abruptly that his stool toppled to the floor. The two of
them glared at each other across the table.

'She's right,' Adam said, standing as well. 'This is her home.
She is mistress here.'

'Oh, is that so?' Robert said, turning to Adam wide-eyed and
incredulous. 'You're fighting for her cause now then? Is this what
happens, when I leave you two alone for a night?'

'At least I was here to protect her!' Adam snarled, feeling the
heat rise to his face. He saw that Robert's teeth were bared, and
his hand had strayed instinctively to the knife at his belt.

'I need no protection from either of you!' Joane shouted,
banging her fist on the table.

The banging was echoed from the far end of the hall, and all
heads turned towards the passageway that led to the door. A
moment of poised silence, then the banging came again, and the
sound of a voice calling for entry.

'It's that Welshman,' said Wilecok. 'What's he doing back so soon?'

'Let him in,' Robert growled, and one of the servants ran to
open the door. 'My apologies,' he said quietly, fists braced on the
tabletop. He glanced first at Joane and then at Adam. 'I have not
rested for some time.'

'None of us have,' Joane said.

Hugh of Oystermouth almost collapsed in through the door
to the hall. He dropped onto one of the benches, seized a mug
of ale from the trestle table and sucked it dry. Then he sagged
forward onto his knees, groaning at the ache in his back and
legs. The servant who answered the door had already gone to
fetch the grooms and attend to the Welshman's lathered horse.

'I galloped here most of the way from London,' Hugh said,
wincing. The cook's boy was already refilling his mug. 'And that
was after riding the distance back from St Albans yesterday.'

'What's happened?' Robert demanded, striding down the hall to stand before him. 'Where is de Montfort? Where is the king?'

Hugh drank again, then stifled a belch with the back of his hand. 'The king,' he said, 'has marched north from Northampton, and the latest word says he's taken Leicester, and probably Nottingham too. Lord Edward has gone with him, and is ravaging the northern shires. Earl Simon trailed in his wake a while, but now he's gone to Kenilworth to meet with his oldest son, Henry.'

'And the army he led from London?' Robert said, with a pained look. 'What's happened to them? Who is in command now?'

Hugh shrugged heavily. 'Nobody rightly knows,' he said. 'The Earl of Gloucester, maybe, or Nicholas de Segrave? Or Humphrey de Bohun? They're falling back on London anyway. There's a lot of dark talk about treachery and conspiracy among them. A lot of dark talk about the Jews as well, and the money they're supposedly hoarding for the king.'

'*What?*' Robert said. He dragged up a stool and dropped to sit facing Hugh, elbows braced on his knees. 'Tell me, how did you hear this?'

'Just the talk among the soldiers as they were passing through Edgware,' Hugh said. 'Some of the knights too. They seemed to think the Jews have hidden gold in tunnels under the city, and have copies of the keys to all the main gates, and they're planning either to shut the gates against the returning militia or to open them when the king arrives with his army. Oh, and a few believe that the Jews have got Greek Fire stored away, and are planning to burn all of London to the ground.'

'Holy Name preserve us!' Robert groaned, and pressed his fists to his brow.

'I rode straight down to London, when I saw the way the wind was blowing,' Hugh said, 'and paid a lad to carry word to Master Elias of what was bearing down on him, then I turned and rode out of Bishop's Gate and straight back up here.' He paused, as if he might expect some thanks or reward. But Robert just answered him with a louring black gaze.

'We have to go,' Robert said, almost as if he were muttering to himself. 'If de Montfort's not around to control his soldiers and the city mob, they'll open the pits of hell itself . . . How long till the vanguard reaches London?' he snapped.

'They should be at New Gate by around this time tomorrow, I'd say,' Hugh replied, a little crestfallen. 'They're not moving with any fixed purpose. I think some still believe Simon de Montfort will return and take charge of them once more.'

Robert was up on his feet again and pacing, scrubbing his fingers through his beard and mumbling to himself.

'We can't go anywhere now,' Adam told him. 'We're all exhausted.'

'True, yes,' Robert said, nodding. He snapped his fingers. 'We leave at daybreak tomorrow. If the roads are clear, we'll be in London well before vespers, and without tiring the horses. Have everything packed and ready to go beforehand,' he told Adam.

'I shall come with you,' Joane said.

'*What?*' Robert yelled, exasperated. 'Of course you will not!'

'You said yourself, it's dangerous to stay here, and I won't go to Pleshey. Let Hawise go and stay there with the countess, and I shall go to London with you.'

'Child,' Robert said, with withering scorn, 'if there is danger for you in this land, then it's at its greatest in London. The city is mad for de Montfort, and Earl Roger is looking very like his enemy at the moment. Humphrey de Bohun, the man who you may remember wants to seize you and marry you, is currently leading an army there. I cannot watch over you when there are greater dangers all around me.'

'I'm sure I will be safe enough,' Joane said. She flung a glance of challenge at Adam.

'Let her come,' Adam said. 'We have no choice, do we?'

Pressing his fist to his temple again, Robert let out a long growl of exasperation. 'Tell the steward he is to conduct the lady Hawise to Pleshey at matins tomorrow,' he told one of the servants. 'John Chyld will go with him, and ride back to report to me when she is safe. *Then*,' he said, turning to Joane with weary resignation, 'we ride for London. And you, my lady, may come or go as you please!'

*

The sun was bright and the air clear the following day, but noon had already passed by the time John Chyld came trotting back from Pleshey with word that Hawise was safely within the protection of the castle walls. The grizzled serjeant showed no sign of fatigue after his repeated journeys, and neither did his stout lumbering cob. Robert gave the order to leave Ware without further delay.

'What is Greek Fire?' Adam asked him as they rode.

'A burning potion, made out in the east, around Constantinople,' Robert told him. 'Like liquid flame, so they say, that burns everything it touches and can never be extinguished, even by water. Nobody knows how to make it, though I once heard it comes from a substance that bubbles up from the ground in certain eastern places and burns with a pretty blue flame.'

'Why would anyone think the Jews of London possessed such a potion?'

Robert snorted a laugh. 'Because they think the Jews are cleverer than them,' he said, 'and so they must know all the secrets under heaven! Although,' he went on a few moments later, 'men tend to call anything that burns hot and fierce *Greek Fire* – I believe something like it can be made of nut oil and hemp flax. Though it's not the true stuff, you understand.'

Behind them, Adam could hear Hugh of Oystermouth talking with Joane in Welsh. The herald had been delighted to discover that she had picked up a little of the language from her mother – the daughter of Llywelyn the Great, as Hugh often reminded Adam – and her maids. Adam had often heard Welsh when he was living at Earl Humphrey's estates in the Marches, but the language was incomprehensible to him, and alien to his ears. 'She speaks it sweetly enough,' Hugh reported. 'But somewhat in the manner of a seven-year-old, which does sound odd at times from the lips of a woman grown.'

Joane herself had brought only a single maidservant with her from Ware, a Flemish woman of her own age named Petronilla, who rode sideways upon a packsaddle. Joane had given her younger sister a lingering embrace before they parted that morning at first light. She had bidden a tender farewell to her hunting falcon too, as it sat hooded and chained on Hawise's gloved hand – London, Sir Robert had stressed, was no place for a barely trained bird of prey – but she had seemed unmoved as they left Ware. She gave no parting glance to the house, the orchards and water meadows. Adam noticed that she had taken with her the illustrated Psalter her father had given her, and from which they had read together so long ago, carrying it carefully in one of her saddlebags.

Shortly before vespers, they crested the last rise and saw London spreading before them. When they reached the church of St Mary Spital, Robert led them off the road and ordered the armour unpacked from its cases and coverings. 'We enter like warriors,' he told Adam. 'So troublesome folk will know we're not to be meddled with.'

In a grove of trees beside the road Adam shrugged into the grease-stained linen aketon and mail hauberk with its coif hood. Then he helped Robert dress in his coat of mail, with chausses beneath it to protect his legs. John Chyld was content with his usual padded gambeson, but he and Adam wore wide-brimmed iron helmets. They fastened their sword belts and shield straps, then swung back up into the saddle, both Adam and Robert mounting their warhorses rather than the weary palfreys. Then, with Hugh of Oystermouth carrying Robert's lance with his red and white pennon, they rode on into London in full martial array.

There were cheers as they came in through Bishop's Gate, people thinking they were the vanguard of some newly arrived magnate's retinue. But nobody challenged them or tried to bar their way. There were other armed men in the streets already, Adam noticed. The army that had marched forth with Simon de Montfort only five days beforehand had flooded back into the city after the retreat from St Albans. But they had neither dis banded nor disarmed. Everywhere there were spears and short swords, militiamen carrying crossbows over their shoulders, others in gambesons and leather jacks lounging outside the ale-houses. Plenty of shields and banners too. A seething energy held London in its grip, leaderless and unbridled, threatening at any moment to burst forth into violence. Adam glanced back at Joane a couple of times, the mail links crunching as he turned, and caught the mingled fear and excitement in her eyes and her tautly alert posture.

In Westcheap the mob parted before them as the iron-shod hooves of their horses rang off the cobblestones. The lane leading to Elias's house was a gulf of darkness, and they heard voices shouting challenges before they reached his gate. Elias had doubled his guard, and his young men were nervous and primed to fight; this time, clearly, they had received no warning of any visitors. By the time Robert had assured them that he came in peace, and a message had been sent to the house and an answer returned, twilight had engulfed them all. They dismounted in the courtyard, the horses skittish. Adam could hear Wilecok whispering avidly to Joane's maid; he turned and saw the woman gasp in trepidation, pressing her hand to her throat. Robert had told Joane that they would be staying with *friends*, and that was all.

'Robert de Dunstanville,' Elias said, appearing in the lit doorway at the top of the steps. 'You are becoming a harbinger of ill tidings, I find.'

'I'm here, am I not?' Robert said, spreading his arms. He mounted the steps, gesturing for Adam to follow him. Below them, Wilecok and John Chyld attended to the horses.

'There's blood in the air out there, you can almost taste it,' Robert said as they paced down the passageway to the hall. Adam was uncomfortably aware that both he and Robert were still wearing their mail hauberks and surcoats, and carried weapons belted at their sides.

'Yes, and whose blood?' Elias demanded, turning on his heel. Now they were in the candlelit chambers, Adam could see how angry the man was, his face darkened with anguish and despair. 'Not the king's blood, no!' Elias cried. 'Not the blood of his *evil ministers* – strange sort of rebellion this one, eh, that targets only those that have offered no threat, no insult!'

Robert made a fanning gesture. *Later*. Behind him, Joane and the others came through from the passageway, and Adam saw Belia enter from the far end of the hall. Quickly they made the introductions, Elias quelling the flames of his anger with practised courtesy and welcoming the lady Joane de Quincy to his home. Adam glanced sidelong at Joane as she took everything in; he saw the swift flicker of realisation, of calculation, of adjustment. They would be accommodated, Elias said, in the adjoining building, where they had stayed before; immediately he ordered his servants to carry hot embers through from the hall and kindle a fire in the hearth of the main chamber. Even in the turmoil of his distress, Adam thought, he was an admirable host.

The others filed quickly along the passageway and through the connecting door, carrying their baggage and chests, Joane's maid Petronilla almost holding her breath and rolling her eyes in fear of the unchristian things that might be revealed before her. Adam made to follow them but Robert gestured for him to stay.

'So,' Elias said, once they were alone. 'Do you know what's been happening in this city, this very evening? My good friend Hagin has been turned out of his home by a mob, beaten and abused, and dragged to prison. The documents, *chirographs*, showing who owes what to whom have already been seized and burned on a fire . . . And this is your Simon de Montfort, your Earl of Leicester, who gives the mob licence to do this!'

'He does not, I am sure of it,' Robert said.

'Oh, you deny it,' Elias said, taut with fury. 'You deny that he is telling his followers that he will cancel all debts owed to the Jews, that he will beggar the Jews?'

'I have never heard him say any such thing,' Robert said, his voice rising. 'If his followers say this, then they are culpable for it, not him.'

'Or perhaps, perhaps,' Elias said, spitting the words, not even listening to Robert, 'perhaps you wish for this yourself, eh? Perhaps you too want to be rid of your debts to us?'

Adam stepped forward. 'Robert has already repaid his debt,' he said. 'He repaid it from what he won at the tournaments . . .' He fell silent abruptly, noticing Robert's grimace and Belia's warning gesture. *Of course*, he thought. There was more than he knew. *Such things are not repaid in coin.*

'It would please me more,' Elias went on, chopping at the air with his hand, 'if you forsook this de Montfort and gave your support to the king. He may be a fool and a spendthrift who delights in squeezing us for every penny he can get, but at least he has the law on his side!'

'King Henry?' Robert said, with a scornful laugh. 'He cares nothing for the law. Five years I've been begging the king for the return of what is rightfully mine. Begging him, and his son too, and his councillors and ministers. Nothing have I had in return but insults and sly abuse! If Simon de Montfort offers the possibility of change, and real reform, then I am his man.'

'Then we are at an impasse, my friend,' Elias said, his voice dropping sadly. 'I no longer know what to say to you, if you would sacrifice all that is right, all those who have helped you and supported you, and sheltered you when you had nothing, for the chance of gain.'

'I'm here, aren't I?' Robert growled. 'Here, standing beside you?'

Elias made a fluttering gesture, then turned and paced towards the rear door. Belia remained, hands clasped and head lowered demurely, her white headcloth glowing in the dimness. Only when her brother was gone did she look up.

'Forgive him,' she said quietly.

Adam caught Robert's slight gesture. He glanced at Belia and saw her nod, then he retreated, silent and discreet, to the passageway, and pulled the hall door closed behind him. He went through to the other building, took some food and drink, but did not remove his armour or sword belt. Joane and Petronilla had been given a separate chamber, and he did not wish to disturb them. But he knew he had to remain vigilant.

After about an hour he went back into the passageway of Elias's house. The door was still closed, and there was silence from the hall. Lowered voices, perhaps; Adam leaned a little closer, listening, but then the sense of intrusion felt shameful and he backed away. He went instead to the main door and walked out onto the steps above the yard, meaning to check on the horses.

The night air smelled of smoke. Not the peat and wood fires of houses and hall, but real arson, and none too distant. Shouts came from the street, echoing between the close-packed houses, and when Adam peered up over the low eaves of the hall and the buildings surrounding the courtyard, he saw a pulse of dull orange light in the sky. From the stables he could hear the sounds of horses whinnying and stamping; they would have smelled the smoke already, and heard the angry voices from the city outside, and their nerves were primed and tense.

Dropping down the steps, Adam paused a moment in the yard, staring into the black gullet of the entranceway. Noises of men shouting, coarse laughter. The closed walls and shutters, the cobbled alleys, bounced the sound and made it impossible to say from where it came. He thought he heard the voices of the guards out in the narrow street beyond the heavy sealed gates.

Drawing a long breath, Adam crossed to the stables. In the warm darkness he did what he could to calm the horses, but they could sense his own agitation. The noise of turmoil from the streets was louder now.

A sudden banging came from outside, and every horse in the stable flinched and stamped. Adam darted out into the courtyard again. Drawing his sword, he advanced into the dark passage of the entranceway. Four steps, then six, and he was almost at the gates. They were solid oak, bound and studded with iron and locked shut with a heavy bar. But any gate can be destroyed, given time.

There were men in the lane, he realised as he listened carefully. Where were the guards that Elias had posted there? Fled, he guessed, or already overcome. He saw the flare of torches gleaming through the cracks around the closed gates. Then another crash sounded against the wood, and a surge of pressure from the far side that shunted the gates back against their locking bar. Adam stepped away, raising his weapon. 'Who's there?' he yelled, his voice echoing in the confined passage.

Shouts from outside, raw and jagged in the smoky darkness. *Open, open*, they were yelling. Another flurry of bangs – kicks, perhaps, or the pommel of a sword battering the woodwork. Then another surging blow, shuddering the gates in their mountings; the men outside were throwing themselves at the studded oak, trying to burst the locks. '*Break them down!*' the voices yelled. '*Bring out the Jews!*'

Retreating into the yard, Adam saw something flash above him, and skipped aside as a burning torch dropped to the cobbles. He peered upwards and saw a figure outlined briefly against the dark sky.

'They're on the roof!' he shouted.

Already figures were spilling from the house, dark rushing shapes against the glow of inner light. Again the shuddering crash came from the gates, then a hacking chop and a coarse cheer. The men outside had hammers and axes, he realised. They were going to break the gates down, then surge into the yard and storm the house.

Robert was beside him, lit by the guttering torch that lay on the cobbles. He hefted his war axe.

'So,' he said, and bared his teeth. 'The dogs have caught the scent of blood!'

# Chapter 17

'Never!' Elias cried. 'Absolutely not . . . I will not be driven from my home by a mob . . . by the scum of the gutters!'

'You're not safe here,' Adam said again. 'Neither of you are.'

They were in the main hall, Elias pacing furiously and clasping his head in anguish. They could all hear the sounds of the mob in the street now, the thunder at the gates. Two of the servants were busy gathering the silverware and draperies and bundling them into chests. Belia appeared to be directing them. She flung a glance at Adam. 'And where would we be safe, do you think?' she said, and it sounded like an accusation. 'Where is there safety in this city now? Where, in this whole country?'

'The only safe place is the Tower,' Adam told them, standing in the doorway dressed in mail, with his hand on the hilt of his sword. 'Hugh Despenser is constable there, Robert says he's to be trusted—'

'Trusted, hah!' Elias broke in. 'This is the same Hugh Despenser who not a month ago led a mob around the city burning and plundering the properties of the Earl of Cornwall? The same Hugh Despenser who acts as de Montfort's lieutenant in London? Him we should trust? Better to trust the devil himself!'

'Yes, Hugh Despenser, the justiciar,' Adam said, keeping a tight rein on his voice. In truth he knew nothing of Despenser, and would not be inclined to trust him either. But this was what Robert had decided. 'Please, I beg you,' he said, directing his words now to Belia. 'You must think of your own preservation. Your own lives.'

'You think I'm going to throw away everything that I've built in this city, everything I've achieved after years of effort?' Elias demanded, stabbing his finger at Adam.

'Elias, please,' Belia said in a low voice.

'*No.* I say again *no!*' Elias yelled. 'I will stay here, and die here if the Lord God directs it. I'm not a fighting man but I swear to you I will not go meekly!' He crossed to the table and snatched up a short thick-bladed falchion.

Ignoring her brother, Belia came to the doorway and took Adam by the arm, her fingers clasping the links of his mail. 'What of Robert?' she demanded. 'Will he stay if Elias refuses to leave? If we all refuse to leave?'

'He'll stay if he needs to,' Adam told her. But he knew that Robert had no intention of leaving; his horses were in the stables, his armour and possessions inside the house, and all the wealth he had gained in the tournaments was secured in Elias's strongroom. There was no time to remove it all safely now, and no way he would surrender it without a fight. But Elias and Belia were a different matter; their lives at least could be saved by a swift departure.

'Let me talk to my brother alone,' Belia whispered, her eyes large and black in the shadows. Adam nodded, and turned away at once.

Out in the yard the crashing blows against the gate had doubled in volume. It sounded like the mob outside had brought something to use as a ram. Between each blow came the battering noise of axes and hammers, the cheers and yells of the angry throng.

'I swear to you,' Robert said between his teeth as Adam joined him, 'if they harm any of my horses I'll lay every one of them in his grave, God help me.'

'Elias won't come,' Adam told him. 'Belia might — she's making an effort to persuade him.'

'There's no time for that,' Robert told him, his gaze not shifting from the gateway. 'Take the lady Joane and the other women-folk. Leave through the neighbouring building — with luck those fiends outside won't have turned their attentions to it yet. Go to the Tower by the shortest route. Wilecok will lead you, he knows the streets. When you get there, find Hugh Despenser and tell him he must send men to aid me.'

'How long could you hold out, if they bring down the gates?'

Robert shook his head, hefting his axe. His shield was slung from a strap over his shoulder. 'Not long enough,' he said under his breath. Then he turned to Adam and seized his arm. 'Take Belia with you at least,' he said. 'Take her, and get her to safety! Go now. And may God's light guide you in this darkness!'

Adam found Belia and one of her maids already waiting in the passageway. Before he could ask about Elias, he caught the brief shake of her head. Then he led both women through the doorway into the adjoining building. Joane was in the next chamber, with her own maid Petronilla, and Wilecok and his Gascon wife. Even here, inside the building, they could hear the noise from the street outside. Petronilla was gasping with fear, and Joane was trying to comfort her.

'You'll be certain to come back soon, won't you, and bring plenty of men with you?' Hugh of Oystermouth asked, with a nervous waver to his voice.

Adam answered with a nod; he had no idea what would hap-. pen when they got outside. He passed Hugh the iron-headed mace. 'If anyone comes up those stairs after we're gone,' he told him, 'hit them with that as hard as you can.'

Joane had a leather satchel over her shoulder, which Adam knew contained her Psalter and a few other precious posses-sions. Some of the others carried bags and sacks too. But all

were dressed in dark cloaks and mantles with hoods, and ready
to move quickly if required.

'Wait,' Joane said, as Belia moved for the far door and the narrow wooden stair that led to the street. With one quick gesture
she gripped the panel of pale linen sewn to the woman's mantle
and tore it off.

'I'd forgotten!' Belia said, wide-eyed. 'Thank you . . .' Then
she turned and removed the identifying marking from her maid's
cloak as well.

'Here, take mine instead,' Joane said, 'in case anyone sees the
marks of the torn stitches.' Swiftly and silently she exchanged
cloaks with Belia, and ordered Petronilla to do the same with
the Jewish maid.

'That's her, isn't it?' she whispered to Adam, as the others
began to descend the stairs. 'Robert's lover? He's never said anything about it to me, but somehow I knew.'

'She is,' he told her. In the dimness of the stairway they stood
close together, and he tried to discern any condemnation in her
voice, any judgement. But there was none. Lightly she took his
hand, squeezed his fingers for a moment, then descended to the
street doorway.

Wilecok led the way, out of the house without a word and across
the narrow street to the dark crack of an alleyway opposite. Adam
went last, checking that every hurrying figure had reached the shelter of the alley before crossing himself. He risked a glance to his left,
towards the gates of the courtyard, and was horrified by the size
of the mob gathered before them. Fifty or sixty men at least, all of
them pressing forward with burning torches and cudgels, some with
spears and blades. The noise was a steady growling roar, cut through
with angry shouts, loud in the narrow street. People were leaning
from the windows of the houses opposite as well, some shouting
encouragement while others merely watched in fearful silence.

Adam's blood chilled, but there was nothing he could do.
Before anyone in the crowd noticed him, he hurried on after the

others into the welcoming darkness of the alleyway. Reaching out to touch the grimy bricks and timber walls to either side, they guided themselves towards the faint glow of the next street. As they reached the far end of the alley Wilecok paused and the rest bunched behind him, pressing themselves against the wall to allow Adam through.

'What's happening?' Belia demanded in a harsh whisper, taking his arm.

Adam shrugged, then joined Wilecok and peered around the corner. He drew a hissing breath. Belia hurried up behind him, and he heard her stifle a cry as she saw what lay ahead. 'Hell has broken loose,' he said quietly.

To the right, the street widened as it met the broader expanse of Westcheap. The glow of fire came from that direction; somebody had kindled a great blaze out in the market area, and the flames threw orange light and huge reeling shadows along the street. There were bodies lying on the cobbles, amid a black tracery of spilled blood. One was a woman; a couple more appeared to be children.

Adam's attention was dragged to the left, where the street narrowed between tilting walls of plaster and laths, and another mob had gathered. Torchlight blossomed in the darkness, silhouetting the figures in the street and the broken doorway of the grand-looking house in front of them. The shutters of the upper windows had been flung open, and men inside were hurling out furniture and possessions. A chest fell, shattering on the cobbled street, and the mob cheered. 'Christ killers!' a woman shrieked. 'His blood is on them all!'

With a shock of recognition, Adam saw that the leader of the gang was Sir John FitzJohn, the young nobleman he had first seen with de Montfort's retinue in France years before. There were other knights with him, and armed serjeants too; the realisation gripped Adam with a steely sense of horror. He had assumed that the rioters, the killers, were faceless members of the urban mob.

But there were knights and squires among them, men just like Adam himself. Shame twisted in his gut as he remembered the stories he had heard and believed about the Jews, only a couple of short years before. Would he have condoned such violence once? Might he even have participated in it? The idea was sickening.

'What are they doing?' Joane demanded, pushing past Wilecok and leaning around the corner of the alleyway. Adam took her arm to draw her back.

'That's Koch's house,' Belia whispered. 'Koch, son of Abraham . . . Oh God, please don't let them take him . . .'

Her prayers were too late. The gang before the house had seized their prey and were dragging him between them into the circle of their torches. The victim was a man of Elias's age, clad only in a linen nightshirt. One of the persecutors ripped it from his shoulders; others struck at him with sticks and ox goads. John FitzJohn was pushing through the throng, and Adam could see the knife gripped low in his hand. In the warping light flung by the torches, the faces of the surrounding men were hideous masks, distorted with hatred.

'I've come to pay my debts to you, as you asked!' FitzJohn snarled. 'Here they are, paid in full!' With his left hand he gripped the man by the throat and slammed him back against the wall. Then he stepped in closer and drove the knife several times into his victim's belly, his elbow pumping as he stabbed.

Belia let out a wailing cry and flung herself from the alleyway, as if she were about to run to the dying man's aid. Adam blocked her with his arm, clasping her tightly and dragging her back into the sheltering dark. Joane was still watching, her hands pressed over her mouth. She took a step forward, out into the street. 'Mistress, be careful!' Wilecok told her, gesturing for her to get out of sight.

'We have to go, we have to go quickly,' Belia's maid was saying in a fervent whisper. 'There are men coming behind us, in the alleyway — we have to move!'

'She's right, there's nothing we can do here,' Adam said, feeling the helplessness pooling inside him like cold oil. Belia was still struggling in his arms, but abruptly her body slackened and he released her. The alleyway was black behind him, but he could hear the noise of approaching footsteps. Retreat was impossible. There was no way they could evade the crowd to their left, who were now pushing through the broken doors and into the house of the murdered Koch.

Wilecok was staring back at the broken doorway, the bodies sprawled on the ground, his mouth slack with disgust. Several of the rioters were still kicking and beating the body of the murdered man. Adam gripped him by the shoulder.

'We have to get to the Tower, as quickly as we can,' he said. 'Which is the most direct route from here?'

'That way,' Wilecok said, pointing to the right, towards West-cheap. 'Open streets all the way, but it's faster than skulking in alleys.'

Trying not to run and draw attention to themselves, they paced quickly towards the fiery glow of the market, skirting the bodies and the blood that ran in runnels between the cobblestones. Joane slipped as her shoe slid beneath her, and Adam took her arm and helped her upright. But they had only gained half the distance to the next corner before the opening into Westcheap filled with the dark shapes of men, weapons in their hands.

'What's this?' a loud voice cried. 'More of the vermin trying to flee!'

The figures were all around them now, made huge by the shadows they threw ahead of them. One of the men, barely more than a youth, carried a flaming brand, and he flourished it at Belia and her maid as they pressed themselves against the brick wall behind them. Another man, stout and red-faced, seized Petronilla by the arm, and the Flemish woman cowered away from him and let out a shriek.

'Take your hands off her,' Joane demanded, throwing herself between her maid and the man who held her.

'That's a Jewish cape she's wearing!' the youth with the torch cried, bringing his flame closer. 'See there – she's ripped off the tabs!'

'Take them all! They're all Jews!' another man yelled. 'Make them say the Paternoster!' growled another. 'Strip them!' shouted a third, his voice slurred by drunkenness. 'Strip them and whip them!'

The red-faced man flung Petronilla away from him and seized Joane instead, gripping her cloak and screwing it into his fist as he dragged her towards him. His teeth were bared in a snarl – but already the tip of Adam's sword was at his throat.

'Release her,' Adam said, holding the naked blade extended. 'Release her now or you die.'

The red-faced man's mouth fell slack, and for three heartbeats the sight of the long blade gleaming in the torchlight stilled the men around them too. Joane tugged at her cloak and freed herself from the man's grip.

'Adam de Norton,' someone said from the darkness. He had not spoken before, but his voice was instantly familiar. Adam stepped back, keeping his sword raised and at the ready. The red-faced man who had seized Joane was backing away from him.

Then the youth with the torch moved his arm, and the guttering light fell on the figure of Richard de Malmaines. 'They're Jews, sir,' the youth said to him, the torch in his fist scattering sparks as he brandished it. 'Some of them are at least, I know it!'

'We are good Christian folk, just like you,' Wilecok replied. He was pressed back against the wall with Petronilla and his Gascon wife. 'You must let us pass!'

'I believe Adam de Norton is a Christian at least,' de Malmaines said. 'Although at times he does not act like one.' He too had a drawn sword, Adam noticed. In the fiery glow, the blade shone dark with blood.

'Best let them proceed,' de Malmaines went on. 'But they should hurry to safety, I think – this is no time to be admiring the stars.'

Adam kept his gaze on de Malmaines. He took a long step back, lowering his sword, then slipped it back into his scabbard. With a gesture, he ordered Wilecok to lead the party on down the street. 'I don't know what you think you're doing,' he told de Malmaines, 'but I see nothing Christian here.'

Richard de Malmaines made a dismissive gesture, then ordered his men on up the street to join the mob engaged in plundering the house of Koch. Adam saw him wiping his blade on a rag and tossing it aside, then he and those with him were lost in the swirl of milling bodies, the flickering light of the torches and the reeling smoke.

There were more fires burning on Westcheap, broken furniture and torn fabrics heaped together with the charred remains of document chests and rolls of records, and left to blaze. More dead lay here too, laid out in neat lines on the greasy paving stones or sprawling one upon another where they had been thrown by their murderers. Men, women and children lay together; whole families wiped out by the fury of the attackers. Many of the dead had been stripped naked, either before or after death.

Joane stood by the street corner, eyes wide, aghast at what she was seeing. 'Who ordered this?' she asked Adam, her voice catching. 'Surely not Simon de Montfort? Who is leading these people?'

Adam shook his head. 'I think only the devil rules tonight,' he said.

Joane pressed a fold of her cloak over her mouth and nodded. Belia and her maid had already hurried on towards Poultry, their hoods pulled up to cover their faces; by the time Adam and Joane caught up with them, they had been joined by a hunched boy of twelve or thirteen, dressed only in linen braies.

'His name is Mosse,' Belia told Adam. 'He's the apothecary's son – if they catch him, they'll kill him . . . he must come with us!'

'Of course,' Adam said, reaching for the brooch at his shoulder. 'Here, he can cover himself with my cloak.'

'No, he can use mine,' said Wilecok, his voice sounding choked. He threw off his voluminous grey mantle and tossed it to the boy. Adam realised that the servant had been deeply affected by what he had seen. Once Mosse had covered himself they formed up once more and set off again, eastwards into the city.

Even here, outside the set limits of the Jewish district, there were angry shouts in the street, weaving torchlight and the sounds of running feet and violent struggle. The night air was charged with smoke, the glow of the flames fogged, and the streets had a gaudy nightmarish quality as they passed through them, like a painting of the inferno. Crossing the greasy cobbles around Stock's Market they entered Langburn Street. Wilecok was leading them along at a jog, halting at every few cross-streets to check the way ahead and ensure they were taking the right path. Beyond St Mary Woolnoth the crowd in the street thickened once more, and again they heard shouts of anger and whoops of savage mirth, the crash of breaking shutters.

'They're attacking the foreigners,' Wilecok said over his shoulder. 'Attacking the Cahorsins and the Lombards, the money-men. Silly bastards!'

Sure enough, the crowd ahead were busily engaged in sacking one wealthy-looking property. A boy in a ragged tunic was leaning from an upper window, yelling into the night. '*Kill all the foreigners! Death to the Jews and the Lombards!*'

'Who are you?' a tall rawboned man in the street demanded, as Adam and Wilecok approached. 'Speak English?' he barked. 'Identify yourselves!'

Adam was in no mood for discussion. He threw back his hood, then drew his sword and raised it before him. 'This is all the identification I need,' he said.

At the sight of the blade, and the mail armour exposed beneath his cloak, the crowd parted. The women followed quickly behind him, and Adam heard the gang in the street mutter and hiss as they passed. He had spoken to them in English, the local dialect too, but he knew they still suspected him. This was not a night to be a stranger on the streets of London.

*

They moved faster after that, breaking into a run whenever the streets were clear enough, and the noise of their footsteps was an echoing clatter in the darkness. Then abruptly the houses fell away to either side of them and they were running in bright moonlight along a dirt track that crossed open ground. The breeze carried the scent of the river's mud, and ahead rose the vast white keep of the Tower of London with its ring of walls and drum towers, ghostly beneath a near-full moon.

A wooden trestle bridge spanned the moat. At the far end was the sentinel tower that stood before the main gatehouse, and before its arched entrance the drawbridge was raised. Adam ran out onto the wooden planking of the bridge, calling to the sentries that he knew must be watching him from the blank slits above the gateway.

'Lower the drawbridge!' he cried, near breathless. 'Lower the drawbridge and allow us entry – my name is Adam de Norton, and I have an urgent message for the constable, Hugh Despenser!'

No reply came from the tower. Adam stood at the brink of the wooden bridge, the muddy water of the moat lost in a gulf of blackness beneath him. He could see a light moving inside the tower, the glow reflected by the archway. Joane and Belia followed him onto the bridge, their cloaks wrapped around them, and their footsteps made a hollow thudding on the planks.

'How many are you?' a voice called from the sentinel tower.

'There are seven of us,' Adam replied. 'No – eight,' he said, remembering Mosse. 'Some of my companions are Jews from the city – they need sanctuary.'

Even as he spoke, the dread mounted inside him, cold and sickening. What if Elias had been correct? What if the slaughter of the Jews really had been ordered by Simon de Montfort? Taking Belia and the others to the Tower would be a death sentence. Just for a moment he pictured them dragged away beneath the gate arches and butchered, their bodies flung in the moat . . .

A cry came from behind him, and Adam looked back to see torches moving in the dark streets surrounding the tower. As he stared he saw running figures appearing in the moonlit open ground, and heard their angry shouts. '*They have a child with them!*' a voice called out. '*The Jews have stolen a child!*' There were many of them, some with weapons in their hands, and they were closing in fast.

Adam turned again and stared up at the sentinel tower. No light showed from within it now. The great fortress beyond was silent under the moon.

Joane stepped up beside him and threw back her hood. 'I am Joane de Quincy, niece of Earl Roger of Winchester!' she cried. 'Hugh Despenser is my cousin — open the gates at once!'

There was a gruff shout from inside the gatehouse, and a moment later the drawbridge groaned, cables straining against counterweights, and began to descend.

'Is everyone your cousin?' Adam asked, mystified.

'Most people turn out to be, in some way,' Joane replied.

As the heavy timbers dropped into place, Adam glanced behind him at the mob of pursuers — some fell back in dismay, while others began to run faster, yelling as their prey escaped them. Adam waited until his small band had crossed beneath the arch of the sentinel tower, and then followed them along the short causeway to the main gatehouse. Behind him he could hear the drawbridge already shuddering upwards once more. There was a knight commanding the gatehouse, a grim-faced man in a white surcoat scored with a black diagonal, and Adam repeated his statement.

'Jews, eh?' the knight said, peering dubiously at Belia, Mosse and the maid. 'There's a fair few of them in here already. Don't see that three more would cause difficulties. Bring them!' he ordered, gesturing as he strode on beneath the double arches of the gatehouse and the raised teeth of the portcullis. 'We've sent a runner to find Sir Hugh, my lady,' he told Joane, in a far more respectful tone.

Through the echoing blackness of the gate passage, they entered the moonlit expanse of the outer ward. Ahead of him Adam saw the keep, the White Tower, larger and more formidable than any castle fortification he had ever seen. They were following a dirt path towards the inner gatehouse, which huddled beneath the flank of the great tower itself.

In the shadow of the inner gates the knight paused, raising his hand. There were men gathered beneath the arches, several wearing mail and carrying shields. Adam and Joane halted, enveloped by the blackness. The others were bunched behind them, all of them waiting in tensed anticipation.

'I would not have said anything back there,' Joane said in a hurried whisper. 'I would have preferred to remain anonymous if I could – but it seemed the only way.'

'I understand,' Adam replied. 'You did the right thing.' He was aware that they were standing very close, and the darkness hid them completely. Adam sensed her movement towards him, then the distance closed between them. She kissed him, and for two stilled heartbeats he felt lifted, suspended in that breathless pause. Then a shout came from the inner gateway, the noise of footsteps, and quickly they slipped apart from each other.

Torches flared, throwing wheeling shadows around the stone-lined passageway, and the guards parted as a trio of men came striding through from the inner ward.

'Joane de Quincy!' a voice cried, booming beneath the arches. 'It's been years since I saw you last, cousin – I pray to God your uncle is here with you!'

'I'm afraid not, Sir Hugh,' Joane replied, drawing herself upright and shrugging back her dark cloak. 'Earl Roger remains on his estates. It was Adam de Norton here who escorted me.'

'A shame, a shame.' Hugh Despenser was a middle-aged man with a look of stern assurance. His flinty gaze fell briefly on Adam, then veered away. 'We have need of Roger de Quincy's support,' he said to Joane, 'and of his men.'

'Is this really Adam de Norton I see?' another voice said. A figure appeared in the gate passage, silhouetted for a moment against the glow of the torches. 'God's blessings upon you!'

The newcomer stepped from the darkness, and Adam saw the face of Sir Humphrey de Bohun, the son of the Earl of Hereford, gleaming in the fiery light. 'I thank you,' he said to Adam with a glad smile, seizing Joane by both hands, 'for delivering my betrothed to me!'

# Chapter 18

They rode out through the gate and crossed the moat at a canter, the hooves of their horses drumming on the bridge timbers. Humphrey de Bohun was in the lead, armoured in mail and mounted on a caparisoned warhorse. Adam rode behind him, on a borrowed rouncey. Three other squires of de Bohun's retinue followed, with four mounted serjeants bringing up the rear, all of them armed and equipped for battle. Across the bridge the nine riders spread out into a column, crossing the moonlit open ground and plunging into the darkness of the city streets.

Sir Humphrey had been adamant that he would lead the expedition himself. 'Besieged by a city mob, eh?' he had said, once Adam had repeated his news. 'Robert de Dunstanville was never one for the more ordinary dangers!'

Joane de Quincy could only watch, blank-faced, as they prepared to depart. Adam could not bring himself to meet her eye. Belia had vanished into the darkness even before Hugh Despenser had made his appearance; Adam saw her shortly afterwards, amid a crowd of other Jewish refugees from the city who had thronged around her desperate for news. Their groans and wails filled the night as Adam followed Humphrey to the stables. De Bohun's own horse and those of his men were already saddled and bridled; he had heard word of trouble in the city and taken due precautions.

'I do not ask, you understand,' he said to Adam, as his squires dressed him in his mail hauberk and surcoat, 'why it was that you and Robert brought Joane de Quincy to London. Or how it was that you came to be sheltering in the Jewry, or that you came to escort her here to the Tower. I do not ask these things.'

Adam had merely frowned in the darkness, as he checked the saddle girths and tack of the horse that had been allotted to him.

'I merely thank God that she is safe,' Humphrey went on, buckling his sword belt. 'And hope that I can prove myself worthy of her approval.'

'You're doing this to *impress* her?' Adam asked, pausing with his foot in the stirrup.

'No, I'm doing this to *deserve* her,' Humphrey replied. With a creak of leather and a crunch of mail he swung himself up into the high-cantled saddle of his warhorse. 'We all must strive to be worthy of great rewards!' he declared boldly, as the horse stamped and pawed the ground beneath him. 'Lord Simon has shown me this – his is the path of virtue and righteousness. Only by following that path, and daring to become a better man, can I deserve to win the hand of a woman like Joane de Quincy.'

Amazed and appalled, Adam turned his face away as he climbed into the saddle. Had Humphrey de Bohun really transformed himself into a chivalric champion? Was the reckless and cruel-tempered nobleman that Adam remembered from his youth now utterly dispelled? He could not bring himself to believe that the change was as deep or as sincere as it appeared. But his heart was crushed at the thought that Joane was now delivered entirely into this man's power, and into his possession. And that he himself had been the agent of that delivery.

But as they rode out from the Tower, the night air loud in his ears and the feel of the powerful horse beneath him, Adam felt his anguish charged with a new and fervent energy. He may have failed Joane, but he could yet rescue Robert. Sir Humphrey was keeping his horse to a steady trot as they moved through the narrow streets, ensuring that their column did not become split up or too bunched together in the confined spaces of the city. Adam wanted more than anything to set spurs to his horse and thunder forward, but he knew that Humphrey was doing the right thing. In places they found crowds gathering in the streets, but the people shrank back against the walls at the noise of the hooves.

Along Candlewright Street they rode in their tight column, keeping to the wider thoroughfares wherever possible. Adam felt the anticipation of confrontation, of violence, like a heat through his body. A fierce anger too: if anyone stood against him he would strike them down without hesitation. If Richard de Malmaines or John FitzJohn dared confront him, he would do everything in his power to destroy them.

Humphrey signalled to the right and they swung into a narrower lane, pedestrians shrieking as they flung themselves back against the walls in terror of the hooves and the clash of armour. A few moments of speeding darkness, walls and shutters flying by only a hand's breadth from his head, and suddenly Adam found himself bursting forth into the open expanse of Westcheap. The fires were still burning, and the bodies still lay strewn on the cobbles. Knots of men lingered in the mouths of streets, most with weapons in their hands, and they cheered and waved as they saw the horsemen and the bright caparisons.

'Which way?' Humphrey bellowed, circling his horse in the centre of the market area.

Adam stared around him, confused for a moment in the darkness and the wavering firelight. 'There!' he cried, pointing to the mouth of the familiar lane, then without waiting for Humphrey and his men he rode on towards it. Reaching down to his hip, he drew his sword.

As he approached Elias's property, he thought for a terrible moment that all was lost. The gates were broken, battered from their hinges and dragged aside, and the mob that had gathered before them had pushed forward into the entranceway and the yard beyond. Enough of them still remained in the street to raise a cheer as Adam came riding towards them, and then to scatter in sudden panic before his charge.

'Get back! Stand clear!' Adam was yelling, hauling on the reins and circling his horse before the broken gates, his sword levelled. He doubted anyone could hear him above the baying roar coming from the entrance passage, where men stood packed together like a bung in the neck of a jar. That at least was cause for hope – they had not yet pressed their attack into the yard, or the house itself.

One of de Bohun's serjeants rode up alongside, and Adam handed the reins to him and threw himself from the saddle. As the rest of de Bohun's company came to a champing whinnying halt in the narrow lane, Adam plunged forward into the mob blocking the yard entrance. He hoped that there were others at his back, but his sole desire was to break through and find Robert. Yelling inarticulately, brandishing his sword above his head, he forged forward with elbow and fist, trusting to his armour to keep him safe and give him the weight and momentum to break through.

Blows hammered at him from either side. The darkness was packed with screaming faces, bared teeth and flying spittle. Adam brought the pommel of his sword cracking down on one piglike face, and it dropped at once into the thresh of bodies and stamping feet. Jabbing with his blade, he goaded the men ahead of him, stumbling after them as they shoved to escape him. These were Englishmen, he told himself – in theory, he was on the same side as them. But the thought vanished at once, and he surged forward with murderous rage in his blood. And suddenly he was through, into a flare of lamplight and a sea of milling bodies.

Robert was on the steps of the hall above him, fully armoured with his shield raised, his axe gripped in his fist. John Chyld crouched beside him, a loaded crossbow resting on the wooden railing and aimed down into the press of men filling the yard. Adam saw Elias behind them in the doorway, clutching his falchion. The tide that had poured in through the gateway had broken at the foot of the stairs and fallen back in angry confusion. Several bodies lay sprawled in the cobbled yard; several other men were wounded, crying out for aid. The smoke of the torches fogged the air, and from the stables came the noise of panicking horses.

How long the situation had been this way Adam could not tell. Robert had the stolid look of a man who had been holding his ground for some time. The mob packed into the courtyard surged and ebbed, some of them pushing forward up the steps with spears and cudgels and then falling back as Robert lashed at them with the flat of his blade. Others had dug up cobblestones and were hurling them; Adam saw one crack off Robert's shield, another strike the wall behind him. Every window in the hall was broken already.

Beside him, Adam saw a man raising a bow, arrow nocked. He jammed his left arm forward, seizing the bowstave and pushing it upwards. The bowman released his arrow with a jerk, and it sailed off over the roof of the hall. Then Adam rammed his elbow back into the man's face and knocked him down.

'Robert!' he cried, raising his sword. '*A Dunstanville! A Dunstanville!*'

Standing halfway down the steps, swinging his axe at anyone who dared advance against him, Robert heard the cry and glanced up. Adam saw a grim smile light his face.

From behind him he heard the tumult from the entranceway. The bellowed voices of the serjeants, '*A Bohun! A Bohun!*'

Then screams, and a panic of bodies scrambling for safety. Iron hooves rang in the confined passage, and Humphrey de Bohun came riding on through into the yard, his mail armour gleaming gold in the torchlight, the blue and white trappings of his horse swirling as he circled and came to a halt. He raised his sword, threatening to strike. But the men in the yard were flinching away from him, pushing against the walls and sliding towards the entranceway before bolting back out into the street against the incoming rush of de Bohun's serjeants and squires. Adam scrambled up onto the stairs to stand beside Robert. But the battle was already won.

*

'You didn't see it,' Adam said. 'You didn't see it, and I did, and so of course you think differently.'

'I saw enough,' Robert replied. 'I saw that mob pouring into Elias's courtyard, intent on all the world's rage and fury. I held them off myself for half the night, until you and de Bohun finally showed up. Broke more than a few heads too.'

Four days had passed since the night of violence. And for those four days, Robert had sat alone, drinking Elias's wine in sullen silence, as if he had wrapped himself in a dark cloak. Now it was the afternoon of Palm Sunday. They had been out exercising the horses on St Giles' Fields, north of the city walls, and as they rode back towards Cripplegate Adam was determined to take this opportunity finally to speak about what had happened.

'But you didn't see the killings,' he said, leaning from the saddle to rub his horse's neck. 'You didn't see corpses lying in the streets – men and women, children too . . .'

'You think I don't know what blood and slaughter looks like?' Robert snarled, rounding on him. 'You think I haven't lived in the world? The things I've seen would surprise you, boy.'

'And you were not at St Paul's this morning,' Adam went on, undeterred. 'You didn't see Simon de Montfort with John Fitz-John.'

Lord Simon had returned to London the day before, and he had taken the place of greatest honour in the Palm Sunday

procession that morning. And there beside de Montfort, walking
beneath the swaying willow branches as the priests carried the
sacramental altar towards the church doors, was John FitzJohn,
whom Adam had last seen knifing an elderly Jewish moneylender
to death with his own hand.

Upon his arrival in the city, de Montfort had issued a procla-
mation that the Jews of London were not to be further harmed
or assaulted, and those who had taken shelter at the Tower were
free to leave and return to their homes. Few, Adam believed, had
taken him at his word. Only that day they had heard news from
Canterbury that Gilbert de Clare's men had attacked the Jewish
community there too, plundering and burning records, killing
any who got in their way. Elias himself had gone to the Tower in
a grim mood, to celebrate the Jewish festival of Passover with
Belia and the others of their community still sheltering there.
He had barely spoken to Robert before leaving, so great was his
anguish.

All this, Adam thought, and still there had been no condemnation for FitzJohn, nor for Richard de Malmaines or any of
those others who had joined them on their cavalcade of bloody
destruction and murder.

'None can be ignorant of what those men did,' Adam went on,
more forcibly. 'Hundreds of innocent people slain – and Lord
Simon embraces them as friends—'

'And what else would you have him do?' Robert broke in,
exasperated, as he turned in his saddle. 'He needs all the support
he can get.'

'Even bloody-handed murderers and thieves?' Adam
demanded. 'And that's not all – Hugh of Oystermouth says—'

'Oh, Hugh of Oystermouth is a sponge for every vicious
rumour,' Robert said, interrupting again. 'I'm thinking I should
be rid of him, and his prattling tongue.'

'Hugh of Oystermouth says,' Adam repeated, 'that Lord
Simon forced FitzJohn and the others to hand over most of what

they'd stolen from the Jews to him. And so he not only forgives them, but makes himself culpable in their crimes.'

'And if he'd cut off their heads instead, what then?' Robert cried, reining his horse to a stand. 'Who would have cheered him?'

Over to their left, in the open ground between the track and the city wall, a mob of young men were running and struggling together, hurling and kicking a ball between them. For a few moments the sounds of their riotous laughter drifted across the field. Quite possibly, Adam thought, those same young men had joined in the attacks on the Jews a few nights beforehand. Sure enough, they would not have relished anyone exacting justice on those responsible. But whenever he closed his eyes, Adam saw the flickering torchlight and the hate-filled faces, the knife in the hand of John FitzJohn as he stabbed again and again . . .

'Listen,' Robert went on. 'Earl Simon has a diverse set of supporters. We don't have to call them our friends, certainly. But neither do we have to make them our enemies. Not yet.'

'But what is Lord Simon's cause, if not truth and justice?' Adam cried, the heat rising to his face. 'How can any cause, any man, be worth fighting for if you must fight alongside murderers and thieves?'

'I'm not fighting for Simon de Montfort!' Robert replied, his voice close to a shout. Adam saw his fists clenching as he gripped the reins. 'Maybe it's true what they say about him – maybe he really is a seducer and a deceiver, and will lead us all to hell with his fine words. No, it's not for his glory or fame that I'm doing this, but for my own!'

'And your honour?' Adam demanded, unable to hold back. 'What about that?'

'*Honour!*' Robert scoffed. He flung out a hand towards the mob playing their ball game. 'Do you think they care about our precious *honour*? Do you think Elias or Belia care about it?'

Adam bit back a reply. Suddenly the anger mounting in his throat made it hard for him to speak, and he did not trust himself to curb his bitter rage.

'If you wanted to be truly honourable,' Robert went on, with a sour grin, 'you would take yourself away from this world and live like an anchorite, where nothing can corrupt you. Honour is worth nothing when you have nothing, do you understand? What use is it, if nobody knows of it?'

'You really believe that, after all you've told me?' Adam managed to say.

Robert shrugged heavily. 'Glory and fame, now – that is worth something. To be renowned in the eyes of one's peers, and rewarded for one's great deeds – that,' he said, raising a finger, 'is the only true victory in this world. You win a good name for yourself, and everything else follows. Lands and security, wealth and prosperity.'

'And love?' Adam said. 'The respect of your friends?'

He saw the barb cut deep. Robert flinched slightly, and turned away from him.

Adam watched him ride on along the path, but for a moment he held back from following. Something caught his eye, away to the right. A whirling scrap of darkness in the air, falling in a swooping dive. Two young men, sons of city burghers Adam guessed, were training a young kestrel with a lure. Abruptly his thoughts veered, and he recognised that his black mood had not been provoked by Robert alone.

Joane de Quincy had been in the congregation at St Paul's that morning too. She had remained at the Tower these last four days, a guest of Hugh Despenser and his wife, and Adam had not heard a word from her. He had not seen her during the procession either, but once they were inside the cathedral he had searched for her as he stood among the crowd of lesser men at the back of the nave. He glimpsed her at last as the priests were singing the Passion; she was kneeling with a group of other ladies, the wives and daughters of barons and magnates, all of them dressed in their finest clothes of silk and samite and fur-trimmed velvet. As he stared she glanced back and their eyes met across the packed bodies of the congregation. At that moment he felt a pulse of feeling, of deep understanding, pass between them, then she mouthed something silently and shook her head.

Outside the cathedral, he had waited in a place where she could not fail to see him, and as she passed with her group of ladies he saw her eye glide over him and catch for a moment. But then she looked away, as if she could not bring herself to acknowledge him again. Had she surrendered to her fate, Adam wondered, and inured herself to marriage with Humphrey de Bohun? Or was she merely avoiding him to protect them both from the wrath of her uncle? Either way, the distance that had grown between them, after their brief unexpected intimacy beneath the gatehouse of the Tower, ached in his heart.

Robert had paused on the track ahead of him, and as Adam rode to catch up he turned in the saddle and addressed him once more.

'Very well,' he said. The heat had died out of his voice. 'I have not lived a good life. I confess it. You think I'm a cynic but I'm worse than that – I'm a liar.'

Adam halted beside him, fighting down the urge to reply. He could see how difficult Robert was finding it to speak, how choked with bitter feeling he was.

'I lie to myself and to everyone close to me,' Robert said, grinding the words in his throat. 'I make love to a woman who is not my wife, knowing that it could bring shame on her, and I can offer her nothing in return . . . But I swore an oath,' he said, rounding on Adam with sudden passion, 'before we returned to England. I swore that I would not hear mass, nor make confession or accept absolution, until I had regained possession of the lands that were taken from me. I would live in a state of sin, at the peril of my soul.'

Adam drew a sharp breath. He opened his mouth to speak, but Robert raised a hand to silence him. 'Because only then, if I win what I seek,' he went on, 'can I help those I love. If I had my lands back again – my own home, my own roof and hearth – then Belia could come with me and live as my wife. None would know she wasn't Christian, and she could feign it if needed . . .'

His words broke off, and he looked away. Adam felt sure that he had not explained this plan to Belia herself, and certainly he would never have mentioned it to Elias. Embarrassment coursed through him. For the first time in all the months and years he had known him, Adam found himself pitying Robert de Dunstanville.

'So, there you have it,' Robert said briskly, as if shrugging off the weight of difficult feelings. 'I fight to regain what's mine, and for what I love, and that is all. And I'm set too far down that road to turn back now. But if you no longer wish to follow then say the word and I'll release you.'

'Release me?' Adam asked, his brow creasing. He felt a sour wash down his throat.

'From your oath to me, your indenture,' Robert said, flinging out his hand. 'You no longer need be my squire. I told you once before that I wanted no unwilling followers – I can't compel you to fight for de Montfort if your conscience will not abide it.'

'You'd simply release me, just like that?' Adam asked him. He was fighting with a sense of painful disappointment that he had never expected to feel. From somewhere behind him he heard the whoops and yells of the ball players, and they sounded like mocking laughter. 'After everything we've done?'

Robert looked at him, his gaze flat and empty. 'What more can I give you?'

'You know what I want!' Adam cried, his voice catching in his throat. 'I want to be a knight – you could offer me that at least!'

'Knighthood?' de Dunstanville said, narrowing his eyes. 'You think it's really such an easy gift? You have to earn it, boy!'

He spurred his horse forward, and Adam started angrily after him. 'You don't think I've earned it already?' he called.

De Dunstanville rode on a short way, then reined in his mount and circled back. Adam glared at him; he was surprised to see the look of intense concentration on his face, something close to anguish.

'Understand this,' Robert said. 'The day you are knighted is the most sacred of your life. More sacred than marriage. It should be done right. In public, where all can see and accept it and none can ever dispute the right. And you should be knighted by a man of honour. A man you can truly respect and follow, to whom you can give your sword.'

He turned his horse again. 'I haven't earned the right to bestow that on you,' he said with grim emphasis. 'Until my war is won, and I have what is mine restored to me, I cannot do anything for you, or for Belia and Elias either. I cannot bestow honour on anyone. I have none of my own to give.'

Adam was unable to look him in the eye. The older man's outburst had left him feeling hollow and strangely ashamed, as if he had provoked it. Words he wanted to say shaped themselves in his mind, but he could not give them speech. Robert was walled with pride, and Adam knew that anything he said would summon only furious scorn in response.

But there was more that he wanted to express. Even as Robert spoke, Adam had realised how much he desired the noble chivalrous struggle that Simon de Montfort had so often promised. Even after all that he had seen and done over these last two years, still he desired the shining prize of knighthood, not as a mere transaction but as something truly won. In his mind he heard Humphrey de Bohun's words, that night they rode from the Tower; yes, he thought, he too wanted to strive to be worthy of great rewards. Even if he had to fight alongside monstrous men like John FitzJohn and Richard de Malmaines, this was the fight he desired, the challenge he wanted to take up. But, like Robert, he would not be fighting for the glory of Simon de Montfort. *For what's mine, and for what I love. And that is all.*

The bells of London were ringing, and when Adam glanced in the direction of Cripplegate he saw Hugh of Oystermouth trotting along the path towards them, his face shaded by his broad-brimmed hat. He wore a little cross of willow sticks pinned to his tunic.

'I come with tidings!' the Welshman called out, reining his pony to a halt beside them. 'No, real tidings this time,' he added, noticing Robert's dark look. 'The sort you might wish to know as soon as possible, I thought . . .'

'Go on,' Robert told him. Adam felt the heat of their argument still lingering in the air around them, but Hugh appeared completely oblivious to it.

'The king is still at Nottingham,' he said, slightly breathless, 'but he's ordered the Earl of Surrey and Roger de Leyburne to seize the castle at Rochester and hold it in his name . . .'

'The Earl of Surrey?' Robert said. 'That's John de Warenne. And de Leyburne's with him too? They know how to fight, at least, and they know the ways of war.'

'Gilbert de Clare,' Hugh went on, 'has already marched against them with his Kentish men and Henry de Hastings, and now Simon de Montfort has called a general muster in Southwark for tomorrow morning, just after matins. He's declared that he'll march to support de Clare, and together they'll take Rochester.'

Adam flicked his attention between Hugh and Robert, watching the older man's expression harden, his gaze sharpen. Roger de Leyburne, he remembered, was one of the knights who had accompanied Lord Edward, and mocked Robert before the tournament at Lagny years ago.

'Then by God, we'll have some fighting soon enough,' Robert breathed. 'Real fighting, I mean – with honed steel, and an enemy in front of us.'

'And we'll be joining Lord Simon, I suppose?' Hugh asked, with a hopeful lift in his voice.

Robert turned to Adam, his saddle creaking beneath him, a question in his eyes. Adam took only a moment to consider. But the answer was already clear.

'Yes,' he said. 'Yes, we will.'

# PART THREE

# Chapter 19

It was the morning of Good Friday when they stormed the bridge for the second time. Across the river, the keep of Rochester Castle was ashen against a smoke-black sky. All night and half the previous day the town beyond it had burned, until the dawn rain dampened the fires. None could say who had set the blaze; it was either Gilbert de Clare's men attacking from the south, or the defenders trying to repel them. Now half of Rochester was a smouldering ruin. But the castle still held strong within its circuit of powerful walls, and Simon de Montfort's army was trapped on the wrong side of the river.

A single bridge spanned the tidal reach of the Medway, and the king's men had torn the wooden superstructure from the middle of it, leaving two of the old stone piers jutting up like rotten teeth from the water. With the timbers, they had fortified the remaining spur of the bridge on the Rochester side of the river, surrounding it with bulwarks and garrisoning it with archers, slingers and crossbowmen to command the crossing. Already the projecting end of the bridge opposite them bristled like a thorn-bush with arrows and bolts.

From the lee of an abandoned building, Adam watched the assault party forming up in a dense column. Most were men of the London militia, stiffened with serjeants and spearmen of the baronial retinues, and a band of Simon de Montfort's own troops. Leading them was John FitzJohn, distinctive in his red and yellow quartered surcoat.

'He might be the devil's own bastard,' Hugh of Oystermouth said, narrowing his eyes, 'but there's no doubting his courage.'

Adam said nothing. Many of the men in the assault party had been drinking all night, while others laboured with adze, saw and mallet, and in the bleary light of dawn they appeared half crazed. They had seen the previous attempt to storm the bridge fail the evening before, and knew what they faced. Courage was not lacking in any of them.

With a great stamping of feet the column surged out onto the remaining length of the wooden bridge, those in the lead hefting big wicker screens before them, the rest bearing overhead the crudely constructed platforms they would use to try and span the gap. Adam saw FitzJohn near the front, urging them on. Part of him willed the man to fall, shot down by a chance arrow. But a greater part of him knew that unless the crossing was taken, de Montfort's campaign would falter and die right here on the riverbank.

As soon as the advancing column approached the broken end of the bridge, the bowmen and slingers on the far side released their first sleeting volley. Impossible to miss such a target; at once the wicker screens and the raised shields of the leading men were battered by arrows, quarrels and stones, and the advance stalled abruptly. Adam saw men drop, either wounded or dead, to be carried back by their comrades. One or two tumbled from the bridge and plummeted into the muddy waters below. But still the fraying mass of troops pushed forward, until they reached the brink of the broken section.

Breath held tight, Adam watched as the gang of men at the front of the column stumbled and swayed, manhandling the heavy timbers forward and edging them out over the gulf as the arrows spat down.

'There he is, look,' Hugh said, nodding to his right, and Adam tore his gaze from the distant turmoil on the bridge. Following the herald's gesture, he caught the blaze of blood-red banners through the damp morning drizzle. Simon de Montfort was riding along the riverbank, accompanied by his household knights. At the bridgehead Lord Simon reined in his horse and stood up tall in the stirrups, watching the struggles of the men at the brink of the broken section as they tried to wrestle the timbers into place.

'They say,' said Hugh in an undertone, 'that he's developing a cunning stratagem for taking the bridge, if this assault should fail. Supposedly he has a *secret weapon*.'

Adam raised an eyebrow, dubious. But Hugh pursed his lips, and did not seem inclined to say more. A flash of light came from across the Medway, and Adam turned to see the sun gleaming through a gap in the clouds, lighting the tall castle keep and the banners that flew from its towers. Squinting, he picked out the red and gold of the king, the blue of Roger de Leyburne, the blue and yellow chequers of John de Warenne. Then the clouds rolled onward, light flashed on the estuary waters, and the next moment the group on the nearer bank was illuminated in a burst of sun. Armour glittered, and the colours of the riders' surcoats and the horse caparisons glowed. Lord Simon raised his hand, and the men assembled along the bank cheered and cried out his name. Even at such a moment, Adam realised, he could still inspire adulation.

Abruptly the clouds closed once more, and the brightness was gone. A cry of dismay came from the bridge, a creak and crash of falling wood, and the crude platform of planks and beams toppled and slid into the river below. A few moments more, and the band of men on the bridge had begun their retreat, carrying their wounded with them. Cheers and yells of defiance came from the fortification on the far side, and a last few arrows came lofting over the gap.

\*

'Hugh of Oystermouth claims that Lord Simon has a *secret weapon*,' Adam said. He and Robert de Dunstanville were sitting outside their tent, armour and equipment spread around them on the patchy grass. The days of rain and drizzle had covered the metal with a thin freckling of rust. Seated on a folding stool, a helmet propped on his knee, Adam was scrubbing at the iron with a coarse rag coated in ashes from the fire.

'He has,' Robert replied, eating raisins from a cupped palm. 'He's making Greek Fire.'

'He's . . . what?'

Robert continued chewing stolidly. 'Don't ask me how, or for what purpose. But he has found an artificer who claims to be able to produce the stuff. He's not Jewish either, before you ask.'

Adam suppressed a shudder. The thought of devilish artificial fire sounded somehow unclean. Surely no Christian would use such a weapon, and on Good Friday too? They needed some way of capturing the bridge, but how fire might assist them in doing that Adam could not imagine.

All around them, the encampment of de Montfort's army spread in a mass of damp canvas and smoking fires, almost engulfing the little riverside settlement of Strood. It resembled the tournament camps that Adam knew so well from the continent, on a far larger scale. But with thousands of London militiamen present as well, it had more the feel of a village fair than a chivalric gathering. Here and there the banners of the knightly retinues rose like islands of gaudy colour in the sodden murk.

The church bells were silent for Good Friday, and without the familiar ringing from near and far to mark the hours, the day felt strangely timeless. But otherwise all thought of religion seemed to have been suspended in the midst of war. In two days it would be Easter, the holiest day of the Christian year – what, Adam wondered, would happen then? Normally it would be a time for confessing misdeeds and being granted absolution; he had last confessed at Cologne, a full year ago, and he felt the black weight of twelve months of sin pressing heavily on his soul. He could not bear to contemplate what Robert must be feeling, with his terrible oath of mortal jeopardy hanging over him.

'Sir Humphrey was asking about you,' de Dunstanville said, finishing the last of his raisins and dusting his palms.

Adam said nothing and continued cleaning the armour. There was a rumour, so Wilecok had reported, that during the riots Robert de Dunstanville and Humphrey de Bohun had seized the treasure of one of the richest Jewish moneylenders in London, and held onto it for themselves. Perhaps, he thought, it was safer for men to believe such things. He had been all too aware, as he rode beside the infantry column on their two-day march from London, that many of the men alongside him must have been among those who launched the attack on the Jews. But none had spoken of it, and since leaving the city all had cloaked themselves in unity and comradeship.

'I don't doubt that if you should ever earn your spurs,' Robert went on, narrowing his eyes in the slanting sunlight, 'de Bohun would be happy to give you a place in his retinue, as a household knight. Not a bad position to take. He could certainly offer you more than I ever could.'

'If such a day ever came,' Adam said, 'then I would not be the household knight of Humphrey de Bohun, or of anyone else. I would be my own man, and seek my own lands and my own fortune.'

'Quite so,' Robert said quietly, inclining his head. He appeared, Adam noticed, impressed and a little relieved. He was conscious that the balance between them had shifted subtly since their angry words on the afternoon of Palm Sunday.

'Has there been any word of what Lord Simon will do now?' Adam asked, eager to change the subject.

Robert nodded briskly. 'He intends to make a crossing of the river tonight, under cover of darkness. All day he's been gathering boats from far upstream. Gilbert de Clare's sent a party of

men across from the Rochester side as well, to guide the assaulting force.'

'You're intending to join them?' Adam asked. Robert had
taken no part in the attacks on the bridge over the last two days.
Apparently he felt there was no glory to be gained in such a
thing.

'Not I,' Robert said with a dry laugh. 'I do not float so well,
you know. De Montfort already has four young knights who've
volunteered to lead the attack. But he wants other men, squires
and serjeants of proven valour and skill at arms, to support them.'

Adam stopped scrubbing the armour and raised his eyes.
Robert was peering back at him with a speculative half-smile.
The memory of that morning's assault loomed in his mind, and
he tried to hide his look of misgiving. To stand and passively
watch such a thing was horrendous, but to be in the midst of it,
struggling on the narrow bridge while the arrows rained down,
would be worse. Any alternative had to be preferable. And if this
was the part he had to play, Adam thought – the test that fate had
decreed for him, perhaps – then he could not refuse.

'Humphrey de Bohun recommended me?' he asked, a shadow
crossing his mind.

'Oh no, there was no need for that,' Robert said. 'But as I
told Sir Humphrey, if my squire wishes to volunteer for such a
foolhardy thing, it is his own decision. I cannot command him.'

*

Simon de Montfort's secret weapon was drawn up on the mudflats beside the river, lodged beneath a rough shelter of thatch
and sticks. The bridge was a mile downstream, and the position
was hidden from the watchers in the castle towers by a bend in
the river and a stand of trees; the shelter was more to protect the
contraption from the rain than to conceal it from the eyes of
the enemy. It was a fishing boat, wide-hulled and flat-bottomed.

A mast was set near the bows, with a big sail of heavy canvas lowered on the yard. Covering the hull from end to end was a construction of sticks and straw, arched over like a vaulted roof. Adam was reminded of a carved model of Noah's Ark he had seen in a church in Germany. But even from ten paces away, he could pick out its particularly repulsive smell, despite the sour whiff of the estuary mud.

'I make no great claims for it, masters,' the artificer said. He was a disappointingly ordinary man, short and jowly, with none of the sinister aspect many had been expecting. 'It is what it is. But it will do what's needed, that I guarantee.'

'What's it made from?' one of the onlookers asked.

The artificer gave a modest shrug. 'There's no real secret to it – merely charcoal and dry tinder stacked inside, pitch and pine resin, several bags of sulphur. And the special ingredient . . .'

'*Magic?*' one of the younger squires asked, round-eyed with wonder.

'No,' the artificer replied. '*Lard*. Slabs of it, laid on thick. Burns lovely, you know, and hard to quench, once the sulphur sets it going.'

That explained the smell, Adam realised. Sure enough, now the man had identified it the stink of rancid pork fat was unmistakeable.

'Pah, this is not the true Greek Fire,' said John D'Abernon, one of de Montfort's household knights. He tugged at his blonde moustache as he turned away. 'I had expected some wonder out of the east, the dragon's breath itself! This is a mere blaze in a hogman's yard . . .'

The others were beginning to drift away as well, repelled rather than fascinated now the mysteries of the device had been revealed. Nearby, a dozen more boats were drawn up on the muddy bank of the Medway, ready to carry them across the river that night. The tide was low, and wide grey-black mudflats stretched from the hummock grass and reeds of the riverbank to the water's edge, where wading birds stepped and pecked in the shallows. Insects flickered over the sheen of mud in the late-afternoon sun.

Adam lingered, caught by an unpleasant premonition. In his mind he saw burned corpses rolling in a dark torrent. With a shudder, he banished the images. But again he found himself wondering whether Humphrey de Bohun had somehow put him forward for this task on purpose, maybe trying to rid himself of a rival for Joane's affections. No, Adam told himself, Humphrey de Bohun had no need of such desperate expedients; he was a great nobleman, with titles and lands, a retinue of followers; the heir to one of the most powerful earldoms in the kingdom. He had the prospect of marriage to a beautiful heiress ahead of him. Adam, by contrast, had nothing but his courage and a strong sword arm – he was expendable, and that was the reason that he had been so quickly accepted for the night's expedition.

Most of the other men gathered along the riverbank were around his own age. Adam recognised a few of the squires from the tournaments in France, or the more recent expedition to St Albans. The four knights leading the assault parties were young men too, aged between twenty and thirty. In their company, Adam felt more secure – like them, he had been chosen for his abilities, that was all. But then he noticed that one of the knights was Richard de Malmaines, and his mood soured. He hoped fervently that he would not find himself in a boat with the man that night, out on the dark waters. His palms itched, like a presentiment of violence.

'*Preudhommes*,' a gravelly voice declared. '*Preudhommes*, gather to me, if you would. All must know how this thing is to be done.'

John Spadeberd was a squat, square-faced serjeant, and Simon de Montfort had placed him in charge of leading the night's attack on the bridge. He stood on a grassy hummock, legs planted and fists on his hips, and waited for the two-score knights and squires and younger men to assemble around him. It was unusual for a mere serjeant to be set above his social superiors, but the forth-coming expedition would be far from usual. Besides, Spadeberd was a veteran of the fighting in Wales, skilled in leadership and all forms of combat; when he spoke, his voice carried an effortless note of authority.

'We take to the water an hour before midnight,' he announced, turning from the waist to address the assembly, 'when the tide is full. Six boats, towing the fireship between them. Oars to be muffled, and none are to speak or make a sound. When we are in midstream we let the current and the turn of the tide carry us down towards the bridge. At my signal, the devils aboard the fireship will set flame to their cargo.'

He paused for a moment, waiting for any questions. There were plenty, Adam knew: how were they to capture the bridge by burning it? And how would they avoid the flaming fireship from burning *them*? But none said a word, unwilling to seem fearful or irresolute.

'Then,' the serjeant went on, 'with luck and prayers – and with the holy blessing – the burning ship will drift downstream and lodge directly beneath the fortification on the broken bridge, and as the tide falls the keel will ground beneath it and the enemy will be unable to float it clear. While their minds are filled with panic and their eyes with the flames, we will land on the river-bank behind them and seize the town gate, overcoming in a rush any who oppose us. We hold it until the London militiamen cross the river in the second flotilla and help to secure it. And this is what Lord Simon has decreed.'

Silence for a few heartbeats after he had spoken. Adam sensed everyone around him drawing a long breath.

'The moon's only a sliver past full,' somebody said, gazing upwards. 'How are we to conceal ourselves from its light?'

'There'll be plenty of cloud come nightfall,' Spadeberd said. 'And our friends on this side of the river will light fires and make commotion to suggest they plan another attack. So, cover your steel, and keep silence. With the blessing, our enemies will be looking elsewhere.'

'And may the Good Lord sow confusion among them!' another voice said, and all turned as Simon de Montfort strode down the riverbank to join their assembly. His horses and attendants waited at the edge of the copse of trees. Immediately Adam noticed the assembled men standing more upright, raising their heads and throwing back their hoods and cloaks. As one they turned to face the Earl of Leicester.

'Friends,' he declared. 'All of you have volunteered for this task, and I thank you for it from my heart.' He pressed his palm to his breast, and his level gaze seemed to touch every one of them. 'On you, our success or failure depends. On your courage, *preudhommes*. Your fortitude and valour.'

Fine words, Adam thought. He had heard them so often before. But at least Simon de Montfort could not be accused of having nothing in the balance. And they were spoken with such force that they sounded sincere. Now de Montfort went to John Spadeberd and to each of the four knights in turn and embraced them – Adam averted his eyes as the earl greeted Richard de Malmaines. He spoke to each one, giving more of his words, more of his assurance and encouragement. Then, as he stared out over the waters of the river, he paused and pressed his fingers to his brow.

Without a word he sank to his knees. There was no bell, no call or sound, but the knowledge passed between the men around him and as one they knelt too. It was nones, the third hour of the afternoon, the hour of Christ's death. And all of them were silent. Out on the river, oblivious to the solemnity, a flight of geese flew southward, their wingtips seeming to skim the water.

After a few moments of prayer they rose to their feet once more.

'Now,' Simon de Montfort said, turning to address them all. 'Make ready as best you can, and wait for nightfall. If God grants us his favour, we will gather on Easter morning in the cathedral of Rochester, and by then the fortress will be ours!'

# Chapter 20

Two hours after nightfall, and clouds covered the moon. Adam stumbled forward, feeling his feet sinking into thick river ooze as the black water swilled around his ankles, then his knees. The tide was high in the estuary, covering the mudflats, and the boats had been pulled up close to the bank between the stands of reeds and the long sedge grasses. Encumbered by a full mail hauberk, the coif laced over his head beneath a wide-brimmed iron helmet, a shield slung on his back and a dark woollen cape shrouding his body, Adam waded forward into the gloom with arms outstretched until he could grab the side of the boat and haul himself aboard.

'Careful there! Careful!' the boatmen hissed, standing waist-deep in the water holding the craft steady while the soldiers clambered forward over the thwarts. Wet boots thudded and scuffed on the timbers, weapons clattered and mail clinked, and all of it sounded far too loud in the darkness. The smell of the river mud was thick in the night air.

Once six or seven men had clambered aboard and scrambled up to perch on the benches between the oarsmen, the men in the water shoved the laden boat away from the bank and out into the river's current. Adam felt the glide of water along the hull, the chill of it in the air, the smell of it rising from his soaked clothes and the muddy puddles filling the bilges. He tugged the dark cape closer around his shoulders, hunching as the breeze whispered across the river's blackness. Oars rattled out, the blades splashing as they met the water, and the rowlocks creaked as the oarsmen bent to their work. When Adam turned his head, he saw the riverbank receding into darkness.

Sounds carried strangely, out on the open water. A light rain was falling, misting the river's surface, and as his eyes adjusted, Adam picked out the shapes of the other five boats gliding out into the stream. The much larger shape of the fireship rose beyond them, a humped darkness on the water, its mast raised and its heavy sail beginning to belly to the estuary breeze. Even from here he could make out the foul trace it left in the air.

Adam became aware of the heavy pulsing of his blood. His palms were sweating so much he feared he would not be able to grip his sword. For the first time he was about to go into battle with edged steel. Only a few hours before he had watched as the armourer sharpened his blade on the grinding wheel, then honed it with the whetstone. Somewhere out there in the night's darkness, he knew, were men that he did not know and with whom he had no grudge, but who he would have to try and kill. The thought of it pressed on him with a terrible sobering weight. But what he feared was not the fighting, not even the killing. Instead he was convinced that he would stumble and trip while getting out of the boat, fall into the black water with a shout that would betray their silent landing to the enemy. He was convinced that in battle he would fumble and drop his weapon, or become confused in the darkness. He feared failure, and disgrace.

The boat was moving steadily downriver now, carried by the current in mid-stream, the oarsmen only making occasional pulls to keep the course true. On the bench beside Adam sat a man in a thick linen gambeson, a crossbow laid across his knees. The man was praying fervently, barely above a breath, and repeatedly kissing a holy medal. Adam set his teeth and tried to still his mind.

'Have no fears, sirs!' a low voice said in the darkness. The serjeant on the bench in front turned and grinned over his shoulder. Adam could smell his rank breath as he whispered. 'Have no fears, for I have a holy string of St Thomas tied about me, and it'll protect us all!'

'A holy string . . .?' Adam said, frowning.

'Yes! Measured it myself, I did, on the saint's tomb in Canterbury. I've worn it ever since, tied tight just here.' He patted his midriff, below his chest, and grinned again. Even in the dark Adam could make out his ruined teeth. 'Protects against all perils, it does, sirs!' he said, to Adam and the quaking crossbowman. 'Proof against fire and water, and steel too!'

The man twisted on the bench, leaning closer to Adam. 'They call me Le Brock, sir,' he said. 'Due to this.' Pulling back his coif he exposed the stripe of vivid white in his lank black hair. 'I'm serjeant to Lord Gilbert.'

'Christ's love will you keep *quiet*!' one of the other squires hissed from near the stern. Adam could make out the tremble in his voice. 'They must be able to hear you in *London*!'

'Remember,' the man named Le Brock whispered, and gave a leering wink as he patted his torso again. 'Keep close to me, sir, and the holy string will see you good!'

The helmsman, standing at the stern with his steering oar, made a sharp sound between his teeth and gestured into the darkness. The clouds shifted, and Adam saw the walls of the castle standing above them on the riverbank, with the pale turreted block of the keep rising high above them against the shredded moon. Over the bows of the boat he could make out the broken bridge, skeletal above the moon's gleam on the water, and ahead of it was the black shape of the fireship with its big sail still driving it on downstream.

'They should have lit it!' somebody whispered harshly. 'Why haven't they lit it? Is it too wet? – oh merciful Christ!'

A chorus of angry hisses silenced him, and all peered into the night and the river's reach. Silent and tense on the benches, the oarsmen steadily backed water in long sweeps to hold them in position against the current as the other boats came up around them.

'There!' somebody gasped, and all drew breath as they saw the spark of flame deep inside the black cavern of the fireship. For a few slow heartbeats the flame wavered, appearing no larger than a candle, then blossomed upwards to light the curve of sticks and straw above it. Adam made out the shapes of figures moving in the depths – *devils*, John Spadeberd had called them. Once the fire was ignited they would tie the tiller of the boat and then slip overboard to swim to safety, trusting the big wetted sail to keep the burning vessel moving unstoppably down towards the bridge.

But the fire was very small, making more smoke than flame. Now the clouds had thinned, the moonlight appeared very bright, striping the river and the walls of the castle. The men in the boats could see other fires burning on the far riverbank, where Montfort's army had assembled to cause a distraction. But already they could hear the shouts of alarm from the watchers on the castle battlements.

Smoke rolled from the burning boat, billowing upwards against the sail and then spilling away over the river's surface. The flames lit it with a sunset glow, and as it thinned across the water and caught the moonlight it turned to a pale roiling fog. Adam realised that he was holding his breath, and forced himself to exhale. The oarsmen were still backing water, but the little flotilla of boats was being carried steadily downstream towards the bridge. At any moment, the men on the castle walls would see them, picked out by the sickly radiance of the burning vessel.

Then came a dull *whoosh* of air, and flame burst upwards from the hull of the ship and curled around the roof of dry tinder, scattering sparks against the sail. Bursts of bright fire came from deep inside – the sulphur catching light, Adam guessed – and then the flames were racing, seething upwards against the damp sailcloth and spilling away into the night. A wave of scorching heat rolled back across the water, and the men in the boats shielded their faces from it.

'Holy Mary protect us,' the crossbowman beside Adam chanted, 'Christ and all His saints protect us!'

'Archers!' another voice cried, startlingly loud. A scream of pain came from one of the other boats. 'Pull for the riverbank!'

An arrow struck the hull of the boat. Another whipped just overhead. Adam struggled to drag the shield from off his back and hold it above him; others did the same, although it was hard to tell the direction from which the arrows flew.

Ahead of them the fireship was blazing, filling the expanse of the river with its flame. Adam saw the great sail ignite and dis-integrate into flying fiery shreds, but the vessel was still moving. Sparks of burning chaff blew from it, hissing and steaming as they dropped into the water, and he could hear the men on the bridge fortification screaming in panic as the hellish vessel bore down upon them. But the boats were moving fast now, sharp prows cutting through the water as the oarsmen heaved, the armed men crowded aboard each one with shields raised, weap-ons readied.

A roar came from along the river; Adam saw that the burning fireship had lodged itself between two of the stone bridge piers, directly below the timbers of the fortification. Already men were running back towards the riverbank to summon help, while oth-ers struggled to draw up buckets of water to quench the flames, or use long poles to shove the blazing craft away.

'Steady!' a voice said from the stern. 'Brace yourselves!'

A rush of water and a grate of mud, and the boat ground to a halt on the riverbank. At once the men in the bows leaped down into the shallows, the others clambering forward over the benches hefting arrow-studded shields and naked weapons.

Almost without thinking, Adam found himself in the bow; he jumped, and splashed down into muddy water. Three sloshing strides and he was climbing the bank, forging through long grass with his shield raised in front of him and his sword gripped tight in his fist.

The bank was steep here, and his shadow threw the ground ahead into total blackness. As he scrambled upwards Adam could see the end of the bridge, the town wall and gate, illuminated by the flames of the burning fireship. And now he could see the cleverness of the stratagem: men were running out through the town gates to aid those on the bridge in fighting the fires. If Adam and the others landing from the boats could scale the riverbank quickly enough in the darkness, they stood a chance of seizing the gates before the defenders could close them once more.

But already the sentries on the walls were raising the alarm. Ahead of Adam a man in a gambeson stumbled on the rutted bank as a crossbow bolt pinned him through the neck. He fell, and Adam leaped over him. Another bolt struck his shield, the iron head punching through the boards just above Adam's forearm. Then a figure reared up ahead of him, wreathed in smoke and whirling sparks. An axe slammed against Adam's shield and he deflected the blow, then swung a low cut beneath the rim. He felt the blade bite, and heard the roar of pain, but already he was shoving his shield forward against his attacker's body. The man toppled, and Adam stabbed down once into the dark and then ran onward. There were others around him, men from the boats yelling as they reached the level ground at the top of the riverbank. *I have killed a man*; the thought pulsed in Adam's mind, then it was gone.

Only ten running strides to the gate. Figures staggered through the smoke, shadows wheeling, and Adam could not distinguish friend from foe. He paused to pull the crossbow bolt from his shield and then he advanced, sword raised, sensing the others that flanked him. The blazing bridge was behind them now, silhouetting them, and to the defenders around the gates they were screaming wraiths of darkness as the billowing sparks arced above them.

The men confronting them now had no experience of war. They were barely fighters at all, just militia trying to defend their town and their bridge. Adam saw them quailing before the onslaught, and his face tightened into a fierce grin. Already he was halfway to the gate, men to either side of him, and their enemy were on the verge of breaking. A spear jabbed at his face and he blocked it, rolling the point and shaft aside. Another spear, clashing against his sword as he parried – he slid the blade down the spear shaft, slicing off fingers. Howls from the dark; he smelled the blood he could not see. A huge figure ahead of him now, a giant in a pale gambeson. Adam caught the blow of a mace on his shield, the impact bursting pain into his left shoulder, then pivoted from the waist as he drove the leading edge of the shield forward, striking the giant in the chest and knocking him back. The following blow flowed smoothly, his blade slashing down across the man's shoulder. Adam felt the blade cut deep, splitting bone and flesh, then the man was down. Hot wetness up his arm as he wrenched his blade free.

It was just like in the *buhort*, when he knew his enemies were routed but still there was a chance they could rally and turn at bay. Adam heard the yelps and snarls of the men around him, like hunting dogs, like beasts. Snatching a glance behind him, he felt the searing heat on his face. A glimpse of billowing fire, the shapes of men throwing themselves from the bridge into the river. The fireship was still burning, great sheets of flame curling up from it and rolling down to the water, fiery flags in the blackness. The air was filled with dancing sparks and swirling smoke.

'*With me! With me!*' Adam shouted, feeling the rasp of the words in his scorched throat. The man called Le Brock was beside him now, hefting an axe with both hands. Together they raced the last distance to the gate. Adam rammed aside the fleeing shape of a man with his shield, stumbled, ran onward. Only moments had passed since they left the boats. Heartbeats, spilled out in bloodshed.

Now they were beneath the gate arch, into the churn of bodies. The gates were heavy oak, banded and studded with iron, with barely the space remaining for a man to pass between them. A mob pressed at either side, every man roaring, shields rammed tight as they shoved. One side was trying to force the gates open, the other to seal them closed. Spears flicked and stabbed in the gap between them, grating against stone, against mail. A man beside Adam screamed as a spearhead darted from the press and ripped open his face. He slumped back, but his body remained upright, caught in the crush.

De Malmaines appeared beside Adam, his face flecked dark red, lit by the fiery glare behind them. 'You?' he said to Adam, and laughed out loud. Together they threw themselves forward, shoulders to the hollow of their shields, trying to burst the knot of men between the gates by brute force. Adam saw iron-studded oak in front of him and threw himself against it. Old hinges wailed; on the far side of the gap the defenders had the big timber locking bar and were shoving it against the gates, trying to force them closed against the press of bodies filling the threshold. Adam felt something strike his ankle. A man beside him screamed and leaped back. He stamped his foot, and his boot came down on the shaft of a spear and shattered it.

'*Bastards!*' Le Brock was screaming into the mob of men packing the threshold, spittle flecking his jaws. 'Sons of dogs! The devil take you all!' He was hewing with his axe, driving great cleaving blows into the gap between the gates. His blade banged off a shield, then rang off a helmet, then chopped flesh.

By ones and twos the men on the far side of the gate were falling back. Then a rush, the attackers surged, and abruptly the pressure was gone. Timbers shrieked as the gates were flung back against the stone arch and the seething mass of men outside surged across the threshold.

Adam stumbled forward, tripping over a sprawling body, and fell to his knees on the greasy cobbles. When he raised his head he saw in the wheeling firelight two men in identical gambesons wrestling on the ground, one of them grimly driving a pointed dagger into the throat of the other. Fear raced through him, the energy of the fight dispelled and cold horror rising in its place. Just for a moment Adam could not move, his limbs weak and his blood still. Then he heard the roar of voices, the triumphant yells, and once again the song of battle was loud inside him. His body was flowing with sweat as he scrambled back to his feet, and his throat felt scorched. Smoke rolled through the arch from the burning bridge.

'Hold back!' an iron voice yelled. 'Hold back – keep to the gateway!' Sir John D'Abernon had pushed through the mob of soldiers and was taking charge now, forming the men into two lines beneath the archway. Already the defenders in the darkened street beyond the gate were rallying, noticing for the first time the small number of their attackers. Barely thirty men had come up from the boats; two had fallen in the attack, but many more were wounded. With the defenders from the bridge fortification gathering in the smoke-filled darkness outside the walls and the town militia massing on the inside, they would be swept away unless they were reinforced.

'The signal,' D'Abernon cried, 'shoot now!' But the sky was full of fire and whirling sparks, and the flaming arrow that one of his men shot upwards was lost to sight almost instantly. From the far riverbank, it would have been invisible amid the larger conflagration. Grimly the little band beneath the gate arch tightened their lines, raising shields edge to edge. Some were already busy trying to heave the big gates off their hinges. Arrows and crossbow bolts smacked into shield boards, clashed against the stone archway; here and there they found a mark in human flesh.

Adam stood hunched behind his shield. Le Brock was at his left shoulder, and John Spadeberd to his right. From somewhere along the line he could hear Richard de Malmaines spitting curses into the darkness, goading their enemies to attack. A flung spear arced overhead, and he heard a shout of pain from behind him. Another arrow struck his shield, and he felt the impact through the bone of his forearm. He willed himself to stay strong, to fight down the fear, but now the momentum of the attack had stalled he felt the cold tendrils crawling in his blood, twining through his limbs.

Shouts from behind him, and fresh sweat broke on his brow and coursed from beneath the rim of his mail coif. Adam blinked, trying to shake the stinging drops from his eyes, his face, but he felt half blind. The voices behind him grew clearer: '*A Montfort! A Montfort!*'

Sudden relief, a great gasp and cry of salvation. Then the reinforcements were thronging among them, surging up the riverbank from the second wave of boats and packing the arch of the gateway. They were Londoners, men of the militia armed with spears and axes, their rough voices echoing beneath the gate arch as they swelled the fighting line behind the wall of shields.

'Now – onward! Go!' cried John D'Abernon, and with a roar the line surged forward, a wave of shields and armoured bodies, bristling with blades. The enemy turned and fled before them. Adam was running, the breath burning in his throat, feeling once more the wild madness of combat powering him. His boots slipped and skidded on the worn and grimy cobbles but he stayed upright. He lashed out at somebody ahead of him, but they were gone before his blow could connect.

More figures, a line of shields in the murk of the street. To the right was the broad grassy moat of the castle, with the castle wall rising on the far side vague in the gloom. Somewhere ahead the wooden bridge and the towers of the barbican. The charge slowed, men closing into a fighting line once more behind their shields. Adam peered into the darkness, his eyes streaming from the smoke and sweat. Yellow shields, marked with something in red.

'*A Hastings! A Hastings!*' a man cried from the opposing lines. Adam heard a cheer from behind him, the answering cry of '*A Montfort!*' and the two lines surged together. Henry de Hastings's retainers had closed up from the south, chasing on the heels of the last defenders as they retreated across the wooden bridge over the moat to the castle beyond.

*

It was past midnight by the time they set fire to the barbican. The breeze had shifted, and sparks and flying smuts were scattering across the town as the troops gathered for the attack. Adam felt the smuts on his face and squinted. Somewhere in the night men were ransacking the priory and plundering the cathedral buildings. From the surrounding streets rose screams, pleas for mercy, wild laughter. The luckier citizens had already fled or taken shelter in the castle.

Through a glaze of fatigue, Adam heard men shouting that the gates were down, the charred timbers burst through with a ram and the portcullis sealing the gate passage beyond levered open. Once again he felt the fierce energy of battle pulsing in his blood. Then he was running, thundering across the bridge towards the smoke-wreathed castle barbican with a squad of Henry de Hastings's serjeants, hardly aware of what was happening or who was leading the attack. Through the funnel of the gate passage Adam charged, scrambling to keep up with the rush. Arrows flickered around him, glancing off the walls, then he was out into the open space of the castle bailey as the cloud shifted and flooded the scene with bright moonlight.

Adam would remember only fragments of the hours that followed. In the dancing shadows, the bursts of firelight and the whirling smoke he saw lines of men clash in combat, fall back and then clash again. He was fighting himself, warding off blows with his shield, his senses drowned with the grate and whine of steel, the copperish stink of blood, the yells of fear and fury and the screams of the injured. His shoulders and back ached from the weight of his mail, his knuckles were grazed and his arms bruised. At some point he found himself snatching a waterskin to wash the reek of smoke and ashes from his throat; the skin contained wine, not water, and he choked and spat, then drank again and swallowed it down.

He remembered slipping on the churned turf, and finding that the blackness beneath him was a lake of spilled blood. A little later – a few moments, a few hours – he seized a half-loaf from a basket and started to eat, only to notice the blood of other men still covering his hands.

Then, later still, Adam heard the clanging of a handbell, and when he raised his eyes from the rutted earth he saw the grey daylight appearing blearily through the grim clouds of smoke. It was the morning of Holy Saturday. A file of men walked slowly across the ravaged expanse of the bailey, priests carrying the holy vessels, with a man with a crucifix going before them. As they passed through the milling throng of fighting men, the wounded and the captured and those still preparing for another attack, all fell still and silent. As one, men knelt and bowed their heads, and the file of priests crossed to the little chapel near the wall of the bailey to conduct the service of morning mass.

When Adam raised his head, everything before him seemed to be part of a dream. Suddenly he felt too weary to get to his feet again. He was scrubbing the black smirch from his face with blood-smeared hands as Le Brock appeared before him.

'See, young sir?' the man said, patting his midriff. 'Didn't it keep you safe, eh? You were right to stay close to me. Kept you safe all through the darkness, it did, just like I said – the string of St Thomas!'

## Chapter 21

The morning of Easter Sunday was a holy truce, and all the bells in Rochester were ringing. In the great cavern of the cathedral the nave and aisles blazed with candles, and on the high altar the crucifix stood proudly, raised from its sepulchre as the choir sang *Christus Resurgens*, on this day of the resurrection. The congregation had been gathering since first light, since matins, thronging the main doors and shuffling in lines, barefoot on the worn paving stones, towards the north transept to make confession, then kneeling in rows before the chancel screen to hear mass and receive holy communion. More like cattle than true penitents, Adam thought as he looked at them. But he was no better.

No, he thought, they were not arrayed in the robes of God. Nor were they clothed in love and charity. These were warriors, the same men that had stormed the gates and the castle barbican, and slain the townsfolk and the king's serjeants in the bailey. The same that had plundered the town and the cathedral close, and stabled their horses in the cloisters of the priory. They were unshaven and mostly unwashed, and they belched and laughed and scratched at themselves as they waited to confess and be shriven. Stinking of smoke and sweat and dried gore, they knelt on the cold stone with bare feet and bare shins, and they showed no shame, no remorse at all.

Adam reached the head of the confessional queue and stepped forward quickly. The confessor was one of several, working in tandem, so great was the number of men waiting to be absolved.

'*Benedicite pater*,' Adam mumbled quickly, dropping to kneel before the seated priest. They were running through the ceremony quickly; already he had seen and overheard a score or more confessions.

'*Dominus exaudiat nos*,' the priest muttered from under his hood, in a flat monotone. *Lord hear us.* But how could he, Adam thought, when so many were speaking at once?

'*Confiteor deo omnipotenti* . . .' He clasped his hands and leaned into the priest's lap, not even glancing up at that tired grey face in the hood's shadow, those hanging jowls. He recited his Creed in a rapid whisper, while the priest nodded and fanned the air above him. Behind him Adam could hear the others in the queue shuffling closer, urging him to hurry up with his sins.

'I acknowledge to God and to all the holy company of heaven that I am a sinner,' Adam mumbled quickly, switching to French. 'I have sinned in thought, word and deed . . . I have not loved God above all things. I have not dreaded him nor worshipped him . . .'

For days he had been thinking over what he would say, how he would phrase his confession. Now it came to the moment, he knew that he should not have been so concerned. The priest was barely listening. He appeared barely awake.

'I have violated the commandments and neglected the holy days,' Adam went on. 'I have sinned with women, and failed to perform the seven works of mercy . . . I have bent my knees more gladly in fornication than in prayer, and hungered more for the acclaim of others than for the blessings and peace of Almighty God . . .'

He was trying to mean what he said, and to feel the contrition in his heart. But these were formulas, not true confessions. He paused, took a breath, and whispered. 'I have killed a man in battle – more than one, perhaps . . .' Better to be sure, he had decided. He had searched among the bodies of the slain the day before, thinking he might recognise those he had cut down, but all had looked equally unfamiliar in death.

The priest had barely moved. Surely, Adam thought, he must have heard such things countless times already that day. He realised that he could confess anything he liked, the most enormous sins, the most heinous crimes, and still the priest would grant him the same absolution he had granted all the rest. Why should he not? He hated them all alike, and doubtless wished them all in hell by the swiftest road.

'I have lusted after a woman who is not my wife . . .' The image of Joane de Quincy appeared to him, and fervently he blinked it away. More troublingly, the image of Belia rose in its place. His voice caught; he could confess no more. 'I beseech my Lord Jesus Christ of his mercy,' Adam went on in a leaden voice, looking up at the priest for the first time, 'and pray for penance for my misdeeds and absolution for the sake of my soul.'

The priest seemed to awaken from a mild trance of discomfort. He raised his fingers and sketched the sign of the cross. 'Make pilgrimage to the shrine of St Thomas, prior to Whitsun, and make offerings worth at least ten shillings,' he said in a croak. '*Ego te absolvo.*'

Already as Adam scrambled to his feet the queue was shunting and the next penitent was creeping forward. He did not feel lightened of sin. Rather, he felt that something heavy had been draped around him, some new burden he would have to carry from this day forward. Instinctively, as he waited to hear mass he scanned the rows of kneeling people, searching for Robert de Dunstanville. Then he remembered the oath the man had taken, and with a pang of remorse he lowered his gaze to the flagstone floor.

*

Later that day the feasting began. With the restrictions of the
Lenten fast lifted, every kitchen and campfire in Rochester
smoked and spat, and the air was filled with the smell of roasting
flesh. Simon de Montfort had laid his Easter banquet in the open
air, in a garden adjoining the best house in town. The sky was
clear and the sun bright, although a chilly breeze whipped at the
smoke from the fires and tugged at the white table linen, and
now and again the servants had to sprint off in pursuit of errant
baskets and trays.

Most of the men seated at the long tables were barons and
magnates, leaders of great retinues. Robert de Dunstanville was
lucky to have been invited at all, even seated at the very far end
of the lowest table. Adam was standing behind him, assuaging his
hunger with boiled eggs and crusts of bread. The scents of the
roast lamb made his stomach sigh, but as usual he would have to
wait for his master to dine first. At least now that he had confessed and been absolved, had taken holy communion and heard
the High Mass, he felt lighter in his soul.

Opposite, on a wooden dais, Simon de Montfort sat at
the high table with his son Henry and his great friend the
Bishop of Worcester. Flanking them were Gilbert de Clare
and Humphrey de Bohun. The apple trees surrounding the
garden had already been hacked down for timber to use in
the siege works, and there was a clear view of the castle walls
and the towering keep. De Montfort and his chief followers
could view their enemy as they feasted and drank, and their
enemy could view them.

'Earl Simon invited their leaders to join him, you know,' one
of the knights at the tables said, raising his chin towards the castle. 'De Warenne and de Leyburne, I mean. Invited them to join
him at table, for the holy truce! They've refused, it seems.'

'A telling sign,' Robert de Dunstanville replied.

'How so?' the knight asked, frowning. He was a heavily built
man in middle age named Ralph de Heringaud, Lord of Eynsford

in Kent. His fifteen-year-old son William stood behind him, acting as his squire.

'They fear the king's wrath,' Robert said, raising his eyebrows.
'Either they expect Henry to relieve them soon, or they are con-
sidering that they may have to surrender. If they intended to hold
out for a lengthy siege – if they had sufficient supplies, sufficient
men and courage to do so – then they would have no qualms
about feasting with their enemy. But they fear that any congenial
acts now may appear treacherous soon enough.'

Ralph de Heringaud pondered this for a moment, still frowning, then gave a loud *harrumph*. 'Maybe so!' he announced. 'Maybe
so indeed. But we shall have a hard fight nevertheless I think, for
the king is far away, and they surely won't yield at once.'

'I doubt you will be doing very much hard fighting either
way, Sir Ralph,' Robert said in a sly tone. Some of the others
around the table smirked and laughed. The overweight knight
could make no reply; all knew that only the younger men, with
the serjeants and the infantry, would be required to assault the
breaches once the war engines had done their work.

To his left, over the stumps of the trees, Adam could see the
high lever arms of three newly constructed trebuchet catapults. Two more were under construction on either side of the
cathedral grounds, and three more on a hill to the south of the
castle. The engines had arrived the day before by barge, brought
from the Tower of London down the Thames and up the Medway, together with skilled artillerists to construct and use them.
Now that de Montfort's labourers and engineers had cleared the
charred wreckage of the bridge fortification and laid a tempo-
rary timber roadway across the old stone piers, the rest of his
army had moved across the river and into the town. Rochester
thronged with fighting men, horses, war engines and wagons of
military supplies and munitions.

'Sit,' Robert said to Adam, shifting along the bench to make
room. 'Join us.' Enough time had passed, it seemed, that social

niceties need not be observed. Adam gladly seated himself, and took a helping of roast lamb from the communal dish. The rich meat, suffused with the flavours of ginger and thyme, was like the manna of heaven. Juices ran down his fingers as he chewed.

'Was it not King John who took Rochester after a siege, back in our grandfathers' day?' asked John D'Abernon, sitting further along the table.

'He did!' Ralph de Heringaud replied. 'After tunnelling beneath the south tower and bringing down half the keep. I doubt Earl Simon will require such tactics. Although King John took nearly two months to subdue the castle.'

'And we must do it in only two weeks,' Robert said.

Again everyone at the table stared at him, nonplussed. 'How do you calculate that?' D'Abernon asked.

'The king is keeping his Easter court at Nottingham, as we believe, yes?' Robert said. 'But he will surely hear that we're assaulting his castle soon enough, and will march south to break the siege. Two weeks from now, at the latest, he will have brought his army here. If the castle has not fallen by then—'

'He'll be able to cut us off from London, and even surround us,' Adam said. 'A siege within a siege.'

Ralph de Heringaud shot him an irritated glance. Clearly he did not expect squires to speak at the dining table. 'So we turn and bring him to battle!' he declared.

'Oh no,' Robert said, shaking his head. 'Not if it can be helped. Battles are very dangerous, Sir Ralph. It is quite possible to *lose*. And in such cases, it is quite possible to *die*.'

'I fear Sir Ralph has not read his Vegetius,' John D'Abernon said with a grin. '*On the battlefield, luck plays a greater part than valour . . .*'

'A coward's maxim,' de Heringaud said, flustered. 'And not at all the way of a chivalrous man!'

Adam kept his head down, concentrating on his meal. When he glanced up again, he saw the men seated at the middle table.

The bullish Henry de Hastings was there — Adam could hear his booming voice as he made some joke or boast — with John de Burgh and Nicholas de Segrave. And beside them, John Fitz-John. From the corner of his eye Adam watched the young nobleman, remembering the bloody scenes in the London Jewry less than two weeks before. Had nobody else here witnessed FitzJohn's savagery? Surely all had heard of it; the young man had made no secret of what he had done. Did nobody else here condemn it, then?

FitzJohn was stuffing his mouth with meat, his jaws shiny with grease as he laughed along with de Hastings's jokes. He took a draught of wine from his silver-rimmed cup to wash the meat down, choked slightly and spat, then ate again. A band of musicians had struck up, drowning the noise of the voices and laughter with a skirl of pipes and rattle of tabor. Meanwhile, most of the squires and many of the serjeants and heralds and others had come to join their masters at the tables, crowding along the benches and adding to the revelry. Ralph de Heringaud's son William slid down onto the bench beside Adam and seized a cup, filling it brimful of wine from the jug and drinking it back.

A hand tapped Adam's shoulder and he tensed, reaching instinctively for his eating knife as he turned. The figure behind him was standing against the light, but stepped back at once and raised his hands. One of the young pages from the high table, Adam noticed as he blinked and squinted.

'The Lord Simon invites you to speak with him,' the page said in a squawk, still unnerved by Adam's reaction as he gestured towards the high table. Adam nodded, getting to his feet, aware that the other men on the benches were regarding him with great interest.

'Be careful what you say,' Robert told him in a hushed voice, turning and taking his arm. 'Remember—'

'I know,' Adam replied with a dismissive shrug, then followed the page over the grass to the dais where the high table stood.

As he approached, he was struck once more by the way everyone present seemed to attend upon de Montfort. The Earl of Leicester sat at the centre of the table, but those to either side of him and all those standing around and seated at the adjoining tables appeared to be directing their attention towards him, listening avidly to every quiet word he said, noticing his every gesture. Adam remembered the gathering in the cellar room before the tournament at Senlis, nearly two years before, when de Montfort had first spoken to him. Lord Simon still projected that effortless and rather uncanny allure, a force that drew all towards him. If anything, it seemed even stronger now.

Adam rubbed at his chin, wishing that he had shaved more dutifully that morning. But most of the men around him still appeared rough and battle-worn, for all their fine clothes and festive air. Humphrey de Bohun was seated at the nearest end of the table, dressed in a tunic and surcoat of bright blue covered with embroidered golden lions. He smiled broadly as Adam stepped up to the dais, standing and clapping him on the shoulder, then passing him a fresh cup of wine. Again, Adam was baffled by the man's warmth. Did he now regard him as an old friend? He was more surprised when Simon de Montfort too got to his feet, gesturing lightly for Adam to follow him as he moved away from the table.

Holding his cup, Adam walked a few paces beside de Montfort. The earl appeared grave suddenly, and slightly distracted. 'My serjeant, John Spadeberd,' he said, 'tells me that you acted with great courage during the attack on the bridge and gate. I've been meaning to commend you in person.'

'Thank you, my lord,' Adam said, trying to hide his confusion. He had been one among many that night.

De Montfort paused, folding his arms across his chest, and gazed up at the castle keep. 'So,' he said. 'What do you think? Can it be taken?'

'I believe any castle can be taken, my lord,' Adam said. 'Or so I've heard.'

The older man glanced at him quickly, a smile tightening his face. 'That's what you've learned from Robert de Dunstanville, I suppose?' he said. 'Well, he's a good instructor, and he's not wrong. Anything can be accomplished, with sufficient courage and strength. And if God wills it, of course.'

'You intend to storm the walls, my lord, once the engines have opened a breach?' Adam asked. It seemed an obvious question, but he felt the need to say something. More than that – he felt the need to impress this man in some way. A vain desire, perhaps, maybe even a childish one, but it burned strongly in him.

'I do, as soon as this holy truce is over,' Simon replied, jutting his jaw. 'And hopefully that will carry it, and we will not have to resort to burrowing beneath the walls, as King John did . . . How I wish this struggle had come decades ago!' he went on, balling his fist. 'Were I even twenty years younger I would be leading the assault myself.'

Adam looked at de Montfort, surprised by his candour. At close hand and in daylight, the marks of age were clear to see. He must be nearing his mid-fifties, Adam realised; his broad rawboned face was lined and pouched, his eyes webbed with wrinkles and his iron-grey hair shot through with paler strands at the temples. But still Simon de Montfort seemed to exude the strength and vigour of a much younger man.

Abruptly he turned to look at Adam, his deep-set eyes sharpening as he took him by the shoulder. 'Understand,' he said intently, 'that it's not for myself that I fight this war. Not for those of my generation – the magnates and barons who follow my banners or the king's. It's for you younger men that I fight. For the bachelors of England – you, and my sons, and all the others of your age. You are the men who will inherit this new realm we are building.'

The word *inherit* seemed to hang in the air. Adam felt de Montfort's hand tighten on his shoulder, as if to stress it.

'You understand that, yes?'

'I do,' Adam replied. 'And I would be honoured to fight beside you for that cause.' He realised as he spoke that he was no longer merely trying to impress; he meant what he said.

'Good,' de Montfort replied, his hand dropping as he turned once more to stare at the castle. For a few moments he said nothing, and Adam wondered if he should take his leave. Then the earl spoke again. 'Remind me,' he said, raising a finger. 'Your family come from near Waverley, is that right? Blakemore or Woolmer area?'

'Yes, lord. My father's lands were just west of there.' *My inheritance*, he thought.

'Then you must know that country well, I suppose?' de Montfort went on, as if he was pondering something. 'I may need to call on your services, one of these days,' he said. 'But I shall ask leave of Robert de Dunstanville first, of course.'

Adam bowed, then turned to go. 'May God protect you tomorrow, Adam de Norton,' de Montfort said.

Making his way back to the lower table, Adam turned over de Montfort's words in his mind. He still did not understand why the earl had singled him out for praise, or what the meaning of his closing comments might be. But the brief conversation had kindled a warm sense of pride in him nonetheless. Foolish, he knew, to be so taken in by the words of the powerful. But he felt himself almost taller and broader as he returned to his place at the bench. And that, he supposed, was how men like Simon de Montfort won others to their cause.

His stream of thought ended as he neared the table and caught the sound of raised voices. Returning swiftly to awareness, he saw the men standing around the table, the others who had risen from the benches, the tensed postures and the angry gestures. With a jolt of alarm he saw that Robert de Dunstanville was at the heart of the confrontation. Robert was still seated on the bench, apparently calm, his hands on the table before him, but

Adam could read the man well and recognised that he was both extremely angry and primed for violent movement.

It was John FitzJohn who confronted him. The younger man had crossed from the middle table to stand before him, one hand clasping his belt and the other resting lightly on the hilt of his scabbarded knife. Other men formed a ring around them, like spectators at a wrestling bout.

'We know well the company you keep, de Dunstanville,' Fitz-John was saying, his face bunched into a sneer. 'We know all about your *Jewish friends*, and where you choose to lay your head . . . You call me Jew killer, is that right? Well, I call you *Jew lover*, and consider it a more shameful name by far!'

'Why should I care about your dirty thoughts, FitzJohn?' Robert said, turning his palm casually. He was not looking directly at the man, but Adam knew he was tracking his every move. 'Why should I care anything for some young pup who only won his spurs, what . . . yesterday, was it?'

'I've done more to earn them than you!' FitzJohn snarled. 'I don't think anyone here has seen you on the field of battle lately. You deserted us on the road to Northampton. You fought against us in London, while we were regaining what was rightfully ours . . .'

'When you were murdering and plundering defenceless people, you mean?' Robert said lightly, with a shrug. 'Molesting women and killing children?'

'Oh, spare us your homilies!' FitzJohn declared, stabbing his finger at Robert. 'There are few here who haven't been squeezed by the Jews. Few here who haven't lost their patrimonies in loan repayments – speak to Ralph de Heringaud there, he knows! How much blood have they sucked from you, Ralph?'

De Heringaud raised his palms in entreaty, mumbling something.

'Or,' FitzJohn went on, with an air of satisfaction, 'speak to Earl Simon de Montfort. Ask him if he opposed my actions. Ask him if he thinks ill of what I did, for the liberation of us all. Those who hate God and the Church and despise the sacraments will always be my enemy!'

Growls of agreement came from the men at his back – Henry de Hastings was one of them, with several other knights. Richard de Malmaines was among them too, Adam noticed. But a rival band was gathering to back Robert now, smaller but no less determined to stand their ground. Adam moved forward to join them, pushing between them until he stood at Robert's shoulder.

'And I have confessed all my sins, on this holy day!' FitzJohn declared, spreading his hands and grinning. 'Confessed and been absolved. Although I do not know that anybody saw you confessing, de Dunstanville. Did you hear mass? Did you enter the church? Are you still a Christian at all, or does your true allegiance lie elsewhere now? . . .'

Robert stood up suddenly, the bench shunting from beneath him, and FitzJohn took a step backwards. Few of those present had swords, but their scabbarded weapons lay beside them, and every man had his knife. Adam glanced down, checking where his own sword lay.

'Enough!' a voice cried. 'Friends, enough!' Humphrey de Bohun came striding through the crowd, spreading his arms to separate the rivals. Adam saw Henry de Montfort, the earl's son, following him, and the bishop too. 'Step back from these accusations, I command you!' de Bohun yelled.

'My allegiance is plain for any man to see,' Robert said, still speaking quietly. 'And you yourself shall see it tomorrow, FitzJohn, when we storm the first breach. Side by side, eh?'

'I shall consider that a challenge,' John FitzJohn said, his face still reddened. 'First man over the wall. First onto the enemy rampart. Let all here witness us. But if you fail us, de Dunstanville, if you shirk, or show your heels . . .'

'Likewise,' Robert said. He leaned across the table and stuck out his palm. FitzJohn seized it, and they glared at each other as they shook hands.

Adam's heart was still beating fast, his reactions sharpened. He began to ease out a breath, and then caught it again as Robert glanced over his shoulder. De Dunstanville's expression was hard and flinty, but there was a look of intense satisfaction in his eyes. As if, Adam thought, he had provoked the confrontation with FitzJohn. As if he had desired that attention, that notoriety. As if he was making a point, somehow. Could it be, Adam wondered, that Robert had envied his own audience with Simon de Mont-fort? Could he even have resented it?

Then a ghastly retching sound came from along the table, and everyone turned to see young William de Heringaud collapse from the bench, spewing up the wine and rich meats he had consumed so avidly.

# Chapter 22

'Baby on the way!' the man in the leather apron yelled, then hauled on the rope. A grate of iron, a click and a jolt. Timbers wailed as the great counterweight began to fall, and the lever arm of the trebuchet, the length of a ship's mast, sprang upwards. A stone the size of a man's torso lay in the leather sling; as the lever arm swung, the stone was jerked suddenly into motion. A smooth rising curve, the arm creaking and the sling whipping up and over, then the counterweight crashed to a halt and the sling released. The stone flew clear across the outer bailey wall, a tumbling speck against the bright sky. From the far side came the distant crunch of impact.

Adam had been watching the war engines all morning, amazed and frankly terrified by their power and precision. Every time one was released he hunched, chest tight, expecting the lever arm to crack, the sling to hurl its massive projectile backwards or sideways into the ranks of the surrounding men, or the whole ungainly timber construction to shudder and explode into fragments. But all morning the crews had hauled down the lever arms, loaded their machines and loosed them. All morning the massive stones had arced over the rampart of the outer bailey to batter the keep and the inner wall still held by the enemy.

Between shots the crews oiled the ammunition channels with liquid grease from the kitchens, tensed and slackened bolts and knots, and watched for the signals from the watchers on the outer wall, who alone could judge where the stones were falling and the damage they were doing. In the moments between the heaving swings and crashes of the big trebuchets outside the walls came the sharper and more frequent cracks of the lighter man-hauled perrier machines mounted inside the bailey, flinging stones at closer range. The keep and the walls of the inner ward were being battered incessantly from all sides.

'Won't be long now,' Robert said. He was chewing his cheek, a tense agitation animating his whole body.

'You think they'll surrender?' a knight beside him asked.

Robert looked at him, witheringly, and shook his head. 'They'll make a breach, I mean, in the wall of the inner ward. A breach wide enough to storm.'

'*Move up! Move up!*' a serjeant was shouting, and the band of archers and foot soldiers waiting by the bridge jolted into motion. Adam joined Robert and the group of knights that accompanied him, and together they jogged across the battered bridge and in through the blackened arches of the gatehouse. The noise of clashing weapons and stamping boots, the heavy clink of mail and the gruff words of command, echoed in the soot-covered stone tunnel between the gates.

Adam had not ventured within the circuit of the castle walls since the night they captured the town gates and stormed the bailey. That bloody and confused combat in the darkness remained fresh in his memory. But the scene before him now appeared totally transformed. Except for the chapel, the buildings of the outer bailey had all been burned and reduced to blackened shells. The open space within the circuit of walls was crossed by lines of wooden mantlets and wicker hurdles, providing shelter for the attacking archers from the arrows, crossbow quarrels and

slingshot of the defenders. Shelter too for the three perrier catapults, and for the troops gathering for the assault on the inner
defences.

The wall that crossed the bailey and enclosed the inner ward
was neither as high nor as strong as the outer ramparts, but
with its gatehouse and battlements it had presented a formidable obstacle on the night that Adam and the other attackers had
first tried to storm the castle. Now the wall too looked very
different: the battlements were in ruins, merlons demolished
and crenels knocked together by the impact of shot from the
perrier catapults. The wall itself was pitted and cratered, and
in places the outer stone facing had broken away to reveal the
crumbling rubble core. As Adam watched, another big projectile
came arcing over from the trebuchets beyond the gatehouse, to
smash directly into the most damaged section of the wall. Almost
simultaneously another stone came whirling in from the catapults over near the cathedral, striking the wall at the same point
on the far side. A cheer went up from the foot soldiers sheltering
behind the mantlets as the wall visibly quaked under the double impact. The defenders were still up on the rampart walks,
preparing to reinforce any breaches, but the siege engines were
working with devastating effect. Another missile fell, crashing
against the wall exactly on target, and the stones shuddered as a
mist of pulverised masonry rose from them.

Adam could taste the dust. His throat was dry, and when one
of the serjeants passed a waterskin he seized it gladly, swilling his
mouth. His body felt oiled with sweat beneath the weight of his
hauberk, aketon and helmet. Most of the fighting men around
him were dressed in the same way. They were not wearing leg
armour, no mail chausses or greaves which would make it harder
to run and to clamber across broken walls and up scaling ladders. Few wore helmets either, just iron skullcaps beneath their
tight-fitting mail coifs, ventails hanging loose from their faces so
they could breathe more easily. Adam noticed John FitzJohn and

his serjeants, distinctive in quartered yellow and red surcoats. Robert and FitzJohn had exchanged glances as they entered the enclosure of the bailey, but there was no time now for exhibitions of rivalry. Tension rippled through them all, every man squinting as he gazed at the rampart, waiting for the wall to crumble.

A yelp of pain came from close by, and everyone hunched instinctively. Arrows were dropping from the dusty air; Adam had not realised they were in range of the archers on the inner rampart. One of the serjeants lay writhing in the dirt, his face corded with pain as he clutched his leg and stared at the arrow pinning his thigh.

'Heads down, shields up!' John FitzJohn cried. His voice sounded thin, youthful compared to the gruff shouts of the veteran serjeants around him. Adam recalled that the man was only a few years older than he was.

The perrier catapults swung and loosed, swung and loosed, faster now that a breach appeared imminent. Crouching in the shade of his raised shield, Adam watched them as they worked. Each of the engines had a crew of eight men hauling on the ropes, dragging the lever beam up and over to sling the stone projectile towards the wall. The crews shouted in unison as they heaved, and the engines cracked and jumped as they discharged their shot.

'Looking nervous, squire,' a voice said. 'You've never stormed a breach before?'

Adam turned to see Richard de Malmaines running a whetstone along the edge of his blade. 'No, I have not,' he said.

'Me neither, to be fair,' de Malmaines said, and let out a cracked laugh. 'But I'm sure it's not as terrifying as men say!'

Then a roar came from the men around them. Adam peered from beneath his shield, narrowing his eyes into the glare. A plume of dust was rolling upwards from the inner wall, about fifty paces to the left of the gatehouse. As it cleared, all could see the section of masonry leaning outwards, stones and rubble jammed together with great fissures running through it. It looked like it would collapse at any moment.

A breathless hush, a double thud from the trebuchets outside the bailey, and everyone craned upwards as two more projectiles sailed across the sky. One overshot, vanishing behind the wall somewhere. The second struck the ground just at the lip of the ditch before the wall, raising a shower of dirt as it bounced upwards to crash directly against the base of the sagging rampart. For a few heartbeats nothing happened. Then the wall section cracked and began to slide, stones grinding as a chunk of masonry ten paces wide toppled forward and crashed down into the ditch in front of the wall. The breach was open, and as the dust cleared the attackers let out a savage roar.

'Forward!' John FitzJohn yelled, raising his sword. 'Everyone forward!'

But Robert de Dunstanville was already running, Adam close behind him, John Chyld and half a dozen other serjeants at their heels. Forward into the rolling dust cloud they ran, armour heavy, breath already rasping as they swerved between the mantlets and hurdles and the knots of archers still lofting shafts against the broken ramparts. The perriers were still cracking away too, whirling stones into the breach to drive back anyone attempting to seal it.

John FitzJohn and his men were on the right of the charge, Robert and Adam on the left. But between and ahead of them were the knights and squires of Simon de Montfort's household, leading the vanguard. Their red shields bore the rampant white lion blazon, and several of them carried long scaling ladders between them.

An arrow banged into Adam's shield as he ran, then a second. A man ahead of him stumbled and fell as he was hit by an arcing shaft. The charging men did not slacken their pace. Suddenly Adam saw the ditch opening before him and staggered down the near side of it, kicking up dust. Rubble grated underfoot, and he quickly realised that he had come down too far to the left of the breach. A stone dropped from the wall above clipped the rim of his helmet, and he felt the kick of it ringing in his skull.

The mound of rubble formed by the collapsed wall was a lot steeper than it had appeared, but already men were scrambling up the tumbled stone and shattered masonry. Arrows and cross-bow quarrels spat down at them from the edges of the ramparts to either side. Holding his shield above his head, Adam began to clamber up the rubble slope. Robert was climbing ahead of him; he could hear his labouring breath. The dust in the air formed a choking yellow-grey fog.

'Christ's bones, I'm too old for this!' John Chyld cried. Adam turned to see him clambering up behind them.

'*A Montfort! A Montfort!*' The household knights were gasping out their battle-cry as they reached the top of the rubble slope. In the breach, a wall of jostling shields and a thicket of spears. The defenders were screaming defiance, shoving at the men climbing up towards them. One of de Montfort's squires was speared in the face and tumbled backwards, bringing down two of the men behind him as he fell. When Adam glanced upwards he saw Richard de Malmaines clambering into the gap, sword raised. From somewhere to his right he could hear the hoarse cries, '*A FitzJohn! A FitzJohn!*'

Ahead of him Adam saw the body of a man who had been struck directly by a catapult stone. The man's upper chest and head had been obliterated, turned into a smear of mashed flesh and blood spattered across the rubble, but the arms still stuck out grotesquely to either side, hooked fingers grasping air. Choking back nausea, Adam scrambled on upwards.

Then he was into the breach, grazing his shins on broken masonry. Staring from beneath his helmet rim he saw the chaotic mass of struggling bodies filling the gap, blades battering shields, maces and axes swinging, no formation or order remaining beyond wild desperate combat. To his right, Robert hooked his axe around a man's ankle and wrenched him off his feet, pausing only to deal a hacking blow at the fallen body before piling forward into the melee.

'Guard yourself!' a voice cried in his ear, and Adam swung his shield just in time as a man in a green gambeson hurled an axe at his head. The spinning weapon struck his shield, the blow almost knocking him off his feet, and already his attacker was on him. The man in green reached down to his belt and drew a long-bladed knife, but Adam shoved forward with his shield and slammed against his chest and right shoulder, pinning his arm across his body. He drew back his fist, levelled his sword and stabbed across the upper rim of his shield, punching the blade in beneath the man's coif and through his throat. The man gaped at him, blood spilling from the wound, but as his legs went from beneath him he seized the rim of Adam's shield and dragged it down with him. Horrified, Adam tried to haul back on the shield straps, but the man's full weight was pulling at him and his sword was still stuck in his throat. *Why would he not die?*

Adam twisted his right hand, sawing the blade in the wound, seeing only the dying man's eyes glaring back at him with a look of utter contempt. The man choked, lips tightening, then blood burst from his mouth. Abruptly the grip on Adam's shield slackened as the man dropped back onto the broken stones.

Staggering upright, the red stink washing over him, Adam drew a gasping breath and pushed himself forward once more, over the wall to cascade down the far slope of rubble. The fight had spilled back from the breach now and across the inner ward towards the base of the great keep. Adam risked a glance upwards; from here the structure appeared enormous, impregnable, a sheer cliff of smooth stone, pierced with arrow slits all the way up to the bristling ramparts and fighting platforms.

Someone barged against him and Adam staggered to one side. The other man glanced at him with a twisted grin on his face — he was one of de Montfort's serjeants, wearing a red gambeson and coif – then a plunging stone dropped from high overhead and burst his head apart. Adam let out a cry as he stumbled backwards, feeling hot blood and bone fragments spatter his face and chest.

Robert seized him by the arm, dragging him aside. 'You're hurt?' he demanded. Mastering himself, fighting down the sudden wave of sickening terror and disgust, Adam shook his head.

'There,' Robert cried, pointing. 'It's de Leyburne!'

Adam stared through the milling bodies, and saw that a party of defenders had sallied from the buildings of the inner ward to drive back the assault. Leading them was a knight in full armour, his blue surcoat and shield decorated with white lions. His face was obscured by his great helm, but Adam recognised the man he had seen at Lagny years before, in Lord Edward's company. At his back was a tight wedge of armoured serjeants, and already they had carved a path into the attacking horde.

They met FitzJohn's retinue first, driving them back across the inner ward towards the rubble-strewn breach. Adam saw John FitzJohn himself limping heavily as two of his squires escorted him clear of the melee. Then Robert charged into the fray, yelling for Adam to follow him.

But John Chyld was quicker. As the remnant of FitzJohn's retinue fell back, the grizzled serjeant dodged towards de Leyburne, swinging a falchion. The knight reacted with practised speed, catching the blow on his shield and turning it, then sliced off John Chyld's hand with a single cut. The serjeant buckled in pain, and de Leyburne wheeled his blade and brought it hacking down through his shoulder to cleave his chest.

Robert halted with a cry of dismay as John Chyld fell. Adam was already darting forward, grabbing the serjeant's bloodied body by the sleeve of his gambeson and dragging it clear of the hacking blades. He tried not to look at the grisly wound. No man could have survived that. Invulnerable in his full armour, Roger de Leyburne strode forward once more, leaving the crippled and the dying sprawled in his wake.

A shout from the breach, and Adam glanced back to see the second wave of attackers swarming in across the rubble, Sir Humphrey de Bohun leading them. De Leyburne saw them too, and just for a moment his steady murderous advance was checked. The men behind him were closing up, raising shields against this new threat. Robert de Dunstanville saw his chance, and struck.

Hooking his axe over the top of the other knight's shield he dragged it aside, then raised his own shield and punched the leading edge of it into the gap below de Leyburne's helmet rim. The knight staggered back, and already Robert's axe was wheeling to chop down on him. De Leyburne got his shield up in time, and lifted his sword to strike. Robert pulled his blow at the last moment, letting the axe skate off de Leyburne's shield and then cut diagonally at the knight's wrist. De Leyburne bellowed as the axe grated along his mail sleeve and his sword fell from his gauntleted grip. It was still hanging by the leather wrist strap, but the knight was reeling now, disorientated, and Robert dealt another hacking blow to his shoulderblade with the axe.

De Leyburne dropped heavily to his knees, his shield slipping from his arm. Robert had time to slam his axe against the side of the man's helmet, denting the iron, before the enemy serjeants closed around their master. Two of them grabbed de Leyburne beneath the arms and began dragging him back towards the keep, while the rest formed a wall of shields and levelled spears.

'Mine! He's mine!' Robert bellowed after them, madness in his voice, but the serjeants had closed up as they retreated, fending off the furious blows of his axe with their shields. Humphrey de Bohun's men came storming into the fight, spilling away to either side to try and outflank their retreating foes and cut them off from the steps to the keep. Two of them seized John Chyld's mauled body and lugged it between them, carrying it back towards the breach in the wall as Robert protected them, swinging his axe at any attacker that approached. Adam could hear the grief in the knight's defiant yells. He felt it himself, a sense of disbelief that clouded his senses, even as the fight grew hotter around him.

Now that the melee had tightened, he could see what lay ahead. At the nearer corner of the keep the stone steps turned at an angle, passing through a projecting turret closed by a single door of heavy studded oak. Above the turret, the stairway ascended once more, up the left-hand face of the keep towards a larger gatehouse. Before this second gate was a ten-foot gap, crossed only by a narrow plank-bridge. Peering upwards, Adam felt his heart seize in his chest. The steps were a death trap for anyone trying to storm them. Truly, the keep was impregnable.

Already, as de Leyburne's men carried their master up the first flight of steps and through the turret gate, the mass of attackers were surging after them. But there were men with crossbows on the turret cap and the gatehouse roof, and at every slit and embrasure above the steps. Stones were showering down from the high battlements too; everyone who could pick up a rock and hurl it was concentrated in the corner above the steps, raining death on the men below.

Adam crouched beneath his shield, feeling the concussion as stones and crossbow bolts struck it. Two bolts had already punched through the shield's leather and wood, their iron heads projecting from the back. Knees bent, he scuttled to the base of the keep and pressed himself against the wall, desperately trying to keep clear of the hail of missiles. Something dark fell from above, and the contents of a chamberpot spattered the ground.

A roar, then a battering noise. De Leyburne's men had managed to retreat through the turret door and force it closed behind them; now de Montfort's men were hacking at the oak with axes and hammers. But Adam could see that the effort would be useless; only a ram could break through that door, and with the

angle of the steps immediately below it there was no room to
manoeuvre one up there or to swing it effectively.

Other men were sheltering at the base of the keep with Adam,
a crush of bodies pressed against the stones, men in gambesons
and mail, several wounded and groaning, others craning outwards to try and see what was happening above them. A strange
hissing sound came from high overhead, then a wave of dry heat
that seemed to roll downwards from the steps. Sudden motion,
shrieks of terror, men scrambling away to either side, some leaping out into the open to brave the arrows. Uncomprehending,
Adam followed the rush around the corner of the keep. When
he glanced back he saw bodies tumbling from the steps amid a
strange whirling brown mist.

Sand, he realised – the defenders had tipped red-hot sand
down onto the men outside the turret door. He felt it on his
face as the breeze carried it, little freckles of fire, and turned
away quickly. But the men who had been struck directly had
no escape. The burning-hot sand was trapped in the links of
their mail and beneath the padding of their gambesons, filtering
quickly downwards until it met flesh. Those who had thrown
themselves from the steps were rolling in agony, screaming like
souls in hell as they tried to rip off their armour and clothing
to escape the searing particles. Some cried for water, but there
was none. Arrows and bolts spat down from above, ending their
suffering quickly enough.

The remaining attackers had fallen back from the steps, most
of them fleeing across the bailey while others leaped down to join
Adam and the others sheltering at the base of the wall. Crouched
beneath the steps, they were sheltered from the missiles from
overhead. But if they stepped out into the open, Adam realised,
every crossbow on the ramparts and the gatehouse roof would
be aimed at them at once.

'I believe we've done enough to satisfy the demands of honour, don't you?' the knight beside Adam said. He turned, and

saw it was Richard de Malmaines. The other man seemed just as surprised to see him there. His bulging eyes and the smear of blood across his face gave him a particularly deranged look.

'We're not going to break into the keep from here, certainly,' Adam said, with a wary glance upwards. They could hear the defenders yelling at them, goading them to show themselves, taunting them with the defeat of their assault. Adam felt the angry frustration boiling inside him. To have got this far and then to have failed – it was maddening.

'We could take one of those ladders and set it against the wall here,' he said, glancing at the discarded equipment littering the base of the steps. 'Climb up to the inner gateway and try to break it down.'

'Excellent idea,' de Malmaines said in a wry tone. 'You go first, and I'll follow right behind.'

Adam turned to him, frowning, and de Malmaines laughed coldly. 'Remember,' he said. 'I'm still pledged to kill you.'

On the far side of the inner ward, another group of men were sheltering in the ruins of buildings along the back of the rampart wall. Robert de Dunstanville was among them, carrying de Leyburne's discarded shield as a trophy; he saw Adam and gestured towards the breach in the wall. Adam saw that the men who had been thrown back from the keep had regrouped there, joined by others from the outer bailey carrying wooden mantlets and wicker screens. But open ground separated Adam and the others with him from that sanctuary. Twenty long strides, Adam estimated, through a storm of arrows, bolts, slingshot and stones from the ramparts of the keep and gate tower.

Another group of men edged around the corner of the keep to join those sheltering with Adam. Humphrey de Bohun was leading them; he had three crossbow bolts jutting from his shield and he clasped the hilt of a broken sword. Adam had seen him earlier, with the party that tried to storm the steps and attack the turret door. Sir Humphrey's face was marked with red blisters from the heated sand.

'Does anyone have water?' he asked, his voice parched. None did. Lips drawn back from his teeth, he tipped his head back and gazed up at the dark cliff of masonry above them. 'We can avail nothing here,' he said.

'We must get back to the breach, lord,' one of the serjeants said, confirming what all of them knew. 'Lead, and we'll follow . . .'

More yells of derision from above them, then came the sound of iron hinges and the bang of the wooden plank-bridge falling into place. The men along the base of the wall leaped up instantly, hefting shields and weapons. Boots crashed on the plank-bridge, then on the stone steps as the castle defenders sallied forth once more to cut them off from their line of retreat.

'Now!' Humphrey de Bohun yelled. 'Back to the breach — with me!'

Shoving themselves away from the wall, the little group of men broke into a sprint across the open ground. Instantly the air seethed with arrows and bolts. Adam saw a man to his right pinned through the foot by a quarrel; two others seized him by the elbows and dragged him after them as he howled in pain. A stone dropped immediately ahead of him, raising dust, and he leaped over it and kept running. He was almost there now, clambering up onto the lower slope of rubble that climbed to the breach. Then he heard a shout, and glanced behind him.

Humphrey de Bohun was sprawled face down in the arrow-studded dirt. For one galloping heartbeat Adam thought he was dead, that de Bohun, the man who would marry Joane de Quincy, had been slain.

Then de Bohun moved, reaching out with one hand and try-ing to raise himself to crawl. Adam was poised at the base of the rubble slope. Other men ran past him, scrambling into the safety of the breach and the line of mantlets.

'Leave him!' de Malmaines cried. 'He's a dead man!'

But already Adam was moving, instinct propelling him. In his mind he heard his own voice telling him he was a fool, that he would be better off by far leaving Humphrey to die; that Joane would be better off too if de Bohun was gone.

Too late. Already he was dropping to kneel beside the fallen man. He had sheathed his sword, but still carried his shield strapped to his left arm. He raised it over them both; at once he felt the impact of a crossbow bolt, then a stone banging off the rim. De Bohun had been struck on the head, as far as Adam could see. Blood was coursing down his face from beneath his mail coif, but he appeared to be merely stunned. Adam hooked his right arm beneath Sir Humphrey's chest and heaved him up, straightening his legs and keeping his shield raised over him. But de Bohun had always been a big man, and in full mail he weighed a lot more than Adam.

Another bolt slammed into his shield. Adam could sense the men on the ramparts and towers spanning their crossbows and whirling their slings as fast as they could, all of them concentrating their shots at the two figures pinned down in the open. Another rock fell, only a stride away from de Bohun's feet. Sir Humphrey grabbed hold of Adam's surcoat and clung on, breath rasping from his throat as he tried to blink the blood from his eyes. Adam was dragging him, hunched over the heavy body as he felt the sweat bursting on his forehead and coursing down his face.

'Stand up!' he hissed through his teeth. 'On your feet, damn you!'

Then suddenly the weight eased as another man grabbed Sir Humphrey's right arm. Between them they lifted him, and Humphrey groaned and kicked his legs, getting himself upright and beginning to stagger.

'By Christ's wounds, I will not let you die!' de Malmaines told Adam, his eyes wide with demented rage. 'Your life belongs to me – not to them!'

Adam laughed suddenly, through the screaming pain in his muscles, the sweat glazing his face, the death raining down all around them. He laughed, his voice cracking, as together he and Richard de Malmaines dragged the body of Humphrey de Bohun up the slope of rubble and over the breach in the wall, where the mantlets were dragged aside and the arms of other men seized them and guided them to safety at last.

*

That night Adam lay in his tent in the cathedral grounds. He could hear drunken singing from the nearby watch-fires, but most of the men in de Montfort's army were too weary and demoralised even to drink. His body ached, his muscles felt raw, and he was covered in grazes and cuts he had not even noticed at the time. In the darkness of the tent Robert de Dunstanville was snoring deeply. Though he had come through the fight unscathed, the death of John Chyld had crushed any satisfaction he might have felt about pressing his advance further than John FitzJohn, or bringing down de Leyburne. Adam felt a similar anguish; he had known loss before, but always at a remove. The serjeant had been part of his life for the last two and a half years, and that sudden and senseless death in the battle had stunned him.

But when he closed his eyes, Adam saw only the face of the man he had killed. The first man he was sure that he had killed, at least. He saw again the look of contempt in the man's eyes as the life ebbed from him, as the blood burst from his mouth. Adam did not regret what he had done. But it was a grave thing, a sobering thing, to take a life. And he had been lucky indeed not to have been killed himself. De Bohun had thanked him, and Robert had appeared warily impressed. But perhaps, Adam thought, de Malmaines had been right all along. He had been a fool to risk his own life to save a man like Humphrey de Bohun.

There would be no swift conclusion to their siege of Rochester Castle. Already men were down in the castle moat with picks and shovels and baulks of wood to begin their mine beneath the castle walls. It would take at least a week just to dig beneath the outer defences, and even with the king and Lord Edward still somewhere far to the north, few believed they had that long.

Lying on his bedroll in the stale gloom of the tent, Adam imagined the labourers deep underground, hacking at the soil. As he slid into weary sleep, he could almost believe that he heard them down there, the scrape of their shovels and the muffled heave of their breath as they dug blindly onward through the dark earth.

# Chapter 23

It was two days later, shortly before compline, that Simon de Montfort summoned Adam to him. The Earl of Leicester had established himself and his retinue in the finest house in Rochester, with a large upper chamber and a gable-end window giving a view out towards the castle. Adam found Lord Simon standing at the window in a mood of deep introspection.

For a few long moments the earl did not register Adam's presence. The servant who had conducted him to the chamber shuffled his feet, then banged his way back down the stairs, and finally de Montfort turned, arms folded across his chest, his face hawkish in profile against the evening light.

'I need you to do something for me,' he said, his voice low in his throat. 'That is, I cannot command you, but it would be a matter of great help to me, and you should have my gratitude. You, and your master Robert de Dunstanville too.'

'You've spoken to Sir Robert already, lord?' Adam asked.

De Montfort gave a curt nod. 'I would not wish to claim the service of another man's squire without permission,' he said.

Adam had already guessed that Robert had agreed to the service, whatever it was. He himself had passed on the summons to this meeting, after all, although he had not appeared at all interested in what it might entail. Since John Chyld's death Robert had remained in his tent, neither eating nor drinking, speaking only a few words. They had recovered the serjeant's body at least, and had carried him over the river to Strood earlier that day. Robert had insisted that they lay him to rest there, rather than see him flung into a common pit with the others slain in the failed assault.

'Ten years that man followed me,' Robert had said, as he stood beside the grave. 'Since Gascony. But I knew nothing of him. Nothing of whence he came, or whoever his people might be. And now I'll never know.'

Adam had remembered what John Chyld told him years ago, about the lying words of knights and noblemen. Had he believed that still, even as he went to his death for Simon de Montfort? The serjeant's words came back to him now, as he stood before the Earl of Leicester himself.

'What would you have me do?' he asked.

For a few moments more, Simon de Montfort's attention returned to the view from the window. The sun had almost set and the sky was a glassy pale blue. Birds wheeled about the castle towers. Earlier that day there had been another burst of activity from the trebuchets and the smaller catapults, followed by another attempt at storming through the breach in the inner wall and attacking the keep, led by Henry de Hastings this time. Once again it had been thrown back, and since then the siege engines had remained motionless, their lever arms upright. Somewhere out there, Adam thought, the miners were still toiling away in the darkness, beneath the outer ramparts by now he assumed. A spike of horror ran through him – would de Montfort order him down into the tunnels, to aid in the excavation?

But the request, when it came, was quite different.

'I need you to carry a message,' Lord Simon said. 'A letter – a personal letter – to my wife Eleanor, the Countess of Leicester. She's been staying at Odiham Castle these last months. We took all our castles back, you know, after we returned from France, and Odiham was always my wife's favourite residence. Since you know that country well and can ride there without need of a guide, I thought I might ask you to be my courier, and to return here to me with whatever reply she gives you. You do know the country, didn't you say?'

'Yes, lord,' Adam said quickly. He had not been anywhere near Odiham since he was twelve years old, and had no idea whether he would still recognise the area at all, but he did not want to appear hesitant or unwilling.

'I'd send one of my own people,' de Montfort said, turning from the window at last and pouring wine from a jug into two small cups. 'But I have nobody with me now as familiar with that area as a native, eh?'

He passed one of the cups to Adam with a slightly strained smile. Adam nodded his thanks and sipped the wine, conscious that there was surely more to this request than he was being told. Any courier could carry a letter, after all.

'I'll need you to leave before dawn,' Simon went on. 'My man can show you as far as Cuxton and put you on the Winchester road, and you'll pick up the route quickly enough from there. You'd go by Waverley, I expect?'

'I would, lord,' Adam said, and peered quickly into his cup.

'Please do give the abbot my sincere greetings.' Lord Simon had crossed to the table, where a large silver inkstand and a heap of quills and blotters lay in the spill of light from the window, and picked up a sheet of parchment. Adam was surprised to notice that the earl appeared to have written the letter himself, rather than dictating it to a scribe. He watched as Simon studied it quickly, folded it several times, then melted wax from a wafer onto the join and applied his seal.

'This letter will be waiting for you in the lower chamber tomorrow, an hour before matins,' he told Adam, holding up the sealed document. 'Carry it safely, carry it quickly, and

I must compel you most strongly to let it fall into no other hands. Deliver it to my wife alone, you understand?'

'I understand, lord,' Adam replied. A nervous heat was rising through him, but he could not tell if it was pride in being selected for such a task, or a presentiment of danger.

'We have six days before the close of Hocktide,' de Montfort went on. 'That should suffice for you to reach Odiham and deliver the message, wait for the reply and convey it back here to me by the swiftest road. You can do it?'

'I can, lord, and I will,' Adam said briskly. He still had no idea how possible it was, but he was determined to try.

There was a wooden bowl of apples on the table too, the last of the winter crop; Lord Simon selected one and studied it briefly, rubbing his thumb over the wrinkled brown skin, then stepped over to Adam and placed a hand on his shoulder. 'I'm putting great trust in you,' he said. The evening light glinted in his deep-set eyes. 'But if you do this for me, my gratitude will bear fruit in time, I promise you that.'

And he bit into the apple with his strong white teeth.

*

Adam slipped away from Rochester the next morning in the dimness before matins, only briefly disturbing the sentries at the gate and on the newly laid bridge. The dawn was chilly and damp, and a mist hung above the waters of the Medway as he rode south towards the little riverside hamlet of Cuxton. Behind him the sun was just coming up, the castle keep a bar of shadow against the bright horizon. His guide took him a little way beyond the hamlet and wordlessly pointed out the way that would take Adam westwards, before leaving him to ride on alone. Away from the river valley the land rose, and by the time the sun was up, Adam had left the misty estuary behind him and was riding along grassy hill slopes on an old track that followed the ridges of the downlands.

He had slept poorly the night before, consumed by thoughts of the letter he must carry and the journey that lay ahead. De Montfort had impressed on him the previous evening the importance of telling no one of his destination, or what he carried. Adam had told Robert de Dunstanville alone a little of what he had been asked to do. But it was a relief to be away from the town, and from the rigours of the siege. He had a good riding horse and a purse of silver to pay for lodgings, fodder and provisions along the way. Lord Simon had left another letter for him as well, to be delivered to the Abbot of Waverley.

The day was warm for late April, the countryside filled with the sounds of birdsong, and in the fields below the track men and oxen were ploughing and harrowing, and cows grazed in the meadows. The grim realities of war seemed very far away. But Adam noticed that the ploughmen and the cowherds scattered as they caught sight of him, fleeing to their villages to seize weapons and shutter houses, in case he was the outrider of an approaching army come to waste the land with fire and sword. News of the kingdom's turmoil had passed through all this country.

Riding at a steady pace, Adam covered the miles quickly. And with every passing mile his mood lifted; he felt almost as if this journey west might be a journey into his own past, his lost childhood, taking him back to places he had not seen since his father was alive. Even so, as he rode his mind was pulled back restlessly to the events of the preceding days. To the death of John Chyld, and to the moment that he had turned back from the breach to help Humphrey de Bohun and carry him to safety. Sir Humphrey would surely have died too were it not for him. Yes, he thought, Sir Humphrey would have died and Joane de Quincy would have been free of him. But what then? Who else would she marry? Not him, certainly. *A mere squire,* Robert had called him once. *A serjeant's son, with no land and no fortune.*

But the day was too fresh, the sun too invigorating, to allow such dark thoughts to gain purchase in his mind. He had saved Sir

Humphrey, and in some way he was sure that was worthwhile. Had he not been prompted by more than mere conscience? The man himself had said little in the days since, beyond giving the curtest thanks – he had seemed more embarrassed at his own weakness and failure than anything – but such an act could not be forgotten, surely?

There were a few other travellers on the road – drovers with flocks of sheep, peddlers with hand barrows, and packmen bent beneath their loads, and once a party of pilgrims ringing hand-bells, who were on their way to Canterbury. But Adam rode on without pause, and shortly before noon he descended from the ridge to water meadows where long-horned cattle grazed in the lush new grass. As he crossed the river, his horse splashing and surging through the shallows, he glanced to his left and saw a group of women washing linens downstream from the ford. They stood knee-deep, dressed only in tunics tied between their legs. One of them stood up and wiped her brow with her pink forearm, grinning.

'Do you wish for a swallow of ale, goodsir?' the washerwoman called to him in English, and gestured to a stone jug cooling by the bank. 'It's fresh. That's if you have a thirst that needs quench-ing . . .'

'Thank you,' Adam said, smiling back at her, 'but I cannot stop.' If he did that, he thought, he might be delayed for some time. He spurred his horse on up the riverbank and into a trot along the road. But soon afterwards, as the track began to rise once more towards the chalk ridge above the valley, he felt the heat of the midday sun and thought again of the jug of ale cooling in the fresh flowing water, and realised how thirsty he was and how far he had yet to travel.

He turned his horse and rode a short way back towards the ford, but as he passed through the last belt of trees above the meadow he reined in quickly. Another rider was at the river-bank, wearing a dark hood despite the warm weather. Adam was suddenly convinced that he had seen the man somewhere before. The rider had halted on the bank and was talking to the washer-women; the woman who had offered Adam a drink was replying to him, pointing away to the west. Adam saw the rider nod, then spur his horse on across the ford without a backward glance.

Gripped by a sudden presentiment, he knew at once that the rider in the dark hood had been asking about him. Pulling on the reins, he turned his horse again and cantered back up the slope, hoping to gain the higher ground before the rider caught sight of him.

All the rest of that day he rode on along the track that followed the ridges, pausing at times to peer behind him until he glimpsed the other horseman far off in his wake. But as the afternoon went on he sighted him less often, and as the light began to take on the soft tones of evening Adam told himself that he had been mistaken, and that the rider was merely a traveller like himself, and had probably reached his destination some miles back. He waited, all the same, beneath a stand of trees on the crest of a ridge, where he could look back over a wide sweep of country. Swigging water from his flask, the horse twitching and stamping beneath him, he stared into the distance until he had convinced himself that nobody was following him. Then he laughed at his own credulity, pulled at the reins and rode on.

Shortly before dusk he reached Merstham, saddle sore and weary, and paid a silver penny for a stable, fodder and a straw mattress in the hay loft above. He lay down for the night with his sword beside him, alert for the sound of a step on the creaking ladder. There were several others spending the night in the hay loft, but all had arrived before Adam and he was sure that the man in the dark hood could not have ridden on ahead of him. For a time his mind whirled, thoughts turning, and he could still feel the motion of the horse beneath him. He started awake, reaching for his sword, then yawned heavily and settled himself on the crackling straw.

The second time he woke he did not open his eyes. His senses were alert at once, sleep dropping from him, but he forced himself to lie still and listen for whatever had woken him. A heartbeat later he heard it again: a shuffling sound in the darkness, a scuffing at the rough floorboards of the loft. One of the other sleepers, Adam thought, making his way to the ladder to go down to the stable and relieve himself . . . But no – whatever was scuffling about in the darkness was doing so with a purpose, and was trying to stay quiet.

Adam reached out slowly, careful not to make a sound, then cursed to himself. He had rolled over as he slept; both his sword and his saddlebag were on the other side of the mattress, and he had his back to them. Instead he slid his hand gently beneath the straw bolster and found the hilt of the belt knife he had placed there. Hardly daring to breathe, trying to slow his heartbeat, he waited until the shuffling noises moved closer. Almost like an animal, he thought, rooting around in the dark. But then he smelled the stale sweat and old wool, a man's breath. Leather creaked, a buckle sliding down to tap against the boards.

His right fist closed around the hilt of the knife and Adam rolled up off the mattress, left arm thrust out. The man was closer to him than he had guessed, crouched over his baggage, and his reaching hand seized him by the wrist. With all his weight behind him Adam threw himself onto the intruder, bearing him down and pressing the honed blade of the knife into the rasping stubble of his throat.

'Peace!' the man hissed. 'Douce, I pray, sir!'

From the far side of the loft another man called out gruffly. 'Quiet there!'

Adam kept his weight on the man, his grip tight on his left wrist and the knife against his neck. He could not see where the man's other hand was – no doubt he had a knife too, probably in his belt. If he moves, Adam thought, he dies . . .

'A mistake,' the man beneath him was saying in a tense whisper. 'I swear to you, God be my witness – I thought those were my own bags . . .'

Blinking, Adam found that enough dim moonlight was seeping into the hayloft to make out the shape of the man's features. Something else as well – a pale streak where his hood had fallen back. 'I know you,' he whispered through his teeth. 'I've seen you before, haven't I?'

'No, sir, no surely you have not,' the man was saying. He was tensed, not struggling but waiting for the moment to use his strength. And he was strong enough, Adam knew that.

'You're a follower of Gilbert de Clare, the Earl of Gloucester, isn't that right?' Adam said. Yes, he thought, he remembered seeing them together on the afternoon of Easter Sunday. 'Did he send you here after me?'

'By the arm of St John, will you *be quiet!*' the gruff voice said from across the loft. Another man made a grumbling sound from the darkness at the far end.

The man called Le Brock was smiling – Adam caught the glint of his crooked teeth, the waft of his bad breath. 'Fair enough,' he said in a hissing whisper. 'My young master sent me. Just to get a look at it – the letter – and see what it says. Why shouldn't we know, eh? Those that follow Lord Simon, and risk their lives for him. Why shouldn't we know what messages he's sending, by a strange courier that none would suspect, what plans he's making? Maybe he's plotting to betray us, eh? Don't you want to know yourself?'

A thudding sound came from the far end of the loft as one of the other sleepers reared up from his mattress, hammering on the low angled beam above him. He was a burly man, and Adam caught the shape of a friar's tonsure in the faint light. 'Christ's wounds,' the man cried, 'I paid a good coin to sleep here, why must I be disturbed!'

'My apologies,' Adam said, and eased himself up to kneel, keeping the knife to Le Brock's neck. 'I caught this thief rummaging through my baggage. Likely he's already pilfered yours!'

The burly friar exclaimed angrily. The third man was fully awake now too, both of them crawling across the wooden floor under the low beams to peer at Le Brock.

'You're right!' the friar said. 'Right enough, by God – this man has come from outside, sure enough. Come to rob us in our sleep!'

'Bastard,' Le Brock hissed at Adam through his smile, and made the word sound like a congratulation. As soon as the knife slid away from his neck he burst into sudden motion, struggling against Adam's grip. He would have freed himself, but the burly friar dropped to sit heavily on top of him and the third man seized his legs and clung on tight. Le Brock was fighting against them all now, wrestling to get away, but even his wiry strength could not prevail against three men. The horses below them stamped and snorted in the stalls, disturbed by the noise.

Adam sat back, wiping his face. The friar had blood running from his nose, and the third, a stringy little groom, was complaining that he'd been cut or bitten, but Le Brock had been beaten into submission, tied with his own hose-laces and gagged with straw and a strip torn from his tunic.

'You're lucky I don't take that holy string from your body and use that to tie you as well,' Adam said quietly, speaking into his ear. He saw the flash of Le Brock's eyes in the darkness. Then the man blinked, nodded and subsided.

Little chance of sleep after that. The night was only half gone, but Adam lay still on his mattress until the faintest wash of grey light showed him the shapes of the bound man and the two other sleepers, and the friar's deep snore sounded placidly. Then he got up, gathering his bags, and eased himself down the ladder. He saw Le Brock's face turn in his direction. Down in the stable he saddled his horse as quietly as he could. Le Brock's mount was tied up by the water trough outside, and Adam drew it by the rein and led it behind him to the edge of the village, then set it loose. Before the first glimmer of daylight he was out of the village and on the road, belly empty but for a swallow of water, heading westward once more.

# Chapter 24

High on the chalk ridge, Adam looked out over miles of sweeping countryside, the stacked woodland falling away beneath him to meadows and fields that stretched southward to the far blue horizon. Here and there smoke rose from scattered villages, but aside from that all that moved were the slow grazing cattle and the clouds rolling across the sky.

As he dropped down off the ridge, a few miles short of Faversham, and rode through the wooded hollows and the folds of the fields towards the river and the abbey, he knew that he must have come this way before, with his father perhaps, the images were graven so deeply on his mind. His father's old manor, once his own home, lay only half a day's ride to the south-west. The temptation to turn aside from his journey and fully steep himself in remembrance was strong. But Adam knew how foolhardy that would prove to be, for all that he felt the hooks of memory and longing dragging at him.

Waverley Abbey was just as it had always been though, golden in the early-evening light in its loop of placid river. The abbot was away, but Adam was shown to the guest hall, where one of the lay brothers rather mutteringly made up the fire. It was a Friday, the day of St Mark the Evangelist, and there were no other travellers staying at the abbey, so Adam took his supper of bread and broth alone. Only once he had eaten did he remember the letter he was supposed to give to the abbot – he would leave it with the porter, he decided. But as he opened his leather travelling bag to find it he glimpsed the other letter, the one he was to carry to Odiham and place in the hands of Countess Eleanor. With a cold shock he noticed that the seal was broken.

Snatching the letter from the bag and studying it in the firelight, Adam saw that the wax of the seal had cracked. An old wafer, perhaps – or maybe Le Brock had managed to break it while he was rummaging in the bag the night before? Either way, the letter was open, and there no way to fix it closed again without destroying the impression of the seal. Sitting beside the meagre fire, Adam turned the square of folded parchment in his hands. Le Brock's whispered words came back to him. He could almost smell the man's breath. *Don't you want to know yourself?*

He knew he should not; it would be a betrayal to read what de Montfort had written to his wife. Words so private, so secret, that he had scribed them himself, to be seen by no other. And yet, he also knew, Le Brock had been right. With a pang of deep guilt he gently eased the folds apart, turning the stiff parchment to the firelight to scan the lines of writing inked upon it. The letter was written in French, which he could read well enough, in a fast and flowing hand. Frowning, he picked out the words, moving his lips as he read them. '*Most dearest of my heart and best beloved companion . . .*'

*

Adam de Norton rode in across the drawbridge of Odiham Castle shortly before noon on the Morrow of St Mark. He had made an easy journey from Waverley, after leaving in the grey of dawn. Odiham was not a mighty fortress like Rochester or the Tower of London, nor was it a sprawling magnate's demesne like Pleshey. A pallisaded enclosure stood on the riverbank, ringed about with moats, with a single octagonal keep rising from the inner-most bailey like a sentinel tower. Adam remembered it from brief childhood visits as a secluded stronghold, hidden amid the woods and marshes far from human habitation, the abode of great men and fine ladies. It was a lot smaller than he had pictured it then, but still it had a feel of quiet and tranquillity. A deceptive feeling, he knew.

And if he had expected the Countess of Leicester to be liv-ing in isolated seclusion, he soon realised his mistake. Odiham was a hive, the baileys thronging with men working and build-ing – many of them repairing the fortifications, Adam noticed – priests and friars coming and going, runners carrying mes-sages, and a great number of paupers: Lady Eleanor, like her brother the king, was a great giver of alms to the poor. Adam announced himself to the men at the gate, then waited in the bailey while his horse was taken to the stables. Finally his name was called, and he climbed the wooden outer stairway to the octagonal great keep.

The Lady Eleanor was resting after morning prayers, the steward told him. Adam could leave the message with him, and he would see that it was delivered to her chamber. 'No,' Adam told the man. 'My instruction was to place it in the hands of the countess herself, and none other.'

'Oh, very well,' the steward said with an irritated flick of his wrist. 'You must wait for dinner, in that case – the countess will join us then. You have just enough time to wash and perhaps change your clothes . . .'

Already the servants were setting up the trestle tables and laying them with white cloths – he would not have too long to wait. The hall at Odiham filled the entire first floor of the keep, and preserved its octagonal shape, with deep windows piercing the walls on four sides, tapestries hanging between them, and a ceiling whose massive beams curved inwards to meet high over-head. Strangest of all was the fireplace; rather than occupying the centre of the chamber it was built against one wall, with a masonry hood over it to direct the smoke out through a shaft to the open air. Adam had seen such things before, but never so large or grand.

He was still studying the unusual fireplace, where a couple of palace servants were stoking up a warming blaze, when he heard one of the tapestries behind him lifted aside. Turning, he saw a tall woman dressed in emerald silk stepping from the arched door of a stairway, a pair of maids and a priest following behind her.

'Where is he?' the lady demanded of the steward as she scanned the chamber. Her eye fell on Adam. 'Is this him?'

Adam stepped towards her and bowed deeply. Trying not to appear too shamefaced, he presented her with the letter. Its broken seal was plain for all to see. He had already explained to the steward that the breakage had been accidental; the man had not appeared convinced.

Eleanor de Montfort took the letter, stared at Adam for a moment with a blank expression, then turned away and paced one of the window embrasures, where a shaft of daylight fell upon a side table. As she read, Adam watched her from the corner of his eye. This was the wife of Simon de Montfort, he told himself. Sister to King Henry, daughter of old King John. She looked, he decided, precisely as impressive as he might have hoped.

She was in her late forties, and tall; almost the same height as Adam himself. Framed by her neat white linen headcloth her face appeared sharp-featured, harsh in repose. A powerful face, immobile as she read the letter, but when she raised her head into the daylight from the window embrasure Adam saw her expression shifting, perhaps pained.

'You read it, of course?' she asked him, an hour later over dinner. Eleanor had invited Adam to sit with her at the high table, and take food from her platter. A rare honour, but one she bestowed without ceremony.

'As I told your steward, my lady,' Adam replied, 'the seal was broken during the journey, perhaps when Gilbert de Clare's man tried to steal it—'

Eleanor made a sound in her throat, a flicker of her eyelids. 'But you read it?' she repeated. 'Later, I mean, when you . . . noticed.'

'I did,' Adam said. There seemed no point in trying to lie. Besides, he had the strong sense that Countess Eleanor could read him very accurately.

'Well,' she told him, 'I'm sure I would have done the same, in your position. Merely sensible, one might say. If rather untrustworthy. But I'd rather my husband puts his trust in sensible men who keep their eyes open, rather than in loyal fools.'

Adam suppressed a smile, and bowed his head. He was uncomfortably aware of his scarred knuckles, his forearm bruised from the shield strap, his unshaven face and unwashed hair. But he was impressed that the countess cared so little about his rough appearance.

As it was Saturday, a fish day, there was no flesh on the dishes sent up from the kitchens. The meal was sumptuous all the same: eel pie and roast trout for the higher tables, red herrings and oysters for the lower. Adam sipped from his silver-rimmed cup; the wine was sweet and golden and came from Spain. The countess kept a large household, as he had first suspected. Sitting at the tables were her household officers and knights, her priests, the confessor and almoner, several visiting friars and the damsels of her chamber. Adam reminded himself that this was a time of war – although the struggles of the kingdom seemed far from this well-appointed table, this rich meal, this graceful company. But, besides the clergy, the men among them were old and long past fighting age. All the rest, Adam expected, had departed to join Lord Simon's army.

'So,' the countess said, wiping her hands on a linen cloth and summoning the ewerer with his basin. She was speaking in a low and confidential tone. 'I have admitted that I would have read the letter, in your position. As you know what it says, how would you react, in my position?'

Adam had not been expecting the question, and took his time before replying. Eleanor rinsed her hands in the basin and dried them again, then turned to him and raised her eyebrows.

'I confess I was surprised, my lady,' Adam said, almost under his breath. 'Surprised, I mean, that Lord Simon seemed to think his situation so desperate. Granted, the siege of Rochester is proving difficult, but the king was near Nottingham when last we had news of him—'

'The king, yes,' Eleanor broke in. 'And his son too. While my brother may not be the most decisive of men, I assure you that my nephew Edward has no such debility. As soon as he hears that Rochester is under threat, he will move like a hound from hell.'

'But even so,' Adam said, 'can you really be in danger here? Surely the king would not try to seize you as a hostage? He's your brother . . .'

Eleanor laughed suddenly, a warm low chuckle, and took another sip of wine. 'My brother Henry wears the mask of a mild and gentle Christian,' she told Adam. 'But do not be fooled. He has sat on the throne of England since he was nine years old, a sovereign anointed by God, and the kingly ire is as strong in him as it was in our father. He can be terrifying when he is roused. And I fear his wrath will be cruel against any who challenge his absolute power.'

Adam suppressed a quick shiver. In his mind he saw rows of bodies dangling from gibbets. Yes, he thought – for the noble prisoners, for Simon de Montfort and his sons, for Gilbert de Clare, even for Robert de Dunstanville there would perhaps be pardon. But for the rest, for the commoners and humble squires, there would be the rope noose. Never before had he so clearly contemplated the consequences of revolt against the royal majesty.

'But you have not answered my question!' Eleanor said, breaking into Adam's thoughts with a slightly mischievous smile. 'How
would you react? Would you flee from here, retreat to the coast,
prepare to take ship for France?'

Adam frowned, the grim mood still gripping him. 'That's not
quite what your husband orders,' he said.

'*Orders!*' the countess crowed, and threw up her hands. She
seemed almost, Adam realised, to be enjoying herself. There
were some who thrived on jeopardy, as he well knew. 'Simon
does not order me,' she went on. 'But he *suggests* it strongly,
wouldn't you say? So – would you run, were you me?'

'No,' Adam said, after a pause. 'No, I would not.'

'Quite right. And you may tell my husband that I will not run
either. In fact, I will come to join him, soon enough. And if he
has strength in his sword arm, he will fight all the better knowing
that I am with him.'

Adam merely nodded. In truth, he had been more shocked
than he had dared to express by what he had read in de Montfort's letter. He would never have expected Lord Simon to have
lost heart so badly, and to believe his situation so desperate that
he would advise his wife to flee the country. If such a letter had
fallen into the hands of some of Simon's baronial supporters, he
knew, its effect could have been deeply demoralising, and could
even have turned them against him. Now at least he understood
the need for secrecy, and why Simon had not used one of his own
couriers.

'And you're sure it was de Clare who sent a man after you?'
Eleanor had asked him earlier, after he told her what had happened on the road. 'It should not surprise me, I suppose. That
boy has the spirit of his father in the body of a callow youth. He
wants more than any man can give him, and he wants it immediately.'

Adam remembered seeing Gilbert de Clare for the first time,
at the reception before the tournament at Senlis. Back then, the

young son of the Earl of Gloucester had seemed an ardent devotee of Lord Simon and his cause. Now he was Earl of Gloucester himself, with a mighty retinue at his command, things were different. Although, Adam remembered, Lord Gilbert was barely older than he was, and still not yet a knight.

'Ah, but they are all alike, these ardent young men,' Lady Eleanor sighed. 'De Hastings, de Segrave, FitzJohn . . . How I wish some of the stronger magnates had found more courage within them! Where is Roger de Quincy, the Earl of Winchester, for example? Has he joined the king too? Oh, but we must use what tools God gives us.'

And Adam had made no reply, thinking of Roger de Quincy, and his niece Joane, and of Humphrey de Bohun whose life he had saved. He thought of the patterns that linked them all, like the intricate diagrams in Hugh of Oystermouth's heraldry of the cosmos. Where, he wondered, did he fit into the plan? Did he have a place in it at all?

'But I am in little danger here for now,' Lady Eleanor was saying. 'Many of the local barons are for the king, granted, but they would not dare harm me. William de Saint John rode off to Oxford a month ago, with both his sons. And Hugh de Brayboef, I think, has gone to follow the royal banners as well—'

'You know Hugh de Brayboef?' Adam broke in, startled from his thoughts.

'Ah yes,' Eleanor said, turning to regard him with narrowed eyes. 'You're *that* Adam de Norton, of course. I should have been more perceptive. Yes, I know de Brayboef – I knew him when he married your mother, may God have mercy on her soul. I knew your father as well, I think. But that was many years ago.'

*And perhaps you remember me too*, Adam thought. He had come to Odiham as a child, although he would have been an insignificant figure indeed back then.

'In any case,' Eleanor said briskly, knitting her long fingers before her. 'I shall write to my husband, and you will carry the letter to him. But I need you to take another letter too — Hugh Despenser is still constable of the Tower, yes?'

'My lady,' Adam said, realising her intention, 'your husband was particular that I should return to him directly, by the close of Hocktide.'

'Easily done,' the countess said with a shrug. 'You may rest a few hours, then I'll have one of my grooms take you to the Black-water crossing at Bredeford. I keep a hunting lodge there where you will stay tonight, and in the morning you can follow the old road to London. You can hear evensong at St Paul's, deliver my letter to Despenser at the Tower, and be back in Rochester before Tuesday. That will be your penance, shall we say, for open-ing and reading the letter. You have a good horse? I can lend you a spare if you need it.'

'No, my lady, that won't be necessary,' Adam replied. Sure enough, he thought, travelling back to Rochester through London might be no delay — he could ride faster on the broad straight highways than he could on the meandering ridge tracks. Besides, that way he would not risk running into Le Brock again; no doubt the man had talents enough to have escaped justice at Merstham, but he would not be well inclined towards Adam.

'Good, then it is settled,' Eleanor said. She tugged the heavy garnet ring from her finger, working it down over her knuckle, and placed it on the table beside Adam. 'You may present that to my husband, when you see him,' she said, 'as a mark of my faith in you.'

\*

Across heath and meadow, through the patchwork of field and forest, the road ran dead straight towards London like a marvel of nature. It was an ancient way, so Eleanor de Montfort's lodge-keeper at Bredeford had told Adam; old even when William the Bastard had first crossed from Normandy. Grass-grown in places and rutted and muddied by carts and beasts in others, the road certainly looked ancient enough. It was Sunday, and Adam had risen at cock-crow and followed the sound of bells through the misty trees to the little chantry chapel for Morrow Mass. Alone, he had knelt on the cold floor while the priest yawned through the ritual. An hour later, he was out on the road and riding, and by noon he was crossing the long causeways and the timber bridge that spanned the Thames at Staines.

Five miles on, the road still running straight as an arrow's flight towards London, Adam passed through a fringe of woodland and saw a shallow river ahead of him. On the far bank, beyond the ford, another trackway crossed the road from north to south. And along that trackway flowed an army.

Adam saw the banners first, fluttering in the bright morning air as he rode through the dappled shadow beneath the trees. Then, as he slowed his horse to a walk, he saw the riders that carried the banners and the multitude that rode along with them. He reined to a halt, dropping down from the saddle and drawing his palfrey off the road and beneath the trees, where he could watch from concealment. He saw knights and squires, serjeants, clerks and mounted servants, some of them wearing mail beneath their surcoats and riding cloaks. There were strings of packhorses heavy-laden with baggage. Men and animals in their hundreds; Adam took them in at a glance, unable to determine their exact number. Most were on horseback, and moving at a brisk pace; a few footmen jogged along beside the pack animals, but any accompanying infantry force must have been marching far behind the cavalry. Squinting, baffled, Adam tried to make out the heraldic blazons on banners and shields.

His heart leaped as he saw the familiar red lattice on white, with a golden lion in the top red quarter – the Dunstanville arms. Then, a short way back along the column, flew the blue banner with the white diagonal and rampant golden lions of de Bohun. Momentarily, the sense of relief and recognition overcame his senses. He took two strides forward, out of the shade of the trees and into the sunlight above the riverbank, drawing a breath to call out.

Then the strangeness of the scene struck him, and poured ice through his veins. Why would de Dunstanville and de Bohun be here, so far from Rochester? Why would they be travelling south? The breath died in his mouth as his chest tightened. With sudden shocking clarity he saw the banners afresh, and realised his mistake. There was no blue bar on the de Dunstanville arms; this was not Robert's banner, but that of his older cousin Walter, Baron of Castlecombe. And the de Bohun arms were not those of Sir Humphrey, but of his father. Sure enough, as Adam's widened eyes took in the details, he made out the familiar form of the Earl of Hereford, riding with his household knights. Alongside them, following the road's verge, was a young squire who Adam recognised at once – he had not seen Ralph de Tosny since his departure from Pleshey years before.

And there, in the much larger band of horsemen that followed, flew the proud golden lions on red, the banner of King Henry himself, with that of his brother Earl Richard of Cornwall just behind him. This was the king's army, the royal host of England, not far away in Nottingham but right here and flowing southward like a mighty torrent.

For two heartbeats, maybe three, Adam remained watching them. It was too long. From across the river he caught Ralph de Tosny's glance, and saw his old friend's face bunch in confusion. More than two hundred yards lay between them, but Adam saw the baffled look shift to one of recognition and then of alarm. Then he heard the shouts. Two of the knights riding with Earl Humphrey had peeled off from the side of the column and were splashing down into the ford, yelling at him to remain where he was.

Adam knew he had to move. If the king's men caught him carrying letters from de Montfort's wife, he would be kicking in the air with a noose around his neck before another hour had passed. Panic flared inside him as he set his foot in the stirrup and swung back up into the saddle. He threw a glance towards the ford; no more than two men were pursuing him, one with a lance and the other with a drawn sword, both of them surging through the water. Others had approached the riverbank, but seemed content merely to watch the hunt.

His horse was jittery, startled by the sudden noise and activity – Adam knew that if he tried to flee along the road, the other riders on their more powerful horses would chase him down. As he heard the thudding of the hooves coming up the slope from the ford at a gallop, he turned his horse's head to the left and spurred the animal into the trees. There was a path there, twisting through the thicket towards sunlit open country on the far side. Head down, Adam let out the reins and kicked with his heels, keeping clear of the low branches as the horse bolted. Crashing through a screen of leaves, he emerged into the open. But instead of a firm meadow to make his escape, he found himself gazing across an expanse of wetland, low boggy hummocks, open water and reeds, fringed by more trees at the far side. Already he could hear the two horsemen shouting as they rode into the thicket behind him. For a moment his hand went to his sword hilt as he considered standing his ground and trying to fight. But he was outnumbered; his pursuers wore mail and carried shields and he did not. Flight was his only option.

Veering to his left, he spurred the horse on along the firmer ground beside the marsh until he had passed the first stand of reeds. Then he twisted the reins again, and the horse plunged into the shallow water. Galloping on through the pool and the reed beds and over the tussocks on the far side, Adam risked another backward glance and saw the two pursuers still coming after him. He had gained a little on them, but one was setting off directly across the marsh to try and intercept him. Birds rose in panic all around them, filling the air with harsh cries.

Onward through the stagnant pools Adam galloped towards the far treeline, expecting any moment that his horse would stumble and throw him from the saddle. Water splashed up around him, and clods of wet dirt kicked up his palfrey's hooves. When he looked to his right he saw the man with the lance threading across the centre of the marshland – his horse was clearly labouring in the morass, but the other rider was still keeping up the pursuit. Adam's own horse was tiring now, but he gave another kick with the spurs and the animal surged through the last of the pools and breasted the slope of the drier land.

He was into the tangled country now, the ground knotted with thorny bushes and high stands of reeds between patchy scrub woodland. Noise of crashing water from behind him, and the shouts of the pursuing riders carrying strangely across the wetland. Not daring another glance back, Adam shortened his reins, slowing his horse's wild canter. He turned to the left, then left again, circling behind a rampart of winter deadfall overgrown with nettles. He could hear the second knight still forging through the marshy pools, drawing much closer now. Slipping from the saddle, Adam took the reins and led his horse on through the long grass into the shelter of a dense stand of brushwood. He halted there, crouching close beside the sweating animal, rubbing its neck and beneath its jaw as it twitched and blew into his palm.

Through the tangle of branches he saw the pursuing knight slowing his mount as he moved between the trees. The man was turning in the saddle, peering around him, his sword raised to his shoulder as if he expected some sudden ambush. Adam had contemplated that – he could surely strike down one of his pursuers, with the benefit of surprise. But he knew that the other rider would be drawn quickly enough to the sounds of combat. It was too much to risk.

Slowing his breath, keeping the horse's head low and calming the animal with a slow caress, Adam watched without blinking as the rider turned and then turned again, seeking his prey amid the tangled scrubland. The man with the lance came up out of the marsh and called to him, and Adam heard his frustrated grunt. Beneath his hands, his horse stirred and flicked its tail.

Then, with a burst of hooves, the two riders were gone and cantering back through the wetland towards the bridge to rejoin the marching column. Adam exhaled hugely, feeling the tension rush from his body. He almost wanted to laugh with relief. Once he was sure the two men had crossed the marsh and were truly gone, he emerged from the shelter of the brushwood, leading his horse behind him. He knew the river was somewhere to his right, and guessed there must be a way of crossing it above the bridge. Pushing through the dense scrub, dragging his horse after him, he emerged once more onto the water meadows beside the river and saw the track open and clear on the far side, only the faintest wash of lingering dust and a mass of trampled dung to show where the royal troops had passed.

Adam forded the river a short way upstream, where the water flowed hock-deep over a bar of sand and gravel. He was aware that there could be further detachments of the king's army on the track behind him, and it would be wise not to be trapped between them. The day was beginning to get hot, and Adam paused a while on the riverbank, drinking from the shallows and splashing his face with clear water.

As he raised his head, he heard the sound of approaching hoof-beats and his heart quickened. There was a horseman coming down the track towards him, alone and riding a dappled mare at a brisk trot. The man appeared intent on the road ahead of him, and with the riverbank grown with bushes and stands of trees, Adam knew he had a few moments until he noticed his presence. Quickly drawing his horse from the shallows, he swung back up into the saddle. A nudge of the spur, and the horse carried him up the bank and into the shadow of a pair of low hornbeams growing beside the track.

The approaching rider was much closer now. He had a broad sweating face and a dark beard shaved above his chin, and wore a finely cut tunic and fur-trimmed hood with a long pointed tail that danced behind him as he rode. Adam waited until the rider had just passed his place of concealment before jabbing the spurs into his horse.

'Yield!' he shouted as he exploded into the sunlight, drawing his sword and brandishing it at the rider. The man glanced back in sudden alarm, the brief thought of flight visibly crossing his features. But already Adam had doubled his palfrey around the flank of the mare and seized the bridle, the sword in his right hand levelled to the rider's throat. 'Yield!' Adam said again as he dragged the horse to a halt.

'Mercy, sir!' the rider cried, dropping the reins and spreading his palms. 'Mercy sir, I beg you! God save King Henry, sir, and I am his loyal servant, I swear it!'

'Down!' Adam cried, gesturing with his sword. He was keeping a tight grip on the bridle, his arm tensed as the other horse tried to toss its head and pull away from him. 'Dismount!'

The man nodded quickly, then slipped down from the saddle. Adam gestured again with his sword, circling his horse until he stood over the captive, and the man dropped to kneel in the dust and dung with his hands raised.

'I promise you, sir, I am riding to meet with the king. I have tidings for him, sir, from Brackley, of my master Roger de Quincy. I am steward of his household, sir . . .' Even as the man spoke, stammering his words, Adam could see the pained realisation dawning on him. 'You are . . . you *are* one of the king's men, are you not, sir?' the man asked.

Adam kicked away the stirrups and dismounted in the showy tournament style, flinging his right leg over the horse's mane and leaping from the saddle to land on both feet, sword in hand. The man flinched back from him, almost tumbling onto his haunches.

'What do you know of the king's army?' Adam demanded, tapping the man's neck with the blade of his sword. 'How many knights are with him? How many bannerets?'

The steward glanced to one side, his face shifting between expressions as he struggled to form an answer. 'I had a good look at them, sir, as they passed near Brackley,' he said. 'Yes indeed! The king has all his household knights, and Earl Richard of Cornwall and all his men, and his son Henry of Almain, and all the marcher barons – Mortimer and de Clifford and L'Estrange, and the Earls of Pembroke and Hereford . . . Fifty or more banners, I would say.'

The steward licked his lips hurriedly, his eyes still darting from side to side. 'Lord Edward is with the vanguard, sir,' he went on, 'and he'll be far beyond the Thames by now. But there are others behind us – I passed them marching on the road, not long after sun-up. The great lords of Scotland, sir – Balliol and Comyn and de Brus, with a host of savage followers. I'd say the king has eight thousand men all told.'

Adam snorted a laugh. The man was nothing if not forthcoming. He peered quickly up the track to the north, but there was no sign of the approaching Scots troops. 'And where are they going?' he demanded, prodding a little with his sword. 'You must know the king's destination, if you were riding to meet with him.'

'To Kingston, sir! He'll cross the Thames there and meet with Lord Edward, and together they'll ride for Rochester, where Lord Simon – may he be bathed in God's holy light, sir, a great man! – is besieging the castle, so they say . . .'

Of course, Adam thought. The king was not marching on London at all – he would bypass the city to the west and then swing south and east to reach Rochester and trap de Montfort's army inside the town. He exhaled loudly, then sheathed his sword and put his foot in the stirrup.

The steward was still kneeling, hands raised, but had a hopeful look in his eyes now. Abruptly Adam paused and stared back at him.

'You said you're the steward of Roger de Quincy?' he asked. 'The Earl of Winchester?'

The man gave a nervous nod, the tail of his hood bobbing.

'And where is he now?' Adam demanded.

'Dead, sir!' the steward replied, widening his eyes. 'Dead these last two days!'

'Dead?' Adam said in a breath, his brow creased.

'Yes, sir, may it please God, my master departed this life on St Mark's Day, at his hall in Brackley. He'd been suffering with a malady for many months, sir, a rotting of the guts, but when he heard the king was nearby he stirred himself to go to him and the effort burst his bowels!'

'*He's dead*,' Adam repeated to himself. Suddenly he grinned, and vaulted back into the saddle. He seized the reins of the steward's dappled mare, and turned his own horse to the south leading the other behind him.

'Wait – where are you going?' the steward cried, stumbling to his feet. 'Who are you anyway? You can't take my horse!'

'I'll loose her a mile from here,' Adam called over his shoulder. 'Run if you want to catch her!'

Then he dug in the spurs, pulling the other horse behind him as the palfrey's pace quickened from a trot to a canter.

'Thief!' the steward cried in his wake, raising his fists. 'You're a thief and a traitorous dog! May the king catch you and cut off your balls!'

But Adam was already riding hard for London.

# Chapter 25

Armed militiamen guarded the tollgate at Holborn. Some clutched spears, a few had bows, and there were more with crossbows leaning from the upper windows of the inn beside the road. All of them levelled their weapons as Adam approached.

'Stand aside,' Adam called to them, reining his sweating horse from a trot to a walk. 'I have a message for the Tower!'

'You don't look much like a courier,' a sturdy bearded axeman said. He wore an iron helmet and seemed to be the leader of the guard here.

'How do we know he's not a spy from the king?' another militiaman said, a reedy youth with a long knobbly neck, dressed in an oversized gambeson and linen coif. There were growls of assent from the other men. They were blocking the road, gripping their weapons with tightened knuckles. Adam almost laughed – Lord Edward and his knights would blast through this little garrison without a touch of their spurs.

'Yes, how do we know you're not a spy from the king?' the axeman demanded.

They were scared, Adam realised. He could see the fear rippling through them. Clearly they expected the royal army to come galloping down the road at any moment. He tightened his knees against the saddle leathers, ready at any moment to drag the reins and pull the horse around and ride clear of them. One itchy finger, he thought, one nervous movement on a crossbow trigger . . . His body prickled all over.

'The king and his troops passed before me at a crossroad not three hours ago,' he told them. His throat was dry, his words hoarse. 'They're going south, to cross the river at Kingston. They're not coming here. Now stand aside and let me pass – I have an urgent message for Hugh Despenser, the constable of the Tower.'

Glances passed between the militiamen, muttered words and questioning grunts. The sturdy axeman screwed up his face, staring hard at Adam. 'For Despenser, you say?' he asked.

'Yes,' Adam told him, his horse sidestepping as he kept the rein tight. Impatience kicked in his chest. 'For Hugh Despenser, then I must ride to Rochester and tell Lord Simon de Montfort of the king's approach.'

'Oh!' the axeman exclaimed. The reedy youth let out a thin laugh. Adam could see some of the crossbowmen at the inn windows smirking, while others shot suspicious glances back at him.

'Doesn't know much, does he, this messenger?' the youth asked. 'Maybe we should give him a message, eh?'

'Stitch him, Addy,' one of the others said. 'Stitch him with a quarrel!'

'Lord Simon isn't at Rochester,' the axeman said. 'He's right here in London, at the Tower. He came marching back here yesterday evening, with his army trailing behind him.'

For a moment Adam was too startled to reply. 'Then . . .' he said. 'Then I must go to him at once!' His mind turned the information over quickly, calculating. If de Montfort was already in London, he must have retreated from Rochester around the same time that Adam arrived at Odiham, or even the day before that. Information of the royal advance must have sped southward much faster than anyone had anticipated.

The axeman ceased his rumination, cleared his throat and spat. 'Reckon this young sir's just as confused as any of us,' he said. 'Open the bar and let him through.'

'Shall we make him pay the toll though?' the reedy youth asked. The sturdy axeman sniffed and shook his head curtly, and three of the others lifted the bar aside.

'Is it true the king has the Scots with him?' one of the others called to Adam as he rode through the cordon.

'And has Lord Edward really promised to hang every man in London, after what happened to the queen at the bridge last year,' another cried, 'then let the Scots take our womenfolk and plunder the whole city?'

Adam just raised an eyebrow as he passed. 'Best keep up your guard,' he called over his shoulder, 'and pray Lord Edward does not come this way!'

He rode on down the hill and across Holborn Bridge, then entered the city by New Gate. Several times more Adam was stopped as he made his way through the streets; there were gangs of armed men patrolling every thoroughfare and guarding every junction. The high spirits and festive mood that had gripped London only a month before were entirely extinguished now, the shops and houses firmly shuttered. The bells of St Paul's were ringing, but nobody was hastening to evensong. The whole city was tensed in expectation of the king's wrath.

\*

'So, it appears that I have been outwitted,' Simon de Montfort said. 'Not by King Henry though, I expect – my brother-in-law is not the cleverest of strategists. No, I believe in this case the scheme was probably devised by Lord Edward. Or Earl Richard of Cornwall – ever the trickster, that one. Both are with the king, you say?'

'I saw their banners, my lord,' Adam told him.

De Montfort grunted, picking up the ring that Adam had given him and tapping it on the table, where the letter from his wife lay, already unfolded and read. It had been easy enough for Adam to find him; the Earl of Leicester had taken up residence in the suite of chambers beside the hall that abutted the riverside rampart of the Tower. He had been conferring with his cofferer and the paymaster of his household when Adam arrived, and he had dismissed them and his other attendants at once.

'We received intelligence some days ago,' Simon told Adam, 'that the royal army was marching on London. Falling like a comet from the north, so the spies said. We were told that some of the burgesses of the city were already conspiring to open the gates to the king, perhaps even surrender the Tower as well.' He shrugged, his face in half profile looking hollow and grey as he toyed with the ring on the table.

'And so I was compelled to lift the siege of Rochester and return here,' he went on, 'to protect my allies in the city. Although I suspected that Henry had no intention of attacking London, in fact, and your information has confirmed it – he'll make a wide pass to the west and south, relieve Rochester and fall on the Channel ports, most likely. He has around eight thousand men, you say?'

Adam just nodded. It was past vespers and he had eaten nothing but a mouthful of bread that day; the remains of the earl's supper still lay upon the table and he eyed the scraps of food hungrily.

'I thank you for bringing me this,' de Montfort said, enclosing the ring in his fist and gesturing to the letter. 'I should not have dared imagine that my wife would desert me, or flee to France. She is far stronger than her brother, of course. But I wrote to her in a moment of weakness and doubt, when I believed that God had deserted our cause. Sometimes, you know,' he said, turning to address Adam directly for the first time, 'when we are parted from others for long periods, our sense of them becomes rather abstract, rather something of our own making. No, I should not have doubted my wife. And now she is coming here to join me . . .'

But Adam's thoughts had veered off, spurred by de Montfort's comment. He was thinking about Joane, and the news he had to give her of her uncle. He had told de Montfort of the Earl of Winchester's death already, one more little nugget of information which, like the others, he had felt he was merely dropping into a dark well. But Adam was determined to tell Joane of it himself – was she still living here at the Tower, he wondered, as a guest of her cousin Hugh Despenser?

'Did Robert de Dunstanville accompany you from Rochester, my lord?' he asked, blurting the question into de Montfort's thoughtful silence.

'Hmm?' de Montfort replied, raising an eyebrow. It looked for a moment that he had forgotten that Adam was with him, or that he had forgotten who Robert might be. 'Oh, not directly,' he said. 'He remained at Rochester until the following day, but I understand he is in London now. I'll find word of him and see it reaches you.'

Adam thanked him with a bow and reversed his steps towards the door. Lord Simon halted him with a gesture, then opened a small casket on the table. For one unpleasant moment, Adam thought that Simon was about to pay him in coin, as if he were a servant. But he just placed the ring inside the casket and closed the lid.

'I'm grateful, you know,' he said. 'For what you've done for me.'

Adam merely bowed again, then slipped out of the door. Once at the head of the spiral stairway he released a breath. He had not truly known what to expect from Simon de Montfort, or what effect the news he had brought might have. But to see the earl so despondent, so burdened with doubts and fears, had left him deeply troubled. Did he still believe that God had deserted his cause, or was he merely trying to pretend that some fresh hope remained? In any case, the earl did not seem inclined to shower him with gifts and blessings. Whatever reward Adam might have expected or desired for the service he had given would have to wait. Perhaps, he thought, it would be forgotten entirely.

At the turn of the stair he met another man ascending. Two men, he noticed, and his shoulders tightened as he recognised the tousled red hair and freckled triangular face of the young Earl of Gloucester. John FitzJohn was directly behind him, glaring up at Adam.

'Ah, the messenger boy has returned,' Gilbert de Clare said. Adam had stepped into the embrasure of a window to let them pass. He had not mentioned to Lord Simon that de Clare's man had tried to intercept the letter; some intuition had stopped him from passing on that scrap of knowledge. Now he was glad of it.

'What news has he brought, I wonder?' FitzJohn said with a smirk as he scaled past Adam. Both men nudged him with their elbows as they climbed.

Adam waited a moment, staring after them as they went up to de Montfort's chambers. He heard another stifled comment, a jagged laugh. Then, easing himself from the embrasure, he dropped down the steps and pushed his way out through the crowd of petitioners waiting at the doorway.

By contrast to the city outside, the Tower seethed with activity, both the outer and inner wards thronging with people, horses and dogs. Most of the surviving Jewish community of London were still living within the protective walls, and many of the barons who had returned with Lord Simon from Rochester had established themselves and their retinues here too. The open areas between the walls and gatehouses were covered with tents, and the smoke of cooking fires hung blue in the evening light.

Adam had seen nothing of Robert since arriving at the Tower, and as he scanned the confusion of encampments he saw no flash of the familiar red and white pennon or shield. But he still had the letter for Hugh Despenser, who he had been told was living in the constable's chambers of the keep. Crossing the plank walkway laid over the muddy churned-up expanse of the inner bailey, he climbed the broad flight of steps that rose to the fore-building of the keep.

Sentries wearing mail hauberks stood at the entrance, but they did no more than glance at Adam as he strode between the huge iron-studded oak doors. Through the inner portals, he entered the great hall. Candles were already burning, but the hall was dim after the lingering daylight outside. Adam had to blink to make out the motley groups of people queuing before the trestle tables: resident paupers, waiting for Hugh Despenser to distribute his evening alms.

Adam approached the far end of the hall and saw Despenser and his wife seated upon the dais with a group of clerks, priests and retainers gathered around them. It took Adam only a moment to pass the letter from Lady Eleanor to one of the attendants and watch it safely delivered. A nod of acknowledgement from Despenser, and Adam was pacing back towards the entranceway once more. The servants were clearing the tables after supper, sweeping the food scraps into the voider baskets for the paupers, but he managed to snatch a bread roll and a lump of cheese from an abandoned platter and bolt them down, washing his mouth with a slug of wine. As he ate and drank he searched the other faces in the dimness of the hall, but there was no sign of Joane, or of Robert.

As he was leaving, a woman entered, shadowed against the evening light from outside. One of the sentries in the gatehouse whistled and she glanced over her shoulder in annoyance, and as she turned Adam recognised her. 'Petronilla,' he said, catching her arm.

Joane's maid appeared startled and pulled herself away from him.

'It's me, Adam de Norton,' he told her. 'Where is your mistress? Where is the Lady Joane?'

Petronilla glared at him for a moment, affronted. Then she nodded, and gestured. 'Out there,' she said, her Flemish accent giving an added brusqueness to her words. 'In the garden, through the little gate. She's with the *Jews*.' And she made a sign of warding against evil.

Outside, Adam hurried down the steps. He quickly found the gate that the maid had mentioned, an arched postern between two of the internal buildings, that led to the outer ward. Another sentry stood there, leaning idly against the doorpost picking his teeth with a twig, but he barely glanced at Adam as he passed through into the furthest corner of the bailey. This was a backwater, away from the main gates and the more prestigious quarters, most of it cluttered with rough buildings, sheds and workshops, and the stables of draught animals. The Jews who had taken shelter in the Tower had been quartered in this corner of the bailey for nearly twenty days now, under the authority of Hugh Despenser and the mayor of the city, ever since that night when so many of their number had been slain.

Close to the postern gate, one small area had been laid out as a garden. Half of it was devoted to vegetables, but in the other half grew herbs and fragrant shrubs, crossed by a path of beaten earth beneath hurdles grown with creeping greenery. Along that path two women were walking, deep in conversation, a boy trailing behind them. Both women wore cloaks and headscarves, but Adam noticed the braided hair beneath the scarf of the younger of the two, the dark copper glow trapping the watery sunlight. It was only as he paced towards them that he realised the other woman was Belia of Nottingham.

'Adam!' Belia exclaimed as he approached, her face lighting instantly with a wide smile. 'When did you get here? Is Robert with you?'

Joane appeared more startled than delighted to see him. Adam halted and bowed to them both. 'Forgive me for disturbing you,' he said, 'I've not been here more than an hour. And I don't know where Robert might be — I was about to ask that of you.'

'He returned from Rochester, surely?' Belia asked, her smile dropping.

'So I hear, mistress,' Adam said. 'But I know nothing more.'

The Jews living in the Tower were compelled by the rule of the constable to wear their identifying marks at all times, so that good Christian people would know to avoid them. Belia's cloak bore the two pale panels sewn to the breast, but she had folded the hem back so they were not too prominent.

'Do send word to me, when you discover his whereabouts,' she said, looking very grave now. 'And tell him . . . tell him I would wish to speak with him. He should not treat me as a stranger.'

Adam, slightly abashed, could only bow his head again. As he looked up, he noticed that the boy lingering on the path was Mosse, the Jewish lad they had saved from the massacre. He seemed to be acting as a page or servant to Belia now.

'Well, we shall allow you two some privacy, I think,' Belia said, with the briefest flash of a smile. Joane opened her mouth to say something, but the other woman silenced her with a glance. A parting nod to Adam, and she gestured for Mosse to follow her as she retreated down the path towards the buildings on the far side of the gardens.

For several awkward heartbeats neither Adam nor Joane said a word. Adam had not spoken to her since the night of the massacre; he had not seen her since Palm Sunday, when she had avoided him so obviously in the crowd outside the cathedral. Now she stood with downcast eyes, twisting the toe of her shoe in the dust.

'You've grown close to Mistress Belia,' Adam said, watching the other woman's departing figure.

'Yes,' Joane replied, following his gaze. 'Strange to find a friend in this place. She's older than me, of course, but I feel a sense of understanding with her. We're both rather like shipwrecked mariners, I suppose, sheltering from a storm that still rages on . . . Or prisoners, maybe, like those poor lions in their pen near the main gate – have you seen them? . . .'

'My lady,' Adam broke in, forcing the words, his mouth suddenly dry. 'Joane, I mean . . . I have some news.'

She glanced up at him quickly, frowning. He could hold nothing back now.

'Your uncle is dead,' he told her. 'Roger de Quincy, the Earl of Winchester, is dead.'

He saw the news strike her, like a physical impact. Joane drew a sharp breath, both hands clasping the cloak across her body. Her lips shaped a silent word.

'This is true?' she asked Adam. 'You're sure of it?'

He nodded. 'I had it from his own household steward, earlier this afternoon. Your uncle died on the day of St Mark, at Brackley.'

Joane stood absolutely still for several moments. Then she let out a wailing cry and doubled over, her hands pressing the folds of her cloak to her face. Stunned, Adam took a stride towards her, his hands raised. He had imagined that she might react in various ways. This was not one of them.

Abruptly she straightened up again, and when she dropped her hands and turned to face him Adam saw the tears in her eyes. 'Dead!' she cried. Laughter burst from her. 'He's really dead? Oh, thanks to Christ and all the angels!'

She was grinning, hugging herself, overcome by wild emotion. 'Do you know what this means?' she gasped, seizing Adam by the arms. 'The ogre that has squatted on my life for so many years is gone! Oh, God and the holy Virgin be praised!'

Throwing herself against Adam, she clasped him tightly. Returning the embrace, Adam felt her body shudder as the trapped frustration of months and years flowed out of her.

'Thank you,' she said, her voice muffled against his chest. 'Thank you for bringing this news to me.' For several long heartbeats they stood together.

'But what happens now?' Joane asked, pulling back from Adam and seizing his hands. 'Am I free? No . . .' she said, thinking as she spoke, 'no, I'm a ward of the king now, surely. A ward of King Henry, in the camp of his enemies!'

Groaning aloud she swayed backwards, keeping her grasping grip on Adam's hands. For a moment it looked as if she would laugh again, or burst into tears of furious despair. As if she had only now become aware of how close they were, she appeared to collect herself, then broke contact and stepped away from him. But there was nobody nearby who could have witnessed their moment of unexpected intimacy. The sun had sunk below the wall and keep to the west, and the shadows of late evening were gathering in the garden.

Joane shivered, pulling her cloak tighter around her shoulders. Raising her head, she stared up at the great whitewashed façade of the keep, the crenellated ramparts and turrets that still caught the last glow of the sun. 'I feel I've been surrounded by walls for too long,' she said. 'I need to see the open sky and the horizon. Will you come with me?' she asked, and gestured towards the battlements. 'Up there?'

Bells were ringing for compline as they passed back through the postern to the inner bailey and climbed the steps to the keep once more. The lines of paupers had gone now, and deep shadow had engulfed the great hall beyond the flickering penumbra of the candles. Hugh Despenser and his officials had left the chamber, and only a few servants still lingered at the long trestle tables. Joane spoke briefly to her maid, who sat with a group of other women, then she gestured to Adam and led him to the far end of the hall, into the gulf of darkness, where a solitary candle lantern illuminated a passageway between the outer wall of the keep and one of the panelled interior partitions. Along the passage they reached a spiral stairway and began to climb. Slit windows shed bars of sunset colour across the curving walls.

'You've been up here before?' Adam called as he followed her. After his long day in the saddle the muscles of his thighs and back were burning.

'Sometimes,' Joane replied. Her voice echoed strangely in the spiralling shaft of the stair. 'It's about the only way one can be alone here. Petronilla says my liking for solitude is morbid, but I've been raised to it . . .'

'And where does this lead?' Adam said, pausing with braced leg to ease the ache in his thighs. The door sealing the arched opening from the stairway was covered in red leather and studded with tiny nails. Peering closer as he fought to steady his breath, Adam noticed that the nail-heads were gilded, glowing in the refracted evening light.

'To the royal chambers,' Joane replied, leaning to peer around the turn of the stair. 'Where the king lives, when he visits the Tower. I suppose if Lord Simon wins his war, he'll imprison Henry in there.'

Adam gave the door another appraising glance, then flexed his limbs and scaled on upwards. Another turn, then another, and they passed a second doorway. But Joane continued climbing, the stair shaft almost in darkness save for a little blueish light filtering down from above.

Just when Adam felt he could climb no more, he stepped out into fresh evening air and saw the sky towering over him, lit by the blush of sunset. They had emerged from a corner turret onto the broad walkway inside the battlements, which surrounded the leaded roofs of the chambers below. Here and there Adam picked out figures around the perimeter, either watchmen or others who desired solitude, but they were no more than dark shapes against the lit sky. Above them, surging flocks of swifts rushed and turned against the glow of sunset.

'I miss my falcon,' Joane said.

'You'd set your falcon on the innocent swifts?'

Adam caught her smile as she glanced back at him. 'I thought there is no sin in nature?' she said.

Together they followed the walkway to the western side, where they could gaze out between the merlons over the expanse of London. Streets and house roofs were lost in the evening haze, the dwellings only picked out by the streams of smoke from hearth fires and kitchens, a multitude of thin dark streaks that rose and merged into a blueish mist over the city. Squinting, Adam picked out the huge shape of St Paul's rising from the packed houses that surrounded it like a great leviathan of the deep. Beyond the cathedral and the city wall, beyond the city's furthest outskirts, a vast indistinct landscape spread to the horizon.

'If Lord Simon wins his war, he will grant Humphrey de Bohun permission to marry me, I suppose,' Joane said.

Adam made a sound in his throat. They both knew the truth of it. 'But if the king wins . . .' he said.

Joane laughed to herself, barely more than a breath. 'I hear you saved his life at Rochester,' she said. 'It was a noble deed.'

'I wasn't even thinking,' Adam replied. 'That is, if I had—'

'You *still* would have saved him,' Joane cut in, with quick emphasis. They were very close together, leaning into the same embrasure of the battlements. 'I would not have you forget your honour on my account.'

'It might have been easier, is all I meant.'

'He's not such a bad man,' Joane said. She sounded as if she were trying to convince herself. 'I mean, he could be far worse. He's old, and not favourable in appearance, but I'm told he's changed his ways, repented his sinful attitudes and become quite virtuous . . . He no longer burns villages, that is, and months have passed since he last robbed a priory or whipped a priest . . .' She broke off with a strangled groan, letting her head drop into her hands.

True, Adam thought, de Bohun could be worse – Joane could
be betrothed to a man like John FitzJohn. Although FitzJohn was
not twice her age, with children of his own. 'You should not have
to do it,' he said, his voice catching.

'What alternative do I have?'

Joane raised her head and leaned into the side of the embrasure.
The sunset colour lit her face, and turned her hair to spun red
gold. Adam placed a hand on her shoulder, and she turned to him
and slid into his embrace. He kissed her, and she returned the kiss,
and for several long moments they were aware of nothing more.

'No,' Joane said abruptly, flinching away from him. She pressed
her palm against his chest. 'No, this cannot happen. You know
that.'

'Oh yes,' Adam said bitterly, recovering himself. 'I know it all
too well.' He dropped forward to lean on the coping of the wall.
From the church down in the bailey he heard the hollow clang
of the curfew bell.

'I'm sorry, I should not have brought you up here,' Joane whispered. 'Forgive me. I was not thinking clearly.'

'I'd say you were thinking clearly enough,' Adam replied,
before he could bite back the words.

Joane took a step back, hauteur rising around her like a mantle. 'What do you mean by that?' she demanded, straightening
her back. 'You forget yourself, I think.'

'Joane,' Adam said, closing the distance between them again.

'No!' she cried. She turned, unable to look at him. 'Remember what you are,' she said, her voice tight in her throat. 'My
cousin's squire – that's all. I thank you for bringing me news of
my uncle the Earl of Winchester, but now I've changed my mind
and I would prefer to be alone . . .'

'Joane,' Adam said again, reaching out to take her arm.

At his touch she buckled, casting herself back against the
stone wall. 'In the name of Christ!' she said. 'Do you think we
are living in a romance? Do you think we can have all we want,

if only we struggle hard enough, fulfil tasks, please our masters? Adam . . .' She drew a long shuddering breath, fighting down a sob, then turned away again. 'Leave me now,' she told him, her voice firm and level. 'Leave and do not come to me again. I will hear no more words from you.'

Before Adam could respond or reply, footsteps came from along the walkway. Adam took a long pace away from Joane, who stepped back along the wall.

'There you are!' a familiar voice said. With a nervous tightening in his gut Adam recognised the solid shape of Humphrey de Bohun forming from the evening shade. 'They told me you'd come up here,' he said as he strode closer. 'Is it true then? Earl Roger's really dead?'

'He is,' Adam told him.

'I shall light candles for him,' Humphrey said, and pursed his lips piously. 'A great man, in his day.'

He halted, appearing to see Joane for the first time, then bowed from the waist in greeting to her. 'God's blessings, my lady,' he said quickly.

Adam noticed that he still had a linen bandage around his head, a wad of cloth covering the wound to his scalp that he had received at Rochester, and his face was freckled with tiny red sores from the hot sand.

'Do you know if Robert de Dunstanville is here?' Adam asked. He was conscious of trying to distract attention from Joane, who was sliding gradually further from him along the wall.

'De Dunstanville? Yes, he's out there,' de Bohun said, flinging a gloved hand towards the sunset and the city that stretched below them. 'At the Jew's house, the place we rescued him from the mob – you remember that night?'

'Of course,' Adam said. Not three weeks had passed since then. He was not surprised that Robert had returned to Elias's house – all that he owned was there, even if all he cared for was not.

Humphrey de Bohun was smiling, his face flushed in the red-dish light. 'They've already sounded curfew,' he said, 'but the gates are not yet shut – if you hurry you can get out before the drawbridge is raised. Come, I'll escort you, in case you have any trouble.'

Both men bowed to Joane de Quincy, who stood stiffly at the parapet like a carved figure on a frieze. Then Adam followed Humphrey de Bohun towards the stairs. They dropped down together, Humphrey saying something over his shoulder about horses, but Adam was not listening. His heart was beating slow and heavy in his chest.

At the dark landing by the doorway to the royal chambers de Bohun halted and turned. His hand fell heavily on Adam's shoulder, pinning him to the spot.

'You saved my life at Rochester,' he said, his voice roughened as the false good humour dropped from him. 'And for that I will be forever in your debt. But I tell you this now – if you touch her again, I will kill you.'

Adam held his gaze, hearing the breath rasp from the man's nostrils.

'I understand,' he said.

# Chapter 26

The news that the king's troops had broken the siege of Rochester reached London three days later. On the approach
of Lord Edward's vanguard, so the few surviving witnesses
claimed, Roger de Leyburne and Earl John de Warenne had led
a sally from the keep and fallen upon the remaining troops that
de Montfort had left to hold the siege lines. They had captured
all the engines, and burned most of them. The fate of the prisoners, even those who had surrendered to the king's mercy, had
been harsh. A few had been hanged, but Edward had ordered
that the rest have their hands and feet chopped off. Adam heard
the news with a cold churn of nausea, remembering his earlier
vision of the gibbet. Such was war, men said. Rebel against royal
authority, and face the penalty. Besides, none of those executed
or mutilated had been knights, as Wilecok wryly observed. But
Adam could not help thinking that Simon de Montfort had left
those men at Rochester as a lure, to keep the king from a direct
march on London.

'It was a shambles,' Robert de Dunstanville had told Adam, on
the evening of his return. 'Simon slipped away from Rochester
by night – we only learned he had gone the following morning,
and it was midday before we discovered why. You can imagine
the panic and confusion, the terror. Everyone expected the

king's army to fall on us at any moment. Anyway, de Montfort left enough of his own men there to keep up the siege, or a blockade at least. There seemed no reason at all for the rest of us to stay, and the London militia were already running back here as fast as their legs would pump.'

They were sitting in the hall of Elias's townhouse, the fire in the hearth sending a fitful glow around the walls and throwing twisting shadows. Robert was slumped in a high-backed chair, a goblet of wine in his fist. Elias sat opposite; he was one of the very few members of the Jewish community to remain in his own home rather than keep to the sanctuary of the Tower. He had his cook and one or two servants with him, and a newly recruited complement of doormen and bodyguards, but aside from that his mansion was deserted. Now Robert and what remained of his little retinue had taken up residence in the adjacent building.

'So was it all for nothing?' Adam asked. 'The attack on Rochester, I mean. The deaths.' All knew that he was referring to John Chyld, whose silent ghost seemed to linger at the margins of the light.

'Not entirely,' Robert said with a mirthless smile. 'Lord Simon intended to coax the king down from the north, and he succeeded. Far better than he'd expected, of course – not even I thought that Henry could move his army that fast. Now, you see, Simon's trapped. If he marches northward, the king and Edward will fall on London and rend it like carrion.'

They stared into the hearth, and Adam recalled the view from the battlements of the Tower. All too easy to imagine the city in flames.

'Personally, I wish the king would come,' said Elias. 'He at least might give us peace. I'm sorry to say it, but your cause will never be mine.'

The moneylender appeared to have aged dramatically in the last few weeks. He had let his hair and beard grow dense and wild, as if he were in mourning, and both were shot with grey.

His house still looked partially dismantled, half his possessions in crates and boxes, the plate and furnishing stripped. Every pane of glass in the hall windows had been broken during the riot, and rough boards covered the gaps. By day the chamber was gloomy as a crypt.

'Don't fool yourself,' Robert told Elias. 'King Henry couldn't give anyone peace, even if he wanted it. No, matters have gone too far for that, my friend. The fire is burning, and only blood will quench it now.'

Robert too looked harried. Adam had been shocked to see him again, and to realise how the events of these recent months had told upon him. De Dunstanville's thin face was drawn, his eyes pouched and his jaw set hard. He looked now like a man at the uttermost limits of his strength and patience, doggedly clinging to a cause, not even knowing if he had ever believed it to be just. He had brusquely refused to visit the Tower, or even to speak of Belia. His pride, Adam knew, would not allow him to indulge that weakness.

'So what will happen now?' Adam asked, after the silence in the hall had stretched too long. 'What can Lord Simon do?'

Robert shrugged, and opened an empty palm. 'Perhaps the chance of open battle is all that remains?' he said. 'A throw of the dice, and a dangerous one.'

'Does this Simon not believe that God is on his side?' Elias said, with a contemptuous sniff. 'Surely that is worth a few thousand men?'

'Maybe so,' Robert said. 'But I would prefer to wait and hope for better news.'

But no good news came. Every day Simon de Montfort sent his scouts to track the king's army. Every day the riders came clattering back through Southwark and across London Bridge to the Tower, rumour whirling in their wake. Master Elias too sent out his spies, and the information they brought was often more reliable, but none of it was encouraging. Following hard

on the tidings of the fall of Rochester came word that the king
had captured Gilbert de Clare's castle at Tonbridge. The royal
army, so the scouts reported, was marching through the Weald
towards the south coast ports; was the king intending to bring
a vast force of mercenaries across from France or Flanders? Or
did he intend to seize all the shipping from Dover and Deal, then
to sail up the Thames with his full force and attack London by
the river?

On the day of Crouchmas there was a change in fortune at
last. Eleanor de Montfort, Countess of Leicester, arrived from
Odiham and rode into London with her full household and an
escort of knights from her western manors, passing through the
streets in grand procession with her train of pack animals and
wagonloads of baggage, to join her husband at the Tower. Her
younger son Guy de Montfort accompanied her, with a band of
men at arms from Kenilworth. It was a very minor reinforcement, but the sight of the countess entering the city so grandly
sent a stir of renewed enthusiasm through the people. Surely
now all could see that Lord Simon would not desert them? And
surely, if King Henry's sister herself was prepared to come to
London in person, across a country in the paroxysms of civil
war, the chances of victory or negotiated truce might be better
than anyone had dared imagine?

Adam saw the newcomers the following morning, as they
attended Sunday mass at St Paul's. He caught Lady Eleanor's
eye briefly through the throng as they entered the cathedral,
but she gave him only the slightest nod of acknowledgement.
Here in the heart of the public world, the Countess of Leicester could have little connection with a mere squire. Adam was
looking more intently for Joane de Quincy; a week had passed
since their conversation on the battlements of the Tower, and the
painful memory of her rejection was a cold stone pressing upon
his heart. He hoped desperately for a glimpse of her, but feared
it too. The thought that he might be spurned by her once again

was sickening, and he was relieved when he learned that Joane and the ladies of the Despenser household had heard mass at the Tower chapel that morning and would not be coming to the cathedral.

It was only as he left after the service that Adam emerged from the gloomy shell of his private thoughts and noticed the new mood that animated the crowd. As Simon de Montfort and Countess Eleanor emerged from the doors of the cathedral a great cry went up from those gathered in the courtyard; this was the first time that Lord Simon had appeared in public since his return from Rochester, and for the people of London to see him here with his wife and his sons and all his most powerful and loyal supporters around him seemed at once to dispel the fearful unease of the last week.

Simon too appeared changed – no longer was he the grim and doubt-stricken man that Adam had spoken with in the upper chamber of the Tower hall. He appeared rejuvenated, fired with an internal heat and light as the acclamation of the crowd rang out around him. It was not just the reinforcement from Kenilworth and the west. Not just the presence of his wife and sons either. No, Adam thought – Simon de Montfort was powered now by the certainty and resolve of imminent battle. No hesitation remained. His life, and the future of the kingdom, were sworn to trial by combat.

'Have you heard the latest news?' Hugh of Oystermouth said, joining Adam as he moved through the crowd and into the northern churchyard. Adam shook his head.

'The men of Kent have attacked the king's army in the Weald!' Hugh told him in a rapid whisper. 'Archers, so they say – they shot at Henry and his army as they marched through the narrow lanes. One of them killed the king's cook, so Henry rounded up a great number of prisoners and had them all put to death! Chopped off their heads, right there and then before his eyes – three hundred and fifteen of them, in a single afternoon!'

Adam shuddered. He had witnessed a judicial beheading once, at Cologne, and remembered it clearly. He tried to imagine what that would look like repeated three hundred and fifteen times. Tried to imagine the quantity of blood. The severed heads knocking together as they were flung onto the growing pile.

'Some of those killed had surrendered themselves voluntarily to the king's peace, so they say,' Hugh went on, 'but to no avail. I've heard it was Lord Edward's doing, or Earl Richard gave the order, but I'm not sure . . .'

'No,' Adam said, with a chilling sense of certainty. 'The king himself ordered it.' He remembered what Countess Eleanor had told him, back at Odiham. *Henry wears the mask of a mild and gentle Christian.* Yes, he thought: and now that mask had been thrown aside, to reveal the face of a truly wrathful monarch.

The story of what had happened in Kent was quickly becoming common currency, Adam could tell. The word had passed through the congregation in St Paul's, whispered and muttered during the long droning passages of the service. There was more too: the outriders of the king's army had reached the south coast, and already sacked and despoiled the abbey at Battle. None were safe from the king's ire, and even the houses of God were prey to the rapacity of his followers.

'Such is the pitiable state of the English!' a voice cried above the heads of the crowd gathering in the churchyard. 'Deprived of all justice and liberty, trampled under a tyrannical rule, like the people of Israel who groaned beneath the harshness of Pharaoh!'

The speaker was a friar, dressed in the grey habit of the Franciscans, standing up on the raised platform of St Paul's Cross. Adam remembered the last time he had seen a friar addressing the crowd, not far from this place. But the reception of the gathered throng to this new speaker was very different. As Adam and Hugh shoved their way through the press of men towards the foot of the cross, they heard cries of agreement and encouragement from all around them. Others stood silent and open-mouthed, nodding along with the friar's passionate address. There were knights and squires among them, and well-dressed city burgesses, members of the congregation who had just left the cathedral. Men from the streets too, from Westcheap and the surrounding area, come to hear the latest news; St Paul's was the very hub of London's turning wheel.

'But God has beheld the suffering of England!' the friar declared, pointing with one finger to the sky. 'In his great mercy he has given us cause for hope. He has sent us this champion, this flower of fame and chivalry, this man so zealous for justice. A shield and defender of the realm of the English!'

'*MONT – FORT! MONT – FORT!*' the crowd began to chant, stamping their feet and raising their fists.

'And what could be more righteous than justice?' the friar called, his voice cracking as he raised it above the tumult. 'What could be more wretched than a king who despises liberty and the law?'

'*Liberty! Liberty!*' the crowd chanted. '*MONT – FORT! MONT – FORT!*'

'And now, with Lord Simon as our true champion, England can hope to breathe again, and pray with every breath for deliverance, and for victory!'

*

'The summons to arms has just gone out from the Guildhall and from the Tower,' Adam told Robert later that day, when he found him in the stables. 'We assemble at St George's Fields in Southwark tomorrow evening and march at dawn on Tuesday.'

'The feast of St John at the Latin Gate,' Robert said quietly. 'A fitting day for departure, I suppose.' He was rubbing down his horse after exercising it on the meadows outside the city. Adam's own horse Papillon was in the next stall; Robert had brought the black destrier back from Rochester with him. He had given

Adam a new hauberk too, with a pair of mail chausses to protect his legs; taken from one of the dead, presumably, but Adam did not ask about that.

The summons to arms had come as no surprise, but still Adam felt a quickening of his nerves, a jump in his blood. Twice before, Simon de Montfort had marched forth from London, and twice he had been forced to retreat. But this time his army would not be assaulting walls or fortifications. This time they would seek out their enemies on the open field of battle. Still Adam felt himself torn. Listening to the friar's speech in the churchyard that morning, he had been reminded of the darker passions of the people, the call to violence and disorder, the furious breath of riot. When he glanced from the stable door into the light of the courtyard, he remembered all too clearly the night that the mob had surged through the gates with murder in their hearts.

Robert de Dunstanville also appeared to have misgivings. In the stable's shadow, his expression was harried. He gave the horse a last few brisk strokes, and then tossed the currying comb aside and planted both hands on the animal's broad back, as if to draw strength from it. Adam saw the lock of tension between his shoulders.

'You know,' Robert said quietly, 'the King of England could lose one hundred battles, and he would still be king. But if we lose once, we are all dead men.'

'We both know that,' Adam replied, frowning. 'Nothing's changed.' For some time he had suspected that Elias's bitter words had lodged in Robert's mind, and that the knight's sense of purpose had been eroded, his valour worn thin. But this was something else, and Adam had never seen it in him before. He snorted a mirthless laugh to cover his dismay. 'All those months and years on the tournament road,' he said, taking a step closer. 'I cannot believe you fear combat now—'

'*Fear?*' Robert said, turning with an outraged grimace. 'What is it you think I fear, exactly? Death – *no*. Shame and defeat?

Maybe . . . But I have already led one man to the grave for a tarnished cause,' he said. 'I *fear* to lead another the same way.'

For several long moments there was silence between them. Adam heard the breath of the horses, the distant noises from the street outside the yard. His heart was slow and heavy in his chest. 'You told me once,' he said, 'that you would not compel me to fight for de Montfort, if my conscience spoke against it. I could hardly expect you to do any differently yourself.'

He saw the brightness of Robert's eye in the shadows, his keenly focussed gaze. 'If you've had enough of this war,' Adam went on, 'then release me, and I will be squire to one of de Montfort's sons, or to Humphrey de Bohun.'

'You thirst so much for battle?' Robert asked.

'You had your own cause for which to fight,' Adam said. 'Now I have mine. Not for Simon de Montfort but for myself, and for what I long to possess. For truth and justice too, if God grants it. But if I had the choice, I would not serve beside any man but you.'

He barely heard Robert's sigh. 'Then I've trained you well,' Robert said, after a pause. 'It does my heart good to know that.' He turned and stepped away from the horse, drawing himself up to his full height. 'One last throw of the dice then,' he declared.

Adam took a long stride towards him, and Robert seized him in his embrace.

'I changed your mind?' Adam asked as they parted.

'Of course not,' Robert said, clouting him on the shoulder. 'But consider that maybe I wanted to be convinced, one way or the other, before making a final decision. Anyway,' he said, pacing to the stable door with a wry grin, 'I wouldn't trust you on your own in a real battle. Not without me to look after you.'

He stood in the bar of sunlight from the yard, then clapped his hands briskly. 'So,' he said. 'We have a day to prepare ourselves, more or less – and we shall make the most of it!'

\*

The following morning, Master Elias ordered his servants to light the kitchen fires and heat pots and cauldrons of fresh water. In the narrow yard behind the main house they set up a big wooden tub, lined it with linen and sprinkled bay leaves and aromatic herbs inside. Then, when the water was steaming, Wilecok and his Gascon wife carried pails of it out to the yard and poured them into the tub. Stripped to his braies, Robert de Dunstanville clambered over the side and lowered himself into the heated bath, letting out a loud sigh of pleasure as the water lapped around his chest and his raised knees. Then he bent his head as Wilecok's wife poured jugs of warm water over him, and scrubbed his body with an abrasive sponge. He had a small cake of Marseilles soap as well, a gift from Elias. Steam rose around him as the water turned grey and sudsy under its floating scum of leaves.

'Not something I hold with, of course,' Wilecok muttered to Adam, his face wrinkling. Adam had also stripped, and stood waiting in braies and linen coif with a rough woollen towel around his shoulders. He would be next for the tub, once Robert had finished bathing. Hugh of Oystermouth would take the third place, after him. But Wilecok was not a bathing man.

'Bad for the flesh, is warm water,' he confided, leaning closer to Adam and tapping his long nose. 'Makes for poor digestion too, and opens the body to bad humours and miasmas! No — hands and face for church and dinner, and a seasonal dunk in a cold river is quite good enough for any Christian . . .' He cast a suspicious glance at Elias's two Jewish servants, who lingered on the timber balcony above them to watch the proceedings.

Wilecok's wife appeared to have no such compunctions, heaving the pots and pails about and splashing the water into the tub with relish. Seeing her clad only in her loose and rather damp linen chemise, Adam realised that the woman was several months pregnant. He had not noticed before, and nobody had mentioned it. Idly he wondered what sort of father Wilecok might turn out to be.

Then, with a start, he shook himself from his reflections. The Gascon woman had paused with her buckets at a signal from Robert, who was sitting upright in the tub and gazing at the balcony, where another figure had joined the two servants. Belia stood for a moment looking down at them all, then tugged her shawl up to cover her face and went back into the house. Adam heard Elias's raised voice from somewhere inside, chiding her for such immodest behaviour.

Robert stood up in the bath, water pouring from his body. He wiped the few wet green scraps of bay leaf from his shoulders and chest, then held out his arms as Adam stepped forward and wrapped the towel around him. Without a word, he climbed from the tub and began rubbing himself briskly.

'Hurry, now!' Hugh whispered urgently to Adam. 'Before the water gets cold!'

By the time Robert had dried himself and Wilecok had helped him dress in fresh linens, hose and tunic, Adam was squatting in the luke-warm bath. Through narrowed eyes, he had time to see Robert climb the wooden stair to the upper chamber; Belia appeared momentarily in the doorway again, and they both vanished into the shadow. Then Wilecok's wife sloshed a pail of warm water over him, and Adam dipped his head beneath the cleansing torrent.

*

Scrubbed, sluiced and dried, Adam dressed himself in clean woollen hose and tunic from a chest in the upper chamber. He was just fastening his belt when a noise from the doorway made him turn, reaching for a knife that was not there.

'I'm sorry to intrude,' Belia said, with a sly smile. 'Your servants are engaged elsewhere.'

Through the open window came the sound of raucous yells and wild laughter. Half-naked, Hugh of Oystermouth was chasing Wilecok around the yard and flicking water at him from a jug, to the great amusement of the Gascon woman and the cooks from the kitchen.

'Please,' Adam said, gesturing for Belia to enter. 'It's your house, after all.'

'My brother's house, not my own,' she said, her smile dropping as she crossed to the far window. 'And it will be a long time until I feel comfortable here again.'

'So you'll remain at the Tower?' Adam asked, joining her by the window. Together they stood in the spill of daylight, close enough to speak in whispers.

'For now, yes,' Belia said, twisting the end of her woven girdle in her fingers. 'It seems safer. And Joane de Quincy remains there too, although she will leave tomorrow for Ware – the justiciar, Despenser, has arranged an escort for her. Now that the armies are moving southward and her uncle is no more, there is less danger for her at her own manor than here in London.'

Adam was nodding, unable to meet her eye. The mention of Joane's name had pierced him through the heart. Over the last few days, he had come to believe that she truly wanted nothing more to do with him.

'She desired that I speak with you,' Belia said, 'before you left to join de Montfort again.'

'She did?' Adam snorted a laugh, shoving back his damp hair to try and hide his expression, but he felt wretched and knew that Belia could read him clearly.

But Belia ignored him, reaching into the purse she wore hanging from her girdle. 'She wanted me to give you this,' she said, taking what appeared to be a small letter or fold of parchment from the purse. 'You might keep it with you, she thought, if you so choose.'

Adam took the parchment from her and unfolded it. It was a page from a book, and for a moment he could only squint at the swirl of ink on the yellowed parchment in the light from the window. Then his vision cleared and he realised what he was looking at. He knew where he had seen this same script, these same coloured capitals and decorated margins.

'*Dicens Domino spes mea et fortitudo,*' Adam read in a breath, translating the Latin as he scanned the words. 'Say the Lord is my refuge and my fortress, my God; in him will I trust . . .' He raised his head, narrowing his eyes as he met Belia's gaze. 'This is a page from her Psalter,' he said. 'Joane's Psalter, that her father gave her . . .'

'She said it had come loose by itself,' Belia said with a slight shrug. 'The binding was not so good – she did no violence to the book. But perhaps God determines these things?'

'*Quoniam mihi adhesit et liberabo eum* . . .' Adam read, holding the page to the light and reading the lines of the psalm. 'Because he has set his love upon me, therefore will I deliver him . . . I will set him on high, because he has known my name . . . I will be with him in trouble . . .'

His voice caught suddenly, and his throat tightened. The inked page trembled in his hand.

'She told me what happened between you, at the Tower,' Belia said. 'What she said then . . . it was harsh, and she regretted it, but she meant to protect you, to shield you from harm.'

'Shield me?' Adam said, anguish rising through the confused fog in his mind.

Belia nodded. 'She understands the world, as do you, I'm sure. Fate does not often deliver us what we desire. Duty compels us. But faith endures.'

Adam looked down at the page again, the lines from the psalm. Her Psalter was one of the most valuable things Joane possessed. The gift was intended as a talisman, he realised. Holy protection against the dangers to come. But it was a blessing too, and a pledge of truth. For a few moments he could do nothing but stare at the page, lost to the warm surging tides of feeling.

Belia laid a hand upon his shoulder. 'She asked me to do this too,' she said. Leaning forward, she kissed Adam on the lips.

The faint scent of Marseilles soap lingered after she was gone.

# Chapter 27

'I'm Simon de Montfort!' one of the boys yelled, brandishing his stick and kicking up dust. 'I'm the Earl of Leicester!'

'And I'm Lord Edward!' another yelled in reply, waving his own stick wildly. The two of them ran at each other, their screams high and bright. The sticks cracked together as they fought. Around them clustered the other children, whooping and shouting for one combatant or the other.

'Those little puppies better watch themselves,' John Spadeberd said, with an amiable sneer. 'Somebody might string them all from a tree if they don't take care!'

'But not us,' Adam replied.

'No, I suppose not us,' Spadeberd said.

Neither of them knew the name of this little Sussex village. Neither had been here before. But the gnarled old oak in the marketplace, the dappled sunlight over the stream and the weir, the straggle of low thatched cottages looked much like any other village in this part of the world. The familiarity was almost comforting.

Spadeberd set his foot in the stirrup and heaved himself into the saddle, leathers creaking. 'Mind you,' the veteran serjeant said through a yawn. 'That lad playing at being Simon does actually look a bit like Lord Edward. Maybe they should swap places?'

Adam mounted his horse, looking more closely at the brawl-ing boys. But it was all too late: the small Lord Edward had already been knocked to the ground, and was snivelling as he picked himself up, his dusty face streaked with snot and blood. The victor pranced, stick held aloft in triumph, but the gaggle of children were rushing away in search of another game.

'If only our own battles were brought to so swift and easy an end,' Spadeberd said. Both he and Adam were wearing full mail hauberks beneath their dun riding cloaks, with swords belted at their sides and shields and helmets slung on their saddles. The nearest enemy might be many miles away, but carelessness could prove fatal.

They rode along the little village street to the barn at the far end, where a wagon was pulled up beneath the trees. A couple of village men and some dismounted serjeants were busy load-ing barrels of fresh-brewed ale, sacks of oats and barley and bundles of firewood onto the wagon bed, overseen by a clerk on a slender palfrey. Unlike the royal troops, who could seize whatever they wanted from anyone in their path, Simon de Montfort's men at least paid for their provisions; the clerk was counting out a handful of silver pennies to the village bailiff, each one stamped with the head of King Henry, courtesy of the king's foes.

Once the cart was loaded, Spadeberd called in the cordon of guards and scouts and they formed up to return to the column. Adam had joined the foraging party that morning, more out of a desire to escape the dust and grinding routine of the march-ing column than anything. After leaving London, the army of de Montfort and his baronial supporters had marched for four days southward over the downs, following another of the ancient roads that scored a straight line across the landscape for mile after mile. At Fletching, a woodland manor belonging to Lord Simon himself, they had rested for two days while the scouts sought out the king's forces and determined their movements.

Then, today, they had moved off again. Southward once more, towards the sea.

Evening was coming on by the time John Spadeberd's provisioning party rejoined the main column, and the vanguard had already halted at the village of Hamsey. Adam left Spadeberd with his wagons and rode on down the road to find Robert de Dunstanville and seek out a camping place before thousands of other men and horses covered every patch of open dry ground in trampled filth. Over the past week he'd had ample opportunity to assess the strengths of de Montfort's force. Compared to the cavalcade of royal might he had witnessed on the road before his return to London, it was desperately thin. Two hundred knights rode behind Lord Simon's banner, with around twice that number of mounted serjeants and squires. The London militias had mustered close to two thousand men, most of them infantry, and there were another thousand archers, slingers and spearmen from the baronial retinues and shire levies. In all, less than half the number the king was rumoured to be leading.

But it was not just soldiers following in the wake of de Montfort. The marching column seemed to swell in numbers with every passing day. Servants and washerwomen, armourers and farriers, cattle-herders and prostitutes, beggars, random children and a vast yapping multitude of stray dogs all trailed along with the army, stretching the column for miles in the dust of the advance. Lord Simon had brought a large wagon along with him as well, plated with iron and mounted with tall pennons; none seemed to know what it was for, although Adam had heard rumours that several city burgesses known to favour the king were imprisoned inside.

With the scouts and outriders and the foraging parties riding out and back, the army flowed across the landscape like a great bustling city on the move. Even after days of marching, the mood of Lord Simon's supporters still remained high, the songs around the cooking fires still ribald and defiant, but none could be doubtful that the odds were dangerously against them.

'They're beginning to snivel,' Robert said, as Wilecok coaxed a flame from a smoking fistful of straw. After even a short day's march, he seemed more than usually truculent. 'I've heard them,' he went on in a low growl, 'the great men, discussing the odds among themselves, assessing the risks. I don't doubt a few of them are already making their plans for an accommodation.'

'With the king, you mean?' Adam asked, dropping his voice. There were figures all around them in the early-evening light, moving through the haze of woodsmoke between the tents and the horse lines. 'Surely we've come too far for that?'

Robert shrugged heavily. 'So any honest Christian might believe,' he said. 'But I'd wager that even our champion himself thinks there's still time for a settlement. Why else, do you think, would Lord Simon have brought so many bishops along with him? Not to say prayers! Why else is he dragging those city burgesses about in his iron cart?'

'He intends sending them to negotiate with the king, you mean?' Adam said, barely above a whisper. 'Even now?'

'Let's not forget,' Robert told him, raising a finger, 'that battle is no small undertaking. Shedding blood – the blood, perhaps, of our king, anointed by God . . . Well, surely such a serious matter should be avoided, if at all possible? Surely there is still time to explain to the king that this has all been a misunderstanding, and for all to stress their loyalty to their sovereign lord?'

Adam was quite unable to tell whether Robert was joking. And yes, he admitted to himself, even now when everything seemed shaped inexorably towards battle – even now, when he could almost feel and taste the shock of combat, could almost relish it, dreamed about it every night with terrified longing – even now, Adam too thought that any way out of the coming bloodshed would be a blessing.

'You told me once that the great men of England know nothing of war,' he said. 'Barely one of them has seen a battle – that's right, isn't it?'

Robert nodded gravely. His beard had grown hard and dark, bristling in the shadow of his cheekbones.

'You've fought in battles yourself though,' Adam said, 'in the holy land.'

'At Al-Mansurah, yes. And the running fights after that too.' Robert was staring fixedly into the spitting flames, as Wilecok fed dry tinder to his blaze. For a long moment dark memories seemed to oppress him. 'But even the tournaments can hone a man for war,' he said. 'There are a few here who know how to handle themselves in the melee. Too many others who think they do.'

'But Lord Simon does,' Adam said intently. 'He understands battle well enough, surely? If any man here knows the risks, and what he stands to lose, it is him.'

'Sure enough. But remember, Lord Simon is the king's brother-in-law. You'll have noticed the way that my cousin Joane de Quincy, for example, seems to be related to everyone in the aristocracy. *They all are.* Every one of these magnates and great barons is related to all the rest, lands and families meshed together like fingers on linked hands.' He knitted his fingers, then flexed them until the knuckles cracked.

'So are you,' Adam told him.

Robert just made a sour face. 'My point is that all of them have a clear road out of this, if they want it. I do not – my connections are less illustrious, and less legitimate too. And you certainly do not. The landless have nothing to lose but their lives, and nothing to save but their souls.'

'What about Sir Humphrey de Bohun?' Adam said, struck by a thought. 'Does his resolve weaken too, do you think?' With Joane now a ward of the king, he considered, Humphrey might see a renewed loyalty as the better course.

But Robert just laughed grimly. 'Ah, not him,' he said. 'Sir Humphrey, you know, my brother in the eyes of God if not men, was issued a safe conduct by the king, summoning him to come and discuss matters with Lord Edward. About the amicable return of his lands in Wales, I expect, and no doubt on the prompting of his father Earl Humphrey. We both know how close to the king's ear he can speak when he wishes.'

'When was this?' Adam said, startled. 'And how did he react?'

'It was last month,' Robert told him. Wilecok passed him a wooden bowl of potage and a hunk of bread. 'And Sir Humphrey ignored the summons. He at least is as firm in his convictions as anyone.'

Adam nodded, obscurely disappointed. Momentarily he had hoped that he might somehow find himself on the opposing side to Sir Humphrey de Bohun. But such a hope was unworthy, he knew. Besides, he had not saved the man's life only to try and take it himself.

'Speak the devil's name,' Wilecok muttered, standing up from the fire with a bowl and a ladle in his hands.

'Sir Humphrey,' Robert said, twisting on his stool and smiling through his beard. 'You come to share our meagre fire, when all the finest hearths are open to you?'

Humphrey de Bohun spread his hands, smiling as he approached. Adam was sitting tensely beside the fire. He had been consciously avoiding de Bohun ever since their last meeting.

'No, don't rouse yourselves on my account,' de Bohun said. He halted a few paces away, one hand resting lightly on his sword hilt. 'And I'm not here to plunder your cooking pot, either!'

'Ha ha,' said Wilecok, sitting back down again with a grimace and a flick of his fingers.

'I've just come from the chapel,' de Bohun went on, disregarding him. 'Lord Simon convened a council of war there, as you know. I thought it best to tell you what I know.' He had lowered his voice to a more confidential tone, or what passed for one to a man like Humphrey de Bohun, but Adam could sense the attentions of those around neighbouring fires shifting in their direction.

'You do us graceful service, brother,' Robert said mildly, and gestured for him to continue.

'It's as we thought,' de Bohun went on. 'The king has his army at Lewes, billeted in the town, and occupying the castle and the adjacent priory. That's only a mile or two south of us here.'

'A mile or two?' Adam said under his breath. His nerves jumped – surely they should not be camped in the open so close to the enemy? The king's men could cover that distance on horse-back before de Montfort's troops could even assemble.

'Don't worry,' Sir Humphrey said, noticing his unease. 'Their sentries have sighted our scouts, but so far the king's made no move to take the field against us. He's in a strong position, sur-rounded by walls. No doubt he is waiting for us to move first, or to seek terms.'

'No doubt,' Robert said, grinding something between his back teeth.

'But Lord Simon wants to send out riders tomorrow at dawn, to scout westward below the ridges.' Humphrey moved his hands in arcs and curves as he spoke, as if he was shaping the land in the smoky air. 'If there's a viable track onto the high ground there, we could flank the town and gain the ini-tiative.'

Robert laughed. 'Never again will I say that the great men of England know nothing of war! Or perhaps they just read books of strategy, hmm?'

'Laugh all you like, *brother*,' Humphrey said, with a sly smile. 'I've already volunteered to lead the scouting party tomorrow. And it was your squire that I intended to join me, not you.'

*

They rode out shortly after dawn, with the dew still wet on
the grass. A dozen men in mail and armed with lances. Most
were knights and squires of de Bohun's own retinue; grooms
and serjeants rode with them. Too many and too strong, Adam
thought, to be a simple scouting or foraging party. The intention,
he guessed, was to flush out any scouts or outposts the king's
army might have placed on the high ground. They rode with the
sun behind them, westward through the little woodland village
of Offham and out into open meadow country studded with
patches of trees and strip fields. To their left the ground rose
abruptly to a high ridgeline, and the sky over the downs beyond
was dark with clouds. The sea was several miles away, but Adam
could taste it on the breeze.

The chalk uplands rose like a billowing wave to the west of
the town of Lewes, cresting at the line of ridges before dropping
steeply into wooded hollows and combes. The local people had
claimed there were tracks that climbed up the steep slopes and
onto the heights, but as he rode across the meadows Adam could
see nothing but unbroken trees clinging to the deep folds of the
land, still dark in night's shadow even as the sun mounted the
sky.

About a mile further on, as the mounted column swung around
to pass closer beneath the ridges, Humphrey de Bohun dropped
back beside Adam. For a few moments they rode together in
silence, their horses at an easy ambling gait. As he was not
expecting a hostile encounter, Adam had left Papillon back at the
encampment and was mounted on a palfrey. De Bohun kept his
restive charger on a tight rein, keeping pace with him.

'What I said to you, the last time we met,' he said, with a
wincing smile. 'It was unworthy of me. You must accept my
apology.'

'Accepted,' Adam said warily. But de Bohun was not finished.

'I'm aware, of course, of your feelings towards . . . the woman
I intend to wed,' he went on. The other riders had moved further

away or dropped back behind them, as if by a silent command. 'I don't blame you for them. Valiant love is a noble thing, in a young man. It's good chivalry too! But you know, of course, that nothing can come of it.'

'Naturally,' Adam said, inclining his head in a stiff bow.

'Ah, well then, good!' Humphrey declared, unable to hide a look of relief. 'I should not want to be forced to . . . well, let us say no more of it. Young women, you know,' he said intently, leaning from the saddle, 'unmarried women, I mean – they're foolish creatures, prone to idle fantasies. Their minds float in the clouds!' He fluttered his fingers in the air, grinning. 'But marriage – to a mature man, that is – brings true wisdom. And Joane de Quincy . . .' He pressed his hand to his breast, his mirth dying abruptly. 'Well, she belongs *to me*.'

Adam kept his expression neutral, and managed merely to nod. But inside him roiled an almost sickeningly violent anger. Yes, he thought, Humphrey de Bohun was a mature man. A man in middle years, of heavy and solid flesh, his face inside the steel oval of his mail coif already pink and glistening with sweat, the freckling of tiny blisters standing out angrily. The thought of such a man taking Joane as his wife, as his property, taking her to his bed, burdening her body and her spirit too with his weight . . . it was intolerable. And yet, Adam knew, that was exactly what would happen. Inside his tunic, beneath his mail and aketon, was stitched the page of the Psalter that Joane had given to him. He could feel it, a slight chafing at the skin of his chest, over his heart. It was all he would ever have from her, and it had to be enough.

He was still crushing his anger inside him when the mounted group broke up, de Bohun ordering two other riders to join Adam in an exploratory foray into the deeper folds of land below the ridge to the east. With John de Kington, one of de Bohun's household squires, and a mounted crossbowman behind him Adam spurred his horse into a trot, through the screen of woodland and over the rising ground.

They entered a hollow, and where the trees broke a grassy sward opened before them, still wet with dew in the early sunlight. Beyond it the land rose steeply, thick with dense scrub and woodland. Rills came down between the trees, and a broken shepherd's hut stood at the far side, but there was nobody in sight.

'No chance of getting up the slope here,' John de Kington said, reining in his horse and peering up at the heights. Adam nodded, pausing to let his palfrey crop at the grass. De Kington tossed him a flask of ale and he took a swig.

The crossbowman cried out a warning, and both men pulled at their reins and turned quickly. A pair of riders were coming through the trees from the lower ground below the ridge. The leading man wore a red surcoat over his mail, and he was followed by a serjeant in a black gambeson. As they emerged into the sunlight, Adam eased his grip on the reins, but did not relax his readiness.

'If you're looking for Humphrey de Bohun, you've come the wrong way,' he called.

'Oh no,' the knight in red replied with a smile. Adam had recognised Richard de Malmaines at once, but only as he approached could he make out the familiar features clearly. 'I was merely exercising my horse,' de Malmaines went on, 'and saw movement through the trees up here.'

Maybe true, Adam thought. But something in the knight's attitude appeared more calculated. Whatever had brought him here, this was no chance encounter.

Stretching, de Malmaines closed his eyes and inhaled. Then he gazed about him, blinking and smiling. 'A fine spot you've found!' he declared. 'What do you say, de Norton – you unhorsed me back at Senlis, could you keep your saddle here?'

Adam noticed that the other man was baiting his horse with his heels, keeping the animal brisk. He had slung his shield from his back as well and slipped his forearm through the straps. Now he raised his lance.

'You see gilding on my spurs, de Malmaines?' Adam called. 'You see my sword hanging from a knightly belt?'

'He's right,' John de Kington shouted from the far side of the grassy hollow. 'This is no time for challenges, sir – and it's dishonourable for a knight to challenge a squire!'

'I do not challenge him!' de Malmaines barked. 'De Norton and I are old friends, you see, old rivals – one day I will fight him and beat him soundly, but this is merely sport – chivalrous sport, and practice. There's no dishonour in it!'

Adam felt his horse twitch and stir beneath him, responding to the tension flowing through his body. He was wearing mail now, and not just the gambeson he had worn at Senlis two years before. But de Malmaines was once again carrying a battle lance, with an iron head that could punch through even the strongest armour if delivered at the charge. Was he truly playing at the joust, or did he intend to strike for real? A cold shudder passed down Adam's spine. Yes, he realised – this was de Malmaines's notion of chivalry: endless challenge, ceaseless violence, the refusal of defeat. And Richard de Malmaines himself was the deranged champion of that ideal. Never would he back down.

But following the chill of that realisation Adam felt a surge of hot anger, the same anger that de Bohun had kindled in him now roaring into full flame. And while he could not strike back against Humphrey de Bohun, de Malmaines held no such impunity. Against him, Adam's wrath was unrestrained.

'Very well!' he shouted, and hefted his lance. He snatched the shield from his saddle bow and shot his arm through the straps. 'Come at me if you dare!'

He had time to hear John de Kington's cry of dismay before he dragged the mail coif up over his head. Then he was turning his horse and lining up for the charge. Richard de Malmaines had cantered to the far side of the hollow and turned as well, his horse kicking at the damp turf. Both men raised their lances, then spurred forward immediately.

Cold air rushed around Adam as he dipped his head low behind the shield rim. Through the saddle leather he felt the hot muscle of his horse, not a trained charger but eager for the fight, as it flowed forward into a gallop. De Malmaines was racing towards him, lance already levelled; this was no sport, Adam knew. And this time he would not get away with trying to seize his opponent and drag him from the saddle.

John de Kington yelled again, his words lost to the battering of hooves and the rush of the wind. Then Adam saw Richard de Malmaines pull up abruptly, his horse stumbling and his lance swinging wide. For a moment he thought the animal had caught a hoof on the rough turf. Then something flashed past his head, and he dragged at the reins and jinked his horse around to the left.

Horsemen were crashing through the screen of trees above the hollow, two mailed knights leading them. There were crossbowmen in the scrub as well – one of their quarrels had lodged into the shoulder of de Malmaines's horse, and he was lucky that the charging animal had not thrown him. John de Kington was shouting again, fumbling with his shield straps as the two mounted serjeants rode up to support him. One of the leading knights carried a shield chequered with blue and yellow; Adam remembered the heraldic pattern from the Rochester siege. These were men of John de Warenne's retinue. *The enemy.*

Swinging out of his charge, Adam felt the muscles of his left arm burn as he dragged at the reins, holding back the power and momentum of his horse, keeping it turning in a tight half-circle. A quick glance back: Richard de Malmaines was still fighting to gain control of his wounded courser, the animal plunging and kicking. Then Adam's curving gallop brought him around onto the flank of the advancing enemy riders, and he let out the reins and dug with the spurs, levelling his lance as his horse leaped forward once more.

The blue and yellow shield was right ahead of him, and Adam aimed for it by instinct. The knight had only just noticed him and was sawing at the reins. Too slow: Adam's careering charge brought him up fast on the knight's left side, his lance smashing into the chequered shield and almost lifting the man from the saddle. The shaft of the lance cracked with the impact, and Adam had time to fling it aside before his horse slammed into the forequarters of the enemy's mount. The other animal screamed, rearing and staggering with the force of the collision, and the rider tumbled back over the crupper. Already Adam was turning again, sweeping out his sword to close and secure his downed captive.

One glance told him it was impossible. Four riders, perhaps five, were closing in around him now with swords and lances readied. Over to his left John de Kington was beset by another pair, one of the serjeants already riding for safety clutching a wound in his side. Richard de Malmaines had vanished. Adam gripped his sword tightly, determined not to flee. Anger still powered his blood. Tugging at the reins he rode to help John de Kington, but the other squire was already raising an empty hand for quarter.

'*A Bohun! A Bohun!*' The familiar cry rang clear in the morning air, and a moment later the first riders came galloping up the lower slope through the trees, the blue pennons flying, the blue shields with the white de Bohun stripe proudly displayed. Adam shouted with relief, grinning as he saw the enemy knights draw in their reins and begin to turn, realising they were outnumbered. Never, he thought, had he been so glad to see Humphrey de Bohun – but here the man was, face gleaming from his mail coif as he yelled his battle-cry and spurred into the attack. At the first blow of his sword one of the enemy serjeants was smashed from the saddle to fall beneath the hooves.

John de Kington wore a shamefaced expression as he rode to join Adam. But the de Warenne knight that Adam had unhorsed had made his escape too, and there was no glory in a mere skirmish. Humphrey de Bohun and his men had driven off the enemy at their first charge, most of the de Warenne riders retreating before contact.

'You found them then!' de Bohun declared, reining his sweating horse to a halt beside Adam.

'They found us,' Adam replied. In the exalting surge of his relief, he forgot all his anger at the man. 'And they almost took us!'

'A good thing we heard the commotion, and were close at hand,' de Bohun said, shoving the mail coif back from his head and seizing a water flask from another of his men. He drank deeply, then splashed his reddened face. 'But no matter,' he said as he wiped his brow and flickered away the water. 'We found the track we need, a short way west of here – so, a successful day, and we have not yet broken our fast!'

From the corner of his eye Adam could see Richard de Malmaines on the far side of the hollow, leading his limping horse by the reins. Two of de Bohun's grooms had gone to assist the injured serjeant. It could, he realised, have been a lot worse. But the rush of combat was in his blood, the keen satisfaction of overcoming an enemy. As he collected his shattered lance and rode to rejoin de Bohun's outriders, Adam felt only the burning anticipation of the fighting to come.

\*

'Lord Edward said this?'

'So we hear,' Hugh of Oystermouth replied, perched on the branch just above him. 'Right there in the refectory of the priory, where the king was sitting in state. He told the bishops that if Simon de Montfort and his followers – his *accomplices in treason*, he called them – wish for peace, they must surrender themselves with their hands bound before them and nooses around their necks, ready to be hanged or drawn as the king might decide!'

Adam exhaled through his teeth. He was sitting in the crook of a gnarled old yew tree, overlooking the churchyard. In the late-afternoon sunlight the area in front of the church was crowded with men, but from their vantage point Adam and the herald would have a good view of what was about to happen. Adam had heard about the first delegation that had been sent to the king that morning, shortly after his return to the camp with Humphrey and his men. That one had been led by the Bishop of Chichester and a party of friars, and had been sent back without an audience. But Lord Simon had persevered, and that afternoon had sent the Bishop of Worcester down to Lewes to negotiate with the royal commanders.

'They say,' Hugh of Oystermouth went on, dropping his voice and leaning closer, the branch creaking beneath him, 'that Bishop Walter was empowered to offer the king fifty thousand marks of silver in compensation, to buy peace in the realm, if Henry would agree to the reforms he once swore to uphold!'

'Fifty thousand?' Adam whispered. It was an incredible sum – where had de Montfort expected to find such an amount? Or had the offer been nothing more than a gesture all along?

Either way, the attempt had failed, and the Bishop of Worcester and his attendants had returned from Lewes carrying defiant letters from the king, Lord Edward and Richard of Cornwall. Letters that proclaimed Simon de Montfort and all who followed him to be perfidious traitors and enemies of the realm, and promising to do utmost injury to them with all their strength and power.

'And now, you see, it's come to this,' Hugh of Oystermouth whispered, his voice tight with excitement. Below them the steady stir of muttered voices had ceased, all falling silent as the men emerged from the porch of the church. First came the bishops of Worcester and Chichester and London, with their attendants and friars. After them came Lord Simon, dressed in mail and with his sword at his side. And following Simon were

his sons Henry and Guy, and the most prominent of his supporters. The silence spread outwards, until all was still. Only the
sound of distant birdsong disturbed the solemn hush.

Simon de Montfort went first. Standing before the assembled
churchmen, he drew his sword and held it reversed, then in a
loud voice made his declaration.

'In the sight of God and of honest men, I hereby renounce my
fealty and homage to Henry, third of that name, by God's Grace
King of England, Lord of Ireland and Duke of Aquitaine.'

After him, Gilbert de Clare also renounced his fealty, and then
Hugh Despenser and Humphrey de Bohun did the same. And
following them came every one of the assembled barons, all of
those who held lands of the king: Robert de Vipont and John de
Vesci of Alnwick, Henry de Hastings and Nicholas de Segrave,
John de Burgh and Ralph de Heringaud and many more. Adam
watched, hardly daring to breathe or stir in case the branches
beneath him creaked, as John FitzJohn stepped up to make his
renunciation. Then, after nearly two score barons and landhold-
ing knights from the greatest to the least had all repeated those
same solemn words, it was done. A great sigh or groan seemed
to rise from the assembled onlookers, a collective exhalation of
breath, then all began to scatter once more.

Adam slid from the branch and dropped lightly to the ground,
Hugh scrambling down after him. Robert de Dunstanville was
leaning against the trunk of the tree, a long stem of grass between
his teeth. As he held no lands, he had no renunciation to make.

'So what happens now?' Adam asked him.

Robert spat out the stem of grass. 'Bloodshed,' he replied. He
shoved himself away from the tree and settled his sword belt on
his hips. 'Best get what rest you can in the next few hours,' he
told Adam. 'Either that, or spend the time in prayer. Tonight,
nobody sleeps.'

# Chapter 28

The path was bone white under the moon. Earlier, beneath the trees that clad the lower slopes, the army had stumbled along in dense blackness, men cursing as they blundered together, horses whinnying nervously. But now they were climbing up onto the broad open expanses of the chalk downs under the dazzling brightness of the stars. A pale fog of dust wreathed them, and when Adam paused and looked back down the trail he saw an army of ghosts rising from the darkened combes below.

But as they emerged into the moonlight he saw a line of white crosses instead; every man in the army, from knights to squires and serjeants, had two long strips of white cloth stitched to his surcoat, front and back. The crosses would mark them out during the night march, just as they would mark them in the battle to come. But they were a holy symbol too. Simon de Montfort's army were soldiers of the cross now, warriors of Christ, dedicated to a higher cause.

'The sphere of the cosmos,' Hugh of Oystermouth said quietly, gazing up at the black and brilliant sky. He and Adam had paused at the summit of the ridge, where the path circled a spur and then levelled out.

'What do the stars foretell, do you think?' Adam asked him, only half in jest.

'Revolution!' Hugh declared, and Adam caught the glint of his widened eyes. 'Great turmoil and violence in the affairs of men and kingdoms. Some rise while others are cast down.'

'Do they tell you who will win the battle?'

Hugh sucked his teeth. 'Ah no, sadly they are not that specific.'

The column of men and horses filed up the path and over the ridge onto the shallower reverse slope, the horsemen all dismounted to avoid presenting a distinctive silhouette against the horizon. Once the men had formed in their retinues, a command came down the columns to begin the advance. They started off slowly and steadily, at the *petit pas*, so none straggled behind and none advanced too far and warned the enemy piquets. Sounds carried eerily: clink of metal, thud of hooves, the creak of leather harness. Adam felt the long grass brushing around his shins like hissing grey water. Above him the stars seemed to turn and spin, and the bright colours of the heraldic banners and caparisons were turned to ash and bone.

The sky to the east was already beginning to pale with the approaching dawn as the advance slowed to a halt. The moon was near full, and by its light Adam determined that the night's march had brought them almost to the edge of the downs. He could make out the shape of walls and towers in the valley below: Lewes, he realised, and its castle and priory. They were less than a mile away from it now. The town still slumbered, unsuspecting, unwarned of their approach.

'I was talking to one of the friars who went down there yesterday, with the bishop,' Hugh of Oystermouth whispered to Adam, coming up beside his horse. 'He told me the king's men had seven hundred strumpets with them in the town and the priory. *Seven hundred!*'

'He counted them all?' Adam asked.

'Just imagine though,' Hugh breathed, still lost in his own considerations. 'He said they were carousing all through the priory grounds, even on the steps of the high altar! Odds are they're all still sleeping it off now, the sinners.'

'Let's pray they are,' Adam said. 'And may the devil sweep them into hell.'

By now there was enough light in the sky for him to make out the forms of the men and horses around him, the army mustering in their thousands across the level summit of the downland. He saw movement away to his right, where the Earl of Leicester, the only man among them all on horseback, was riding slowly between the gathered contingents. Adam knew that de Montfort had spent the last hours in prayer, and had only now come up to join the army on the downs. The earl dismounted, then paused to confer with the Bishop of Worcester, and Adam found himself drawn towards the great ring of men surrounding them.

A line of figures appeared from the early-morning twilight. All were dressed in white unbelted tunics, ghostly in the dimness. Adam saw that the leading figure was Gilbert de Clare, the young Earl of Gloucester. Behind him walked de Montfort's younger son, Guy, and following them were squires of both their retinues and several other younger noblemen. Halting, de Clare knelt before Simon de Montfort, and Adam caught the sound of words carrying through the stillness. A slap, loud and sharp, as de Montfort cuffed the young earl across the face. Adam had seen the ceremony performed often enough before, and dreamed of experiencing it himself. Gilbert de Clare stood and raised his arms, hands pressed together as if in prayer, as Lord Simon fastened the knightly belt around his waist and two of his attendants buckled the gilded spurs to his ankles. Then Lord Simon kissed the young earl on both cheeks.

De Clare stepped away, and Simon repeated the ritual with his own younger son. One by one the others came forth, seven more young men kneeling before Lord Simon and then standing as he belted them with the sword and made them into knights. In the half darkness, beneath the illuminated sky, the whole performance had the appearance of a dream.

'Your time will come,' a voice said quietly. Adam turned his head to see Robert standing at his shoulder. 'Just stay alive long enough.'

Robert's tone was softened, and as he spoke he patted Adam lightly on the shoulder. At his touch a shudder coursed through Adam's body. He was older than Gilbert de Clare by several months, older than some of the others by a year and more. By knighting them now, and by knighting men of their retinues as well, de Montfort was rewarding them for their loyalty to him, and making them full partners in his cause. But after he had rewarded the powerful young men whose support he needed, there was nothing left to give to others. Adam understood, but still he felt hollowed inside.

Now the priests were calling men to confession and absolution. Day was nearly breaking, and already the first cocks were crowing down in the darkened valley as they sensed the approach of the sun. The multitude gathered on the downs divided into groups, men seeking out the bishops and the priests, the attending friars, and kneeling before them to confess their sins and be shriven, before facing the test of battle. '*Ego te absolvo! Ego te absolvo!*' the Bishop of Worcester declared, his voice loud in the stillness, as he paced slowly along the lines of kneeling men, planting his crosier before him and forming crosses in the air with two fingers.

'Go,' Adam said to Robert.

Robert shrugged, and Adam saw him turn his face away. He took the older man by the shoulder, then seized his hand. 'Please,' he said. 'Kneel and be shriven.'

'I can't,' Robert said. 'I took an oath . . .'

'Break the oath. In the name of friendship, I ask you.' He tightened his grip on Robert's shoulder. 'I took an oath as well, you remember? I swore to your cousin Joane de Quincy that I would protect you, and would not let you die in a state of sin. You remember that?'

'I'm surprised you do,' Robert said, and twitched a smile. It was light enough for Adam to make out his face clearly.

'Do this for me,' Adam told him.

Robert held his gaze for several heartbeats, then nodded abruptly and pulled away from him. Adam watched as he walked stiffly and knelt. He heard his voice as he mumbled his confession to one of the priests. '*Confiteor deo omnipotenti . . .*' Nobody was paying any attention to the words. Except God, Adam reminded himself. The bishop walked on along the line, crossing the air before him.

'*Ego te absolvo! Ego te absolvo!*'

Then Adam knelt too, and confessed, and was shriven.

When he stood up again the sky above him was glowing sapphire, and a rim of brightness was opening the horizon above the hills to the east. Simon de Montfort, mounted once more, his horse clad in a bloody-red caparison adorned with rampant white lions, rode before the army. With the glow of daybreak behind him he turned to address them, stretching up in his stirrups as if every one of the thousands who stood before him on the broad downland might hear his voice.

'Beloved friends,' he called. 'This struggle today is not mine alone. We fight for our country, for the honour of God and of the saints, and of our holy mother church. Let there be one faith amongst us, brothers, one will in all things, and one love towards God and all the realm of England!'

Some men spoke out in agreement, but the spell of silence still remained. The rest just breathed the words, nodding. A multitude of hushed voices repeated what they had heard to those behind them.

'We do not fear,' de Montfort went on, walking his horse steadily along the front ranks, 'to offend the king, or to die in the name of justice. But let us pray together now, to the King of All, that what we do this day pleases him, and he aids us in overcoming the malice of our foes. As we belong to God, let us commend our bodies and our souls to him!'

Dropping from the saddle, Lord Simon turned to face the bright horizon. As one of his squires held his horse, he lowered himself to the ground and lay face down with arms outstretched. In a wave of motion, like grass falling to the scythe, knights and squires, serjeants, archers and militiamen alike followed his example. Adam fell to his knees and then stretched himself on the springy turf, feeling the freshness of dew beneath him as he spread his arms.

'Grant us, O Lord, a mighty victory this day,' the bishop cried, beseeching the heavens with upraised crosier, 'to the honour and glory of your name!'

Together they lay, thousands of men stretched cruciform on the ground as the first sun broke in the east, spilling bright daylight across the sky. Adam heard fervently muttered prayers from all around him. One of the voices was Robert's. As he whispered the words, Adam could feel the fold of parchment pressed against his breast, the holy psalm written there. *Say of the Lord, He is my refuge and my fortress . . .* How many others, he wondered, carried holy charms and relics and tokens? He remembered Le Brock, and his string of St Thomas. Surely many of those around him felt similarly protected. But their prayers, their collective abasement, had a power nonetheless. Adam felt it gathering around him, like a charge of thunder in the air, a tremor running through the ground beneath them.

'Up now,' somebody said gruffly. 'Up and make ready!'

A chorus of cock crows was sounding from the valley. Stumbling to their feet once more, brushing the grass and dirt from their surcoats, the men summoned their grooms and servants to them. Adam slid his legs into the chausses, then stood holding the raised hem of his hauberk as Hugh secured the mail leggings to his girdle strap. Once Adam was fully armoured he turned to assist Robert, lifting the leather corselet lined with iron plates over his shoulders and lacing it securely at the back. Robert had seldom worn a coat of plates over his mail to protect his torso during tournaments, but in battle it was the only thing that might stop a lance delivered at the charge. When the coat was secured, Robert pulled on his surcoat, with the large white crosses stitched prominently both front and back. In the clear wash of daylight his helm and armour gleamed, freshly polished and immaculate. Beside him, Adam fastened the broad-brimmed iron helmet over his coif. The armour weighed heavily, but as he stared into the sunrise he felt a pure confidence rising through him, an absolute surety of purpose.

All along the front ranks of the army men were mounting, grooms handing them pennoned lances and banners. Once he was secure in the saddle, Robert took off his helm and propped it on the saddle bow. Hugh passed Adam his shield and he slung it over his shoulder by the strap.

'Listen,' Robert said, lightly tugging the rein so his destrier took two steps towards Adam's. 'If things go badly today – if you see me fall, or I'm captured . . . Get yourself clear, you understand?'

'I wouldn't flee the field—' Adam began to say.

Robert reached over and seized his hand in a mailed fist. '*Listen to me!*' he demanded, then went on in a hushed urgent voice. 'This will be a bloody day, I have a sense of that.'

Adam nodded, a ripple of chill running through him.

'Do not sacrifice yourself for me,' Robert went on, 'and not for Lord Simon either! If things go badly, you ride like the flames of hell are at your heels. And you feel no shame for it. Do you understand?'

Then Robert grinned, and pulled him closer. Leaning from the saddle, they embraced. Mail links grated together. 'Remember,' Robert said. '*Fame and renown* – that alone is why we do what we do.'

They separated, and Robert nudged with his heels to walk his horse forward. The whole army was moving in formation now, lines of mounted men rolling across the crest of the down.

Robert and Adam were in the right flanking division, led by Sir Humphrey de Bohun and Lord Simon's two sons, Henry and Guy de Montfort. The panorama opened as they advanced. A river of mist was flowing along the valley, cloaking the contours of the land, but the battlements of the castle and the gatehouse caught the first rays of sun. To the right, where the land dropped to broad meadows, the priory stood within its quadrangle of walls, the spire of the church rising into the glow of morning.

As they rode up to the brink of the slope above the town, Adam saw figures running across the area of grassland between them and the walls of the priory. Men on horseback pursued them. Dawn cloaked the scene in a shimmering haze, but Adam made out the horsemen cutting down one or two of the fleeing fugitives.

'Enemy foraging party,' Humphrey de Bohun called as he joined him, and grinned. 'They've had a surprising start to their day!'

Squinting, Adam followed the last few running figures as they raced away down the path towards the gates of the priory, which still lay deep in mist and shadow in the valley below them. Over to his left, he saw the massed formations of knights and serjeants drawn up along the brow of the slope. This would be what their enemies would see, he realised, as they were roused from their beds by the cries of alarm, and gazed up in shock and confusion from the gates and walls of Lewes. A whole army, appeared as if by a miracle on the heights commanding the town, fully arrayed for war with banners raised and surcoats marked with the holy cross, awesome and terrible in the first gleam of the sun.

A few moments later, all the bells in the priory and the churches of the town began ringing wildly.

*

It took almost two hours for the king's troops to rouse them-selves from their billets, spilling forth in milling confusion to assemble before the walls of the town. Massed cavalry formed the front lines, with the infantry drawn up behind them. Trumpets brayed, and hoarse yells drifted up to the men waiting on the brow of the hill, as the bells kept up their constant clangour.

'You see him?' Humphrey de Bohun asked, riding over to join Robert and Adam. He raised a mailed hand and pointed down at the enemy's flanking formation as they mustered on the slope above the priory.

'I see him,' Robert said quietly.

It took Adam only a moment to realise what they were looking at. The enemy flank division, opposing theirs, was led by the king himself. Knights of the royal retinue formed a great block at the centre, beneath the golden lion banner, and Adam could almost make out the crown mounted on the helmet of one of the leading riders. But just behind the king's array he saw the familiar blue and white banner of Humphrey de Bohun, Earl of Hereford, the lord that Adam himself had served for so many years. The father of Sir Humphrey, and of Sir Robert too. Adam wondered if the king had placed Earl Humphrey there on purpose, to demoralise them. It seemed a great impiety to set father against son. But perhaps the earl had chosen the position himself, so the shame of his family should not be expunged by another man?

'By the chin of St David, there's enough of the buggers,' Hugh of Oystermouth said, as he stood beside Adam's horse holding his lance and shield. 'How many do you reckon?'

'Six to eight thousand,' Robert said without hesitation. His practised eye had already calculated the enemy strength. 'More than enough for everyone.'

'That must be Lord Edward over there on the far flank, look, with the Marcher Lords with him,' Hugh went on, shading his face with a levelled palm. His sight had become blunted after too many long hours staring at inked script by candlelight, and he needed to squint and peer to make out the banners. 'Then

Earl Richard of Cornwall leading the central battle, just in front of that windmill on the road to the town gate,' he said. 'And the Scottish lords with him too. That will be the great crowd of their infantry right behind them.'

'What's that strange banner flying next to the king's standard?' Adam asked, staring down at the gathering mass of the royal household troops opposite them. 'The red one, with the long streaming tail?'

'Ah, that would be *the dragon* . . .' Hugh said, his voice faltering.

Adam frowned at him. He had never heard of such a thing.

'It means the sentence of death,' Robert explained crisply. '*No quarter.*'

Horns were wailing from the left flank of de Montfort's array, where Henry de Hastings and Nicholas de Segrave led their retinues and the London militia. On top of the ridge, the newly knighted Gilbert de Clare commanded the centre, with John FitzJohn supporting him. A short distance behind them, further up the slope, Lord Simon himself was stationed with Hugh Despenser and the reserves. Between the mounted men, groups of archers and slingers waited to rain arrows and shot on the enemy as soon as they came within range.

It was just like a tournament, Adam thought as he sat in the saddle, slightly dazed by the bright sunlight glaring in his eyes. The two great lines of mounted knights drawn up facing each other, just waiting for the signal to charge. He almost expected to see the marshals striding up the slope between them, consulting their lists and flourishing their batons. Taking a flask from Hugh, he swallowed back wine. Nervous tension massed in his spine and shoulders, and he fought to calm himself. The verses of the psalm he wore stitched inside his tunic came to him once more. In his mind he seemed to hear Joane de Quincy's voice reading the words. *A thousand shall fall at your side, and ten thousand at your*

*right hand; but it shall not come near you . . . Because you have made*
*the Lord your refuge . . .*

Breathing the verses to himself, Adam traced a cross across
his breast. He had noticed many of those around him doing the
same. Humphrey de Bohun drew a crucifix from the neck of his
mail coif, kissed it, then tucked it back into place.

'What's de Segrave doing?' Robert said abruptly, standing in
his stirrups and craning his neck to the left. 'He and de Hastings – they're pushing too far forward and leaving their infantry
unprotected.'

A couple of other men heard him and gazed towards the far-
left flank as well. Ralph de Heringaud, the stout knight that
Adam had encountered at the feast in Rochester, cursed loudly.
'Somebody needs to pull them back,' he said. Sweat was flowing
down his face in runnels from beneath his coif. His son, riding
behind him as his squire, appeared pale and half sick with nerves.
Up at the front of the formation, Henry and Guy de Montfort
were turning in the saddle, frowning in confusion at Humphrey
de Bohun.

'Adam de Norton,' de Bohun ordered. 'Ride at once over to
the left flank and tell de Segrave and de Hastings to pull their
cavalry back up the slope and close the gap with the militia,
before they unbalance our whole line!'

Adam glanced at Robert, who nodded his agreement. Without another word he tugged at the reins, swinging to the left
and spurring Papillon into a gallop across the slope. Passing the
rear of Gilbert de Clare's and John FitzJohn's men, he emerged
above the left flank division. At the fore were the black banners
of Nicholas de Segrave's retinue, the red on yellow of Henry
de Hastings. From his position on the slope, Adam could see
that they had advanced too far downhill towards Lord Edward's
huge host, which waited in formidable strength across the meadows below them. A space of several hundred yards had opened
at their backs, before the ranks of the London militia covered

the brink of the downs. The Londoners were raising a great din, cheering de Montfort's name and yelling abuse at Lord Edward and Richard of Cornwall. Their massed shouts rolled down the slope towards the silent ranks of their enemy.

Then, before Adam could determine the position of the baronial leaders, he heard another noise. An eruption of trumpets from the opposing lines, an iron roar of voices shouting from inside helmets, and then the massed formation of Edward's division broke into motion. Reining to a halt, Papillon prancing beneath him, Adam watched in awestruck horror as Edward's horsemen came powering up from the meadows, pennons streaming as they lowered their lances to the charge. Armoured riders in tight formation, most of them on armoured horses, they slammed into de Segrave's wavering front ranks. The noise of screaming men and horses, and bellowed cries of defiance, echoed across the hillside.

First de Segrave's formation buckled and split, then Henry de Hastings's retinue broke before the storm of steel and horseflesh. Up the slope above them the ranks of the London militia were in turmoil, some of the men turning to flee while others tried to form a defensive line. But Adam could see how the fight would unfold. Edward's leading riders had already crashed through the disintegrating left division of the baronial army, and were galloping hard towards the disordered ranks of the Londoners, swords raised. With a jolt of intuition Adam recalled the stories he had heard, the threats issued by Edward against the men of London for the insults they had heaped upon his mother the queen the year before. Now, before his eyes, those threats would be realised. The Londoners would be bloodied chaff before the tempest of royal vengeance.

Papillon reared as Adam hauled at the reins, turning in the air with kicking hooves. Then, without a backward glance, Adam was riding hard the way he had come. A ripple passed through the rear of the central division as every man turned to stare at the disaster unfolding on their left flank. Already Adam could hear the trumpet signals, and see the banners waving in the bright air. Breathless, he swung his horse back around to join de Bohun's men on the right.

'Lord Edward's smashed our left division,' he cried as he cantered up beside Robert and Sir Humphrey. 'The London militia are breaking . . . if they flee, the king's men will be able to swing around our flank and get behind us.'

'Christ preserve them, we can do nothing for them now,' Robert said. He pointed down the slope, and Adam saw that the king's household retinue, with Earl Humphrey's banners accompanying him, had begun their advance.

'Here they come,' Hugh yelled. 'Hot as hell and smiting like the devil!'

Heart thundering, blood beating in his head, Adam seized his lance and shield from the herald, who turned and ran back to the rear. To the left, de Clare's division was already advancing down the ridge towards the centre of the enemy line. Below them the men led by Richard of Cornwall and the Scottish lords were in motion too, gathering momentum as they pushed forward along the road from the town.

Sir Humphrey de Bohun had ridden up to the front of the formation to join Henry de Montfort. Adam saw him turn in his saddle and raise his lance to the three hundred horsemen behind him.

'May the Lord give us *glory*!' de Bohun yelled.

Walking their horses forward, the knights of the baronial army reached the brink of the slope, then broke into a trot. Rolling downhill, their advance gathered speed, their horses stretching out into a canter and then into a plunging charge. The noise of the hooves was a steady thunder through the earth beneath them. Riding directly in Robert's wake, into the bursting sunlight, Adam felt the tension in his body lift suddenly, all the dread and anxiety burned away at once and replaced by a rush of pure violent exhilaration.

Not even God could hold them back now.

# Chapter 29

A horse went down ahead of him, either stumbling or shot by an arrow, the rider flung from the saddle. Robert veered around the fallen animal and Adam followed, the speed and momentum of the charge carrying them on down the slope towards the opposing army. Suddenly Adam felt the terror bursting over him like a storm of frozen hail, the chill of it seizing his body and crushing him down onto the saddle. Ahead lay an advancing torrent of bloody-red banners and shields and roaring golden lions, of powerful horses and armoured men, the finest warriors in England under the standards of their king. The charge of de Montfort's knights appeared puny by comparison, scattering over the hillside at the gallop. They would be engulfed, consumed. And no avenue of escape remained.

Adam kept his head low, staring out through the narrow slit beneath his shield and his helmet rim, lance held upright to avoid spearing the men ahead of him. In the moment before the reckless plunging charge met the enemy front line the royal knights appeared to part before them, opening a lane. Hope ignited in Adam's mind. *Maybe they could survive this* . . . But there was no safe passage, only the mesh of combat, and suddenly he was right inside it.

An explosion of noise: the smash of lance into shield, of armoured bodies in collision, of iron meeting flesh. The first few riders went down under the lances and the hacking blades, like meat fed into a grinder as they tumbled beneath the threshing hooves of the horses.

Robert swerved, his lance angling, and struck an oncoming knight at full tilt. The impact blasted the man up out of his stirrups and sent him tumbling back over his horse's tail, the animal rearing and plunging in shock and kicking out with its hooves. Robert swerved again, his lance broken, galloping clear as Adam's horse jinked around the panicking animal without faltering. As they met again Adam swung his lance towards Robert, intending that he take it as he had done so many times before in tournaments. But Robert was already reaching for his axe.

'Go!' he yelled, waving Adam onward, '*Go!*'

Adam just had time to swing the lance down and couch it beneath his arm before the second line of enemy riders were upon him. Papillon had slowed only slightly from the galloping charge; now the big destrier surged forward once more. Adam hunched behind the lance, aiming the head straight and true at the unshielded right side of one of the opposing knights. He saw the man notice him – too late – and try to turn. Then the lance struck, the impact shoving Adam back against the high saddle. His angle had been too high, he realised, and the man was wearing a coat of plates under his mail; the honed tip of the lance grated upwards from the knight's chest and rammed into the folds of his coif beneath the rim of his helmet.

The knight screamed, his own lance swinging to clout Adam's shoulder, but the head of Adam's weapon was trapped in the links of his mail coif and Adam was pushing at him, their horses circling wildly. Dragging back on the lance, Adam tried to stab the point into the man's throat, but it was securely caught. Pulled forward, the knight almost fell from the saddle. Then he reared upright again, his sword drawn, and hacked at the shaft of the lance.

A blow cracked against Adam's back, right at the base of his spine. He lost his grip on the lance, the knight bolting clear and dragging the weapon after him with the head still trapped in his mail. Another rider was pressing up on Adam's flank now, raining down slamming blows with a mace. Adam twisted in the saddle, both arms behind his shield as he absorbed the force of the attack. The two horses were fighting beneath them, Papillon kicking and trying to rear, the other animal twisting its neck to bite. Adam reached down for his sword, fumbling for the grip. The mace slammed against his helmet, and hot white pain burst through him.

Then a figure appeared behind the other rider, an axe swinging down to cleave the mail and the iron skullcap beneath it and bite deeply into his head. The axe ripped free again, spraying a pale mist of blood, and the man was tumbling dead from the saddle even as Robert galloped on past.

Stunned, pain blooming through his body, Adam raised a mailed hand to wipe the spatters of blood from his face. Papillon was still moving beneath him, carrying him on deeper into the melee, but for a few long moments Adam was almost unaware of it. Then his sense sharpened, forcing down the pain, shrugging off the binds of horror, and he was back in the fight.

By now the opposing charges had turned and intermeshed, swirling into a vast moving gyre of combat. Adam saw men on all sides of him, the gaps between them steadily consumed until his knees were pressed against those of the other riders, their horses surging at each other in wild frenzy. Impossible to determine who was fighting whom; here and there a white cross appeared, or an upraised banner. The noise was incredible, all-consuming. *The ironworks.*

Adam struck out to left and right, trying only to forge a path through the crush. The low sun threw blinding shards of

light between the struggling bodies. *I'll die here*. The thought
was clear and cool in his mind. No, he refused it. *A thousand
shall fall at your side, and ten thousand at your right hand* . . . He
hammered the pommel of his sword at a rider shoving up on
his left side, and the man reeled back and then hacked at him
with his own weapon. Adam caught the blow on his shield,
then slashed at the exposed oval of the man's face, his blade
opening a bloody gash. Then he got his shoulder behind his
shield and shoved, teeth clenched as he forced the injured man
from the saddle.

A lance darted from the press, the tip slamming against his side.
He felt the impact deep in his ribcage. Reeling, he hacked back
and down by instinct, his sword shearing through the lance shaft
before it could stab at him again. The rider collided with him,
tumbling forward, his great helm almost smashing into Adam's
face before he pulled himself back again. His horse reared and
struck down with its hooves at Papillon's rear quarters; Adam
clung to the saddle as the warhorse staggered beneath him, then
he was up again and turning, reins short on his fist as he hacked
back at the enemy rider.

His sword was a blunted mallet, beating at iron. No way of
telling if his blows were having an effect. Already his right arm
was numb and aching, jarred by repeated impacts. The other
rider veered away, his maddened horse snaking out around Papillon's rear. Adam dragged a breath through his teeth, winging
his shoulder to try and work the blood back into his right arm.
Something clipped his helmet but he barely felt it. He needed to
get clear of the crush, before it sucked him under.

Daylight to his left, a clear channel opening between the surging horses and men. *Move*. Dragging at the reins in his fist, Adam
gave one kick with the spurs and Papillon bolted, carrying him
out of the melee in three long strides. Open ground before him,
littered with broken spear shafts. He was further down the slope
than he had expected; away to his right was the stream at the foot

of the hill, with the walls of the priory beyond, and the spire of the church rising from the sun-shot haze.

But then he saw his mistake.

The open ground was seething with enemy foot soldiers. Fifty strides away, a line of crossbowmen had already seen him, picking out the white cross on his surcoat and raising their weapons to shoot. Closer, spearmen closed in on him at a run. Others carried axes, grain flails, scythe blades mounted on poles, even wooden clubs. A quarrel struck the top of Adam's thigh, punching through the mail to lodge in the padded gambeson beneath. Pain flowed up his leg into his groin, but already he was turning his horse, keeping his shield up. A second quarrel banged into it, and a third clipped his helmet.

Away to his right another rider was surrounded by infantry. Adam recognised the blue shield and surcoat, the golden fish blazon of Ralph de Heringaud. His young son was still with him, trying to control his capering palfrey as the foot soldiers jeered. Before Adam could ride to their assistance he saw de Heringaud seized from behind and dragged from the saddle, one foot catching and twisting in the stirrup as his panicking horse shied. A man in a filthy gambeson and linen coif raised a long dagger and stabbed it down through the eye slit of his helmet. Ralph de Heringaud was dead before his foot slipped free of the stirrup, and his armoured body was dragged down into the dirt. The soldiers closed around the fallen knight, hacking with axes, beating with clubs and flails. Adam saw de Heringaud's son riding clear, his face blanched with terror and streaming with tears.

Papillon had turned fast, but the tide of enemy infantry had swarmed up on all sides now. A spearman thrust at Adam and he turned the strike with his sword and then slashed back, his blade hacking through the man's forearm. Two more were stabbing at his legs from the other side, but his mail chausses took the force of the blows. His horse was backing and shying as the spears closed in a ring, reddened snarling faces on all sides, eyes tight

with rage, bared teeth flecked with spittle. Striking out, Adam
warded off blows and sent men stumbling away from him, but
still more were pressing in. A man leaped up at him, trying to
seize the rim of his shield and drag him from the saddle. Adam
slammed him back, then brought his blade swinging down to
chop at his shoulder. The sword sheared down through the man's
collarbone. Pulling the blade free, Adam twisted as another
attacker grappled him from his right. Slipping his foot from the
stirrup he raked his spur across the man's chest then shoved him
away.

Papillon surged forward as a man tried to snatch the bridle,
jolting Adam in the saddle. One kick with an ironshod hoof
demolished the man's jaw. Furious now, the big horse bucked
and kicked out again with both rear hooves. Wary, the spearmen
shrank back, and Adam saw his chance. Planting his foot back in
the stirrup, he jabbed with the spurs and Papillon leaped, soar-
ing clear of the ring of attackers.

*

The air was fogged with dust, churning in the bright morning
sun. Adam's face was matted with it, a mask of dirt and drying gore, runnelled with sweat. His whole body pulsed and
ached. His horse was injured too, a long cut on the neck. Not
deep, but the blood was flowing down the animal's forequarters. Leaning forward, Adam rubbed at Papillon's mane and
the uninjured side of his neck, but the horse was trembling and
twitching, blowing hard.

Adam was riding across clear ground, the packed melee swirling away to his right, fierce knots of combatants up the slope to
his left. Fatigue dulled his shock as he noticed the bodies strewn
beneath him. Some were infantrymen cut down and left to die,
but there were knights and armoured squires among the fallen,
crawling wounded or sprawled dead. A multitude of dead horses

too, some with spears still stuck in their bodies, or with hideous belly wounds, dead on their backs with legs canted grotesquely upwards, some still alive and struggling to stand as their entrails dragged in the dirt. All around, the trampled turf was black with blood. Adam's stomach roiled, and he fought down a chug of nausea.

Then he saw Robert away to his right, in the lock of the melee, standing in the saddle to hack down with his axe. Drawing a long breath, his throat dry and swollen, Adam tugged at the reins and spurred his weary horse back into the heart of the battle.

Almost at once he lost sight of Robert. Trumpets called high and brassy through the tumult, and when he raised himself in the stirrups he saw a banner tossing above the throng directly ahead of him. Red and gold, the lions of England. The king's own personal standard. The crowd of men and horses parted, and Adam saw beneath the banner the figure on the mailed war-horse with the red and gold caparison, his gilded helmet flashing in the sunlight, the crown set upon it burning gold. A storm of household knights surrounded the king, but Adam had a clear view through the throng. For one long moment of amazement he saw the armoured horse stumble and fall to its front knees, a lance jutting from its neck. He saw the crowned figure sliding from the saddle, toppling sideways into the billowing dirt.

At once men were dismounting all around the fallen king. One of the household knights took him by the arms and lifted him bodily into the saddle of his own horse. Within moments the king was up again and away, hunched in the saddle as his bodyguards closed around him. The knight who had dismounted stood his ground, legs planted – and the next moment Robert de Dunstanville's axe slashed down and split his helmet open.

'Back, back!' Robert yelled as he saw Adam in the crush. Adam recognised the trumpet calls he had been hearing. '*Rally!*'

\*

'Where are we?' Humphrey de Bohun was shouting hoarsely. 'Where's Lord Simon? How far are we from the town?' He had ripped off his battered helmet and flung it to one of his squires. Now he was tipping water from a flask over his reddened face. Adam almost fancied he could see steam rising from the man's body and from the flanks of his horse.

'We almost took the king!' one of Henry de Montfort's knights was yelling, grinning as blood ran from his scalp. 'The king himself!'

The trumpet was still bleating the signal to rally, but only a handful of Sir Humphrey's company had rejoined his banner. Adam had followed Robert up the slope, both of them battered but so far uninjured. The royal knights had seemed content to let their opponents disengage and regroup, after seeing their king brought down right in front of them.

Adam stretched up in the saddle, gazing into the low hazy sunlight. To his right were the spire and roofs of the priory buildings down on the meadows, where he could see the king's forces rallying, forming up once more beneath their banners. But what had happened to Edward? Adam had last seen his division away beyond the ridge, storming up the slope to attack the London militia. By now he should have swung around into the flank of de Montfort's reserves. Craning his neck, Adam almost expected to see the golden lion banners streaming over the ridge near the windmill he had noticed earlier, Lord Edward and the Marcher Lords, their thirst for blood unslaked, ready to fall upon them from the rear and annihilate them utterly.

'The devil take them, they're not breaking!' John de Burgh cried, as he rode up to join them with only a couple of serjeants left of his retinue. 'They're too strong for us!'

'It's your faith that lacks strength!' de Bohun snarled back at him. He seized his helmet and pulled it on again. Guy de Montfort had joined them too, alone and riding a blown horse, his face waxy with shock and pain. But he managed to dismount and exchange horses with one of his squires.

'Look at them!' de Burgh said, flinging his mailed hand towards the king's reformed array. 'One more charge and they'll drive us off the field!'

'No,' said Robert. 'No they won't – not yet.' He was pointing with his axe, and everyone turned to follow his gesture.

Adam's heart felt tight in his chest. Just as he had imagined, a host of armoured horsemen was bursting across the ridge and plunging down into the fray. But their red shields bore the fork-tailed white lion of de Montfort, not the prowling golden lions of Lord Edward. Bellowing cheers broke from the men of Humphrey de Bohun's company. The Earl of Leicester was leading his own troops onto the field at last, bringing his reserve division down the slope at the charge, straight into the exposed flank of the royal array.

*Where was Edward?* Had de Montfort already beaten him, up there on the top of the ridge, while the main battle was raging on the slope below? It seemed impossible. But Adam felt his blood singing in his body, fresh strength flowing through him. Simon de Montfort's men were carving a bloody path through the enemy infantry, foot soldiers fleeing before their charge. Down the slope, the king's banners were wavering as his squadrons turned to counter the new threat.

Robert leaned closer and grabbed Adam by the back of the neck. 'Ready?' he said. His helmet was propped on his saddle bow, and he had a flask in his hand. Adam nodded, and Robert passed him the flask.

Wine, *God be praised*. Adam drank, then swilled his mouth and spat. His head was ringing, but at the sound of the trumpet his horse stirred beneath him, head up and ears back. The wound in Papillon's neck was still bleeding, the blood very red against his dark hide, but the horse appeared to feel it no longer.

'Yes,' Adam said. 'Yes – *ready*.'

\*

It was a ragged sort of charge. Barely fifty men, few with lances, and many of them wounded. But they rode screaming, brandishing swords and maces and axes, goading their weary horses from a trot to a flat gallop down the slope to crash into the king's array as it thinned and stretched to the left to confront de Montfort's reserves.

Adam felt the wind at his back. He wondered if this was what it felt like to be truly led by the divine spirit. Against his chest he could feel the leaf of Joane's Psalter, soaked now with his own sweat and blood no doubt, bound to his skin, to his heart. And around him were his brothers, his fellow warriors. Robert de Dunstanville, John de Burgh and Guy de Montfort, even Humphrey de Bohun, who led the charge. He was one with them. He heard their yells of fury, of near-joyous defiance, and realised that he felt no fear at all now. No pain either, all fatigue gone — only the frenzy of battle, the fierce desire for glory, remained.

The king's men saw them and turned to take their charge on their left, the shielded side. Many still had lances and couched them, angling them to strike. But de Bohun's riders came down on them like a summer thunderstorm, weaving in among them and blasting apart their front line with sheer violent momentum. Adam saw Robert smash a lance aside with his axe, then cut the rider from the saddle on the backswing. He dodged another lance himself, sliding his sword along the shaft until he could stab over the shield at the face of the serjeant gripping it.

As the formation buckled, the melee began its mad swirl once more, veering riders crashing together and staggering apart, hacking and slashing from the saddle. There were infantry between them too, and many of them were wearing the white cross on surcoat and gambeson; de Montfort's own foot soldiers, Adam realised, had swarmed down the hillside and joined the fight.

Ahead of him a rider with a blue shield yelled and raised his sword as he saw the cross stitched to Adam's surcoat. Adam swung his own shield up, catching the blow and turning it aside, then slammed his blade into the opening of the rider's coif, piercing his neck. For the space of a heartbeat their plunging horses jostled them together. Ralph de Tosny gazed back at Adam, eyes widening in recognition. With an anguished cry Adam dragged his arm back, and as the blade tore free, blood gushed from the wound. A heartbeat longer, Ralph's eyes clouding, then the body toppled from the saddle and fell beneath the stamping hooves. His breath tight, Adam pulled Papillon around and leaned from the saddle, but the body of his former friend was lost amid the turmoil of the melee. Then he dug with his spurs and was moving again.

He was into broken country now, the ground cut up with ditches, hedgerows and strip fields. Cheering from his left, and as he leaped a shallow ditch Adam saw de Montfort's red and white banner streaming in the air ahead of him, Lord Simon's household knights riding in a close wedge beneath it. They were driving the king's troops even further down the slope, towards the meadows and the priory precincts. Around a hedgerow and into a narrow strip of open ground, Adam saw another knight ahead of him, a man wearing the white cross on his red surcoat, beset on both sides by mounted serjeants. The knight was hurt, buckling in the saddle, his weapon gone, and the serjeants seemed determined on making an end of him. One grappled his arms, while the other slammed repeated blows with a mace across his bent back.

Adam spurred forward immediately, drawing breath to shout, but he had only closed half the distance when he realised that the stricken man was Richard de Malmaines. He drew back the reins, slowing Papillon to a trot and then circling to the left. For a few long moments he considered how satisfying it would be, how convenient, simply to let the man die, right now, in front of his eyes.

The idea was a flicker of malice, of justified retribution. Then it was gone, and Adam was spurring his horse forward once more, sword raised. The two serjeants had their backs to him, and did not turn as he galloped closer. One stinging blow knocked the mace from the first man's grip, then Adam slammed into him with his shield and toppled him from the saddle. The second had noticed him now, but did not have time to draw his sword before Adam leaned and struck at him across de Malmaines's hunched back. Bellowing, the serjeant jinked clear of his blade, but Adam managed to seize the reins of de Malmaines's horse with his shield hand. The fallen man was stumbling to his feet, and Papillon lashed out and kicked him hard in the torso. Then Adam was turning, dragging the other horse behind him, de Malmaines barely clinging to the saddle.

Back up the strip of open ground and into the cover of the hedgerows Adam rode at a canter, only slowing once they were clear of the two attackers. Then he reined to a halt, reached across to the other horse and dragged de Malmaines's head up from his protective crouch. Blood was flowing down the man's face from a head wound, and he bared his teeth in a grimace of pain as he blinked and stared at Adam.

'You?' he managed to say. Adam swung his sword around and levelled it at his neck; just for a moment he remembered the night of the massacre in London, and the temptation to plunge the blade into de Malmaines's throat was almost overwhelming.

'You owe me your life,' Adam snarled at him. 'Our feud is at an end!'

De Malmaines began to laugh, then his body buckled with pain. He raised a bloodied hand, the mail mitten dangling loose from his cuff. 'It's over,' he croaked.

'You give me your word?' Adam demanded, seizing the edge of the man's mail coif and dragging his head up to stare into his eyes.

Richard de Malmaines pressed his tongue against the back of his teeth, spitting a little bloody froth. 'You have my word,' he said, wincing.

'Then go,' Adam said, shoving the man away from him. De Malmaines fell forward over his horse's neck, and for a moment looked like he would slide from the saddle. Then he jogged at his reins, kicked weakly with his heels, and his blown horse stumbled forward again, in the direction of the ridge and the open land beyond.

Adam watched him go, breathing hard, the fierce heat of anger still burning in his throat. Perhaps it would have been better to let the man die, or even to take his life in vengeance for the evils he had committed. But it would have lain hard upon Adam's conscience if he had. And a word of honour had to mean something, even for a man like de Malmaines. Even if the battle was lost, Adam told himself, he had won his own sort of victory.

*

The battle was not lost, not yet, but it was hard to tell who was winning. Over the half-mile or so of churned turf between the slope of the downs and the priory meadows the horsemen charged and rallied, spinning into sharp melees and then scattering once more. Adam flicked a glance towards the high ground to his left. He could see fierce fighting around the windmill and the little church to the right of it, where the yellow banners with the red chevrons of Gilbert de Clare's retinue were swaying against the sky. No way of telling what was happening on the far side. He kept moving, twisting in the saddle as he rode, hunting for any sign of Robert. Renewed fatigue was aching through him, dulling his senses and slowing his reflexes. His sword and his right arm were brown with blood. More blood spattered the forequarters of his horse. The top rim of his shield was so deeply notched that one of the straps was coming loose from its mounting.

Somewhere up ahead, the king's royal standard tossed and waved over the jostling surge of combat. Simon de Montfort's red and white banner was there too; as Adam watched, it dipped, as if the bearer had stumbled or fallen. A moment later it was lifted high once more, streaming in the gritty breeze. Trumpets sounded, high through the rush of battle. *Rally*. Adam stood in the stirrups, peering back over his shoulder. There, to the left: the blue banner with the white diagonal of Humphrey de Bohun. He turned his horse towards it.

Only as he drew closer did he snap from his daze of fatigue. The banner had no *fleur-de-lis* upon the white stripe. It was the standard of the Earl of Hereford, not his son. But already Adam was close enough to see the eddying whirl of mounted men fighting around the banner. Earl Humphrey himself was mounted high on his powerful mailed warhorse, blue and white caparison swirling beneath him as he fought. Tensing with horror, Adam saw that one of the two knights he was fighting was Robert de Dunstanville.

Stooping low over the saddle bow, taking a tighter grip on his battered shield, Adam urged Papillon deeper into the swirl of the melee. But then, moments after he had first noticed them, he saw Robert reach for Earl Humphrey's horse, trying to seize the bridle. Robert's helmet was gone and he wore only his mail coif, and he was shouting – urging his father to surrender, perhaps? Adam could not hear the words. But he saw Earl Humphrey's helmeted head turn in Robert's direction, saw the sword in his mailed fist rise. With one savage downward stroke the earl slashed Robert across the face, then kicked with his spurs. His horse leaped forward, carrying him free of the mounted combat, away from his own standard bearer and the beleaguered knot of his retinue knights and off into the open ground, riding hard for the priory meadows.

Adam brought his horse round in a tight circle and rode up alongside Robert. The knight was lying across the neck of his destrier, but he raised his head as Adam took his bridle. Blood flowed from a gash across his cheek, but he was alive, and not blinded. 'Don't . . .' he managed to say.

'Robert, I'll lead you to safety,' Adam told him.

But Robert shook his head, dragging his hand free of his gauntlet and pressing it to his cheek. 'No,' he said, through bared teeth. 'Don't stay with me . . . Go! Go on!'

For a moment Adam was intent on refusing him. Then he saw the fire in Robert's eyes, and knew what he was asking. He tightened his jaw and nodded. Releasing Robert's horse, he pulled at his own reins and brought Papillon round again. The black destrier whinnied and blew, then saw the open ground and the race ahead. One surge of his powerful back legs, and the horse burst forward into a canter, then a gallop.

Down the last ebb of the slope, they splashed through the little stream that edged the meadow. The water was already flowing ruddy brown, dead and wounded men sprawled along the banks and floating face down in the shallow pools. Up again and over the hoof-churned bank they rode out onto the flat meadow. Adam could see the Earl of Hereford up ahead of him, the blue and white caparison of his horse swinging heavily, encumbered by the mail skirts beneath. There were plenty of other men riding back towards the priory; off to his left Adam saw the royal standard coursing down the slope towards the stream as well. But when he looked in that direction he saw what the earl had not: the priory had only one main gateway, a large fortified structure already mobbed with a crowd of men trying to get through and into the walled precinct. And the gate was away to the left, around the corner; Earl Humphrey had crossed the stream too early and was riding for a blind section of wall.

He was halfway across the open meadow when he realised his mistake. He slowed his horse, and Adam saw his helmet turn to left and right as he scanned the wall before him for another entrance. Trapped, he turned at bay, and it was then that he saw Adam riding at the gallop towards him.

The earl had no lance. For a heartbeat he could only sit in the saddle watching Adam approach. Then he dragged the reins around, kicked with his heels and swept out his sword, a savage roar coming from his helmet vents. Adam too had his sword drawn; only now did he comprehend how steeply the odds were stacked against him. Papillon was labouring, close to the limit even of his great strength. Still he pressed onward, shield up and sword raised. If he could strike one blow, one good hit with all his remaining force and fury, from the core of his body . . .

Earl Humphrey waited until Adam was almost upon him, then he let out his reins and his armoured destrier ploughed forward. Too late Adam realised that the earl was intending simply to ram him aside. Too late to turn, or to slow, Adam tightened his knees on the saddle, gripping the barrel of his horse as the bigger destrier slammed against him. Papillon screamed, rearing back and kicking, and Earl Humphrey leaned from the saddle and hacked down at the horse's head. Adam's sword fell from his grip, and he threw himself forward onto the streaming mane as Papillon staggered back and then collapsed beneath him.

Kicking his feet from the stirrups, Adam flung himself from the saddle as the horse fell. He landed hard, taking the impact on his shoulder and then crashing onto his back. For several panicking heartbeats he could not breathe, his chest crushed tight, and he thought he was dead.

Opening his eyes, he crawled his hand through the grass until he felt the hilt of the sword lying beside him, still secured by its wrist strap. The feel of the worn grip in his palm was a reassurance. He forced himself to breathe, tasting blood in his mouth as he expanded his chest. Pain burst around his ribcage, but when he flexed his limbs he felt no breaks or sprains. With a gasp of agony he sat upright.

Papillon lay a few yards away, crashed down on his side, his steaming belly motionless. Groaning, Adam rolled onto his side and then pushed himself up, getting his legs beneath him. The mail chausses weighed massively, but he struggled to his feet and stood swaying. Only then did he see the other fallen horse.

Earl Humphrey's armoured destrier had come down only twenty paces away from him. Adam guessed the horse had stumbled, or that one of Papillon's rearing hooves had struck the other animal. It was still alive, twitching and blowing bloody froth from its nostrils, but one of its front legs was clearly broken. Adam took a few more paces, tightening his grip on the sword.

The downed rider lay pinned beneath the fallen animal. He had managed to drag himself from the saddle and lay on his back, but his foot was caught in the stirrup and he could not get free. Adam heard the old man's muffled curses and gasps of pain from inside his helmet as he strode closer. Then he stood over him.

'Yield,' he said.

Earl Humphrey lifted his gauntleted hands to his helmet and dragged it free. The face beneath was flowing with sweat, corded with pain, eyes narrowed in the sunlight.

'I know you,' the earl said through his teeth.

'Yield,' Adam repeated, levelling the notched and blunted sword at the man who had once been his lord and master.

Humphrey coughed a laugh. His horse stirred weakly, kicking its rear legs. 'You were my squire,' he said. 'One of my squires . . . some runt of a boy, from somewhere . . .'

Adam felt the anger burning through him. 'What's my name?' he demanded. 'Tell me that and I'll let you go free.'

The earl smiled, almost closing his eyes. 'How am I supposed to remember that?' he said wearily. 'Besides, I'd never yield to you! You're just a squire. The Earl of Hereford does not surrender to a mere squire!' He slumped back onto the turf, still laughing through his bloodied teeth. 'You'll have to kill me,' he said. 'Kill me . . . or just walk away . . .'

Adam became aware of others around him, the shadows of men and horses moving across the grass. But he could not turn away from the figure of the downed nobleman. The anger was fierce in him, the humiliation. Could he really kill this man?

'Adam de Norton,' a voice said.

He turned, and saw the group of riders gathered behind him, and the banner under which they rode. The man who had spoken swung down from the saddle and took three strides towards him. Yes, Adam thought, this was how it must be. One earl would surrender to another. At least he had played his part.

'Come here,' Simon de Montfort said, gesturing to Adam. He had taken off his helmet and passed it to one of his squires. Adam noticed that he had a string of captives with him, royalist knights taken in the melee, now under the guard of de Montfort's own men. Was the battle won then? Had the king and all his forces really yielded, or fled the field?

'Come,' de Montfort said again, and this time Adam obeyed. His feet dragged in the rutted grass, and he thought at any moment that he would stumble and fall. He wanted to weep with sudden overwhelming fatigue. 'Kneel,' de Montfort said.

Adam dropped to his knees before him. He heard the words that the man spoke, as if from a distance. They seemed to have little meaning. Then he felt the sting of the slap upon his cheek. 'Awaken from evil dreams,' de Montfort said. 'And remember your oath always. Now – rise, Adam de Norton, and be a knight.'

Stumbling to his feet, Adam felt the brightness of the sun in his eyes, the wetness on his cheeks. He raised his arms as one of de Montfort's squires removed his worn old sword belt, and another removed his spurs.

'Bring me Sir Henry de Hussey's sword,' Lord Simon ordered, snapping his fingers. 'He shall have that one, I think.'

Adam glanced towards the group of captives, who sat watching the ritual from the saddle with expressions of grudging disinterest. 'Take good care of it,' one of them called. 'That blade is Solingen steel.'

Another of the squires joined them, carrying the sword in its belted scabbard, and a pair of gilded spurs taken from one of the captives. Adam stood still, eyes closed and palms pressed together, as Simon de Montfort buckled the sword around his waist and the squire fastened the spurs to his heels. But even now, at the moment of his greatest honour, Adam heard the words this man had spoken years before. *Some of us know what a debt is worth.*

De Montfort took Adam by the shoulders and kissed him quickly on both cheeks. 'Now,' he said as he stepped away. 'Go and take what is yours.'

Adam bowed his head, then turned and paced the short distance back to the fallen horse and rider. Earl Humphrey's destrier had ceased its struggles – Adam guessed one of the squires or serjeants had ended the animal's suffering. But the earl still lay where he had fallen, flat on his back with his teeth bared to the sky. He struggled up onto one elbow as Adam approached.

Adam closed his hand around the grip of the sword, feeling the fine green leather under his palm. Honed steel whispered from its sheath. Three times he sliced it through the air, hearing the steel sing.

He stood over his captive, eclipsing him with his shadow. Then he brought the sword's point to Earl Humphrey's neck.

'*Yield,*' he said.

# Chapter 30

Henry, third of his name, by the Grace of God King of England, Lord of Ireland, and Duke of Aquitaine, wore a harried look on his pale features. The king sat upon a tall throne of gilded wood, in the centre of the panelled and painted chamber of the bishop's palace at St Paul's in London. Surrounded by splendour, he had a greyish pallor in the light falling from the tall windows. Lifting his hand from the arm of his chair, he worried nervously at his curling grey beard, then remembered himself and let his hand drop once more. The crown upon his head appeared slightly crooked, but nobody wanted to straighten it for him.

The king's unease was understandable, Adam thought. In the six weeks since his crushing defeat on the battlefield of Lewes, Henry had seen his government overturned, his wife and closest friends driven into exile, and his sons and brother imprisoned. All his most powerful supporters had fled to France or submitted to the new regime. Either that or, like the Earl of Hereford, they too were captives awaiting ransom. Henry was king now in name alone. His kingdom was in the hands of the barons, and their leader, Simon de Montfort.

But still the rituals of fealty had to be observed. Adam stood straight, one hand resting lightly on the silvered hilt of his sword, until he heard the presiding steward of the court clear his throat quietly and gesture. Then he paced forward across the tiled floor and knelt before the throne. Raising his hands, palms together as if in prayer, he extended them towards his king. Henry leaned forward slightly, pressing Adam's hands between his own. The royal palms were cold, and slightly clammy. The words came easily, echoed into silence. Then Adam received the royal kiss, stood once more and reversed his steps with bowed head.

Over to one side of the hall, a trio of clerks were busy at a long table, recording the acts and pronouncements of the day. One of them, before long, would record in his roll that the king had accepted the homage of Adam de Norton, son and heir of the deceased James de Norton. They would record that, once the said Adam de Norton had rendered his rightful payment to the king's exchequer, he was to have without delay possession of the lands of which his father had been tenant in chief, and which had been taken into the hands of his stepfather Hugh de Brayboef upon his mother's death. Hugh de Brayboef could not protest; he too had fought on the losing side at Lewes. And who could dispute the judgement of God?

Yes, Adam thought; truly the victory was sent from heaven. How else could Earl Simon's outnumbered and inexperienced force have won the day? Only a week after the battle, as he passed through Canterbury, Adam had heard confirmed reports that several people had witnessed heavenly beings entering the fray: St George and St Thomas, mounted and bearing shining holy banners, riding before Earl Simon's troops as they vanquished the royal retinue.

All knew the truth, of course. All knew that Lord Edward's powerful right division, unable to restrain their thirst for blood, had kept up their pursuit of the fleeing London militia for many miles, cutting down the Londoners by the score. Then, unable to restrain their lust for plunder, they had circled back and fallen upon Simon's baggage train, attacking the strange armoured cart in the mistaken belief that Simon himself was hiding inside. By the time Edward and his companions had gathered their wits and returned to the field the battle was lost, the king and the Scots barons sheltering within the sanctuary of the priory. All that remained for Lord Edward was to help negotiate the royal surrender the following morning.

A heavenly victory indeed. Surely, such amazing good fortune came only from the Lord? Even if that victory had fallen into the hands of the unjust, the murderous, those men like John Fitz-John and Gilbert de Clare, who now vaunted in the hour of their triumph. The winners of a trial by combat, Adam knew, must always have the blessing of God, even if they are the worst of men.

But he could not forget the scene on the evening of the battle, as he had walked back up towards the ridge. The mounds of bodies, men and horses cut down in the melee and strewn on the blacked turf. The almost overwhelming stink of blood and viscera, and the pitiful cries of the wounded. Amid that great slaughter he had searched for the corpse of Ralph de Tosny, hoping that he might give his old friend the honour of a decent burial at least. But he found only the unknown dead. Already the people of the town were moving between the bodies, robbing the slain and the dying alike. This was the reality of war, he had told himself as he stumbled uphill in the gloom of dusk. Behind all the words, the talk of glory and chivalry, lay this overwhelming truth. It had been many days before the stench of the slaughter left him; at times he thought he would never be free of it.

He had not digested the unexpected change in his own fortunes either. Adam did not, of course, still hold the Earl of Hereford as his prisoner. Even with his new knightly station, he lacked the means to secure and maintain such a powerful and prestigious captive in a fitting way. Instead he had sold the ransom to Sir Humphrey, the earl's son, who had taken his father gladly into his custody for a promised sum of five hundred marks of silver, to be paid into Adam's hands. Only a mere fraction of the true value of an earl's ransom, of course, but more than enough to equip Adam as a knight and allow him to pay the customary tax on taking possession of his lands.

And now, Adam thought as he paced back towards the doors of the hall, Sir Humphrey de Bohun was formally betrothed to Joane de Quincy, with the blessing of Earl Simon and the king. Nothing stood in the way of their marriage, and they would be wed as soon as Sir Humphrey had recovered from the wound he had taken in the last hour of the battle. That knowledge alone cast a shadow over the glimmer of Adam's joy. He still possessed the leaf of Joane's Psalter, so heavily stained by blood and sweat it was almost illegible. He had the St Christopher's medallion she had given him too, so many years ago. But he had lost Joane herself, and that brief strange intimacy that had flicked between them was extinguished now. Or so he had compelled himself to believe. But as he passed through the doors of the hall, through the gathered people waiting in the next chamber, he caught a glimpse of her with Lady Despenser and some of her maids. For a fleeting moment their eyes met, and he knew that the bond between them remained unbroken.

'Look at you,' Robert de Dunstanville said to him, striding from the gathered throng and planting his palms on Adam's shoulder. 'Proud as the devil now, eh?'

Adam could not suppress his grin. Robert was smiling too, if crookedly: the scar across his cheek had not yet fully healed. Already he had given his homage to the king, and had been granted possession of his lands in Shropshire once more. He conducted Adam out into the courtyard, where Hugh of Oystermouth was waiting for them with the horses.

'Well then,' said Robert, taking the reins and swinging himself up into the saddle. 'Let's leave these lordlings to their deliberations. We have our own fortunes to seek!' He gave a nudge with his spurs, jogged the reins, and rode across the courtyard towards the street outside. But Adam lingered a moment, glancing back into the dimness of the hall.

Soon enough, he knew, the victors of Lewes, with Simon de Montfort at their head, would set about reforming the government. Guaranteeing liberty, so they claimed, and righting the wrongs of the past. Already a Great Council of Barons had been convened, and soon there would be a new parliament too, with members drawn from all the knights and clergymen of the kingdom.

A bold dream, it had seemed once. Perhaps it was still. Perhaps all anyone could do was to pray that the new rulers of the land proved just and fair, and fulfilled the great boasts they had made, for which so many had suffered and bled. Because if they did not, Adam thought with a chill of premonition, as he paused with one foot in the stirrup, then very soon the armies would be mustering once again.

And all that they had gained could be swept from their hands by the storm of war.

# Historical Note

'In the year of grace 1264, on the Wednesday after the feast of Pancras, the English bore the shock of a very grievous fight at the castle of Lewes; for to wrath yielded reason, life to the sword.' So the contemporary verse known as the *Song of Lewes* describes Simon de Montfort's greatest victory. 'Now England breathes again, hoping for liberty . . .' its anonymous writer proclaims. 'The English likened unto dogs were become vile, but now have they raised their head over their vanquished foes.'

Composed in Latin shortly after the battle, probably by an eyewitness, the *Song* praises de Montfort and his cause in a blend of poetic and religious imagery. It gives a unique insight to the political beliefs of the time, and the ways that they might have been expressed. It also inspired the title of this novel.

Simon de Montfort himself remains one of the most controversial figures in medieval history. To some he was a hero, a man who stood up for justice and liberty against a corrupt and oppressive royal government, and laid the foundations for parliamentary democracy. To others he was a self-serving and unprincipled adventurer, a religious bigot whose stubborn pride and ambition propelled England into a bloody civil war. Either way, he was certainly a man of great energy and charisma, capable of inspiring people throughout society, and his influence on the era was immense.

The battle at Lewes, and the campaign that led up to it, are described by an array of medieval sources, not all of whom agree on the details. My fictional recreation draws largely on David Carpenter and Christopher Whittick's paper 'The Battle of Lewes, 1264', updated in 2014 and currently available online from the Sussex Archaeological Society. Other aspects of the military situation resist easy comprehension. The attack on the bridge at Rochester, featuring de Montfort's fireship, for example, is particularly obscure – the medieval chroniclers who describe it take more delight in listing all the flammable materials that went into the vessel than telling us what Simon did with it – but hopefully my version of events at least makes sense.

By the 13th century, the cultural divisions between the native English and their Norman and French overlords had largely dissolved, especially after the loss of the major continental territories of the English crown by King John. While Anglo-Norman French remained the language of the court and the knightly class, English was widely spoken, and may have been the first language of all but the very highest aristocracy. Sources from the period speak of the 'community of the realm', or *communitas regni*, for the first time encompassing both nobles and commoners in one national body. Unfortunately, one of the earliest and most vivid manifestations of this new sense of English identity was an upsurge of violent xenophobia. Simon de Montfort was himself a Frenchman, but this did not stop many of his followers from launching murderous attacks on anyone they considered to be 'alien'.

De Montfort's attitude to the Jews has also blackened his reputation, although his intolerance was widely shared at the time. First brought over from France by William the Conqueror, partly to help finance his royal government, England's Jews were barred from most occupations besides money-lending. Many thrived even so, albeit under oppressive regulation and against a backdrop of relentless and often hysterical popular hostility. The debts that so many English knights and nobles owed to Jewish financiers only increased their resentment, while viciously anti-Semitic church rulings gave their rancour a pious veneer. This growing intolerance led to a wave of brutal attacks on Jews by Christian mobs, including the bloody massacre in London in Easter week of 1264, described in this novel; contemporary sources put the number of dead at several hundred.

The story of England's medieval Jewish community often makes for grim reading. But for all the severity of law and custom, relations between individuals were perhaps rather warmer: a mandate banning Jews and Christians from sharing meals or living under the same roof hints that this must at least have been a possibility, while the ruling that classed sex between a Jew and a Christian as a form of bestiality suggests that in private things were not always as hostile as they might appear.

For all the frequent brutality of their behaviour, many members of the knightly class did, at least in theory, hold themselves to high standards. The ideals of chivalry are often misconstrued today, and frequently derided, but to many in the medieval world they seemed real and vital enough. Developing from a practical code of battlefield conduct in the 12th century into something like a moral ideology by the 13th, chivalry may more often have been honoured in the lapse, but the massive popularity of courtly romances, the tales of King Arthur and Charlemagne, attest to a widespread belief in the code of the virtuous Christian warrior.

One of the main arenas for the display of this martial code was the tournament, which was at the peak of its popularity at this time. Many people today probably consider tournaments as synonymous with jousting. In the mid-13th century, however, the joust was only just coming into vogue as a popular side attraction; conducted in the open field and with no dividing barrier, it was both showy and extremely dangerous. The main event of the tournament was the melee. Possibly the most violent form of field sport ever devised, these mass mock battles often featured hundreds or even thousands of mounted combatants and spilled out over miles of territory. Injuries, and even deaths, were commonplace, but the champions of the melee field were the megastar sportsmen of their day.

In writing this novel I have drawn on a wide range of scholarly histories. These include several excellent modern studies of Simon de Montfort, by J.R. Maddicott, Sophie Thérèse Ambler and others, and of both Henry III and his son Edward. Maurice Keen's *Chivalry* and Saul David's *For Honour and Fame: Chivalry in England 1066–1500* were invaluable in reconstructing the ideals and attitudes of the 13th-century knightly class, while David Crouch's wonderful book *Tournament* provides all the detail anyone could need about the melee-based events of the 12th–13th centuries, supported by translations from original sources.

Robin Mundill's *The King's Jews* is a brief but detailed survey of the Jewish community in England, while both Margaret Wade Labarge's *A Baronial Household of the Thirteenth Century*, and Louise J. Wilkinson's *Eleanor de Montfort: A Rebel Countess in Medieval England* throw a revealing light on the household of the Countess of Leicester, and the lifestyles of the wider medieval aristocracy.

One very recent book that proved particularly helpful in filling in the background to the story was Nicholas Orme's *Going to Church in Medieval England*. The everyday religious rituals, experiences and beliefs that permeated and gave shape to the lives of the people of the Middle Ages are often invisible to us today, and all too often overlooked.

# Acknowledgements

While the planning, researching and writing of this novel was a solitary business, it has since become more of a communal effort. My thanks go to my agent, Will Francis at Janklow & Nesbit, for his dedication in placing the book with a new publisher, and to my editor, Morgan Springett at Hodder & Stoughton, for his enthusiasm and attention to detail over the process of polishing and refining the manuscript. Any ragged edges and errors that remain are entirely my own responsibility. But most of all I thank Narmi, for lending me *Chivalry*, and for persuading me that this was the book I really wanted to write.